D0019845

THE HERETIC

Liam McIlvanney

THE HERETIC

Europa
editions

Europa Editions
1 Penn Plaza, Suite 6282
New York, N.Y. 10019
www.europaeditions.com
info@europaeditions.com

Library of Congress Cataloging in Publication Data is available
ISBN 978-1-60945-741-9

McIlvanney, Liam
The Heretic

Book design by Emanuele Ragnisco
www.mekkanografici.com

Cover photo: Jim Umberger / Stockimo / Alamy Stock Photo

Prepress by Grafica Punto Print – Rome

Printed in Canada

CONTENTS

For Isaac

Footfalls echo in the memory
Down the passage which we did not take
Towards the door we never opened . . .
—T. S. ELIOT, "Burnt Norton"

THE HERETIC

SUNDAY, 22 JUNE 1975

She wakes in the night knowing something is wrong. Up on one elbow, straining to hear. She turns her head to check on the girl. The girl has kicked off her covers on her side of the bed, lies sprawled in her shorts and grubby white vest. Denise reaches over to place a palm on her daughter's head and the heat makes her gasp. Has the girl caught a fever? She lays the backs of her fingers against the girl's cheek—burny, rough—and blows on the sleeping face, rotating her head to let the breeze play over forehead, eyes, nose, cheeks, chin. The girl stirs, flips her head to face the window.

For weeks now the city's been a sweat box. That's the trouble with these old tenements: can't heat them in winter, can't cool them in summer.

Denise flops back and stares at the ceiling. She wonders what snapped her awake. Sometimes the young team go on sprees late at night, smashing the windows of derelict flats. You hear their laughter, pounding feet, cheers going up when the glass shatters. Her own building is mostly empty. Just herself and wee Kirsty up here and old Mr. Stewart on the floor below. But all the breakable panes have been smashed and anyway she's out of easy stone-throwing range up here on the fourth floor where her white net curtains—her flag of truce— and a wilted aspidistra on the windowsill testify that somebody lives here.

There *is* a noise, now that she's properly awake, but it's not the hard laughter of youths, nor the drunken singing of the old jakeys who sometimes set up camp in one of the empty flats. It's a soft noise, but strong too, a kind of gentle roaring, like a river in spate or like a wind has got up and is buffeting the building. A summer storm?

And now she registers what's been troubling her all along. It's too bright. There's an odd glare, as though the sun has decided to rise in the night. Drawing back the covers she steps out of bed and now she gasps again. The floor. The wooden floorboards are hot, they actually sting the soles of her feet like the planks of a sauna. There is no way to make sense of this and so she tiptoes to the curtains and pauses. Then she jerks them apart.

Orange.

The whole world is orange and black and yellow and crackling. The warehouse next door is ablaze. Fire blooms through the latticed roof where slates have crumbled and beams have collapsed. The roaring is the noise of the flames, pouring in spate, like upside-down waterfalls from the top-floor windows.

But why is the floor hot? How can she feel next door's blaze on the soles of her feet? She unsnibs the window—the metal catches already hot between finger and thumb—and hauls the juddering sash upwards. Hot air is sucked into the room, sparks and soot, and she pushes her head through and leans out and down, the ground swinging sickly up at her, too far to jump, far too far, and she sees it now, the evil tongues of flame licking out from the floor below, Mr. Stewart's flat. Her own building is on fire.

She goes to shake Kirsty awake but a thought stops her and she slides as if on castors to the little hallway and presses both palms to the door. Her forehead comes to rest between her palms and she knows, from the sickening heat between her eyes, she already knows.

She fumbles at the chain and draws the bolt. She hauls the door open and a scream catches in her throat. Swooping and diving and wheeling round the landing are ravens, bats, demons—no, *shadows*—thrown madly about by the flames that clamour and climb to clutch and pluck at them from the stairwell.

Denise approaches the bannister, leans fearfully into an updraught that blasts her cheeks and singes her eyebrows. The stairwell's an inferno. Hell's been installed in a Tradeston tenement.

She staggers back to the flat, slams her door, slides the bolt and then the chain as if the blaze will be deterred by something a well-placed boot-sole could obliterate. She snatches towels from the laundry basket—two, three, four—soaks them at the jawbox sink and lays them along the bottom of the kitchen door. She retreats across the blistering lino and the hot boards to the bed-recess where Kirsty is rousing and moaning. Denise climbs back into bed and takes the child in her arms, laying the girl's sweaty head against her chest. She hears a crash from somewhere below. She presses her daughter's head even tighter to her chest and squeezes her eyes tightly shut.

Old Mr. Stewart. You stupid bastard, she thinks. You stupid fucking bastard. You have left a chip pan on, or you have fallen asleep with a fag in your hand and your stupidity is now going to kill us all. I hope you die in agony, burned in a hell of your own pig-stupid making, but maybe it was not Mr. Stewart at all. Maybe it was jakeys, ripping up floorboards in an empty flat, burning them in a brazier. And she pictures Mr. Stewart in his inevitable herringbone jacket with the worked-in birdshit on the shoulder, she sees his gappy grin and boxer's nose, his Santa Claus beard and his flat balding head, she sees him turning this way and that in his shabby flat, his hands holding his head, his hands with their uncut nicotine-yellow thumbnails. He stinks like a midden but he doesn't deserve to die like this. None of us do.

Too far to jump. Four storeys. Far too far. Would they do it together, when the time came? Could she plunge from this height with the child in her arms? But they'd be saved before then. Any second now she would hear them, sirens, splitting the night. Blue lights whirling. Up the stairs they will stamp, the firemen in their gear, striding through the flames, taking their axes to the front door, shouldering through the splintered wood, bearing them away to safety. But suddenly she knows what it was, the crash she heard, she knows it was a section of the stairwell.

Nobody is coming. Nobody will be climbing those stairs to their rescue. They are on their own, stranded in the square box-bed. The box-bed will be a raft on a raging, burning sea. Could they float off, she wonders, float out into the night, float off over the city's streets, riding the breeze until a zephyr deposits them on the coast somewhere, still in bed, side by side, on the dunes of Prestwick or Troon?

Oh God.

Kirsty is squirming now, straining to lift her head, *It's too hot, Mummy*, and she pushes the wet hair from the girl's face, *I know, sweetie, I know*, and blows on the girl's hairline. I will do anything, she promises. *Light from light, true God from true God.* If you just keep us safe, I will do whatever you ask, I will go back to Mass, I will get back together with Gordon, I will take him back, I will do that much. *And his kingdom will have no end.*

She can hear the sirens now but they seem so far away and the smoke is seeping through the towels beneath the door and it is seeping up between the floorboards, *We look for the resurrection of the dead*, and she can hear the crackling of the flames. I will take him back. *And the life of the world to come.*

Keep us safe.

I
A WORLD OF SPECULATION

TUESDAY, 1 JULY 1975

1

D uncan McCormack was running. Like a man possessed, like a man with the Furies at his heels. Up Hyndland Road past the parish church, then down Novar Drive with the big chimney of Gartnavel Hospital rearing up over the tenements.

Left down Lauderdale Gardens with his breath pegging in ragged gasps, his knees jolting. Past the bowling club with its perfect square of turf, its green-and-white timbered pavilion, and round into Queensborough Gardens before cutting sharp left down a lane between tenement blocks. He never entered this lane without thinking of that other lane, the one in Battlefield where they found the Quaker's first victim.

Bursting out onto Clarence Drive he heard, too late, the mosquito drone of an electric milk float that braked to miss him—chink and rattle of bottles and crates, muffled curse of the driver—and McCormack raised his hand in apology before sprinting off past Hyndland Academy, looping round a leafy crescent of villas and back onto Partickhill Road.

He stopped at the junction with Gardner Street and checked his watch. Twenty-seven minutes and twenty seconds. He had shaved nearly a minute off his time in the past two weeks.

He planted his hands on his knees and bent over, sucking lungfuls of air, feeling the blood pool in his face and head, sweat spotting the pavement. Finally he straightened up and took it in.

The view.

The best view in the city, the view that made the run worth-while. The sandstone canyon of Gardner Street dropped away like a ski-jump. The city's steepest street. Down at the foot of the hill was the early traffic on Dumbarton Road. If you raised your eyes you could see the river and the cranes and the green hills of Ayrshire down to the south.

The South.

If you kept going, down past the Borders and Yorkshire and the English Midlands and Oxfordshire, you would reach the grey spreading stain of London. And Peckham. And the lit-tle brick house with the wooden gate on Marsden Road. And the stone-flagged path to the green front door with the cracked pane of stained glass and maybe a head bobbing into view behind the glass, a head with curly brown hair above green eyes, eyes that crinkled at the corners when the mouth creased in a smile.

Fuck it. Stop. He turned away from the view. Lifted the hem of his T-shirt and wiped his face with it, the breeze chill-ing his sweat-slick ribs. He set off down Gardner Street, turned left onto Caird Drive. There was no point thinking about that. Brown hair. Green eyes. No point thinking about what you'd lost. Think about what you still had to find. What you'd come back to find. The job was to find Walter Maitland. This was how he thought of it. Not nailing Maitland or catch-ing Maitland. Finding Maitland.

In one sense, finding Walter Maitland was easy. He lived in a big house in Bearsden. You could march up his driveway and knock on his door. But finding Walter Maitland in his crimes? That was the challenge. McCormack thought of all the malfeasance in the city—drugs, protection, gambling, girls—stretching in all directions like a dark labyrinth. And the beast who prowled it, the Glasgow Minotaur, was Walter Stuart Maitland. McCormack had been stalking its corridors for months, turning down its dog-legs and dead ends, doubling back on himself. No nearer, it seemed, to the beast at its heart.

He was climbing the short flight of steps to number 43 when a car door opened.

"Sir!"

McCormack whipped round. "D.C. Nicol?" He made a show of scanning the street. "People will talk. Parked outside the boss's flat at seven in the morning?"

She smiled tightly, looked at her watch. "Twenty past, sir."

"What's the word, then, Detective? What's happened?"

She was standing beside the car now. "A murder, sir. Down Crawford Street. A man. Haddow's assigned it to us. You were on the way, so I thought I'd stop."

"O.K. Look, come up to the flat, have a quick cup of tea. I'll get changed."

Nicol checked her watch. McCormack rested his hands on his hips. "He'll still be dead in fifteen minutes, Nicol. Come on."

She locked the car. He led the way up the stairs, conscious now of his sweat, his laboured breathing, shaking loose his bunch of keys.

"Sorry, it's right at the top."

"It always is, sir."

McCormack nodded. It was true. "Every call-out. Fourth bloody floor. Why does nothing happen at ground level in this city? It's as if crime rises, like the bloody heat."

When he reached the top landing, McCormack saw that the postie had been. He scooped the letter from the mat and knew without looking that the envelope would bear the fluid, looped handwriting, the London postmark: SE15.

He showed Nicol into the kitchen and stowed the letter in the hallstand drawer alongside the other unopened envelopes.

He found his inhaler and grabbed a couple of puffs. He

poked his head into the kitchen. "Tea and coffee in the cupboard behind you, Nicol. I'll take a quick shower. What?"

Nicol was smiling. "Nothing, sir. It's just . . ." She gestured round the room. "It's like the 1930s in here. Not exactly *Ideal Homes*."

McCormack glanced around the kitchen. He'd inherited the flat from his gran when he was twenty-six; he'd changed nothing in the twelve years since. Now he studied the kitchen, with its mint-green wall tiles, chipped enamel bread-tin, its range cooker on the green-and-yellow chequered lino and he rubbed a hand against the bristles on his jaw.

"What can I say, Nicol? Quality never goes out of style. Ten minutes." He paused with his fingers clamped to the door frame. "What the hell were you doing in the office at this hour anyway?"

She shrugged. "Getting a head start, sir."

"You'll go far, Nicol. Further than most of the lazy bastards in Glasgow CID. Me included. Right." He slapped the door frame twice. "Ten minutes. Tops."

Fifteen minutes later they were turning onto Dumbarton Road.

"The locus is Crawford Street?"

"One of the backcourts, sir, as far as I understand."

A Corporation bus pulled out sharply in front of them, the green-white-and-gold livery stippled with dirt, and Nicol pumped the brake and slammed the horn with the heel of her hand. The driver's arm emerged from the bus window, hand up in acknowledgement.

"So what did he say?" McCormack asked.

"DCI Haddow?" Nicol focused on the road for a spell. "He said we'd had long enough on the Maitland case, sir. It was time to move on."

"That sounds a little diplomatic for Haddow. You sure that's how he put it?"

"The phrase 'pissing taxpayers' money up against a wall' may have been used, sir. The phrase 'fannying about.'"

McCormack shook his head, breathed the word *arsehole* in a weary sigh.

"Still, at least it's on your home turf, sir." Nicol glanced in the rearview. "A murder on your doorstep."

McCormack snorted. "It's the other side of Dumbarton Road, Detective. That's a foreign country down there."

As Nicol drove, McCormack told her about Partick, the history of the district. The medieval village, mentioned by King David I in 1136 when he granted the lands of "Perdyc" to the church. How the archbishop built his summer palace here, before the old village of kirks and mills was swept away by the tide of industry. Shipbuilding. Dyeworks. Printworks. The district split in two then, with the workers housed on the low ground by the river while the middle classes climbed the slope to the north. Coal merchants would charge different prices when they crossed Dumbarton Road. The half-crown bag in the worker's slum became a five-bob bag in a hilltop apartment. There was the "hauf-croon" side of Dumbarton Road and there was the "five-bob" side.

"And I," McCormack said emphatically, "come from the five-bob side. Don't you forget it."

"I thought you were a Highlander, sir," said Nicol.

"I am," he said. "I was brought up in Ballachulish. But my grannie lived here. I used to come down and stay with her every summer. Get summer jobs. Knock about the city. So I'm a Glasgow Highlander, if you like." He smiled. "The best kind of Highlander."

A uniform flagged them down on Crawford Street. McCormack flashed the warrant card as he stepped from the car, clamping the brown trilby onto his head.

"It's over here, sir." The uniform was leading them across the wasteground, where one side of a great black square of tenements had been demolished. Already the smell was catching at their throats. The backcourt at Crawford Street was a vast open-air rubbish dump. A tip. A cowp, right in the heart of a built-up area. An inland sea of putrefying garbage, with gulls pecking and squawking, lifting and settling with angry flaps of their wings.

The uniform hoisted the red-and-white police tape and they ducked under. A path had been cleared through the mounds of black bin bags and boxes. McCormack thought of the Red Sea as he tramped towards the little clearing.

A second uniform and a plainclothes CID man waited by the body. The uniform nodded, stepped back to give McCormack room, uttered a begrudging "Sir". The plainer—he was from the Marine police station on Anderson Street and Davin or Devine or something was his name—said nothing. McCormack knew him from the Quaker investigation, back in '69.

"D.I. Duncan McCormack, Serious Crime Squad," McCormack said, though both of these men would know who he was. Both would resent him. This had been their murder. Now it was his.

McCormack dropped to his haunches, tugging the knees of his trousers. It was a physical act he repeated at the scene of every murder he'd attended and it brought them all flashing through his mind, all the corpses he'd scrutinized—beaten, choked, shot, stabbed.

By the looks of things, this one was beaten. A tall man in a boiler suit that was two sizes too small. Probably from a thrift shop, or scavenged from somebody's rubbish. It bunched at the crotch and fell short at the sleeves and the trouser cuffs. The man's feet were bare. The two smallest toes on his right foot were bloody and raw. An accident. Possibly rats, if he'd been here that long. The feet were livid and blue.

The boiler suit was the kind with stud-fasteners rather than a zip. The studs were undone almost down to the crotch. The man didn't appear to be wearing anything under the boiler suit and there was bruising and grazing—splotchy and raw—on the exposed regions of the man's torso.

His hair was longish and white and there was a silvery glint of stubble on the chin and throat. Beyond that, it was difficult to gauge much from the face. You could tell it was a face. Beyond that, you were struggling. He'd been bludgeoned repeatedly, possibly with one of the bricks or half-bricks littering the ground or with one of the broad-bottomed wine bottles bobbing on the sea of rubbish.

The man's hands were bruised and swollen, fingers black and purple, blood or mud under split nails. He wore a pinky ring with some kind of ruby or garnet on his left hand and a signet ring on his right ring finger. There was an upturned "V" engraved on the signet ring—or, no: the compasses and square. A Freemason.

McCormack glanced up. Right in his line of vision was the gable end with the huge mural that was in all the papers last week when it was finally finished. A wee boy in old-fashioned clothes riding a big brown and white dog while a yellow bird swooped down at them from a blue sky filled with puffy white clouds. It made about as much sense as anything else in the immediate scene. He straightened up. "Who found him?"

The CID man jerked his head to where an old tramp in a Crombie overcoat stood hunched against a tenement wall, a uniform watching over him.

"The old boy? The vagrant?"

"I know. World's first public-spirited jakey. Walked to Dumbarton Road and phoned it in."

"Does he know who it is?" McCormack asked, and the CID man's name floated into his consciousness: *Devlin.* "Can he identify the body, D.S. Devlin?"

"He says not. Says he's never seen him before." Devlin paused. "He says the body was hooded, sir. When he found it."

"What?"

"It was wearing a hood. He took it off to, you know, check. I'm assuming that's the hood right there."

McCormack saw it. A black canvas sack of some sort, beside the bloodied head. He lifted the sack between finger and thumb, passed it on to Nicol.

"Get that bagged, D.C. Nicol."

He heard footsteps behind him, a jaunty whistle: "Comin' Thro the Rye".

"It's true then." Martin Seawright, the forensic pathologist, was picking his way through the garbage. "The bright lights of London couldn't hold you."

The police photographer was at Seawright's heels. And Jardine the procurator fiscal bringing up the rear. The three wise men, thought McCormack. The Coming of the Magi.

"I missed you too much, Martin. Your sunny demeanour. Your rigorous professionalism. Not to mention the pure northern air. I just had to come back."

"Right then." Seawright took a dishtowel-sized oblong of tarp from his bag, spread it on the ground and knelt beside the body. He nodded at the corpse, as if making its acquaintance. He pulled on a pair of surgical gloves, placed two fingers on the victim's neck, just under the jawline, and looked off across the sea of rubbish with no expression on his face. After a few seconds he checked his wristwatch and jotted something in a black leather notebook. When he started on the examination, McCormack left him to it, wandered off a few yards and lit a cigarette. The crowd behind the police tape was larger now, standing there with the usual glum vigilance, mothers and children, elderly men. He spotted the bobbing blond curls of Fiona Morrison, the *Record*'s crime reporter.

If they cleared this up quickly, they could have another run at Maitland. Haddow was pissing them about by throwing this murder into the mix but maybe they would clear it without breaking stride. It was the vagrant, most likely. The one who called it in. Posing as the innocent bystander. If not him it would be another derelict. A fight over the dregs of a bottle. A drunken tussle that spiralled out of hand. The hood was a troubling detail, certainly. And why was the victim still wearing his rings? One gold, the other an authentic-looking ruby. But they would sort it out. They would blitz the door-to-door, round up all the jakeys in the district. Then they could get back to Walter Maitland. Back to something that mattered.

McCormack finished his cigarette and ground it underfoot.

"Inspector! Inspector!"

Fiona Morrison looked like she was flagging down a taxi. "Inspector! Can we have a quick word?"

She always used the first-person plural, as if the corporate might of the *Record* stood behind her every word. McCormack bowed his head and crossed the patch of waste ground. Morrison detached herself from the little crowd and they met across the sagging incident tape.

"Murder?"

There was never much in the way of social nicety from Morrison.

"Well, we await the pathologist's report. But, yes, suspicious."

"Stabbed? Strangled? What?"

"Again, the pathologist will determine that."

"Male? Female? Age?"

She would be hoping for a woman, McCormack thought. Young, pretty. A sex murder. The Quaker all over again. "The deceased is an elderly man. I'm sorry to disappoint you."

Morrison had her notebook out. She glanced up from her writing, hard-eyed. "You can be a real prick, D.I. McCormack, you know that? He got a name?"

"Not as yet, no."

"He a vagrant?"

"You mean as opposed to a real person? We're keeping an open mind, Miss Morrison. You ought to try it some time."

He turned on his heel and crossed back to the body. Seawright was packing up his bag. The police snapper was on his tiptoes, angling for a vertical shot of the body.

"Any thoughts?"

"Many, many thoughts, Inspector McCormack." Seawright snapped the clasps of his bag, rose to his feet. "Thoughts that will be in the forefront of my mind when the PM's underway. If, however, you are asking for preliminary findings . . . ?"

"I am," McCormack said.

"Then in that case I would suggest that the cause of death is very likely to have been blunt force trauma to the back of the cranium. Possibly inflicted by a hammer or similar instrument. By a perpetrator who is left-handed. Time of death to be determined, though I would estimate that the victim has been dead for between six and twelve hours. Place of death unknown."

"He wasn't killed here?"

"He was killed somewhere else and dumped here. There's not enough blood around the body. This looks messy, but the real mess is somewhere else."

Seawright smiled with his lips pressed tightly shut, used his free hand to straighten his raincoat. McCormack noticed that Seawright's glasses had an amber tint, as if he wanted to put as much filter as he could between himself and the sights of the day.

"O.K., Martin. How are we fixed for the PM? Maybe look to get it done tonight?"

"You got an ident already, D.I. McCormack? My, that was quick work."

"Not as yet, no."

"Well, you know the drill, Inspector. No ident, no PM. Not until this gentleman"—tipping a finger at the procurator fiscal—"says so. I'll await your call. Good to have you back."

He strode off with the snapper and the fiscal at his heels. "That's not sarcasm, by the way," he called. "I think I actually mean it."

Nicol at his elbow: "Shell's here, boss. We ready for them?"

McCormack looked round to where the dark van had parked beside the perimeter wall. The shell was like a black ambulance, a Commer van with no rear windows. The driver and his mate hovered by the vehicle's rear.

"Aye, we're about done here."

Nicol beckoned and the driver opened the rear doors and he and his mate got to work. They laid a stretcher down beside the body. They spread a polythene sheet on top of the stretcher and laid a body bag on top of the sheet. Then they lifted the body into the bag, setting it down like something breakable, zipped the bag, wrapped the whole thing in polythene and carried the stretcher into the shell.

Nicol slapped the side of the van and they were off, nudging gingerly through the knot of onlookers, then turning right onto Sandy Road. McCormack pursed his lips as he pictured their destination, the white-tiled room with the cold steel tables, the slick grey floor with the drainage holes.

He got the keys from Nicol and sat in the car while he radioed in. He arranged for an incident caravan, and uniforms to help with the door-to-door and check for evidence in the vacant flats. If Seawright was correct and the victim had been killed somewhere else, then the vacant flats were a good place to start.

"Oh, and we'll need some kind of truck," he told the dispatcher.

"A truck?"

"The body was dumped on a rubbish tip. We'll need the rubbish bagged, in a five-yard radius of the locus. Need a team to go through it."

"Right. Well. You'll be Mr. Popular."

"I always wondered what they called me behind my back. Thanks for your help."

They crossed to where the uniform stood with the vagrant. McCormack took the uniform aside.

"What's your name, Constable?"

"Buchan, sir. Eddie."

"He tell you anything, Eddie?"

"Just his name, sir. It's Joseph Turner. Joe."

McCormack stepped towards the old vagrant. The stench, even in the middle of a rubbish tip in high summer, rocked him like a force-field, a burning reek, ripe and sour, that had McCormack breathing shallow through his mouth and stepping back a pace. The man watched him through his dirty fringe with sidelong flicks of his coal-dark eyes.

"Mr. Turner. I'm Detective Inspector Duncan McCormack. You took the hood off the body."

The man looked at McCormack and back at the ground. "I wanted to check. To make sure, like. That the guy was deid."

"It's all right. Anyone would have done the same. But listen, did you take anything else? Was there nothing in his pockets?"

The man's greasy locks swung as he shook his head, his eyes still fixed on the ground. "Nut. Nuthin."

"I'm wondering about the rings," McCormack said. Turner just shrugged. "Why didn't you take the rings? Could've got something for them at the pawnie, couldn't you? Or swapped them for some tinnies, a bottle of El D?"

"He was deid when I found him," the man said. "I never did it."

"O.K., Joseph. Where are you dossing this weather—one of these flats?"

Turner jerked his thumb over his shoulder. "Up there. Third floor."

"Alone?"

"Mostly."

"Right then, Joseph. We'll talk to you later. We'll need to ask some more questions." McCormack gripped the constable's elbow as he passed, leaned in and spoke low. "Take him to Temple. Have him searched at the station."

"Righto, sir. Will do."

The rain came on then, big spare drops, pattering onto discarded cardboard boxes, snapping against the tightened skins of bin bags.

"Come on, then." McCormack strode off across the rubbled ground. "Let's get started."

After ten yards he stopped, turned. Nicol hadn't moved. She looked as if she was trying to remember something. "We're doing the door-to-door, sir?"

"You've got other plans, have you?"

"But don't the uniforms . . . ?"

"Nicol. If you learn nothing else, learn this. The biggest chance of a breakthrough in a murder case is now. Right now. While the body's still warm. Yes, the troops'll do most of the legwork, but all due respect, Nicol—we're the detectives. Folk here don't need much of a reason to stonewall the polis. Let them get used to the idea of a body in their backcourt and they'll tell us nothing. Shock's the best weapon. *Body was dumped here last night. What do you know about it? What did you see?*"

"Right, sir. Got it."

They picked their way through the towers and pyramids of rubbish. The rain fell like a blessing on the baked asphalt and the simmering bin bags.

"Was that your first?" McCormack asked.

"Sorry, sir?"

"Murders, Nicol. Was that your first one?"

She thought about it. "Not my first body. But, yes, it was my first murder. At least the first I got to attend the scene."

"Good. You did well."

Nicol said nothing.

"Sorry. That sounded glib. I mean, you did better than I did. My first one. Stabbing in Blackhill. Messy. Guy had been plunged in the stomach with a breadknife. By his missus. He was sitting there in his armchair as if he'd been watching *Match of the Day*. Puddled in blood. His lap sopping. Chucked my guts in front of the pathologist. Not Seawright, thank Christ."

Nicol nodded. She was thinking about the bodies. No murders, but plenty of bodies down in Ayrshire when she was still in uniform. Housefires. Kids trapped in upstairs bedrooms. The unthinkable smell. You learned after the first one to requisition a new uniform straight away. The smell never left the old one. That fire over in Tradeston the other week—there was a kid involved in that one, wasn't there?

Housefires were bad, but housefires were not the worst.

The worst was Traffic.

Traffic, by a very long way. That clear, frosty night on the A77. Head-on collision near Fenwick. The driver of one of the cars had come through the windscreen. He was lying on his back on the central reservation like the effigy on an old church tomb. Apart from one detail. His head was missing. They found it under the car, like a lost football. The staff at the mortuary sewed it back on, put him in a high-collared tunic for when the family came to identify the body.

They had reached the cliff of black tenements. Nicol stopped. "Can I ask you something, sir?"

"Go on, then."

He was expecting some query about procedure, what happened next with the body. When the PM might take place. What she said instead was simply, "I never asked you, sir. Why *did* you come back?"

McCormack plunged his hands in his raincoat pockets and looked at the rubbish-strewn ground. He blew out a sigh. What could he tell her? That he was tired of London and tired

of the job and thought a change of scene might make a difference? That he couldn't hack it anymore in a proper city and
had to skulk back here to this jumped-up village? That he'd
split with his lover of three and a half years and could no
longer bear to wake up to the wallpaper, the streets, the fucking underground stations and ratty cabs of a city where he'd
been—of all things—in love? That he'd opted, in a stroke of
bitter genius, to return to a place where the kind of love he
sought was not even legal?

Or maybe he could tell her the truth?

He looked up and smiled.

Nah. That would never do.

"I got tired of my accent," he said.

2

E very morning, Detective Chief Inspector Alan Haddow sat at his desk and scoured the *Glasgow Tribune* for lies about the Force. He looked at the splashes, the side-bars, the court reports. He read the paper from masthead to the back-page sport. He even glanced through the crossword, as if a cop-bashing message might have been coded into its clues.

He was a Fifer by birth and had never taken to Glasgow. You could live in a place for twenty years, you could clean up its streets and lock up its neds. Didn't mean you had to like it.

Today's splash was Bugner's defeat to Ali in Kuala Lumpur: "Ali keeps title in easy victory." Trust a Glasgow paper to lead with a boxing match. Everything arse-backwards in this fucking town. The trivial was news, the news was trivia. And Bugner? If big stumbling, lumbering Bugner had punched him out, laid Ali flat on the canvas, that might have been front-page news. As it stood, this was Dog Bites Man.

Still, they might have a better splash tomorrow, depending on how this Partick thing played out.

He took a sip of his coffee and turned the page. Some things never change, he thought. Here was Scotland Yard making an arse of itself again. Under the headline "Lucky Lucan", he read of how two Scotland Yard detectives had returned from France, where sightings of the missing English Lord had been reported. "We're pleased with the results," a DCI was quoted as saying. "We think we may well be on the right track." What track's that? thought Haddow as he flicked through the pages. The fucking dog track? Chasing the hare?

There was little in the rest of the paper to vex him. No aspersions cast on Strathclyde Police. Ringo Starr had divorced his wife. There were twenty arrests at an Orange Walk. A Glasgow MP was calling for an inquiry into alleged abuses at Auldpark Children's Home, which shut down last year. A sidebar revealed the momentous news that Ted Heath had been left out of the British yachting team for the Admiral's Cup.

We all have our crosses to bear, thought Haddow. Cataloguing the ex-premier's recent run of ill-fortune, the article continued: "In the last year, Mr. Heath, who captained the British team to victory in 1971, has lost a general election, the Tory leadership, had a yacht wrecked at sea, and had his Belgravia home bombed."

On the plus side, thought Haddow, he hasn't had to deal with Duncan McCormack.

McCormack was a problem. Worse, he was a mistake. A mistake that someone else had made, but one that Alan Haddow would have to fix.

Six years ago, McCormack was walking on water as the cop who cracked the Quaker case. The Quaker. A multiple murderer, preying on women who went to the dancing at the Barrowland Ballroom. The city was obsessed with the murders—*addicted*, it sometimes seemed, to the endless news reports about the dapper killer, the Dance Hall Don Juan. Everywhere you turned you saw posters featuring the artist's impression of the killer, or the sinisterly handsome identikit photo. The Quaker was a celebrity, more like a footballer or pop star than a killer. And McCormack caught him. Or, rather, since there were two men involved—a local government clerk called William Bickett who courted the women, and a gangster called McGlashan who did the actual killing—McCormack caught them both. But he also brought down Peter Levein, the head of CID for the City of Glasgow Police, and he did it with what many people—Haddow among them—considered an unseemly glee. Levein topped himself in Saughton a couple of years back. Shrunken husk of a man. And now the pricks at St. Andrew's Street had brought McCormack back, poached him up from London, to show how squeaky clean they were. Welcome the whistleblower back with open arms. Install him in one of the plum jobs.

The pricks at St. Andrew's Street might peg McCormack as some kind of hero. Everyone else knew what he was. A grasser-up of his fellow officers. An airer of dirty linen in public. A scab. A tout.

He was also, Haddow reflected bitterly, the reason why he himself was in charge of this shower. When Peter Levein was still head of CID, when his move to the Big House looked assured, certain agreements had been reached. Certain under-standings. It was understood that when Levein became chief constable, Alan Haddow would take over as head of CID. But then Duncan Dogood McCormack waded in with his Sword of Justice and that was that. Levein was sent to a different Big House and all bets were off. The big job went to somebody else and Haddow had to settle for head of the Serious Crime Squad, out in the bloody wilds of Anniesland with a parcel of primadonnas.

Still, there was one primadonna whose time was almost up.

We'll see who's still standing when the bell rings, Haddow thought. Who's Ali here. Who's Bugner. You should have stayed gone, McCormack. Like Lord bloody Lucan.

Haddow shook his head, kept turning the pages.

Some people saved the sports pages till last. Or the letters page. Haddow savoured the obituaries. Nothing made you feel more alive than reading about those who'd newly carked it. Their litany of achievements could be as lengthy as you liked.

It didn't matter. They were dead, and Alan Haddow wasn't. He read each obit to the end and mentally added the same three words to each of those final lines: "He is survived by his wife Gloria, their three sons, and seven grandchildren." *And Alan Haddow.* There was no doubt about it: obituaries fairly bucked you up. He was reading about a professor of Hydraulic Engineering who died on a mountaineering expedition to the French Alps when the knock came at his door.

"Come."

It was Iain Shand. One of McCormack's team, specially chosen by Haddow.

"D.C. Shand." Haddow abandoned the *Tribune* with a sigh. He didn't ask Shand to sit. "Our Highland friend; how's he taking it?"

"The Partick tasking? I don't imagine he's too happy. But he's doing it. He's out now with D.C. Nicol. She picked him up on the way."

Haddow nodded. "Well. You know what to do, son. Keep me posted. If he cuts any corners, I want to hear it. Plus, I'll be telling him to drop the Maitland inquiry for the time being. I want this Partick thing cleared up. If he tries to keep Maitland on the boil, you let me know."

"Sir."

"And Shand?"

"Yes, sir?"

"Remember who's got your back here, son. O.K.? Don't get taken in by McCormack's us-against-the-world horseshit. Remember whose gang you're in."

Shand nodded, closed the door behind him.

Haddow took a slug of coffee. It was cold now but he didn't care. He went back to reading about the engineer, a little smile tugging at his mouth, like the obituary was a joke whose punchline he already knew.

"You thought it would be different, didn't you?"

Nicol was smiling; McCormack could see the glint of her sharp little teeth from the tail of his eye as he turned the wheel: Crow Road, straight lines of tenements.

"What would be different?" McCormack asked.

They were heading back to Temple Police Station through the landscape of a Second World War newsreel. The dustcart drivers' strike was entering its fourth week. Bags of rubbish lined the pavements, pecked at by hovering gulls. Broken prams, discarded fridges, cardboard boxes in tottering columns. The mounds were five or six feet high in places, turning the pavements into secret alleyways, cutting off sunlight to the ground-floor flats.

"I mean with me. You thought they might talk because I was there. Because I'm not a proper polis. Because I'm a woman."

"Who said you weren't a proper polis?"

"You want a list of names? Every polis in Glasgow, minus two or three."

"Minus four. They don't talk because they don't talk. Because this is Glasgow. Cause that's how it works, Nicol. Nothing to do with you. Or me."

The house-to-house had been pointless. Nicol had stood beside McCormack at a blurring sequence of doors as he gave his polis knock, three measured blows, the kind of summons that Death might attempt with the butt of his scythe. No one gave them the time of day. Word had gone round. Everyone knew about the body, no one had witnessed a thing. The only anger McCormack and Nicol encountered was directed at them, not the killer. *Cunts've been dumping stuff out there for fuckin weeks. It takes a body to get youse off your arses. How do you know it's just the one? Could be the fuckin Thistle back four buried there for all you cunts care.* Still, at least they'd get the chance to question Turner properly when they got back to the station.

They drove on in silence. Away from the city centre. Away from the action. He'd been heading that way for two months, thought McCormack. Ever since he'd come back from London. He'd spent six years at the Met, with the Flying Squad mainly, the Sweeney, all that swagger, long hair and leather jackets, trying to look like their own outlaw gang. Succeeding. And now he was back in Glasgow. Flett had coaxed him home, DCI Flett, his old St. Andrew's Street gaffer. Come back up the road, son. Forget all that Quaker shit, all that business with Levein. Be part of the new Serious Crime Squad, head up one of the units.

But then Flett had suffered a heart attack at a midweek match at Ibrox, carted out on a stretcher past the craning necks of football fans. He retired with immediate effect. And his replacement, Alan Haddow, had made it known that McCormack wasn't his blue-eyed boy. Wasn't rated. Not quoted. So now McCormack found himself heading up a unit of waifs and strays. As well as himself (D.I. Duncan McCormack, the Highland Thief-taker, Grasser-up-in-Chief, yesterday's man), the unit included: D.S. Derek Goldie, McCormack's old offsider from the Quaker case, fat, blond, disgruntled; a cocky young pretty-boy dipshit D.C. called Iain Shand; and Elizabeth Nicol, the token female D.C. that every four-strong unit now required under the bright new dawn of integration.

McCormack pulled into the driveway and swung round towards the car park at the rear, stowing the Rover in the converted stables. The Serious Crime Squad of Strathclyde Police was quartered in Temple Police Station on Bearsden Road. Clearly, someone possessed a sense of humour. There was nothing serious about Temple Police Station. The location—in the docile wilds of suburban Anniesland, with a timber yard on one side and a stretch of respectable tenements on the other—was a joke. The building itself—a two-storey sandstone structure with a one-storey cellblock adjoining—looked like something from a children's picture book. The cellblock was a miniature version of the main building: the same red stone edged in smart white mortar; the same symmetrical windows; the same pitched and slated roof. The cellblock—which also housed the reception and the two tiny offices used by McCormack's unit—was known as the Byre, while the main block was the Big House. Temple Police Station looked more like a station-master's cottage than a cop shop. You half-expected window boxes and hanging baskets.

As McCormack and Nicol pushed through the front door, though, the place was in uproar. There was shouting and bang-ing from the cellblock and no one manning the front desk. They stood frowning for a minute and the desk sergeant came shouldering through from the main building with two judder-ing buckets, brimful of water. He sluiced them into the cell-block, one after the other, and the shouting and cries got louder.

D.S. Derek Goldie emerged from the office as the desk ser-geant disappeared back into the main building.

"The hell's going on, Derek?"

"It's the jakey, sir," Goldie said. "The witness you sent back from Partick."

"What about him?"

"Maybe it was the heat. I don't know. But when he got into the cell, well, Jesus, that's when it started."

"For Christ's sake, Derek. That's when what started?"

"Man's crawling. He's *alive*. And they all came pouring out of him, out of his hair and beard, the lice, bugs, fleas, whatever. The whole cellblock—well, it's overrun."

"Oh, for Christ's sake."

The desk sergeant was back with another two buckets. McCormack pushed through to the little office that his unit shared.

"We need to get the pest-control in, sir," said Nicol. "And a barber."

"Can't get a barber, Nicol. You can't cut their hair until they've been tried. What?"

Iain Shand was hovering. "Boss wants to see you, sir. Wants an update on the Partick case."

McCormack shook his head. He wanted to pace round the office but there wasn't room. He stood in front of the cork-board with its poorly exposed photographs of Walter Maitland and his close associates. Big, bluff, surly faces that seemed to sneer out at him from the walls.

"Fuck this."

He was off, the door swinging back on its hinges. He plunged through the corridor to the main building, into Haddow's office, no knock.

"McCormack. What the Jesus?"

"You're out of order." He was snorting with anger.

"Sit down, McCormack."

"Pure spite. You're doing this out of spite."

"Sit down, Detective! Now!"

"The job was Maitland." McCormack dropped into a plastic chair and smacked his palm with the back of his hand. "That's why they brought me back. Now you're saddling us with this? At least be honest. At least admit what you're doing."

"You've been at this since you came back. Months you've had. What have you got, exactly?"

"If you're giving us a tasking, give us it. Don't give us it and then take it away."

Haddow looked down at his desk, lips tight. There was a glass paperweight on the desk and he moved it gently, an inch to the right. He kept his eyes lowered. "You maybe want to watch your tone, Detective. 'Do this, do that.' Did you get a promotion I somehow missed? Did you?"

McCormack ran his tongue across his upper teeth. "No. Sir."

"Right. Then you might bear in mind which one of us is in the big chair, son. Anyway, it's done. Marine are stretched and they need our help. That's the job, Detective." He looked up. "Assisting Divisional CID with our specialist knowledge." There was a trill of irony on those last two words. "Man of your experience should clear this up in jig time. You can get back to Maitland when you're done."

"Hamill's team couldn't do it?"

"They're busy. The Byres Road bank job. From what I hear, they're getting somewhere."

"Armstrong? Patterson?"

"The weak link's you, son. Face it. Your unit. Everyone else is doing a job. Let the Maitland stuff lie. Just for the moment."

"Let it lie? And what happens when the Quinns hit back? He torched their warehouse, sir. Killed four folk in the process. You think the Quinns are gonnae, what, take the philosophical view?"

"What are you saying, Detective?"

"I'm saying it's Pearl fucking Harbor, sir. It's an act of war. The Quinns'll hit back. And then all bets are off. Meanwhile, I'm stuck with this?"

"*This*, Detective, is a man dead. Murdered. You want back to Maitland, you need to clear this Partick thing up. You get an ident?"

"Not as yet, no."

"Well, that's the priority. Get the ident. Take it from there."

McCormack was at the door when Haddow called his name. He turned back.

"You know something, McCormack? I keep asking myself why you came back. I'm wondering how Flett must have pitched it. It's six years ago, son, it's all water under the bridge, the Force has been reorganized, it's a fresh start. Something

like that? Because you know what? That's a pile of shite."
Haddow leaned forward. He jabbed his finger at the window.
"It may say Strathclyde Police on the sign out there. But far as
I'm concerned? This is still the City of Glasgow Police. My
mate Pete Levein is still dead. And you're still a fucking rat.
Now, go and do your job."

The smart thing was to leave now. Bite your tongue. "And
your mate Levein," McCormack said. "What was he, if not a
fucking rat?"

Haddow was on his feet, leaning over the desk. "You don't
grass your own! For fuck's sake, McCormack, how's anyone
supposed to trust you now? Who's gonnae believe that you've
got their back? No cunt. That's who. No cunt." He slumped
back into the chair, shaking his head. The *Tribune* was lying
open on his desk and he pushed it violently away. "Go on, son.
Get out my sight."

3

In the end McCormack phoned the procurator fiscal to request a special dispensation, and a grimly competent little man in a brown nylon tunic arrived with his chromium attaché case and got to work with his clippers. Turner's greatcoat and his other garments were inspected for blood before being sent away for incineration.

When McCormack and Nicol sat down across from him in the interview room that afternoon, the vagrant looked like his own younger brother, possibly like his own son. His head had been shaved and the beard was gone. The lean jowls shone, the scrubbed cheeks ruddy. He wore a flannel shirt in red-and-blue checks, black slacks from lost property. The fingers he drummed on the tabletop were long and lean, the nails clipped and squared.

"Joseph Turner?" McCormack consulted his notes.

The man cleared his throat. "That's me, chief."

"How are you feeling?"

"Been worse." He shot the cuffs of his flannel shirt. "Nice gaff you're running here."

"Aye?"

"I'd recommend it to friends. I mean, assuming I had any."

The man grinned. The new look didn't extend to his teeth.

"Well they'd have to wait, wouldn't they? We're undergoing renovations. Some of the rooms are getting fumigated."

"Ah now." Turner grimaced. "Did you really need to bring that up?"

The pink smell of carbolic wafted out as he spread his arms, the baked aroma of laundered clothes. McCormack was having trouble equating the man in front of him with the shambling tramp at the Crawford Street dump.

"At Crawford Street, Mr. Turner," D.C. Nicol cut in, all business; "when you found the body: what time would you say that was?"

Turner looked at McCormack and back at Nicol. "Well. I havenae got a watch but I'd say around dawn. Just after dawn. It's the best time. For raking the midgies. When it's light enough to see but there's no one around."

Midgie-raking: one of Glasgow's venerable, disreputable pastimes. It meant sorting through other people's rubbish, looking for something worth keeping. Since the dustcart drivers' strike, midgie-raking had become Glasgow's national sport, a universal pastime.

"You got much competition?" McCormack asked.

"Well, aye. But no at that time in the morning. They're all out for the count, sleeping off the Lanny."

Lanliq Fortified Wine: tipple of choice for your discerning derelict.

"And you're TT, are you?"

"Band of Hope," Turner said proudly, thumping his chest with the side of his fist. "*That I may be my best and give my best in service, God helping me, I will abstain from all alcoholic drinks.*"

"God help us," said McCormack. "Congratulations, though. Tickety boo. Now, Joseph. When the police arrived, there was no identification on the body."

Turner nodded. "O.K. Right."

"But you got there first. I mean, look, Joseph, if you snaffled his wallet and planked it somewhere, I can understand that. Just tell us where it is and we'll say no more about it."

"God's my witness. There was nothing. I looked in the fella's pockets: there was nothing there."

"Why did you not take the rings? I would've taken them, in your position."

Turner's eyebrows climbed. His shorn skull made his eyes look huge, the eyes of a baby. "I just didnae. Didnae seem right."

Nicol chipped in: "And why did you take the hood off him?"

"I told you. Make sure he was deid."

"You've never seen a dead body?"

"I was at Monte Cassino, missy."

"So you knew he was dead, then," Nicol insisted.

"Well. I wanted to see if I knew him."

"And did you?"

"Never saw him before in my life."

"He wasn't local?"

"Did you no hear me? I've never seen him."

McCormack took over. "You were sleeping in one of the vacant flats, Joseph?"

"Aye. One of them condemned blocks."

"Did you see anything during the night? Hear anything?"

Turner paused. He fingered his smooth cheeks, studied the desk. McCormack's voice dropped a soft octave. "Come on, Joseph. Tell us what you saw. We'll send you on your way."

"There was a van. Like a wee bus. Bright headlights."

They waited.

"You mean like a minibus?" Nicol prompted.

"Naw. It had a flat front, like a single-decker bus. But shorter."

"Anything else?"

"It had two colours. A dark colour and a light one."

"Two-tone. You couldn't see what the colours were?"

"It was the middle of the night. I think the dark was on the bottom, the light on top. Maybe the other way round. I don't know."

McCormack spoke softly. "And what happened, Joseph?"

"A man dragged something out of the back and dumped it on the rubbish heap."

"A body?"

"I thought it was a roll of carpet or something. I don't know."

"It could have been a body?"

"Maybe."

"And the man?"

"I don't know. White shirt or T-shirt. Dark trousers. That's all I saw."

"Big? Small? Thin? Fat? Young? Old?"

"Young, I think. Twenties or thirties. He moved like a young man, looked like he was fit, you know. In shape. Medium height. Shorter than you, anyway."

"Hair?"

"Looked like he was wearing a hat. A cap, maybe."

"O.K. You're doing well, Joseph. You thirsty? You want a cup of tea?"

"Oh, now you're talking, son." The ruined grin was back.

They broke for a few minutes. The desk sergeant came in with a tray bearing three cups of tea and a plate of shortbread fingers. McCormack passed out cigarettes. As he was lighting Turner's smoke he asked him, "How much money did you have on you last night?"

"What, you want to borrow a fiver, son? I'm a bit short right now."

"Just answer the question, Joseph."

"Twenty pence."

"And you used two pee to call it in?"

Turner sensed a trap; the eyes narrowed. "So what? Anyone would have done that."

"You think so? *I* wouldn't." McCormack folded his arms. "I was in your position I'd have got off my mark. Get the hell out of it. Leave the body for someone else to discover. Why'd you call it in, Joseph? Why'd you walk three or four hundred yards and use some of your pot to call it in?"

He ran his hand over his shaved head. "I thought maybe someone had seen me. I thought you'd track me down."

"You've got a record?"

The man nodded, looked at the ground, sucked on his cigarette.

"What did you do, Joseph?"

"I got in a fight. Years back." He looked up. "Bloke died. It wasnae my fault."

"You killed a man?"

"I punched a man. Lucky punch. Unlucky. Wasnae trying to kill him. He picked the fight with me. Got what was coming."

"This was when? Recently?"

"Nah. Sixty-one."

"You go down for it?"

"I did eight years. Peterhead, mostly. It wasnae too bad. Manslaughter, mind. Not murder."

"He started it. That's your excuse?"

"It's true."

"Right. Well. I'm surprised you weren't acquitted then. I mean, all you did was beat a man to death, Joseph."

"See, this is what I was worried about. I didnae beat a man to death. I knocked into a bloke in Sammy Dow's, spilled his pint all down him. The good suit ruined. He starts shooting his mouth off, bobbing and weaving, trying to smack me. I lamped him. Once. No my fault he died."

"O.K., Joseph. You wait here for a while."

They went back to the office and Nicol typed up Joseph Turner's statement. McCormack went with her when she took it through for Turner to sign. He watched as Turner took the pen. Turner signed the statement with his right hand.

"The man in the van," McCormack asked him. "What did

he do after he'd dumped the body? I mean, did he just drive away?"

Turner passed the statement to McCormack. "Aye. Well, he lit a cigarette first. Took a couple of drags."

"Was he facing you?"

"What?"

"When he lit the cigarette, Joseph. Was he facing you?"

Turner spread his hands. "Aye, he was. But I mean I'm not gonnae remember his face. I was a hundred yards away, maybe more. It was dark. And the match—it went out in a second or two."

"That's not what I mean, Joseph. What hand was he holding it in? The match? And then the cigarette?"

Turner closed his eyes. He raised a hand, opened his eyes and looked at it. "The left," he said. "He was holding the fag in his left."

McCormack walked Turner out to the street. He pulled a pound note from his wallet. "Get something to eat, Joseph. A proper lunch. Not one that comes out of a bottle." He watched as the man crossed Bearsden Road and shuffled to a halt at the bus stop.

Back inside, D.C. Shand looked up from his desk as McCormack crossed the squad room.

"Message came when you were with the witness, sir." Shand's expression wasn't easy to read.

"Spit it out then." McCormack hovered at the door to his office.

"English bloke, sir. London accent. Wouldn't give his name. He'd been trying to get a hold of you for hours, he said."

"Right." McCormack paused with the door open, waiting for Shand to continue. "And the message?"

"Well, that's the thing, sir. He didn't seem to have a message at all. He seemed upset. He sounded, well, he sounded as if he was crying, sir. Didn't leave a number."

McCormack nodded slowly, as if this was something he'd expected.

"Thank you, D.S. Shand."

He let the door swing shut behind him, flopped into the chair behind his desk.

4

McCormack lifted the phone and dialled the *Record*'s number.

"Fiona Morrison," he told the switchboard operator. And then, "Detective Inspector Duncan McCormack."

"No need to phone," Morrison said brightly when she came on the line. "A simple spray of roses would have done the job. Yellow, for preference. Box of Milk Tray. Nonetheless: apology accepted. We move on."

McCormack snorted. He told her about the witness, the slim man dumping something from a vehicle, two-toned, a minibus, possibly a VW camper van. He mentioned the rings—the Masonic signet and the pinky ring. If he had a photo of the rings sent over could she give it a decent spread in the morning edition? Help identify the victim?

"And you'll give me the scoop on any new leads?"

"If the picture gets us leads, you get the scoop. Owe you one, Fiona."

They were waiting for him in the outer office, his unit: waiting for his pep talk, his instructions. Words of wisdom. A nest of fledglings: *feed me, feed me.*

He stood at the corkboard with his hands on his hips. He'd been standing up there for the past four months, giving chapter and verse on the way to nail Maitland. For all the bloody good it had done them. It was almost a relief now to have a straightforward task. Here's a body. Find the killer. He laid out the state of play: victim, locus, probable cause. Turner's sighting of the VW camper van.

"And you've just let him go, sir?" Shand was incredulous.

"It's not the vagrant, D.C. Shand. It's not Turner."

"Previous conviction for violence? Eight-stretch for manslaughter? Come on, sir. He's a stick-on."

"He walked half a mile to phone it in," McCormack said. "Why doesn't he just get off his mark?"

"Double bluff?" offered Goldie. He had started on his lunchtime sandwiches and he wagged one rhetorically in the air. "Maybe he knows someone saw him."

"This was a savage beating," McCormack said. "Vicious. Prolonged. If he did it in that backcourt, half of Partick would have heard him. He wouldn't be hanging around. Anyway, Seawright says it happened somewhere else. The killer beats the victim's head in, then brings him to Crawford Street to dump him in the rubbish."

"Which rules out Turner," Nicol said.

"Rules out nothing," Shand said. "He probably killed him in one of the derelict flats. Dragged him downstairs and dumped him."

"We spoke to the uniforms after the door-to-door," Nicol said. "There's nothing in any of the vacant flats to suggest a killing. No bloodstains. No freshly broken windows. No sign of a struggle."

"Or maybe he killed the guy round the corner. The whole area's a bombsite. He's got form, this guy Turner. Why are we looking elsewhere?"

"O.K., D.C. Shand." McCormack stood there with his arms folded. "If it makes you happier, look into Turner's conviction. See if there's more to it than he told us. See if anything connects it to this one. MO, circumstances, victim's age, whatever."

He raised the subject of the rings once more. The ruby pinky ring and the gold signet with the compasses and square.

"You're saying Turner didn't take them?" Goldie asked. "What is he, soft? Superstitious?"

"And the dead man's a *Brother*?" Shand said.

Traffic sounds came through the open window as they thought about this. A man with a Masonic signet ring wasn't a vagrant. He might be many things but he wasn't a vagrant.

"Could be a cop," Goldie said quietly.

"Could be lots of things," McCormack said. "Still, it narrows things down. Probably a Prod. Probably not short of a bob, if the ring's a ruby and it's real. We've got uniforms sifting the rubbish round the body—we'll see what emerges from that. Meantime, Shand—you check Turner's previous. Nicol: get the details of the boiler suit. Find out if there's anything distinctive there. Who makes these boiler suits. Where they get sold. Derek: contact the Masonic lodges, citywide; see if anyone knows of a missing Brother. Fiona Morrison's running a photo of the rings in tomorrow's *Record*. Not much else we can do till we get an ident."

"Right. Good thing we've got Walter Maitland to be going on with, then," said Shand.

"Aye, well. Haddow wants us to lay off Maitland. For the time being, he says."

McCormack glanced down at the floor as he said this; it was easier than meeting their eyes.

Shand snorted. "Lay off Maitland? Jesus Christ. We'd be as well hoisting the white flag right now, give Wattie Maitland the freedom of the city."

He's already got it, McCormack thought. What he said was, "Look, we keep our hand in with Maitland as well as this Partick thing. But we do it under the radar. And we need to focus, here. What's our line of attack? What's our best chance of success?"

"Success? You think he wants us to succeed? Bloody Haddow." Shand was pushing at his rolled-up sleeves. "How do we know he's not one of them, eh? Maitland's tame coppers. Bought and paid for."

McCormack turned quickly, sighting down the barrel of his extended arm, his pointing finger. "I'm going to pretend I didn't hear that, Detective. That sort of talk helps no one."

Shand turned his palms up. "Well have we no touts in Maryhill, then? Folk there must want him off the streets as much as we do. Show them we mean business, that we're gonnae put him away for good, and they'll be queuing up to grass him."

Goldie wiped his mouth with a paper napkin. "You ever been to Maryhill, Iain? Could you find it on a map?"

"Yeah, yeah. The fucking code of silence. It's a code of fear, mate. Take away the fear, it's not a code anymore."

"It's not fear," McCormack said.

"How's that, boss?"

"Because it's not. Iain, does it never occur to you that people actually like Maitland? That folk in the schemes see the point of what he does?"

"He's a parasite, boss."

"What you've got to remember," Goldie was speaking slowly, as if to a child. "A lot of people got houses through Maitland."

"Right. The Housing Office scam." Nicol nodded. "The one he worked with William Bickett."

"What's that got to do with anything?" Shand was glancing between all three of them with quick, indignant twists of his neck.

"Few years back," Nicol said, "when Maitland was working for McGlashan, they had a scam going with the Corporation housing department. You wanted a council house, you gave Maitland a bung. Fifty quid gets you to the top of the waiting list. Get your nice wee three-bed in Knightswood or wherever."

"What's your point, Nicol?"

"The point is," McCormack said. "The point is, people remember that stuff. It counts for something."

Shand dug in his jacket pocket for his smokes. "Counts for what, sir? Come off it. They remember Maitland ripping them off? They remember paying fifty quid for something should have cost them nothing."

"No, son." Goldie was shaking his head, the patient schoolmaster. "Something they would never have got, if it wasn't for Walter Maitland."

"So they're grateful. So what? Suddenly they're Maitland's soldiers? Give me a break."

Goldie pursed his lips, looked at McCormack.

"Look, Iain," McCormack said. "It's the little things, O.K.? The wee favours. Maitland needs something hidden. 'Can you watch this box for me? Keep it under your bed for a few days?' 'No problem, Mr. Maitland.' Or maybe someone needs to disappear. 'Can my friend doss down for a few days?' 'No problem, Mr. Maitland.' Or somebody needs an alibi. 'Oh yeah, I saw him in the Duke last Thursday. He was there all night. Never moved from the spot.' You see how it works? He's got an army of civilians ready to help. Are they going to commit murders for him? Rob banks? Of course not. But they do the little things. The things that keep it ticking nicely over. He's not 'ruling the streets with fear', that's a bullshit *Record* headline. He's ruling the streets with favours. He helps people. Helps them more than we do. That's what we're up against."

Shand seemed to think about this. He tugged his nose with forefinger and thumb. "Ah, fuck it. We should do what they do with the Taigs."

"The Taigs, Detective?"

"The fucking Irish, sir." Shand was putting a cigarette out in the metal ashtray with repeated angry stabs. His black hair swung over one eye. "Those IRA bastards. Hold them for a week. No warrants or lawyers or any of that shite. Show them what's what."

McCormack waited till Shand had extinguished his cigarette. Then he leaned forward and gripped Shand lightly by the wrist. He spoke softly. "Now understand something, son. There are no shortcuts here. O.K.? A shortcut's just more work in the long run. Covering your tracks. Getting your story straight, sticking to it. We do proper police work here, D.C. Shand. We do things right. And if it takes a little longer, then that's fine. It takes as long as it takes."

He released Shand's wrist.

"With respect, sir, that's bollocks. How long till Haddow works out we're still going after Maitland? A week?"

"Then we do what we can in a week. That's the job, son. There's no magic bullets. If we run out of time, we run out of time."

"Right. Do they ever run out of time, sir, do you think? Walter Maitland and his mates."

"You don't beat them by stooping to their level, son. They've won when that happens. Oh and by the way, son." McCormack clapped Shand on the shoulder. "Taigs? You're working for one."

Goldie and Nicol were laughing. Shand held up his hands. "Ah, Jesus. Look, boss. I didn't mean anything by it. I was just . . ."

"Leave it, son. You've got your big day coming up in a week or so. The Glorious Twelfth. You can put all that shite away for another year when that's over. O.K.?"

"Right, sir. Absolutely." Shand was nodding like his neck was on a spring. "Nae danger. Again: no offence, boss."

Shand's cigarette butt was still smouldering in the ashtray. Goldie was watching the wavering line of smoke. "The fire," he said. "The Tradeston fire. Must be some way to nail him for that?"

"It's a dead end, Derek." McCormack sat on an empty desk. "We've been through it. F Div's been all over it. There's no witnesses, no evidence."

"Four people dead. Burnt to a cinder."

"I know. A wee girl among them. And we've got the funeral on Thursday."

Nicol looked up. "Whose funeral?"

"The mum and the wee girl. Haddow wants us to show face. Myself and Derek. Represent the Force. For all the good it'll do."

"Burnt to death in their beds," Goldie said.

"Aye. And Maitland ordered it. No question. But did he set the fire himself? Do we know who did? Come on, Derek. Maitland's too cute to get his hands dirty."

"Right. Everything goes through his brother Hugh. And his dogshit cousin—McPhail."

McCormack was on his feet again, stalking to the window. He could see the gasometers by the canal, their delicate framework of hoops and girders standing stark against the sky. It was a view that calmed him usually, but not today. Goldie was right. Walter Maitland could burn four people in their beds and you couldn't touch him for it?

"Are we kidding ourselves here?" He turned sharply in the tight space. Three faces pointed up at him—sullen, sad, like scolded dogs. "Serious Crime Squad. Elite fucking unit. Haddow's right. We've had months to make a case against Maitland. The fuck are we doing?"

The other three shifted in their seats. Goldie was the senior figure, it was up to him to respond. "Iain's got a point, though," Goldie began. "I mean, maybe not Haddow, but somebody's feeding Maitland the inside scoop. He's always that one step ahead. We do what we can, Dunc. But if the game's rigged . . ."

"Then we've got to rig it, too," said Iain Shand. "In *our* favour. That's what I'm saying, boss. Take the war to Maitland. Take it to these scumbags."

"Can you hear yourself, son? Take the war to Maitland!

What was your bright idea? Cigarette smuggling! Where did that get us, again? How did that pan out?"

Maitland was sourcing untaxed smokes. Woodbine. Embassy Filter. Offloading them in his pubs and brothels, selling them from Maryhill flats. They'd managed to disrupt the operation a couple of times but they couldn't find the source. The Wills cigarette factory on Alexandra Parade swore blind that there wasn't a leak.

"There's other interests, though," Nicol said.

Goldie frowned. "Protection? Sharking? We've tried it."

"I was thinking more about prostitution, actually," Nicol said. "That's still not legal. Last time I looked."

McCormack and Goldie exchanged a look. "Go on," McCormack said.

"Well, we know he's expanding in this area. Or certainly his brother is. Why don't we focus on that for the time being, see what we can come up with?"

Shand had found a packet of ready salted crisps. He tore open the side-seam and set them in the centre of his desk. "Maitland's expanding in all areas. What's so special about hoors?"

"He won't be expecting it, for one thing. No one's tried to disrupt that side of his business in years."

Hoors, McCormack thought. He'd gone with one, years back, he must have been twenty years old. Back when he still held out hope. It was the wrong girls, he'd decided. The girls he'd been with were inexperienced, they didn't know what they were doing. A pro would take him in hand. A pro would iron him out.

On a breezy night in August he took nearly half of the earnings from his summer bartending gig (he didn't know what a woman cost and he didn't want to find himself short) and walked into town. On Blythswood Hill, by the only square of grass in the whole city centre, she was standing on a corner, one foot propped on the wall behind her. She took him into West Regent Lane, to a recessed doorway plastered with graffiti. Someone had markered a big cock-and-balls at eye-level and it seemed to mock the woman's efforts. She was patient and kind, but finally, long after McCormack wanted to slither down between the bars of a drain and be washed away to sea, she tucked him gently away and pulled up his zipper. Don't worry about it, she told him. Stage fright. Everyone gets it. Once you break your duck there'll be no stopping you.

She'd been right, it turned out, though not quite in the way she'd imagined.

"Come on, Nicol," Shand was saying. He spoke with a mouth full of crisps. "You ever tried to get a conviction for living off immoral earnings?"

"Yes, I know. That wasn't my—"

"Weeks of surveillance, it takes. We havenae got weeks."

"I know that, Iain. I was thinking more about the girls, the women themselves."

"What about them?" McCormack said.

"Well. In my experience they pick things up. They hear things."

"The hoors?" Goldie looked up from his sandwich. "Who would tell a hoor anything?"

"The *women*," Nicol said. "You'd be surprised. Or maybe you wouldn't. Guys get careless in situations like that. Possibly they've got other things on their mind."

"In your experience?" McCormack said. "You're saying these women have touted for you?"

"Some of them have, yeah."

"There's the question of credibility, though, isn't there?" Shand put in. "I mean as witnesses."

Nicol turned her bright smile on him. "Oh, I see. Bank managers, are they? Kirk elders? Knights of the realm?"

"Who?"

"Your stable of touts," Nicol said. "You obviously move in different circles than me. Look, sir." She turned to McCormack. "It's just an idea. I've got a bit of experience in the area. Professionally, I mean."

I bet you have, thought McCormack. Women cops got all the sex cases. All the indecencies and child assaults. After integration it was supposed to be different, but it was hard to change the culture. When a sexual came in, it went straight to the woman on the squad. She did her share of all the other stuff too—there was integration so far as that went—but she did the sexuals on top of that.

"You're in touch with women who work for Maitland?"

"I don't know. Maybe. They come and go. There's new girls starting all the time."

"So what's the plan? Let's hear it."

Nicol set out what she knew about Maitland's brothels. She gave a run-down of the various types of prostitution practised in the city, largely for the benefit of D.C. Shand, who seemed to believe that hoors were hoors.

On the contrary, Nicol informed him. There are hoors, and there are hoors. First you've got the independents. The high-class hookers. One-woman businesses, operating out of private addresses in good parts of the city. Regular clients, mostly professional. Everything discreet and hygienic. These are the places the polis never know about, except by chance.

Then there's the saunas. Again, high-quality girls. Good hygiene. Bit of glamour. Nice surroundings. The girls give up most of their wages to the gangsters who run the places, but they've got some muscle behind them if something goes wrong. It's a damn sight safer than working the streets.

Next step down is the proper brothels, the knocking-shops in the dodgier schemes. Nitshill. Govan. Blackhill. A bit rough and ready. Clients are the local punters. Again, there'll be a gangster on the premises, keeping the women "safe". Again, the women give up most of the money in return for security. It's not a sauna but it's not the streets.

And then, finally, bottom rung of the ladder, there's the streets. Women out in all weathers in Blythswood Square, Bothwell Street doorways: D.C. Shand's "hoors". Poor women not presentable enough for anything else. Working the streets to feed their weans. Maybe seasonals, in the run-up to Christmas. They take whatever comes, they run all the stupid risks. These are the women who turn up dead.

"It's a hierarchy like any other," Nicol told them. "You get a bit of movement. Sometimes a sauna girl lets herself go, gets too fond of the drink, ends up on the streets. Or maybe a young lassie starts out on the streets, gets spotted, finds herself working the saunas. But basically it's a caste system; you keep to your level."

McCormack nodded. "So what do you suggest, D.C. Nicol?"

"Simple. We focus on the saunas. The women at the top, the lone hookers; they work for themselves, they've got nothing to do with gangsters. The women at the bottom are the same; they're out trying to feed their weans, or some scumbag boyfriend's pimping them out. The brothels? O.K., sometimes the women might hear something; it's a criminal milieu. But the proper gangsters aren't screwing these women; they're not seen as classy enough. The saunas are different. The top boys all use the women in the saunas. It's a perk of the job. Freebies. Those are the women we want to target."

"So we hit one of Maitland's saunas." McCormack was nodding to himself.

"Not exactly 'under the radar', though, is it?" Goldie asked. "What if Haddow wants to know why we're raiding Maitland's brothels?"

"We're following a lead," McCormack said, "from the Partick case. The victim may have been in the area to buy sex. Possibly he was a frequenter of local saunas. It's thin, but it'll do." Something struck him. Local? He frowned. "Do we know where they are, though? These saunas?"

Nicol grinned. "We do, as it happens, sir. *We* know exactly where they are."

5

Diamond in the mud. That was the Duke of Perth amid the sooty drabness of Maryhill Road. Between a barber's and a bookie's, the pub announced its name in bulbous gold letters on a bottle green background. On either side of the name was a gold fleur-de-lis in bas-relief. Half-frosted plate-glass windows bore the words "WINES" and "ALES" in gold-leaf paint. But the glittering dream couldn't escape the reality of Maryhill; across the frosted windows lay an elaborate grillwork of wrought-iron bars, painted a rich burgundy, which gave the place the air of a luxury stockade.

Inside, the pretensions collapsed entirely. Cracked red lino like cheap cuts of steak, scarred wooden tables clamped to the floor, a bare wooden bench down the length of one wall. Twin taps on the counter: lager; heavy. A gantry of fortified wines and blended whiskies with names like "Glenkinnan" and "Clan Gathering". The people who drank here were not connoisseurs. They came to the Duke to get drunk, fast. If their drink was wet and alcoholic, that was plenty. There was something selfless and ascetic—a kind of monastic dedication—in the prevailing approach to drink.

Aside from the holy drinkers, there were those who came to the Duke as a show of loyalty to the landlord. The pub may have been named for the Duke of Perth, but the real power in the land had his name in much smaller letters over the lintel: "Licensee: W. Maitland". At the far end of the pub, behind a door marked function suite, was the inner sanctum, the room where Walter Maitland held court with his key lieutenants—his brother Hugh first of all, and then four men whose names could produce little pockets of silence in pubs right across the Northside. Below these men was a cadre of younger thugs in sharp suits who called themselves the top boys and hung around in the public bar. Below the top boys were the hangers-on and fringe players, and below them the civilians. This hierarchy was reproduced in the floor space of the pub—Maitland's soldiers at the far end, civilians near the door.

Christopher Kidd sat in the civilian end of the Duke of Perth twirling a beermat through his fingers. His half-pint of heavy was finished and he didn't know whether to buy another. The pub was lunchtime quiet but Maitland's boys held their spot at the far corner of the bar. In their pinstripe high-waisters and platform soles they looked like a pop band more than a gaggle of wannabe gangsters. Kidd tapped his beermat on the table.

Was it only ten days back he'd sat here with John McPhail and told his story? McPhail had listened while Kidd told him how he'd been visiting his cousin across the river, down in Govanhill. Kidd was walking back into town along Victoria Road when a lorry pulled up beside him. Did he want half a day's work? The delivery crew were short-handed and the next thing Kidd was grasping the gaffer's forearm and being hauled up into the cab. Not the hardest tenner he ever earned but not far off it. Rolling big barrels up a pair of planks to the first floor of a warehouse in Tradeston. The gaffer was a big man in a black leather jacket, hair swept back in a widow's peak. The men called him "Denny".

"Denny *Quinn*?" McPhail asked. "You were working for Denny Quinn?"

"Well, I think so. I mean, I'm not a hundred per cent, but, aye, I think so."

"Six-footer. Built. Black goatee beard, looks like the devil?"

"That's the fella, aye."

At that point McPhail went into the back room and came back with another bloke and the two of them sat down opposite Kidd.

"Tell him what you told me."

When Kidd finished his story, the bloke looked at McPhail and then back at Kidd.

"And it's the Quinns?"

"I think so, aye. Denny Quinn anyway."

The bloke nodded, looking away across the crowded pub to the light in the half-frosted windows. He was talking to himself now. "It's the whiskey from their Irish connection. They know we've clocked the Allison Street gaff so they've moved it to this new place." He looked back at Kidd. "You ready to earn some money, son?"

Kidd grinned.

So it was agreed right there and then that Kidd would do it. At a table in the Duke of Perth, McPhail and the other bloke talked him through it. How you looked for a wall heater or plugged-in radio or lamp to set up your materials. How you splashed a trail of water from the source to the doorway, *before* you laid down your trail of petrol, so that the petrol floated on top and couldn't be detected later. The aim was to make it look like an accidental fire. The Quinns would know it was Maitland, but no one could prove anything. There was nothing to it, they said. Piece of piss, so long as you kept your head and followed instructions. Which Kidd had done, to the letter. So why the fuck was McPhail now ignoring him?

McPhail had seen him; that was certain. Kidd looked bitterly up the pub to where Maitland's crew stood. One of them seemed to have cracked a joke. The four heads reared back in laughter and McPhail turned to scan the pub and stared straight at Kidd, the laughter gone, blinking slowly, photographing him with his eyes. Then he turned back to the others.

Kidd lit a match, watching the yellow sail of flame climb the blackened stick. He had pictured this scene many times. How it would be when he had proved himself to Maitland and could take his place at the end of the bar, standing and joking with the top boys. He'd pictured himself pushing through those doors in a mohair suit, tipping his chin to Jack the barman, the magic circle at the end of the bar parting to welcome him. A wee goldie lands on the bar-top in front of him. He pulls a cigar from his breast pocket and somebody thumbs a lighter. He leans in to the flame and puffs it alight, tips his head back to send a plume of blue smoke to the ceiling, nodding like a judge, scanning round the pub with his cool, hooded eyes.

The match was burning his fingers and he shook it out hastily. McPhail was striding down the scuffed red lino towards him. Kidd straightened in his seat but McPhail kept his head down, buttoning his jacket, and made for the Gents.

Kidd followed. He could hear McPhail's piss drumming on the steel trough. He stood and waited for McPhail to finish, for McPhail to shake himself unhurriedly, zip his fly. McPhail crossed to the steel sink. Only when his hands were lathered did he decide to notice Kidd. He studied himself in the mirror, twisting his jaw as if to check the closeness of his shave, raising his voice above the running water.

"Just tell me one thing, Chris. What the fuck are you play-ing at?"

Kidd glanced around: the trough, the empty stalls, the Durex machine. "Where was I supposed to get you? It's been four days, John."

"I can count, Chris. I know how many days it's been. But you need to use the heid, mate. You cannae be here. What if Walter came? What if somebody saw you with Walter? After what you've done."

People see Walter with you, Kidd thought. And we all know what you've done.

"I did what was asked," Kidd said. "Did exactly what you told me."

"Is that right?" McPhail had finished washing his hands. He yanked the towel rail three or four times. "We asked you to kill four people, did we? A mother and a wee lassie among them? Burn them tae a crisp. I must have missed that bit. When did we ask you that, Christopher?"

"I did what was asked," Kidd said again.

"And, what? You think you're one of the boys now? You think Walter will welcome you with open arms, give you a route? You think that's how it works?"

You think I don't know how it works, Kidd thought. You think I don't know about gangs? The staff at Auldpark Children's Home were a gang, after lights out in the dorm, when they hauled you out of bed. The fucking church is a gang, with the pope as its leader-aff. You boys are nothing special.

"Look, Chris. It's nothing personal. You just need to disappear. All right?"

Kidd gaped. He felt behind him for the cold tiled wall, subsided against it. "What?"

McPhail laughed. "Jesus, son. Get a grip of yourself. I mean you need to get out of the city for a bit. What did you think I meant?"

"Nothing. Where would I go?"

"We'll sort it out, Chris. Go home and lie low. Someone'll come round and see you in a day or two. Tell you the plan. All right? Take this for now."

McPhail was peeling tenners off a roll: three, four, five. He pushed them into the top pocket of Kidd's jacket, jabbing them down with stiff fingers. He gripped Kidd's lapels in his fists, shook him lazily, slapped his jaw, twice, the way you might bring a drunk man round. "All right, man? You need to sober up here, Chris. You need to keep the heid, pal. All right?"

Kidd's head hung low, like a sulking child. He looked at his feet. What choice did he have? "O.K., John. Understood." He made as if to shake hands but McPhail was already moving past him, clapping him on the shoulder. "Now get the fuck out of here. All right?"

Out in the street, Kidd narrowed his eyes against the afternoon sun. He spat on the ground and stamped down on the buckled metal of the cellar-grille as he set off down Maryhill Road, the springy give of that hollow square of pavement tingling in his ankle as he walked.

6

Woodlands Road was the kind of indeterminate street—not quite city centre, not quite West End, snaking between the upscale purlieus of Woodlands Hill and the tenements of St. George's Cross—where you were likely to find a sauna. Back in the Fifties most of Glasgow's vice was confined to the centre. The yellow light from the late-night coffee-stalls drew the punters coming out of the clubs and casinos, the dancehalls and flicks. From the shadows round the hatches the girls would step forward into the drunk men's line of vision, lead them up the alleys, do the business for a quid. But a crackdown in the late Fifties shut the coffee-stalls and shuffled the girls up the hill to Blythswood Square and West Campbell Street. That's when the saunas came into their own.

Healing Hands had the mirrored window, the neon sign (disembodied jazz hands in bubble-gum pink), and the doorentry system.

McCormack thumbed the buzzer.

"Evening, sir. Can you confirm your appointment?"

"Don't have one."

A pause. "I'm afraid we're fully booked this evening. Perhaps you could telephone to schedule something."

"Right. In fact, I think an opening may have come up." He was holding his warrant card up to the screen.

A longer pause. "One moment, officer."

It was several moments—a good two minutes by Nicol's

watch—before the buzzer sounded. In the meantime the receptionist would have punched the button under her desk, sounding a bell in all of the basement cabins, and the hookers and their clients would have hightailed it to the fire door into the alley, where two uniforms were waiting to shepherd them back.

McCormack and Nicol were in the foyer with the hard-faced receptionist—lavender tunic, hoop earrings—when the getaway troupe came straggling up the stairs. Hair awry. Misbuttoned shirts. Shirts on inside out. Even the receptionist let a smile of sorts flicker across her glossed lips.

As if by some accord the punters and the women had separated, the men huddling in a rumpled cluster beside the vending machine. Four men. Three business types and one in polo shirt and jeans.

"Gentlemen. I'm Detective Inspector McCormack. This is Detective Constable Nicol. We need to see some ID, please."

One of the suits was reaching into his inside pocket when the man beside him stepped forward. "Now hold on here." The man was chubby, with jowls that juddered when he shook his head. His swept-back hair was thinning. His shirt was half open. He wore a St. Christopher medal on a gold chain. "Hold on here just a minute."

It was hard, McCormack thought. Hard to stand on your dignity when your shirttail was poking out of your unzipped fly and you were carrying one of your shoes. Hard, but then some of us rise to a challenge.

"There is no requirement," St. Christopher was saying, pointing an empty brogue at McCormack like a hand-tooled, soft-leather pistol; "no requirement that we furnish our identities."

McCormack looked at the other men. The one who'd been reaching for his wallet had frozen in the act and now he drew his hand out empty. McCormack ran his tongue along his upper gums, breathed through his nose. The chubby man's eyes were bright with defiance.

"Put your shoe on," McCormack told him. "Clarence Darrow. 'Furnish your identities'! What if I arrest you right now for obstructing a police officer in the pursuit of his duty? Get your names that way. How would that be?"

"The law of Scotland regards sexual transactions as a private matter between two people," the man intoned. "You have no right to require our names."

The other men were enjoying this now. They were straightening their clothes, tucking in their shirts, coming back to themselves with each properly buttoned cuff. The man in the polo shirt and jeans was hanging back, McCormack noticed, head down. He caught McCormack's eye and looked away, and in that moment McCormack knew he was a cop. He didn't know him; he just knew he was a cop. Nicol jerked her chin at McCormack and he tilted his head to her whispered counsel. He nodded. Nodded again.

"O.K., gentlemen. You're free to go. The officers here will escort you to your cars, see you safely on your way." McCormack turned his gaze to the uniforms, who nodded briskly, ushered the men out into the street.

When the uniforms came back, they had car registration numbers for three of the men. The fourth—the man in the polo shirt and jeans—claimed to have travelled by bus.

"You're finished for the night here," McCormack said to the receptionist. She had a name-tag on her tunic. "Annie. Say hello to Walter, Annie. Tell him Duncan McCormack sends his regards."

"Who's Walter? Don't know any Walter."

Out on the pavement, the women were getting into the cars. McCormack stepped back into the street and looked up at the cliff-face of tenement looming above the ground-floor shops. They'd be up there somewhere. Not Maitland himself, but Maitland's men, sitting in a room, playing cards perhaps, ready for trouble. He was surprised that the panic button hadn't brought them down, but maybe Annie had phoned them before she opened the door: *Polis are here; I've got it.* A shape moved behind a first-floor window, the figure of a man blocking the light, then he was gone and the curtains pulled shut.

Almost as soon as they arrived at Temple, as the women were being processed at the charge bar, you could see the weak link, the one you'd detach from the herd. The hunted eyes, the hunched shoulders. The hiss of her bangles as she rooted for her ciggies. Nicol saw it too. He let Nicol do the interview, she was the expert; he just sat beside her on their side of the table.

"Yvonne Gray," the woman said.

"And how long have you been working at the sauna, Yvonne?"

"At this one? Two year. Aye, two year."

"And before that?"

"Different saunas." She tossed her head. "Different places. Ye know?"

"The man you work for, Yvonne. Met him, have you?"

"Who? I don't know." She wiped her nose with the back of her hand.

"But you've heard of him, right? You've heard of Walter Maitland?"

Yvonne looked at the desk, eyes darting. She didn't know what to do with this. Everyone had heard of Walter Maitland. "We work for Annie Symes," she said. "That's all I know."

"You know what Walter Maitland does, Yvonne? I mean, apart from ponce off women, obviously."

She shook her head again. She kept glancing at the door as if someone was coming through it to rescue her. She didn't want to be here. She didn't want to be the one who was talking to the polis about Walter Maitland.

"Look, I need to get back. Honest. I've got a kid at home." She raked her bare arms with her nails, raising pink scratch marks. "Can I go now?"

"Soon, Yvonne. We won't be much longer."

Yvonne nodded. She sat there in the starched white snap-button tunic like a nurse, though it was she who looked sick, sallow, bluish under the cold white lights. And it was Nicol who probed like a doctor, seeking with her steady questions to fathom the source of her ailment.

"Do you know this man?" Nicol asked. "Have you seen him in the sauna? Can you tell us his name?"

There were six photos on the desk, face down. Nicol had taken them from the corkboard in the squad room. The Maitland brothers and their four lieutenants. She had turned the first one over and Yvonne Gray shook her head.

Nicol flipped the others, one by one. Yvonne Gray would know all of these men, they would be regulars in the sauna, but she pursed her mouth sceptically and shook her head until the last face stared up from the table. It was the meaty, brutish face of a man in his forties, greying hair swept back. There were deep grooves dropping from the sides of his nose and his top lip was folded in a sneer. He looked as though he'd been interrupted at a task he enjoyed or maybe somebody had asked him a stupid question. When Yvonne Gray saw the face her own face tightened. Her whole body braced and clenched and her breath caught, a clipped hiss.

"Did this man demand sex from you, Yvonne?" Nicol kept her voice even, low. "You're not in any trouble, we just want the truth."

Yvonne was scratching her arm again. She kept her head down. "Nope. Never seen him."

"But you recognized him, Yvonne. This is Alex Kerr. He lends out money for Walter Maitland. You know who this is."

"Naw. Mebbe. Look, I thought I knew him. But I don't.

There's too many, to be honest. They all blend into one. Cannae help you."

She had closed up completely now. Whatever chance there might have been had gone. She wasn't going to tell them anything. The thought came to McCormack, madly, to offer her money. Wasn't this her thing? You please men who give you money. Give them what they want. But he stopped himself in time.

"O.K. then, Miss Gray." Nicol was holding a business card between finger and thumb. "You remember what this man did. Or anything else you want to talk about, you call that number. I'll come to you. I'll help you. O.K.?"

Yvonne Gray took the card; Nicol kept a grip of it until Yvonne nodded, then she let it go. Yvonne stowed it in the breast pocket of her tunic.

Nicol walked her out. McCormack could hear Nicol's voice and Yvonne Gray's heels dwindling down the corridor. It was time to call it a night.

On the way home he picked up an early edition of tomorrow's *Record*. Back at the flat he poured himself a large Springbank and slumped down in the armchair with the paper. There it was, page seven:

BODY FOUND IN CITY DUMP.

Fiona Morrison doing her best to make it sound like a gangland slaying. There was a long-lens snap of the locus with the red-and-white incident tape bisecting a cluster of figures, McCormack among them. And a close-up of the dead man's rings. They gave the telephone number for the incident room at Temple Police Station at the end of the report.

That was something, McCormack reflected. The phones would be ringing tomorrow, maybe someone would have seen something. He rose and crossed to the sink to add a little water to his whisky. When he sat back down a dead weight of lethargy pressed him to the chair. A long day but, Jesus, all of the days seemed long. Maybe he was past it, maybe it was time to pass the reins to a younger man. He thought of Iain Shand, all cufflinks and cockiness. His smirking face. Shand didn't rate him, McCormack knew. Probably thought of him as dead wood. Yesterday's man. Damaged goods.

Who's gonnae trust you now? Haddow's jibe came back to McCormack as he sipped his whisky. The papers might call you a whistleblower, but that was just a fancy way of saying "rat". There was a reason why the partner you worked with was called your "neebor". Neighbours might bitch about one another, they might indulge petty jealousies and rivalries. But ultimately they lived in the same street. They had each other's backs. And you needed that in the polis. You needed that solidarity. You couldn't function without it. Civilians didn't understand what it was like. Sometimes a suspect made a false accusation. Sometimes your split-second decision turned out to be wrong. Sometimes you had to cut corners. Sometimes a witness needed a little additional persuasion. That's what life was like. If you were too much of a kirk elder to accept that, then you had no business being a polis. McCormack did accept it. What he didn't accept was that a polis like Peter Levein—who spent five years in a gangster's pocket, who colluded with serial murder—deserved the same protection as everyone else. Levein had put himself out in the cold when he did what he'd done. But no one else saw it like that. Now McCormack was out in the cold for what he'd done to Levein. What McCormack had done was heresy.

Fuck it. At least Goldie and Nicol had his back. He hoped. And Greg Hislop did too. He smiled at the thought of the crabbit old bastard. Hislop might be retired but his legend hadn't faded. The old CID Inspector was still revered in the station canteens and polis bars across the city. He'd cracked the heads of the Billy Boys and the Norman Conks in the Thirties, given the Boche the same treatment during the Second World War, helped put Peter Manuel and Jimmy Boyle behind bars. He was a Highlander, from Ballachulish, like McCormack. And though he'd left Balla when McCormack was a kid, Hislop had played shinty with McCormack's father. McCormack worked under him at C Div. Jesus, McCormack remembered: what days those were. He and Hislop had terrorized the East End neds and the older man had become mentor, drinking buddy and surrogate dad all rolled into one. When he came back to the city, the first thing McCormack did was seek Hislop out. Now he met Hislop every Thursday night in the Park Par on Argyle Street. More often than not, it was the highlight of the bloody week. Roll on Thursday, McCormack thought, as he raised his glass to Hislop in a silent toast.

WEDNESDAY, 2 JULY 1975

7

Liz Nicol took the knife and pushed it through the shell. It made a satisfying crackle. The yolk looked up at her like a surprised eye. She finger-tapped a few grains of salt onto the yellow disc—neither runny nor chalky but rubbery. Just as she liked it. *Go to Work on an Egg*. She glanced at the clock. Second day of a murder inquiry. Don't be late.

Second day, but it felt like the first. For Liz Nicol, it always felt like the first day. Did a time come when you felt you had made it, when you stopped having to prove your worth from scratch each day?

She finished the first half of the egg and started on the smaller half. Its little pebble of yolk came away and then she scooped the rest in a clean whole, the slick perfect curve of the albumen bluing in the light from the kitchen window.

A murder inquiry. Maybe now they'd get to see what Duncan McCormack was all about. She'd been excited to come and work under McCormack, the man who caught the Quaker. Up until now, the team's brief had been building a case against Walter Maitland, but that was like bottling smoke. Now their goal couldn't be clearer: find the man who killed the man in Crawford Street.

She smoothed her skirt in front of the hallstand mirror. It was enough to make you pine for uniform. Days when you reached into the closet for the bluebottle tunic and skirt, the cap with the Sillitoe tartan. It was no problem for the men. In

CID they just changed to a different uniform, a row of suits in the closet. Choose a tie each morning and you were done.

She had gone for the look she always went for. Businesslike but not stuffy. Wide-collared cream satin blouse with two buttons undone, a chocolate-coloured suit with long jacket and below-the-knee skirt. Tan tights and slingbacks. She stared intently at the frowning woman in the hallstand's glass.

In some ways integration had made things worse. As a detective, Nicol had been in with the men for years, on the book, working the rota like anyone else. But the integration of the uniformed branch had changed the atmosphere, even for the plainers. An edge of resentment was creeping in, a sense that female detectives were muscling in, taking the jobs of men with families to feed. Already she'd overheard herself being called "Mrs. Thatcher" in the canteen at Temple. Jesus, you had to laugh at that. A woman might be leading the Tory party. Who knows, in time she might become PM. But a woman heading up the CID? Or even a divisional unit? Be the Twelfth of Never when that happened.

She plucked her car keys from the dish on the hallstand and stepped lightly over the gravel. Since her marriage foundered last Christmas, she'd been living in the grounds of her parents' villa in Newton Mearns. The gate lodge had been converted into what her mother persisted in calling a "granny flat".

Nicol closed the car door and started the engine as quietly as she could. She did this, not out of consideration for her sleeping parents, but because she knew that, if her mother was awake, she would be staring down at her daughter's departure with a look of insufferable pity.

Nicol eased out of the driveway and headed up to Ayr Road. She wondered, fleetingly, how her mother referred to her when chatting with her keep-fit friends. *Poor Lizzie*, probably. Poor Lizzie, the prodigal daughter. Not just unmarried but divorced. Damaged goods, to her mother's way of thinking.

The traffic was light on the road through Giffnock and she opted to cross the Clyde by the Kingston Bridge. The Tunnel was quicker for Temple, but she liked how the approach road lofted you over the river and onto the bridge. It felt like a runway, like your plane had taken off and you were soaring over Glasgow, the sun silvering the Clyde, the whole city spreading out to the east and the west.

What would it be like now, she wondered; starting in uniform in the general force, with no more Women's Dept? She was grateful, in a way, that she'd missed all that. Getting into CID when she did, she was pretty much accepted for who she was. Maybe her partners would have preferred to be neighboured to a man, but they never treated her any different. There was a stupid initiation thing in some stations where they used the office stamp on your backside, to show you were now the "property" of that station. But once that was over you were one of the boys, you could more or less forget you were a woman.

Which wasn't too hard, she reflected. Lately, she was getting plenty of practice in that department. In the six months since Kenny left, she'd been living like one of the Poor Clares. Sister Elizabeth of Temple. Men weren't keen on dating cops at the best of times. But divorced cops? The only upside was that you never had to explain why you divorced. People just assumed it was the pressures of the job. Nicol didn't correct them. Sometimes she almost believed it herself.

When she reached Temple, the gang was all there in the Byre: Shand perched on his desk, Goldie swinging on the legs of his chair, McCormack standing in his office doorway. McCormack had been for his run that morning; his hair was still damp from the shower.

"So what do we think?"

"The blonde skinny one," Goldie said. "Yvonne something. Something spooked her."

"Gray," Nicol said, dumping her bag on the desk. "Yvonne Gray."

"She's, what, thirty? Thirty-two?" Shand was swinging his legs, polished toecaps winking in the light. "Been round the block. Must've been lifted a dozen times. Why's she acting like a rabbit?"

They all turned to look at Nicol. She sat at her desk, opening a box-file of witness statements. "Liz." McCormack jerked his chin at her. "Any thoughts? You're the expert."

"Really?" She laughed shortly. "The only woman in the room knows more about pros than the men do? We sure about this?"

"Just answer the question."

She had touched a nerve. "O.K., sir." She shoved the box of statements aside. "Could be something, could be nothing. These women, they see things. Things happen around them. They get pretty superstitious, some of them."

Goldie's fingertips were resting on the desk edge. He kept pushing himself off and returning as he swung on his chair legs. He looked like he was playing chords on the piano. "You mean don't walk under ladders? Black cats are unlucky?"

"Unlucky? All pussy's lucky." Shand was grinning. "Whatever the colour."

"How do you mean 'superstitious'?" McCormack asked. "Like they've got their little rituals?"

"They do, but I was thinking more of the stories they tell. Sort of urban myths. A bogey man who murders prostitutes. Never gets caught. *Can't* get caught."

"Like Jack the Ripper?" Goldie said.

McCormack frowned. "They make up stories to scare each other, you mean?"

"I wouldn't exactly say that, sir. Stories like that are real, to a point. Prostitutes go missing. They wind up dead. Only it's not one man who's doing it. That's the fairy story part."

There was a lull after Nicol's words. The three men were conscious of a shared unease. Nicol was the authority in this particular field. They recognized that. But they wanted to believe in the story. They wanted its reassurance. A single man, killing women. A bad man, a bogey man. A one-off. Not a whole phalanx of men. Men like them. They were like the Lost Boys waiting for the Wendy Bird to tell them a different story. It was Shand who spoke up, with a perplexed half-laugh. "So how many are there, in your opinion? I mean, how many men? Running round, murdering women?"

"Well how would we even begin to know?" Nicol looked round the three faces. "Do we know how many prostitutes go missing? Does anyone keep track of missing girls? Do we even pretend to give a shit?"

McCormack leaned against the doorjamb. He was thinking about the Quaker. His last big case before he left for London. They used an identikit photo, an artist's impression. The face was everywhere, the name on everyone's lips. What spooked the whole city was the idea that anyone could be the Quaker. Your next-door neighbour. The man who read your meter. The bloke behind you in the post office queue. That was bad enough. But if your neighbour did turn out to be the Quaker then at least it freed the others from suspicion. But what Nicol was proposing was something different. A football team of Quakers. A male voice choir of Quakers. Men who could hold down a job and go to the football and tuck their kids in at night and fuck and kill a prostitute.

"We're getting off track here," he said, but Nicol wasn't finished. She held up a finger. "Two years ago," she said.

"Oh Christ. It's *Jackanory* again." Shand turned to McCormack, jerked his thumb at Nicol. "Can she not make a point without telling a story?"

"Two years ago." Nicol raised her voice. "I was working in A Div."

Shand groaned. He ran his hand through his hair, shaking his head. But he slumped back in his seat with his hands hanging loose in his lap and glared at Nicol, *get on with it*. She leaned forward, her arms folded tight on the desk, leaning into the story. "Seven in the morning. I'm heading back to Turnbull Street, cutting through a lane near the Broomielaw and I see this black bin bag in the gutter. Only it's moving, And there's a noise coming from it."

"And it's a bag of kittens somebody forgot to drown. Where's my violin?"

"Screw you, Iain Shand. It's a woman. She's wearing a cheap black plastic mac and it's pulled up over her head. I go over to look." Nicol flicked a tongue-tip along her upper lip. "Her head's been stove in, the hood of the raincoat's all soggy with blood. Thick, sticky blood."

Shand said nothing, reached for his cigarettes.

"So I call it in and the ambulance guys—well, it's a lane near Argyle Street, woman victim, early morning: they know it's a pro. And they take their sweet time. And finally, when we're in the ambulance heading for the Royal, they radio ahead: *O.K., we're bringing in a slapper who's got bashed.* I can hear them. *She* can hear them. And that's what they call her."

Shand shook out his match. "They're there to save lives, Nicol. That's their job. Not to make folk feel good about themselves. Slapper's a slapper."

"Slapper's a woman, shithead. Somebody's daughter. Somebody's mum."

"Your mum was a slapper? That tells us a lot."

"That's enough," McCormack barked. "Shand: shut the fuck up. You're out of line. Nicol: finish your story."

Nicol breathed through her nose, eyes on Shand. "Anyway," she drawled out the word. "Four or five days later, she's well enough to talk. Tells me what happened. She's gone with this punter. They've done the business and then he's hit her with a crowbar he's stashed in the lane. But the best part? Sometime during the night, she's lying there with a fractured skull, and a Traffic car rolls past. She shouts for help and the window comes down. The cop looks at her: *You're a fucking hoor. What do you expect?* And away they go. Leave her for dead."

Shand snorted. "Yeah. Like that's how it happened."

"You think she was lying? The bastards didn't even bother to check. She was a hoor lying in an alley. Fuck her."

"Well, if you're gonnae take the word of a hoor over a fellow officer . . ."

"Aye, I'll take the word of a hoor. Every time. Over the likes of you? Every time. What would you have done, D.C. Shand? Would you have stopped to help her? 'Slapper's a slapper.'"

"They know the risks, Nicol. They want to get into cars with strange men, it's up to them."

"Right. Because they've got so many other options. Do you practise being this fucking stupid? Does it just come natural?"

"Sir!" Shand's arms were aloft, a striker appealing for a penalty. "Am I gonnae have to listen to this?"

"You give it out fast enough." McCormack refused to meet Shand's imploring gaze, staring fixedly at Nicol. "Try taking it now and again, son."

Shand shook his head. He smiled falsely at Nicol. "So what happened, then? To your wee pal?"

"Like you give a shit. Did she die, you mean? Aye, she died. Not then. A year later. Sleeping pills."

"And I'm to blame 'cause a hoor topped herself?"

"No, Iain. You're to blame because you're too thick to appreciate what these women go through. Women like Yvonne Gray. Because you won't make the effort to understand."

"Right. That'll do, Nicol." McCormack walked between their desks, slapped his palm down on Nicol's. He'd let it go too far, partly because he shared Nicol's distaste for Iain Shand

and wanted to give her a chance to state her case. But there came a time when team cohesion had to mean something.

"We've enough enemies at the end of that corridor." He jerked his head at the door. "Let's not start on each other, all right? Now. First thing. We need to find Yvonne Gray. Pay her a visit, find out what's eating her. Who took her address?"

Shand snatched up his notebook with a sidelong glare at Nicol, riffled through it, held up a page for McCormack to see: "Seventy-eight Shamrock Street."

"Shamrock Street?" McCormack crossed to the map of the city pinned on the wall. "That's in Garnethill, isn't it?"

"What was the number again?" Goldie had stopped swinging on his chair.

"Seventy-eight."

"Seventy-eight? My brother lives in Shamrock Street. They demolished that end of the street two years back. For the motorway: seventy-eight's gone. It doesnae exist."

McCormack had found it: Shamrock Street. The map was out of date. He traced his finger along the thin black-edged line to where it met St. George's Road. But out there in the city, the multiple lanes of the M8 motorway had smashed through Garnethill, truncating Shamrock Street and many others.

McCormack thought about this. Yvonne Gray was hiding something. If they charged in and lifted Gray, her bosses would twig that something was up. Maitland would know.

"We need to play this carefully, Nicol."

"Sir."

"Go back to the sauna and get her real address. Get all the addresses, so Gray's not being singled out. Find out where she really lives. What the score is. You manage that?"

"On it, sir."

"Oh and take Lager Tops with you." Shand scowled down at his desk. McCormack and Nicol shared a grin. "Seeing as you're getting along so well. And Iain?"

Shand was on his feet now, shrugging into his jacket. "Boss?"

"Did you look into Turner's conviction?"

"It was just like he said, sir. Fight in a pub. No hoods, no boiler suits. No similarity to Crawford Street."

And no reason, therefore, to be holding Turner, McCormack thought. No need for your earlier outburst. But he said nothing. He let the silence speak for itself.

8

T he motto for the City of Glasgow Police was two words long. In Glasgow, two words are often enough. Sometimes no words are needed.

Semper Vigilo.

That was the official motto. *Always alert*. The polis in the squad rooms and canteens favoured an alternative version, though theirs required an extra word.

The job's fucked.

This was the true motto, the mantra, the refrain, whenever cops from the UK's oldest police force gathered together to bitch about the brass.

The job's fucked.

D.S. Derek Goldie sat in the silence of the Byre, typing up statements from the Crawford Street door-to-door. He could see through the open door of the inner office to where McCormack sat at his desk stoically doing the same. It seemed to Derek Goldie, surveying the wreckage of a twenty-four-year career, that the job was more fucked now than ever, and in more ways than you could count. For one thing, it was fucked by amalgamation. As of May 1975, the City of Glasgow Constabulary ceased to exist. It was bundled together with seven other forces to form Strathclyde Police, with a territory stretching from the Highlands to the Borders. What the fuck did a city cop have in common with some sheep-shagger from Inveraray?

The job was also fucked by integration. Since the start of

the year, the women's section had been disbanded and female officers embedded into every division of the mainstream Force. "Embedded" almost raised a bitter smile but, Jesus, the way Goldie looked now he'd have a better chance with the sheep.

And now, to top it all off, the job was fucked by the strike. Bloody dustcart drivers had left the entire city looking like Paddy's Market on a bad day. Lakes and seas of garbage. Mountains and drifts of dreck. Great hillsides of plastic carriers, spilling their innards of burst teabags, used nappies, banana skins, crushed beer cans, sanitary pads, crisp packets, the contents of ashtrays and Hoover bags.

Sometimes you felt that the smell would never leave your clothes. Then again, it felt to Goldie as though he'd been standing in a pile of rubbish for the past six years. Since Duncan McCormack left. Rubbish of McCormack's making. All the baggage of being the right-hand man of the polis who took down the gaffer.

He remembered the first time he encountered McCormack. He'd been working the Quaker murders and the investigation was going nowhere, costing the bloody earth, and McCormack was sent in to "review" it—which everyone took to mean shut the thing down. Everyone on that inquiry hated McCormack, none more so than Goldie. They had come close to blows, he remembered, one night in The Smiddy, over a game of pool. And then the Quaker killed again and instead of shutting down the investigation McCormack was part of it. He was neighboured with Goldie and the two of them cleared the damn thing, nailed the Quaker. But they took down Peter Levein in the process, Head of Glasgow CID, and that—it was made clear to Goldie in myriad contexts and manifold ways over wearisome months and laborious years—was not a smart move. Too many people found their shelter under the spreading limbs of Pete Levein's tree.

And because of that, Goldie's own name was mud. Now, when polismen gathered in pubs and canteens to bitch about things, he himself would be another reason why the job was fucked. No loyalty. No one watching their neighbour's back. Look at that fat cunt Goldie.

McCormack being in London hadn't helped. When it all blew up with Levein, McCormack headed south, starting afresh with the Met. Goldie faced the backlash alone. There were postings where he'd felt like a human Flying Fortress, catching a barrage of flak. So when McCormack came back, and requested Goldie for his new unit, Goldie had a wee bit of thinking to do. In the end, he figured, why the fuck not? They would bitch about his McCormack connection anyway; why not give them something to bitch about? If they're planning to hang you for stealing a sheep, you might as well shag it.

Goldie's thoughts were interrupted by the slamming of a car door in the street, a commotion in the corridor, the clack of heels, raised voices, a posh one, high, rising over everything.

"Which one is it? Is it this one?"

McCormack met Goldie's gaze, held it, neutrally, both of them cocking their heads.

The door flew open and clanged against a filing cabinet. A woman stood on the threshold in a summer dress, squeezing her purse in both hands. Stripes of red along her cheekbones. The desk sergeant's anxious face bobbing at her shoulder, Brian Imrie, struggling to reclaim his authority.

"Look, miss. You can't. I mean, there's no—"

The woman cast fiercely round, looking for a seat.

McCormack rose slowly and pulled out the chair on the far side of his desk, gestured for the woman to sit.

"It's all right, Brian. I've got this."

The desk sergeant withdrew and the woman stilted towards the chair and sat, slamming her purse down onto the desk. She wore a gold chain, a pendant that sank down into the neckline of her screen-print dress. The dress was cream, patterned with large, heavy-looking roses that seemed somehow too intimate and pink under the glaring striplights. There were dull gold hoops in her ears. Her chin was twisted in a tight little knot, quivering slightly.

"Take your time." McCormack leaned back in his chair. He could smell the woman's perfume—something opulent and floral, as if it issued from the pattern on her dress. "All the time in the world. Can we get you some tea? Coffee?"

"It's my father," the woman blurted. "Gavin Elliot. The man on the rubbish heap. The man on the news. It's my bloody father."

McCormack and Goldie exchanged another glance. Goldie rose from his desk with a notebook and pen, drew a chair up at the short end of McCormack's desk.

"You mean you recognize the rings?" McCormack asked her.

She nodded shortly, hand in front of her mouth. "It's him. It's my father."

"O.K. We're just going to note down some details, miss. I'm Detective Inspector McCormack. This is my colleague Detective Sergeant Goldie. Could we have your full name, please?"

"Eileen Elliot," the woman said tartly, batting impatiently at her hair, flicking it over her collar. There was no gold on her hand to match the gold at her ears and neck.

"And you think your father is the man whose body was found?"

"He's been missing five days. Only nobody knew. He was supposed to be up at The Croft. We have a house in the Highlands, up near Ullapool. He calls it The Croft. *Called* it The Croft. Jesus."

Her gold earrings caught the light as she shook her head, massaging her temple with finger and thumb.

"We'll get some tea." McCormack gestured to Goldie, who started to rise from his seat.

"I don't want tea!" she said savagely. "Look, I'm sorry. I just want to get through this. There's no phone at the Ullapool house. No way of getting in contact. That's how he liked it, but it meant that nobody knew. Everyone thought he was up at The Croft."

"I see." McCormack paused to let the woman explain. He had her pegged at around thirty, thirty-one. "Who is 'everyone', Miss Elliot?"

"I'm sorry? Oh, I see. Me. My sister in London. And, I suppose, Julia Ferris. She's dad's secretary." Her voice wavered sardonically on the last word.

"And your mother?"

"Dead. Seven years back. Cancer."

"I'm sorry."

"Don't be. She wasn't. She grabbed it with both hands. Like a bloody lifebelt." She laughed shortly. "The choice was cancer or the rest of her life with my father. She took the easy way out."

No one knew what to say to that. There was a lull before McCormack spoke. "Miss Elliot, if the Ullapool house doesn't have a phone, how do you know he's not there?"

Eileen Elliot flicked a hand impatiently. "The neighbour has a phone. He went over to check. There's been no sign of Dad—no sign of anyone—for weeks."

McCormack was looking at her expectantly.

"What? Oh, the neighbour. John Urquhart. U-R-Q-U-H-A-R-T. He lives out on Ardmair Road. My father's house is half a mile further west."

Goldie wrote down the details. McCormack's thoughts had wandered to the Saltmarket, to the white-tiled mortuary slab room where they cut up the bodies. We've got the ident, he was thinking; now Seawright can get to work. We can cut the man open, peel back his skin, fossick around in his entrails, take the buzz-saw to his cranium. Work out what's what. Then he noticed that the woman's head was tilted and she was staring pointedly at him. Clearly, she had asked a question.

"I'm sorry, what was that?"

"I said, did he suffer much?"

McCormack blinked. He felt a little chill in his guts. He didn't know which answer the woman in front of him was hoping for. He cleared his throat. "It's difficult to say, Miss Elliot. We won't know until the post-mortem takes place."

"Which will be when?"

"Well, today, hopefully. I mean, once you've, well, once we know it's him."

She snatched her purse from the table, clutched it in her lap, sitting bolt upright. "Shall we do that now? The identification?"

McCormack nodded slowly. "Right. Well, I'll need to make some calls, Miss Elliot. Make some arrangements. We'll send a car to pick you up at your house. If you'll write down the address."

She snatched the notebook from Goldie, dashed something down in a fluid, looped hand.

"Miss Elliot." McCormack spun the notebook round to read the address. A good one: Albert Drive, Pollokshields. "What did your father do?"

"Do?" Eileen Elliot looked confused. She brushed the hair from her face with the back of her hand. "Do? He was Gavin Elliot. That's what he did."

"*Gavin* Elliot? Gavin Elliot the . . ." McCormack hesitated, unsure how to finish the sentence. In the intensity of the moment, he hadn't registered the significance of the name. The body in the boiler suit wasn't that of a tramp—the teeth and the gold signet ring and the pinky ring told you as much. But he'd never had dreamed that the ruined head might belong to

Gavin Elliot. Former Tory MP and city councillor. Slum landlord. Restaurateur. Charity fundraiser. Knight of the Realm.
"Gavin Elliot the . . . businessman?" he asked.

"Well, exactly." The woman smiled bleakly. "The businessman."

Goldie had stopped writing and the pen hung limply from
his fingers. McCormack was slumped back in his seat, hands
dangling in his lap. Eileen Elliot looked from one to the other.
She smiled at McCormack. "Isn't this where you ask me if Dad
had any enemies?"

9

Gavin *Elliot?*"

McCormack was obscurely pleased that Haddow's response was the same as his. Maybe everyone who heard the name of the Crawford Street victim would feel this need to repeat it a couple of times, the way you might test the trueness of a coin by rapping it on a counter.

"*Gavin* Elliot?"

Haddow was out of his chair now, shaking his head, stalking to the window. "Jesus Christ, McCormack. You don't do things by halves."

"I didn't actually perform the killing myself, sir. I just attended the locus."

"No but it's typical of you just the same. Christ, McCormack. Gavin Elliot? You're sure?"

"I know, sir. It'll make a lot of noise. The papers'll give it a show. It's still a murder though. It's still a dead guy. Motive, means, opportunity."

"It's not that. Or it's not just that. I knew him, a bit."

"You knew Gavin Elliot?"

McCormack thought of the rings again—the Freemason's compass and square. Probably Elliot and the boss attended the same bloody lodge.

"I investigated him." Haddow was looking out of the window. McCormack could see his boss's ghost in the glass but he couldn't read his expression. "Never came to anything."

"What was the complaint?"

Haddow turned. "Ach, it was a sexual, McCormack. Rape allegation. Turned out to be malicious. Wee lassie looking for an easy payout."

"Blackmail?"

"That was the ploy. One thing I remember, though." Haddow sat back down at his desk. "That man had plenty of friends. When I was looking into the lassie's allegations it was made clear to me that people were watching. I mean, I went ahead and established the facts, without fear or favour. It was all on the level. But those friends won't have gone away, McCormack. You understand me? They'll be watching to make sure that whoever did this is caught. You better see that he is."

He left a pause, presumably so that McCormack could express his eagerness to please. McCormack said nothing.

"I'm tasking another two units to assist you. Armstrong's team and Patterson's. You'll continue to work mainly with your own guys. But every morning you'll brief the whole task force and Armstrong and Patterson will distribute the tasks to their teams as they see fit. Understood? That's all, McCormack."

On the way back to the Byre, McCormack stopped at the canteen for two teas. He placed one in front of Goldie and stood with the other, leaning against the filing cabinet.

"Haddow's got a firework up his arse," he said.

"Yeah?" The slicing of the typewriter keys was wincingly loud. Goldie was typing up statements again.

"Says we'll be under scrutiny. Elliot had powerful friends."

"Right. Well, you'll know all about that."

The keys bit into the patten.

McCormack pulled a chair out from Nicol's desk and sat down opposite Goldie. "What happened here, Derek?"

Goldie frowned. "You mean with Elliot's daughter, earlier? She's a cold one, all right. Shock, probably."

"No. I mean what happened *here*. With us. With you." McCormack waved a helpless hand.

"Oh, right." Goldie pushed his half-drunk tea into the centre of the table. "You're trying to say you don't know?"

Of course he knew. What happened to Goldie was Duncan McCormack. The scab who brought down Peter Levein. When McCormack left for London six years back he'd no time to fret about anyone else. Saving himself was the order of business. Over the years, though, he'd thought about Goldie, left behind in Glasgow. Everyone knew how close he'd been to Goldie. And with McCormack gone, who else was going to suffer the backlash, the whispers, the snide asides in the station canteen?

"Ach, I suppose I'm asking, how bad was it?"

Goldie snorted. "It's taken you this long to even ask? Really?"

"I'm asking now. How bad was it?"

"You mean, how many friends did Levein have? How badly did they miss him? A lot. O.K.? A lot of guys did well out of Levein. They were onto a good thing, Dunc. Did they appreciate that coming to an end? Not greatly, it has to be said."

"But that was me, Derek. I mean, if anyone was to blame, it was me."

"Oh, don't worry. You got the credit all right. But then, you weren't around, were you? To receive the adulation."

McCormack had been in nicks where a guy wasn't liked. He knew how it worked. He'd been that guy himself. Still was. "Why didn't you leave? Put in for a transfer?"

"You mean come down to the Met?" Goldie laughed. "I actually thought about it. But come on. Jenny. The kids. Her folks. My folks. Never gonnae happen."

McCormack leaned his elbows on the table. "Then why come to Temple, Derek? Why come and work for me?"

"I don't know." His right hand opened like he was balancing

an object on it. "I don't know. Like they say, I suppose: in for a penny. Ah, look, fuck it, Dunc. I've got six years till I've done my thirty. Take my pension and go. The job's fucked. I'll be glad to see the back of it."

McCormack remembered something Greg Hislop had said to him, six years back, during the Quaker case. *Are you just doing the job to put siller in your pocket?* he'd asked. *Because there's easier ways. This is not like other jobs. If you're not making a difference,* Hislop had said, *you're just in the road.*

"Look, I wasn't here, Derek. You were. You bore the brunt. I'm not pretending I know what that was like. But if you're giving up the ghost, for Christ's sake finish this one job before you do. Finish what we started six years ago. All right? Catch whoever killed this Gavin Elliot. Put Maitland away. For old times' sake."

Goldie held his gaze. He was a fat, tired, disappointed man in a cramped, shabby office. His yellow hair was whitening, thinning. The teeth revealed by his jutting lip were grey and stained. But there was a flare of contempt in his bloodshot eyes.

"I'll do it for my own sake, Duncan. I'm not out to pasture yet."

McCormack nodded, drank his tea.

Shand moved up a gear and put the foot down on a clear stretch of road. "Why are we trailing round after hookers? At this late stage of the game. Have we not got better things to be doing?"

Nicol felt that this was a rhetorical question and continued to watch the city spool past, the terraces of Great Western Road, the stalls of fruit outside the grocers' shops, apples and oranges and pears like something out of a kiddie's book, the sagging bags of rubbish. Shand clicked his tongue against his teeth and drove.

"He's clutching at bloody straws," Shand said, shaking his head.

"She knows something about Maitland, Iain. Otherwise, why was she spooked? And she recognized Alex Kerr in the photos."

"No surprise there. Probably sucks him off every day."

Nicol emitted a non-committal "Hmm". The sky above the tenements was restless and overcast, with silver glints between clouds, a patch of vivid yellow shot through with misty grey. Rain was on its way. Rain would be good. Rain would damp down the smell of all the rubbish.

They were driving to the massage parlour again, for Yvonne Gray's home address. Nicol sat in the passenger seat and felt the hum of the engine, the car's suspension joggling her towards a state of weightless relaxation in which the where-abouts of a prostitute, the whereabouts of the Crawford Street killer, seemed rather abstract problems. She tipped her head back against the headrest and let the sound of her breathing fill her ears.

"Listen, Nicol. That stuff last night."

She opened her eyes. Shand rubbed a hand across his mouth and cleared his throat.

Here we go, she thought. *An actual apology from Iain Shand. This'll be good.* She shuffled up straighter in her seat. But no. He pulled out to overtake a bus. "I didn't mean to upset you. I wasn't trying to wind you up."

"Not even trying?" Nicol whistled. "You're just a natural then, Shandy boy, aren't you?"

"Well, look. If you won't accept an apology—"

"That was an apology? My mistake. Generally the words 'I'm sorry' feature somewhere in an apology. That's kind of how you know."

They drove on down Great Western Road. Mid-morning quiet. Rain clouds sagging onto dirty tenements. Shand shifted his hands on the wheel. "I'm sorry, Liz. O.K.? I'm sorry. I mean it."

The rain came on then, a thunderplump, fizzing on the tarmac, drumming on the car roof. With the windscreen wipers thrashing, they moved through the torrent. The light in the car changed, became more intimate. It felt like they'd been sitting there for hours, side by side, like some old married couple on a bench. Plus the fact he'd called her *Liz*.

"It's just easier if we get on, Iain. You know? We'll do a better job. And I know it takes some adjusting. The whole integration thing. I know it hasn't been easy for everyone . . ."

"Whoa," Shand said. "Hold on here. You think this is because you're a woman? You're playing that card?"

"Right. Because you're absolutely fine working with a woman, Iain. That's been really clear."

Shand was pushing back against his seat as if flinching from an imminent crash and now he swung the car abruptly to the kerb, stamping on the brake so that Nicol bounced against the seat belt, flailing back into her seat.

"Now wait a fucking minute," Shand said, wrenching the handbrake with a savage rasp. "Have I given you the slightest reason for thinking that?"

Nicol, still surfacing from the shock of Shand's emergency stop, gaped wordlessly.

"Because you're a fucking liar if you say I have. Oh I know the kind of things they say. I've heard them myself. 'You're taking the job of a man with kids, a breadwinner.' Bullshit. If you can do the job, you deserve the job. I've never said anything different."

Nicol straightened up, fixed her seat belt. "Jesus, Iain. O.K. Point taken." She pushed the hair out of her eyes. "Thanks."

Shand swung back out into the traffic. "Anyway, we should be rounding up Maitland's goons. Putting proper pressure on them."

"The old rubber hose, is it? I don't think that's McCormack's style. Anyway, we tried bringing them in. It never worked. They're more scared of Maitland than they are of us. The gaffer's right. No mileage in going off half-cock, trying to cut corners."

Shand said nothing, stared straight ahead.

"Oh, Iain." Nicol turned slowly to look at him. "Iain. Jesus. What did you do?"

"I'm saying nothing."

"You're gonna get us *all* fucking jottered, you know that? What did he tell you?"

"It's fine, Liz. Honestly. It's no biggie. I'll bring you in on it if it pans out. Look. We're here already."

There was a space right outside Healing Hands. Shand swung the Velox into it.

"Just so you know." Nicol placed two fingers on Shand's wrist as he turned to open the door. "You're on your own with this, Iain. Whatever it is. I want nothing to do with it."

Annie, the receptionist from the night before, buzzed them in. The pink tunic had gone. Now she wore a grey sweatshirt, jeans and off-white trainers. A silver crucifix caught the light as she stooped to collect the mail.

"Can't keep away, eh? We're not open for another two hours."

"We need a couple of addresses, Annie. Couple of the girls last night. They gave us false addresses."

"I can't be giving out employees' addresses." Annie clutched the letters to her chest, looked scandalized at the very idea. "It's policy. We don't do that. These girls take enough risks without everyone knowing where they live."

"We're not everyone, Annie," Nicol said.

"You're everyone to me."

A door slammed down the corridor and a woman's voice rose tunelessly in song.

"You want the squad car parked outside all day," Shand said. "You want the unmarked car across the road with the big telephoto lens poking out. We can do that. See what that does for your business."

Annie looked at Nicol. "Whose cage did you rattle, hen? Getting stuck with this arsehole for a partner?" She went behind the desk and plucked a ledger from beneath the counter, started flicking through it. "Who was it anyway?" She kept her eyes on the flicking pages. "Somebody getting something off their chest?"

"We're just dotting the Is, Annie. Crossing the Ts. We get a false address, we chase it up," Nicol said. "That's all."

"Just routine inquiries, is it?" She shook her head at Nicol. "Here we are."

She spun the ledger. There were two pages with girls' names and addresses, phone numbers beside most of them.

Shand tore the pages out of the ledger.

"Hey! That's private property!"

"Put in a complaint, Annie." Shand was folding the pages, stowed them in his inside pocket. "I'm sure Her Majesty's Inspectorate of Constabulary in Scotland will make it a priority."

Yvonne Gray's address was in Dowanhill. They drove back up Woodlands Road, up the slope of Gibson Street towards the uni campus, perched on the crest of the hill. The rain had stopped and the streets were shining. They drove down past Kersland Street and on to Byres Road.

The flat was a basement bedsit in Bowmont Terrace. They thumbed the buzzers till the front door clicked. Room 6 was one of two in the basement. They rang the bell and waited. Shand slapped the door with his palm.

"You're too late."

A man had emerged from the room across the hall. Thirties, thin. Grey flannel trousers and a red checked shirt. Maroon braces. Thinning hair greased back, a three-day beard. The usual Glasgow dentistry. "She's already gone."

"You mean she's left for work?"

"I mean she's gone, mate. She's outta here. Wild blue yonder. Must've known youse were coming."

He laughed softly. Shand nodded. "How could you tell? That she's gone for good?"

"I've seen a midnight flitting, mate. She took the wean, two suitcases. Coupla bin bags. She's skedaddled."

"What time was this?"

"Like I said. Last night. Midnight. Maybe one in the morning."

Nicol felt once more the magical strangeness of her job. You moved around the city and people opened their doors and gave you little glimpses of their lives. Like she was still six years old and playing with her doll's house, swinging the hinged facade, peering into all the different rooms.

"Know her well, did you?" Shand asked the neighbour.

The man shrugged. "Knew her to pass the time of day with. Or night, usually. She kept odd hours."

"Aye?"

"Aye. Worked up west, she said." He looked slyly at Nicol. "Masseuse. Got in at all hours. What's she done?"

"She had, what, one child?"

"Ah now, don't get me wrong. She looks after that kid. The kid's always clean, nicely turned out."

Nicol was scribbling in her notebook. "She worked late hours, you said."

The man shrugged. "Goes with the job, doesn't it? Jobs."

"What do you mean, jobs?"

"She did bar work, too. Up in Maryhill. The Barracks Bar, I think. She wasn't scared of work, I'll say that. Not like some around here. So what's the score, then? State secret, is it?"

The Barracks Bar, Nicol thought. Hugh Maitland's pub.

"So who looked after the wee one?" Shand asked. "While she was out?"

The man's glance strayed to the staircase. "There's a woman upstairs. I think Yvonne paid her to watch the wee fella." He read the expressions on the cops' faces. "Ground floor. On the right as you come in the door. The flat directly above Yvonne's."

"She got a name?"

"Name on the door's Bissett. Never looks the road you're on. Stuck-up bitch, you ask me."

They climbed the stairs, rapped on the door. No joy. Nicol wrote *Urgent. Please phone this number* on her business card and slipped it under the door.

Driving back up Great Western Road, both Nicol and Shand were silent, thinking it through. Finally Nicol craned round in her seat. "We bring her in and she flits the same night? Works in Maitland's brother's pub?"

"Let's not get carried away, Nicol. There's lots of reasons she could have shot the crow. Maybe she owed money. Maybe she couldn't make the rent."

"She gets a tenner for every cock she sucks, Iain. Twenty for full sex. Even when Orphan Annie takes her cut, she can make the rent on a one-bed flat."

"A habit, then. She's in debt to a dealer."

"You heard the neighbour. The boy was clean. Happy. Nicely turned out. His mum's not a junkie. It's what I thought: she knows something. Maybe she was planning to leave town anyway. But we spooked her last night and she's jumped the gun."

The rain had come on again while they talked. Shoppers on Great Western Road huddled in doorways, sheltered under grocers' awnings. The bin bags lining the pavement leaned on one another like drunks.

"Good thing she did," Shand said.

"How do you work that out?"

"Well, if her card wasnae marked already, it's marked now."
'Cause we asked for the addresses at the knocking-shop?"

"Anyone could spot that Yvonne was the weak link. Wee Annie'll be straight on the blower to Maitland. By dinnertime, half the neds in Glasgow'll be looking for Yvonne Gray."

"Well then." Nicol zipped her jacket. "The answer's easy. We need to find her before they do."

Back at Temple, Shand parked the car in the old stable-block, killed the engine.

"You know what gets me, though?" He had his hand on the key ring, still dangling from the ignition. "It's not the fucking altar-boy routine. It's the hypocrisy."

Rain was spitting the windscreen.

"He's not a hypocrite," Nicol said. "He's a lot of things, but he's not that."

"Really? You know why he came back from London then? Why he left the Met?"

Nicol sighed. Take your pick, she thought. He'd fucked his guvnor's missus. He was on the take. He fluffed a drugs bust. He punched out a Super. The Yardies put a price on his head. The Malties ran him out of town. Everyone had a reason why McCormack left. Everyone had a theory, though hard evidence seemed to be in short supply.

"A death in custody," Shand said. "Gen up. I got it from a mate who works in Vice down there. McCormack wasn't the only one present, but he was in charge. Things got out of hand. Prisoner died. On his watch. So, yeah. I'd say that makes him a hypocrite."

Nicol opened the door. "If it's true," she said, "maybe it explains why he wants us to go by the book. Maybe it explains why we should." She was off then, dashing through the rain for the station doorway.

Shand caught up with Nicol in the corridor to the Byre. "What we talked about earlier. In the car . . ."

"I'm not a grass, Iain. But don't ask me to cover for you. This goes tits up, it's your card they'll be taking, not mine."

McCormack and Goldie were waiting for them, McCormack in his raincoat, patting his pockets. He looked like someone waiting for an overdue bus.

"Keep your jacket on, Nicol. We're off to the Saltmarket."

"The High Court, sir?"

"The mortuary, Nicol, the mortuary!"

"We got an ident?" Shand asked. "The jakey on the rubbish tip?"

"Some jakey," Goldie said. "Gavin Elliot. How's that for a jakey?"

They looked blank for a second, then Nicol twigged. "The Tory MP? Jesus Christ."

"Ex-Tory MP."

"Gavin Elliot?" Shand whistled. "Gavin fucking Elliot. Oh, ya dancer. Haddow'll be spitting blood."

His grin fell as McCormack crossed the floor in two steps, brought his face up close to Shand's. "Ya dancer? A man's dead, son. Get a fucking grip."

"Well, he was taking the piss, wasn't he?" Shand stepped back and shrugged out of his jacket, hung it on the back of his chair. "Haddow. He was trying to humiliate us. Make us work this nothing murder. Bloody message boys for the B Div plainers. And now this. This is front-page news, above the fucking fold. And it's ours."

"It's not news, D.C. Shand. It's a human bloody being. If he'd been a jakey he'd still have been a murdered man. We don't rank murder victims here, son. It's not a league table."

"Aye, O.K., boss. Everyone's equal. In the eyes of God, maybe. In the eyes of the DCI, though? In the eyes of Turnbull Street and the Secretary of State and the *Daily* fucking *Record*? We'll have the press boys camped on the doorstep. This is big league."

Shand rolled his shoulders. He was in his element now, the star of his own private movie, the detective cracking the big-time case. Nicol tightened the belt of her jacket, followed McCormack out to the car.

10

T he High Court of Justiciary commands a corner site on the north bank of the Clyde. Its porticoed entrance looks across the Saltmarket to the central avenue of Glasgow Green and the massy grandeur of McLennan Arch.

In the shadow of the High Court, facing north, squats a less distinguished building, long, low, in blood-red brick. Its large frosted windows are criss-crossed with bars.

This is the Glasgow City Mortuary.

McCormack stooped under the low lintel and followed the attendant down the corridor. In the anteroom, he shrugged into a gown and flexed his fingers into rubber gloves and stepped out of his slip-ons. The choice of Wellingtons lined up against the anteroom wall was meagre but he found a pair that didn't pinch too badly. He took a deep breath and entered the slab room.

As always, with its tiled walls, its white-clad attendants and its chemical fug, the slab room reminded McCormack of a municipal swimming baths. The room was busy. Haddow was already in position, standing to attention in his white Wellingtons. Seawright was there, too, scowling slightly. McCormack wondered what was eating him until he spotted the tall figure of Professor Alistair Agnew, the chief pathologist. Agnew would be conducting the PM, with Seawright in attendance to corroborate the findings, as the law required in cases of murder. Even Jardine, the procurator fiscal, had turned up. Nicol and Shand were on hand to bag and label and log the dead man's belongings and items of clothing.

McCormack exchanged nods with the others, catching Haddow's eye and jerking his head very slightly towards Jardine. Haddow nodded. As a matter of courtesy, the fiscal was kept informed whenever a PM was scheduled, but he rarely bothered to show. The fact that he was here, in his white scrubs, with his surgically gloved hands clasped behind his back, showed how seriously the high-ups were taking this.

"Gentlemen." Agnew flexed his gloved fingers and smiled round the faces. "Lady": he inclined his head graciously to Nicol, flicker of a smile. "Shall we begin?"

Agnew cut away the boiler suit and passed it to Nicol and Shand, standing back with his gloved hands raised to let the police photographer get shots of the body.

Gavin Elliot's white hair pegged him as a man in his sixties or seventies, but his body was that of a younger man—sinewy, slim, with a tight flat belly. He was suntanned, with a triangle of white around pubis and hips. There were no tattoos, no birthmarks.

"Well." Agnew walked round the body, something birdlike in the way he dipped his head down for a closer look and then straightened up. "If we didn't already know, I think we could safely conclude that this gentleman wasn't a road-mender. His hands have been beaten and two of his fingers broken, but the finger ends are smooth, without calluses. The dentistry is good, expensive. This chap was wealthy, he was good to himself."

"He didn't get a tan like that in Glasgow," Haddow said.

"I would assume not."

"And the boiler suit wasn't his?"

"We can safely say, I think, that a boiler suit was not Mr. Elliot's habitual attire."

"I mean the size, Professor. It was too small for him."

"Very possibly. Now." Agnew raised his arms to shoot the loose cuffs of his surgical gown. He looked like a moorland prophet, arraigning the heavens. Then he got down to business, the business that McCormack still found hard to watch, despite all his years of experience. Maybe because of them.

When it was over, McCormack cornered the chief pathologist at the big steel sink.

"Professor Agnew. The blows to the head—that's the cause of death?"

Agnew peeled off his gloves with an air of disgust, balled them and binned them. "We'll need to wait on the toxicology, but for now I'd say the cause of death was the trauma inflicted on the skull by at least three heavy blows with a blunt instrument."

"He was battered to death."

"As I say, test results may change the picture. But that's best guess at the minute."

"O.K., Professor. Anything else?"

Agnew raised his voice above the running water as he soaped his hands with pink surgical scrub. "There were fibres embedded in the wounds. From the hood, most likely."

"He was hooded when they killed him?"

"It looks like it. In addition, there is extensive bruising on the torso and upper arms. Some of the bruises are more developed than others. Considerably so."

"You mean they're older? They belong to an earlier incident—nothing to do with the killing?"

"Conceivably." Agnew drew the word out, tilting his head. He dried his hands with paper towels. "Or maybe the killing itself was more . . . protracted than we assume."

"I don't follow."

"Inspector McCormack, I'm suggesting that Mr. Elliot here was tortured. He was held for three or four days and tortured."

"You're basing this on old bruises?"

Agnew shook his head. "There is also the question of faecal residue, around the anus and backs of the legs, and on the boiler suit."

"But that's what happens, isn't it? That's normal."

"The bowels tend to evacuate at death, Inspector, yes. But in this case the faecal matter is, again, considerably older."

McCormack put his hands behind his head, twisting his neck in disbelief. "They kept him in his own filth?"

Agnew nodded. "I'm afraid so. The urine stains would tend to confirm this. I think he was taken somewhere, placed in this boiler suit, beaten repeatedly, denied access to sanitation."

"Jesus Christ." McCormack glanced down at his white rubber boots. He felt the sudden urge for a cigarette. He could see Haddow from the corner of his eye, beckoning him over. "Is there anything else?"

"There is, yes. The gall bladder was markedly distended with bile."

McCormack waited. "Words of one syllable, Professor. You're dealing with a big thick teuchter here."

Agnew winced. "Well. It may mean nothing. But it may indicate that the deceased hadn't eaten for some days."

"You can't tell that from the stomach?"

"No. Not at all. Food takes around four hours to leave the stomach. An empty stomach just tells you that the deceased hadn't eaten in the past four hours. But this. Well. You see it sometimes, in cases of malnutrition, starvation. Normally the gall bladder empties of bile as food reaches the small bowel. For a gall bladder to reach this size, well, it suggests that no food has passed through the bowel in a number of days."

"He was being starved?"

"As I say, it's a possibility. Also, there is circumferential linear bruising and abrasion around the right ankle."

"Professor, for Christ's sake . . ."

"He was manacled, Detective. Somebody chained him to a wall or a post in the ground. He was shackled like a dog."

McCormack nodded. That was certainly clear enough. Agnew drew off his surgical gown. He looked older in his three-piece grey suit, the angled bars of his club tie. "This wasn't an easy death, Inspector. Somebody wanted this man to suffer. And suffer he did."

He turned away now, as if McCormack had been complicit in the victim's pain.

McCormack stepped out of the mortuary into the summer morning, sucking down big gulps of air. Nicol came after him. They crossed the street, walked under the big stone arch into Glasgow Green. The city's oldest park looked preternaturally bright in the sunshine. They walked along towards the big obelisk of Nelson's Monument. McCormack had come here as a boy sometimes, to play long, sprawling games of football on the pitches by the bend in the river, games that lasted deep into the summer dusk, till you played by sound and touch in a blurring world that felt like the blue lull before you dropped off to sleep. And then when he was older he would come here too, in the same blue dusk, to play a different game, with older boys, or men, a game for two that had something of the same dreamlike urgency. But that had stopped. Since he'd come back to Glasgow, all those games had stopped.

He was aware of Nicol almost trotting to match his stride. He slowed his pace.

"That was pretty ropey back there, Nicol." He turned his head sharply to check her expression. "You did well. How are you feeling?"

"I'm fine, sir. But how do we tell Eileen Elliot what happened to her father?"

"I don't think we'll ever quite know what happened to her father," McCormack said drily.

They walked on. It was the school holidays. Some kids were having a kickabout on the grass beside the walkway, cheering, groaning, calling for the ball, absorbed in the game, a self-contained universe marked out by jackets for goalposts and invisible touchlines.

McCormack cleared his throat and spat on the ground, dabbed his lips with his handkerchief. "There was real pleasure involved there, Nicol. Someone's enjoying himself. He's got the bit between his teeth."

"You think he's going to do this again?"

"If he hasn't already."

The ball broke and came skittering towards them across the grass. McCormack trapped it neatly and stroked it back, side-footed, between two trees.

"Cheers, mister!"

"You don't think it's personal to Elliot?" Nicol asked. "It looked pretty personal."

"Oh, Elliot's not random. I don't mean that. Whoever did this bore a grudge against Elliot. He wanted to break Elliot, degrade him. Dumping him on the rubbish tip is part of that. But there's too much . . . *craftsmanship* here. He's going to find an excuse to do this again. This isn't the end of it, Nicol." He shook his head, frowning at the ground. "It's maybe not even the beginning."

11

I t gets better," McCormack said. "Worse. They kept him in his own filth. For four or five days. Shackled to something. A radiator, probably."

"Jesus Christ. So, what are we looking for—a soundproofed basement? Some sort of lair?"

"Could be." McCormack nodded. "Could be a farmhouse. Isolated cottage. Something like that. Anyway, it's organized. It's planned."

"You think maybe he's done this before?"

"I think it's highly likely. Check the records, Derek. Strathclyde, the other forces. We're looking for hooded corpses. Corpses in boiler suits. Corpses dumped in public places. Evidence of torture. Victims of a similar age to Gavin Elliot."

"Righto, Dunc."

"Nicol." McCormack was wrestling into his raincoat. "Get on to Companies House. Make a list of Elliot's business associates. Start talking to them. We're looking for possible enemies, deals gone bad, failed businesses, that sort of thing. But before you do that, get your coat. You're coming with me: we're going to see Elliot's daughter. Shand: get down to the *Record* and the *Trib*. See what they've got on Elliot in their morgues. Back here at four for a debrief. What?"

Shand was looking puzzled. "PM's already been, sir. You were there. What am I going to the morgue for?"

McCormack was buttoning his raincoat, looking at Shand, breathing through his nose. "Jesus Christ, son. Where did they find you? No, I wasn't at the morgue because I don't live in the United fucking States. I was at the Glasgow City Mortuary. Newspapers, on the other hand, *do* have morgues, for reasons I don't have time to belabour. Nicol: I'll get the car. You tell him." And he was off, stamping down the corridor, crashing through the fire doors.

"The fuck was that about?" Shand turned petulantly to Nicol.

"The morgue," Nicol explained, all sweetness and light, "is where a newspaper files its clippings. It's organized by person. Every time you appear in the paper, every time your name is mentioned, a copy of the article is cut out and kept in a cardboard file. When a journalist needs to write an article about you, they go to the morgue and look at your file. The morgue files on Elliot will maybe give us some pointers. Get them photocopied, bring them back. Simple."

"Would it have killed him to explain that?" Shand snatched his raincoat from the coatrack on the way out the door. "Thanks, by the way!" he shouted, gruffly, from the corridor.

Goldie and Nicol shared a grin. Nicol headed out to join McCormack.

The morgue at the *Tribune* was an actual room, a storeroom up the back stairs, under the eaves. The news editor himself—stooped, bearded, with a knitted, square-end tie—took Shand up and unlocked the door. It looked like some kind of punishment cell. A wooden chair, a desk, a bare light bulb, and rows of filing cabinets lining the walls.

"I'll leave you to it," the news editor said. "You find something useful, let me know—I'll get someone to run off a copy."

"Hold on." Shand's raised hand stopped the news editor in the doorway. Shand gestured helplessly round the room. "Is everybody really in here? I mean, everyone who's been in the paper?"

The news editor smiled. "Well. Not everyone in the paper. Not the sports pages, or the classifieds. But everyone who's been in a news report or a feature for, say, the past fifty years? Yes, they're all in there. Have fun."

After closing the door, the first thing Shand did was locate the "S"s and start hauling open the heavy drawers. *Shadwell*, *Shaefer*—Christ! Here he was. Right before the bulky folder marked, "Shand, Jimmy" was a slimmer version with his own name. Shand felt a surge of relief, a pulse of gratitude. Iain Shand existed. He mattered. The file featured trial reports, with paraphrases and sometimes direct quotations of Shand's testimony. It gave him a little thrill to see his words there in black and white. And right at the back of his file was a photo feature: Shand's graduating class at the Police Training College at Tulliallan. The passing-out parade. Shand's strained smile beneath a chequered hatband, his name there in bold in the photograph caption.

Shand remembered the day, the high wind that tangled the bunting on the platform and swallowed snatches of the CC's speech. All the ladies on the platform kept their hands on their hats and looked almost as though they were saluting. Shand's father had missed the whole thing—getting fou in the pub, more than likely—but his mum had been there, in her best green twinset, her court shoes polished to a shine as high as Shand's. She brought a present—a striped, regimental-looking tie—and told him that his dad had picked it out. But when Shand thanked him later, the old man just smiled vaguely and Shand had the familiar sense of being both invisible and somehow at fault. After Tulliallan it took Shand less than three years to make it into plain clothes as a detective constable, but his father—a career soldier who reached major before retirement—seemed to regard all civilian ranks as a childish parody of the real thing. Still, if Shand managed to stay on Alan Haddow's good side, or if he helped to bring down Maitland, he'd make D.S. before too long. That would be something. Plus, he had his other little iron in the fire. Things were going to happen. Nothing surer. For now, let's just enjoy being Iain Shand, Serious Crime Squad detective.

He turned his attention back to the morgue, the drawers and drawers of ordered files. Almost reverently, he replaced his own file, closed the drawer and leaned against it. The room seemed suddenly magical, as if Shand was God and all the souls in the city were ranked at his disposal. He pulled out another drawer and started flipping through the files.

On the drive across the river, Nicol thought about telling McCormack. But what could she say? Shand's up to something? You better watch him. She needed more than that. Like, maybe an idea of what the hell it was that Shand was up to. Better hold fire. Do some digging.

"Here we are." McCormack killed the engine.

"Daddy's Girl doing all right for herself," Nicol said. "Money gets money."

She unfastened her seat belt and climbed out of the car.

"What is that, some kind of biblical thing?" McCormack said.

She looked at him. "You mean 'For whosoever hath, to him shall be given'? I suppose it is."

McCormack looked blank. Nicol smiled. "Your side of the house don't really rule by the book, do you?"

"Who needs the book?" McCormack said. "We've got grip, Nicol. Grip. The intercession of saints."

They were parked in the driveway of Eileen Elliot's Pollokshields villa. Discreetly fortified behind a high stone wall and a row of half a dozen mature trees, the house on Albert Drive reared its blond sandstone bulk. Foursquare and elegant; double bay windows on the ground floor and a stone balcony overhanging the entrance. At one corner of the house was a round tower topped with a witches-hat roof. A weather-vane pointed to some less fortunate quarter of the city.

A girl in her mid-teens answered the door. She smiled uncertainly at Nicol and McCormack.

"We're looking for your mum, dear. Is your mum in?"

The girl kept smiling but her mouth closed and a crease puckered the space between her eyes.

A deep dirty laugh came barrelling towards them from the hallway and Eileen Elliot appeared, laying a slim hand on the girl's shoulder. "Thank you, Sarah. I'll handle it from here."

The girl turned and wandered off down the hallway.

"I'm sorry. I shouldn't laugh," Eileen Elliot said. She had changed her outfit. In place of the morning's business suit she wore a round-necked navy sweater and pleated charcoal slacks. Court shoes with a low heel. Pearl earrings.

"She's not your daughter," McCormack said.

"I should take offence, D.I. McCormack, but you looked so gormless standing there. I'm sorry. Sarah helps me round the house. Come in, the pair of you."

They followed her down the hallway to a big bright lounge at the back of the house.

"Can I get you something to drink? Coffee? Tea?"

Sometimes it was better to deliver bad news quickly, without dragging things out. Equally, shocks were better absorbed with a hot drink. It gave you something to do with your hands.

"Tea would be very nice," McCormack said. Nicol nodded: "Same, thanks."

Eileen Elliot went out to see to it. They looked around the room. It was a long, large room down the side of the house, three windows along one wall. There was an elaborate cornice round an electric chandelier, big blocks of dark wood furniture offset by the bright floral print on the sofa and chairs. On a dresser beside the marble fireplace there were Lladro figurines—a Flamenco dancer among them—and photos in plain silver frames, mostly of a handsome middle-aged woman with something wounded in her smile. There were no photos of Gavin Elliot.

"It's a lovely house you have here," Nicol said, when Elliot returned.

"Thank you. I was holding out for a 'Greek' Thomson, but this is a tolerable substitute." Elliot took her seat and crossed her legs, tugging down her hem.

McCormack nodded at the painting over the fireplace, a seascape with roiling breakers of aquamarine and white Hebridean sand. "That's not a—"

She smiled at him. "Peploe, Inspector. It is, yes. But I don't imagine you're here to debate the merits of the Scottish Colourists."

"I'm not, no." McCormack took his seat at the other end of the sofa from Nicol. He looked down at the carpet between his knees, knocking his knuckles softly on the chair-arm. Then he looked up sharply. "We have the preliminary findings from the post-mortem, Miss Elliot. I'm afraid the pathologist confirms what we suspected. Your father was murdered."

Eileen Elliot nodded tightly. "Go on."

"The cause of death was a blow to the back of the head. Your father was struck with a heavy object." McCormack grimaced. "Repeatedly."

He looked down at the carpet once more. Eileen Elliot cocked her head. "But there's something else, Inspector, isn't there? Something you're not saying."

McCormack cleared his throat. "Your father was mistreated before he died, Miss Elliot. Tortured, we think."

Elliot looked at Nicol as if giving her a chance to contradict this. Then she looked away across the room towards the French windows and the green expanse of lawn. A child's swing stood splay-legged on the grass, its chain wound tightly round the crossbar so that the red plastic lozenge of the seat was clamped tight against the crossbar. Sarah came in just then with a clanking tray. She crossed the carpet like a tightrope walker and set the tea things down on a low lacquered table.

"Thank you, Sarah," Eileen Elliot said, without shifting her gaze from the window. They busied themselves with the tea. There were silver tongs for the sugar, apostle spoons with elaborate handles, a milk jug adorned with a pheasant in flight.

"When you say tortured . . ." Eileen Elliot said.

"He was beaten, burned. His teeth were broken. We think he was held somewhere for three or four days. Shackled. Probably starved. They treated your father like a dog, Miss Elliot. I'm very sorry."

Elliot nodded again. "The poppy-seed cake is very good, Inspector. I get it from a deli down in Giffnock."

McCormack and Nicol waited.

Elliot shook her head. "A man of sixty-nine," she said. "Who would do that to a man of sixty-nine?"

"Whoever did it," Nicol said. "We will find them. We will put them away. That's a promise, Miss Elliot."

Elliot looked at McCormack for confirmation, and nodded when he did. "Thank you," she said simply.

"Miss Elliot. I'm sorry, but I need to ask you about your father's career. Possible enemies. His politics, for example. Not hard to make enemies in that game."

"Oh no." Elliot shook her head briskly. "He gave that up long ago. He hasn't stood for office in, what, five years. It's not politics, Inspector, whatever it is."

"Three years, in fact." McCormack had his notebook out. "He last stood for the Corporation in 1972. Lost his seat."

"Thank you, that's right. What I mean, though, is that he'd given up before that. He was going through the motions, Inspector. He hadn't taken a real interest in politics since he left the Commons. He regarded his work as a councillor here as, well, as more of a hobby, if you see. Politics was the big stage, to my father; this was just pottering about in his garden."

"I see. You'll understand, though, that we need to check every angle. What about business, then? Are there business associates who might have occasion to resent your father? Rivals?"

"Resentment, Inspector?" Eileen Elliot hooded her eyes like a hawk. "You said my father was tortured. That's a bit beyond resentment, wouldn't you think?"

"Miss Elliot, I'm looking for help here. If you want to argue about my choice of words, that's your prerogative. I want to find whoever did this to your father."

She dropped a hand onto the seat-cushion beside her, a little slap that bounced a slim gold lighter into the air. "You're right, Inspector. I'm sorry. It's just, my father kept his business interests very much to himself. I wouldn't know any more about them than you do. I took little interest in his affairs, and he, I have to say, returned the favour."

Nicol cleared her throat. "What is it you do, Miss Elliot?"

"Retail," she said curtly. And then, as if she was surprised at her own brusqueness, she added, "I own a few fashion boutiques. Not central; suburban. Giffnock, Newton Mearns, Eastwood. A specialized market."

Nicol gestured vaguely at the room. "And you do fairly well?"

"We do quite nicely, thank you. To answer your question, Inspector, my father was a hotelier. He also had interests in property and construction. He enjoyed some success, so, yes, I've no doubt there were people who resented him. He was also, at times, a deeply unpleasant man. Enemies shouldn't be hard to find, though whether they would go to such lengths . . ."

"Do you have names, Miss Elliot? Names of men who were your father's enemies. Business rivals."

"Oh, I wouldn't know, Inspector. It's all faceless companies now, isn't it? In hotels and construction. Your guess would be as good as mine."

She walked them to the front door. As they crunched down the driveway, McCormack turned to look back at the house. An upstairs curtain had been plucked aside. The face of the girl, Sarah, looked down at them. McCormack smiled, threw his hand up in a wave. The girl never moved, never smiled, just continued her sullen vigil.

The *Daily Record* building was one of the architectural treasures of Glasgow. So Iain Shand had been told by his old art teacher at school. Pausing under the big sandstone arch over the entrance, Shand decided he would have to take Mr. Jackson's word for it. It wasn't that Shand had no opinions about architecture. It was just that the location of the building, in a narrow cobbled lane behind Central Station, left no vantage from which to view it. Shand craned his neck to take in a dizzy cliff of white and blue glazed bricks studded with mullioned windows, before hauling open the double doors to the lobby and crossing to reception.

Shand flashed his card to the woman at reception and asked to be shown to the morgue. Ten minutes later he was leafing through a folder of Gavin Elliot clippings when the door flew open and a woman with curly blond hair strode towards him and planted her palms on his desk, leaning pugnaciously forward.

"Janey told me you were here. What, you were just gonnae pretend I don't exist?"

For a jarring moment, Shand wondered madly if this was an old girlfriend or one-night stand, a spurned lover come to demand why he hadn't called. But he'd never seen this woman in his life.

"I'm sorry. What—"

"D.C. Shand, isn't it? You're one of McCormack's boys."

"Uh-huh. And you are?"

"I'm Fiona Morrison, sweetheart. I'm the woman who wrote the splash you read with your cornflakes this morning. With a nice big close-up of your victim's rings. And you're here to tell me what's what. Like your bloody gaffer promised."

It was starting to make sense to Shand, just not quite quickly enough. As he saw Morrison's attention drop to the clippings on the desk, he closed over the folder, let his forearm come to rest on the cover. He forgot, however, that the folder with the Xeroxed *Tribune* clippings was also on the desk and it was this that Morrison opened.

"Elliot?" She sounded puzzled. Then she glanced sharply at Shand. "The victim's Gavin *Elliot*?"

"Now, wait a minute. We haven't said that."

"Jesus Christ." Her knuckles rapped the desk. "Has the PM been done? It bloody has, hasn't it? The PM's been done. What did it show?"

"Look. Miss Morrison. A statement will be issued. We'll do a presser this aftern—"

"Iain! Iain! Sweetheart." Morrison lifted a chair from her side of the desk and thumped it down at the corner with Shand. She sat down and leaned forward to grip his wrist. She leaned so close that he couldn't see her properly and he thought of the building's facade in the tight little lane. "Let me tell you how this works, O.K.?" He could see a glossy smudge of her lipstick, the light catching a big hoop earring. "You're still new to this. But there are times, in a detective's career, when you need the help of someone like me. To move things along. With a case, I mean. You need someone to spin the details a certain way, maybe try to provoke a suspect. Panic him. Or get a clue out to the public, like your gaffer did with these rings."

She left a space for Shand to agree. He nodded tightly.

"Now when that happens, I'm your woman. D.C. Shand

gets a direct line to the *Record*'s front page. But this is a two-way street, D.C. Shand. You need to help me too. You see that, don't you?"

It wasn't till Shand nodded once more that Morrison sat back. There was a notebook on the desk and a pen had materialized in her hand. She pointed it at Shand.

"So. Let's confirm this right now. The murder victim is Gavin Elliot."

Shand glanced down at the Xeroxed cuttings: Elliot on the rostrum at an election count, flanked by rival candidates, three suits with rosettes. Morrison had already drawn her conclusions. She was watching him with a flicker of a smile. She would find out at the presser anyway, Shand thought. What harm would it do to give her a jump on the other papers? And what harm would it do to D.C. Shand to have a journo in his pocket?

"Correct," he said decisively. "The victim's name is Gavin Elliot."

"Good." Morrison ran a hand through her hair and tossed her curls. The hoop earrings waggled. "And the PM was this morning, wasn't it? Now. Let's hear about that."

C hristopher Kidd sat in the living room of his tenement
flat and watched the sky. It was an old flat with deep
sills and he perched in a window, leaning back against
the frame, one leg cocked on the sill. He'd barely moved for
the past two hours. An old Golden Virginia tobacco tin sat on
the windowsill, just beyond his right foot. Sunlight played on
the green-and-yellow logo on the lid.

He closed his eyes, focused on his breathing. A fat mosquito whine, faint at first, grew steadily louder. Kidd craned up
to see a motorized hang-glider crossing a slice of sky. Sharp
chevron wings in silhouette; the tiny prone form of the pilot.

What would Maryhill look like from the air?

About as flash as it looked from the ground, Kidd supposed. The barrack squares of tenement blocks, the oblong
roofs of the high-rise flats. Big swathes of waste ground.

He sat up, swung round, grabbed the tobacco tin, prised
off its lid. Inside were five or six cigarette ends, a packet of
Rizlas and a Bic lighter. Taking each cigarette end in turn, he
pulled off the blackened tip and snapped off the filter. Then
he crumbled the tobacco into the flimsy trench of a Rizla
paper. The tobacco wasn't moist and springy like fresh rolling
tobacco; it was gritty and brittle. His finger ends were ashy
and black and the musk of stale tobacco brought juices to the
base of his gums. He rolled the Rizla, licked and gummed it,
lit it with the Bic.

He still had the fifty McPhail had slipped him. He could

buy a hundred packets of smokes if he wanted. But he'd developed a taste for it, over the years. Pre-smoked baccy. You got into the habit of making things last, eking them out.

Outside, a cat was picking its way through the backcourt bric-a-brac. An abandoned mattress, odd shoes, a blue quilted anorak, a white pram-wheel. The cat shrank down on its haunches, shivering with indecision, before it sprang onto the wall of a midden and stood for a moment, tail swishing.

McPhail had told him to wait.

Well, O.K. Let's wait.

He thought about traipsing up Maryhill Road to the Duke, having it out with McPhail. He saw himself walking into the toilet again, the top boys crowding in after him.

It was better to wait.

Waiting wasn't a problem for Kidd. Growing up in Auldpark, you were an expert on waiting. You waited outside the warden's office for six of the best when you'd done something wrong. You waited for the meagre meals. You waited for the holidays to drag to a close, killing time in the grim Christmas corridors. Every second Sunday you waited for a visitor who never showed. You waited for your sister Izzy to finish entertaining the "Friends of Auldpark" when they came around for their monthly dinner. You waited just to grow the hell up and get the fuck out.

And then, a few years later, when they got you for the Gallowgate newsagent's job, you waited all over again, for a five-stretch in Barlinnie's B Hall.

Waiting was bread and butter to Christopher Kidd. Meat and drink.

Only this time he wondered what exactly he was waiting for. Would McPhail even send someone? Kidd tried to view it from their perspective, the boys in the Duke. Would he come and help Christopher Kidd if he was them?

Maybe they would find it easier to put the word out: it was

Chris Kidd who started the Tradeston fire. Tip the polis. Tip the Quinns. Either option would take Kidd off their hands. Either option would take Kidd down the Saltmarket. High Court or mortuary, one or the other.

Kidd smoked his cigarette and thought about this. The prospect didn't faze him, either way. He had killed four people. It seemed unlikely—none of the cons he'd encountered in the Bar-L had killed that many—so he said it out loud.

I killed four people.

The words seemed to hang in the air, one for each victim. There was something almost liberating in having caused the death of four people, even if you hadn't meant to. It made the vengeance of the Quinns or of the courts seem trivial, beside the point. It put things in perspective, was another way of phrasing it.

You were bomb-proof. You didn't give a fuck.

It was like nothing mattered. If it ever had.

Except Isobel.

He smiled in the empty flat at the mere shape of her name. Isobel. They had gone into the Home together, after their Da left, once Mum couldn't cope. Isobel was three years older. That meant she remembered more. In the Home he would keep on at her to tell him about their da. About the time before their da left, when they were still a family. There were memories he had, he wasn't sure if they were things he really remembered or things Izzy had told him. He was jealous of her memories. He knew it annoyed her when he asked her to tell them again and again, all the old stories, but he couldn't help it.

Outside, the cat had lain down on the midden roof, sunning itself. It raised its head imperiously and craned round before lying back down with its legs outstretched.

When Isobel turned sixteen she left Auldpark. Kidd felt bereft. He ran away a couple of times but they always caught him and brought him back. Isobel never wrote, never came to see him. By the time he left Auldpark, he hadn't seen Izzy in over three years. He got an apprenticeship with a firm of painters and decorators, worked hard, rented a flat in Maryhill. One night in a pub on Great Western Road he met a bloke he knew from primary school, Brian Gavaghan. When he mentioned that he'd been looking for Isobel, Gavaghan looked at him queerly and looked away. Eventually he told him that Izzy was working for Walter Maitland, in one of his East End brothels, out in Dennistoun.

Christopher went there, asking for Isobel. He was shown through to a damp bedroom with a one-bar fire. He sat on the candlewick bedspread and a woman came into the room and knelt on the floor in front of him. She was two inches taller than Izzy and her eyes were the wrong colour. He batted her hands away and buckled his belt. "Who cares?" she said. "I'm Isobel if you want me to be."

Kidd finished his cigarette, stubbed it out in the baccy tin. There was no point fretting. McPhail would send someone or he wouldn't. Maybe the Quinns would come. Or the polis. He had a plank of four-by-two wedged under the Yale lock. It wouldn't hold for long but it would give him a chance to get his act together if somebody started to kick down the door.

When the brothel proved a dead end, he was back to where he started. Then he went down for the Gallowgate job. Five years later, all he had was that Izzy had worked in the Dennistoun place, a place run by the Maitlands. And then it struck him. Maybe he could make himself useful. To the Maitlands. Get close to them. He started drinking in the Duke, getting his face known. His plan was to prove his worth, maybe get taken on by the Maitland crew. And the encounter with Denny Quinn gave Kidd his chance. Now he could do something for them. And once he was established, once he'd claimed his corner spot in the Duke, he could start to ask around. About Izzy. Someone might remember her. Maybe

they'd know where she'd gone. Down to London or up to
Aberdeen. It was the best part of a decade since he'd seen her.
There was always the off-chance that Izzy was dead. You had
to face that. But maybe she'd just got scunnered with Glasgow,
fucked off to try her luck someplace else. Boarded a sleeper at
Central. Jumped on a bus at Killermont Street. Who could
blame her?

He looked out the window. The cat was gone. There were
footsteps in the close, echoing up the stairwell. Kidd eased
himself off the windowsill, stepped softly across to the door.
The footsteps were climbing the stairs. There was a ball-pein
hammer on a ledge above the doorjamb and Kidd reached up
softly and took it down. He flexed his fingers on the dimpled
rubber that sheathed the handle, let his arm hang loose to
sense the heft of the faceted head. He licked his lips. The steps
were coming closer. Come ahead, then. Don't be shy. They
came to a stop just outside the front door.

13

M cCormack was leafing through the PM report. He could hear Professor Agnew's voice in the dry, circumspect prose. Eileen Elliot's question was running through his head as he read: *Who would do that to a man of sixty-nine?*

Who, indeed? The question bothered him. Torture wasn't Walter Maitland's style. Maitland was ruthless, would take people out as soon as look at them if he saw the need. But he did it clean. You heard about it from touts, how so-and-so had disappeared, the body never found. He never did it like this. Torture a man for three or four days and dump his corpse in a backcourt.

He looked up: Nicol at the door. "Sorry to bother you, sir. We just heard back from Companies House."

He waved her in. "Any joy?"

"I think so. We asked for details of Elliot's companies, and all his directorships and appointments. There's a company called Wyndford Property Limited. Gavin Elliot was director. You might recognize one of the others."

McCormack leaned back in his seat, hands behind his head, fingers laced. "Oh, aye? A celebrity?" He chewed his lip. "Now my mind's running away with me here, D.C. Nicol. You're going to have to put me out of my misery. Would it be too much to hope that this celebrity was someone we take an interest in?"

Nicol sucked some air in through her teeth. "Would it, sir? No, no, I don't think that would be too much at all."

"It's not Himself?"

She shook her head. "Close, though. Carol Havlin."

McCormack's grin fell. "Carol Havlin? Who the fuck's Carol Havlin?"

"Legal spouse of one H. Maitland, Esquire."

"Hugh Maitland? Walter's fucking brother." McCormack shaped his lips to whistle, then stopped short. "We sure it's him, though? It's the same H. Maitland?"

"The address is a flat in Garrioch Road. Above the Barracks Bar."

"Hugh Maitland's pub. Bingo. The Maitlands and a murdered city businessman. The Maitlands and a former city councillor. Ex-MP. That good enough for you, DCI Haddow? Get in."

"Oh and, sir? I forgot to say. The neighbour we spoke to when we went to Yvonne Gray's flat? Says she did bar work, too. Up in Maryhill. The Barracks Bar."

McCormack thought about this. "That's proper police work, Nicol. O.K.: tell the others."

"Not just a pretty face, then?" She stood in the doorway struck a cheesecake pose, biting her lip, head held high.

McCormack was back with the report. He glanced up. "Just tell the others, Nicol."

Later they discussed it in the Byre.

"What do we do now, boss?"

"What do we do? We go and see them. Put the hard word on Glasgow's so-called hard men."

"The Maitlands?" Shand was on his feet, grinning like an idiot. "The bloody Maitlands?"

"That's the general idea, D.C. Shand. Being as how we're the Serious fucking Crime Squad of Strathclyde fucking Police."

"Well, when?"

"I don't know, D.C. Shand. I was thinking maybe a fortnight come Tuesday might be a suitable time, if everyone's diaries permit. *Now*, Detective. We do it now."

"You want me to . . . ?" Shand jerked a thumb at the door.

"Yes, Iain. Bring the car round. We're going on an outing."

When McCormack and Shand had left, Nicol drifted through to see the desk sergeant.

"Oh, Brian. I've managed to leave my locker key in my other bag. Could you give me the master?"

"Too many handbags, Liz. That's the problem. They're paying you too much." He reached behind him to a line of hooks.

"Aye, I've noticed that, Brian. Lighting my fags with burning fivers, that's me. Thanks a million."

"Bring it back, though, eh?"

"Two minutes."

The little alcove for the station lockers was in the corridor to the main building. It was empty when Nicol approached. Iain Shand's locker was right next to Nicol's. Even if someone appeared they'd never clock what she was doing. She put the key in and turned it.

They drove in silence, Shand at the wheel and McCormack lost in thought as they climbed Switchback Road.

Six years was a long time.

When McCormack left Glasgow, Walter Maitland was a bouncer. Or a "dancehall supervisor", as he preferred it. Six years later there were barely any dancehalls to supervise—it was all glitzy discos attached to pubs. Glitterballs. Lassies writhing on little checkerboard handkerchiefs of dancefloor. And now Maitland was the boss.

Walter Maitland ruled the whole city. Or anyway, everything north of the river.

It seemed a steep promotion. Then again, there were no training schools for Glasgow gangsters. No degree programmes or vocational placements. You fought your way up from the streets, and chucking drunks out of the Barrowland was as good a route as any. If you saw your chance, you took it.

And Walter Maitland had taken his. The villa on Manse Road in the suburb of Bearsden sat in grounds that could have housed a smallish hospital. To call it "detached" seemed slightly begrudging. The houses on either side were forty feet away, screened behind stands of mature trees. There were so many trees in this part of North Glasgow, so tall and thickly planted that it felt to McCormack like driving through a forest.

"This is us."

Shand signalled and swung the Velox between weathered gateposts—one of them capped with a black shag of ivy—and onto the driveway of Maitland's property.

"Jesus." Shand slowed the motor and they crackled up the curving drive.

McCormack nodded. He knew what Shand meant.

There was nothing fancy about the house. It was just a boxy farmhouse in pale blond stone, symmetrical, with two bay windows on either storey and a single slim pane above the pedimented porch. No towers or battlements or crow-stepped gables. It was purely the size that made you gasp. It rose like the cliffs of Dover into the Bearsden sky.

They parked behind a racing-green E-type Jag. As Shand climbed the steps to ring the bell, McCormack buttoned his jacket and turned to take in the grounds. The rounded rectangle of lawn slid away in front of the house towards the trees at the boundary wall. It was completely empty. You might have staged a football match or a battle re-enactment on its manicured expanse. Its vacancy felt to McCormack like a statement. It was vast, carefully tended and used—apparently—for absolutely nothing.

The front door opened and McCormack turned.

Walter Maitland stood on the top step, shoulders squared, chin jutting out. He had thickened since McCormack saw him last, the torso filling a pale blue linen shirt. Beneath the tailored ecru-coloured shorts his skinny shins dropped down to leather slip-ons. His dainty, sockless ankles looked comically slight beneath his carthorse bulk. Still, nobody was laughing.

"The Highland Laddie. Like a bad fucking penny. And who's your girlfriend?"

"This is D.S. Iain Shand, Mr. Maitland. We were hoping for a word."

"Yeah. I kinda figured that."

They followed him down a dark wooden hallway, their footsteps muffled by a scarlet runner, to a bright airy space at the rear of the house. The French windows were open to the gold evening sun. Maitland flopped into an armchair and waved his hand for them to sit. McCormack and Shand sat on the sofa, side by side.

The room was furnished in a hard man's idea of a gentleman's club. Armchairs in green buttoned leather were arranged loosely round a circular coffee table bearing a spread of magazines. The walls were half-panelled in dark wood. Etchings of racehorses. Deco standing ashtrays. A brass poker-and-tong set glowed on the hearthstone. Some sort of antique musket was mounted over the marble fireplace.

"Mr. Chekhov's, is it?" McCormack nodded at the gun.

"You want to see a licence?"

"Forget it." McCormack fished out his notebook. "Nice place."

"Can we get to the point?"

"It *is* nice, though. I've been in a room like this before." McCormack was nodding, glancing round. "Southside. St. Andrew's Drive."

"Is that right?"

St. Andrew's Drive was where John McGlashan had lived, the man Maitland succeeded as the King of Greater Glasgow.

"Aye. I mean, not exactly the same. Obviously. This other room had a walnut desk. You know, with the green leather top? More bookshelves too. Classy. Oh, and a guy with his face blown off on a rug in front of the fireplace." McCormack nodded. "Same taste in whisky, though." He looked at Maitland while pointing to the corner where two rows of bottles stood on shelves behind an L-shaped bar.

There was an empty glass on the bar-top, a bottle of whisky beside it. Glen Grant.

Maitland ran a hand across his hair, patting it down. His hair was still thick, still black, though a stain of grey was spreading at the temples. "If you want a drink," he said, "you only have to ask. Is this going somewhere?"

"Sadly, no," McCormack said. "On both counts. No, we're here about another dead friend. You seem to collect them. This one's called Gavin Elliot."

"No friend of mine."

"Just a business partner, then," Shand said. "You look quite pally here, though."

Shand had slipped a Xeroxed newspaper cutting from his folder and laid it on the coffee table in front of Maitland. Shand had retrieved it from the *Tribune* morgue. It showed Walter Maitland with his arms round two men. One was Hugh Maitland. The other was Gavin Elliot. All grins and tuxes at some charity smoker in a city-centre hotel. They were holding an outsize cardboard cheque for eight thousand pounds made out to Auldpark Children's Home.

Maitland ran his hand through his hair. "We've been in the same room. Gold star for the boy detective."

"Same room. Same company." Shand put the Xerox back in his folder. "Wyndford Property Limited."

"That's my brother, wee man. That's not me. Take it up with Hughie."

"We plan to," said McCormack. "But a man might be forgiven for assuming that you keep an eye on what your underlings get up to."

"Hughie's four years older than me."

"And that makes him the boss, does it? He runs the family?"

"He ties his own shoelaces. He's his own man."

"Right. 'Am I my brother's keeper?'"

"Am I what?"

"Oh, I'm sorry. It's in the Bible, Walter. Cain and Abel. Imagine a Taig having to tell you that."

"The Bible, aye. It tells you to pray for those who persecute you, too. Don't hold your fucking breath."

McCormack found this funny. He turned to Shand to bring him into the joke, jerked his head at Maitland. "He thinks this is persecution. You think this is persecution? We're just getting started, Walter. This wasn't one of your scumbag gangster pals we're talking about. This was an ex-MP, Knight of the Realm. You don't get to so much as blow your nose without Strathclyde Police checking the hankie. Not till this thing's sorted."

"You've had months," Maitland said. "Months trying to get something on me. And what have you got? The square root of fuck all. And now this? Suddenly it's my fault someone got mugged? On the half-crown side of Dumbarton Road?"

"That's where he was found. He was killed somewhere else. Somewhere secure. He'd been worked over. Tortured. Kept for days in his own filth. A man of nearly seventy. It's not a mugging, Walter. It's someone who knew him, hated him. Someone with a grudge."

Maitland stroked the bristles on his cheek with the backs of his fingers, stared out the window.

"It's personal," McCormack went on. "It's revenge. It's about some kind of betrayal, maybe. Maybe a business deal gone sour."

"If you've got an accusation to make," Maitland uncrossed his legs, planted his feet a yard apart on the parquet. "Let's hear it. Otherwise, could you maybe get to fuck out of my house?"

"O.K. Well, thanks for your hospitality, Mr. Maitland. We'll be seeing you again soon. Probably at our place."

McCormack and Shand rose to their feet. Maitland did too. "You know, you people should be congratulating me, what I do for this city."

"Congratulate you for what? For killing four people in a Tradeston tenement."

"The fuck you on about now?"

"The Tradeston fire, Walter. Who else would have set that fire to burn down the Quinns' warehouse?"

"The Quinns? Are you a halfwit? It's an insurance job. Fuckin thieving tarriers. Oh, wait. I forgot: you're one of them."

"I'm a Highlander, *a mhic ifrinn*."

"And I'm an entrepreneur. I bring money into this city. What do you bring?" Maitland shook his head. "Why are you even here? Didn't you fuck off to London? Still, not everyone can hack it down there."

McCormack was moving to the door, Shand behind him. "You'd know better than me."

There was a rumour that Maitland had been down in London the previous year, looking to muscle in, establish a foothold, noising up the East End teams, the Maltese round Soho. Word was they'd sent him packing.

"Why'd you come back then?" He wasn't done needling McCormack. "Unfinished business?"

"Don't flatter yourself, Maitland."

McCormack and Shand were making their way down the hallway, but Maitland wasn't finished.

"No? I hear you've got my photie on your wall, out in Anniesland. Fucking pin-up. Bring it in and I'll sign it for you."

McCormack shook his head. He knew Maitland had tame cops, everybody knew. But tame cops on the Serious Crime Squad?

"Maybe I'll type up a confession. How you torched the Tradeston warehouse. Killed four folk in the building next door. Get you to sign that."

"This is your idea of police work? Throw slanderous accusations about and hope something sticks? No wonder the Met got shot of you. Here, son." They were at the front door now, the three of them, and Maitland turned towards Shand, jabbing his thumb at McCormack. "You want to get anywhere in your line of work, don't follow this guy. He's fucking lost it. He's yesterday's paper."

They drove back down Switchback Road towards Temple. Neither spoke for the first few minutes.

"What was that about the whisky?" Shand asked, finally.

McCormack opened the window an inch to flick his cigarette end into the wind. "When McGlashan got topped we found a glass at the scene. Well, two glasses. One had Glash's dabs on it and a half-inch of Macallan at the bottom. The other glass was empty but contained traces of a different whisky."

"Glen Grant?"

"It's all Maitland drinks."

"Maitland topped John McGlashan? Holy Christ."

"There were no dabs on the glass. Nothing else to tie him to the locus. But, you know. It made all kinds of sense. Peter Levein was trying to tidy things up, get rid of loose ends. Biggest loose end was John McGlashan. Maitland was helping him out."

On the way home that evening, almost as if the car itself was in charge, McCormack found himself bearing left at the Botanic Gardens, onto Great Western Road. He skirted the city centre, headed east along Cumbernauld Road before dropping down to join the Gallowgate. He parked outside the Eastern Necropolis and walked through the gateposts into the beautiful green gloom of the trees.

A short way down the hill he came to a stop in front of a plain grey stone. They hadn't changed the name; what would they change it to? The stone still said what it said six years ago:

HELEN THANEY
19 May 1941–10 August 1969
RIP

The woman in the coffin had been buried at the Corporation's expense. Helen Thaney had no kin in Scotland, and no friends to take charge of her body. There was a father back in Ireland but he'd packed her off to the nuns when she was sixteen years old and cared no more for her in death than he had in life. That left the Corporation, who had at least gone the length of those extra three letters—RIP—that identified the woman's religion.

But the trouble was, McCormack reflected, as he squatted down to tug the clumps of overgrown grass from the foot of the stone and stood again, wiping his hands on the skirts of his raincoat—the trouble was that those three letters might turn out to be superfluous. The woman in the coffin may have been Catholic or she may not. But one thing was certain: she wasn't Helen Thaney.

McCormack rested his hand on the rough-hewn granite headstone. The facade of the stone was glossy and polished, it threw back your own blurred reflection. But the stone's curved top was jagged and rough. It chafed McCormack's palm as he drew his hand across it.

When you closed a case there was always something left over. A piece that didn't fit. The Quaker case was like that. It was neat enough at the finish. There were three key players. John McGlashan was the gangster, the killer; he'd murdered three women between May 1968 and August 1969. William Bickett, the Corporation housing clerk, was McGlashan's accomplice, luring the women from the Barrowland Ballroom. And their police protector was Peter Levein, head of CID for the City of Glasgow Police.

Levein had killed McGlashan before the Quaker Squad could get to him. But Levein and Bickett had both gone down. Levein later killed himself in prison. You could call it a result, of sorts. But the woman in the coffin was the remainder carried over once you'd finished the sum. She was the reminder that you never got everything right. McCormack wasn't naive enough to think that he could come back after six years and square it all away. But one of the reasons he came back was the woman in the coffin.

That night, back at the flat, McCormack poured a Spring-bank and slumped in the armchair, stocking-soled feet up on the coffee table. He sipped the whisky. The Maitland interview had gone about the way he'd expected, but Eileen Elliot? That was different. He'd had enough experience to know that people reacted in differing ways to the murder of somebody close. Some shut down; others opened up. Some grew an instant cara-pace; others turned to mush. But whichever way it took them, genuine grief was hard to fake. You watched their eyes, you got some kind of handle on their feelings.

Not so with Eileen Elliot. He thought about her reaction to the PM report. When McCormack disclosed the details, the chapter and verse of her father's mistreatment, Eileen Elliot closed her eyes, drew in a long, deep breath through her nose, paying it out through the "O" of her mouth. It could have been her way of absorbing the blow, but it looked to McCormack much more like relief. How could that be? Had she expected worse? Had her imagination worked up some catalogue of hor-rors that made the actual details a blessed relief?

He swirled the oily liquid, sniffed the brassy, tart aroma. Was there something else behind Eileen Elliot's response? She stood to gain from her father's death. An estate of half a million could turn someone's head, make them act in unusual ways. But Eileen Elliot was already rich. She lived in a Pollokshields mansion. Her Merc was still glossy with showroom wax. Whatever she might be planning with her father's inheritance, she wasn't—so far as you could tell—in urgent need of cash. "Comfortable" was the word McCormack's parents had always used, when discussing people with money. Eileen Elliot was certainly comfortable. As he himself was, in a different sense, sitting here with his feet up, a ten-year-old malt at his elbow. He thought about Iain Shand, stuck in the cramped Velox, out on surveillance in the wilds of Maryhill. Good enough for him, McCormack thought. He took another sip of malt, let it roll across his tongue, the lovely burn.

Maybe it was the whisky, maybe it was the little victory of making Walter Maitland lose his temper, but in that moment it didn't seem too bad. Life. The job. The whole shooting match. He turned the glass under the light, watching the golden liquid find its level. The faceted crystal impressed itself on his skin and suddenly the rough feel of the headstone under his palm came back to him. The woman in the coffin. She was one reason he'd come back. Aye. But she wasn't the only one. He wasn't just coming back to Glasgow, he admitted. He was running away from London. As a cop you couldn't afford to be vulnerable. You couldn't afford to have doors in your life through which the bad guys could get to you. And Victor was one of those doors. Solid fucking dependable bloody Victor. McCormack thought about the unopened letters in the hallstand drawer. He pictured the hand that had addressed those envelopes. After three years in London, McCormack had given up hope of finding anyone. Week by week he took his perfunctory pleasures in the parks and public toilets of South London. It wasn't such a bad way to live. And then, without warning, here came Victor Fraser into his life.

McCormack's flat on Peckham Rye had developed a leak

and the handyman sent by the landlord to fix it was Victor. He knew straight away. He knew without a doubt that Victor was interested. Once the leak was fixed—it was a blocked down-pipe that caused it—McCormack offered Victor a beer. They drank bottles of Bass on the little brick balcony with its view of the Rye's drab expanse of grass. Victor talked about himself. He had served with the army. His father was a Glasgow man and Victor considered himself Scottish too. Indeed, the regiment he'd served with was the Royal Highland Fusiliers. He even did a passable Glasgow accent that had the two of them laughing, clinking bottles. After the second beer, McCormack walked Victor to the door and then when Victor turned to say goodbye they were suddenly kissing, tugging at each other's clothes.

It developed from there. Before long McCormack was spending three or four nights a week in Victor's little semi on Marsden Road. Victor was like a wholesome, unflappable, highly addictive drug. McCormack had never felt this way before. It was pretty much what he'd always wanted and for that reason it started to frighten him. He knew that, before long, if he was forced to choose between the job and Victor, he would choose Victor. And so, while he still could, he chose the job. He took the offer from his old CID boss and transferred to Glasgow. Back up the road. Serious Crime Squad. He only told Victor the night before he left; didn't give him a chance to object. That, he supposed, was what the letters were. And whether they were anguished pleas or bitter denunciations, they were right. They were right and they were unanswerable and that's why McCormack couldn't read them. Fuck it. He downed the *uisge beatha* in a oner and stumbled through to bed.

THURSDAY, 3 JULY 1975

14

H addow strode into the squad room waving a paper in the air, like Chamberlain after Munich. Only it wasn't peace in our time.

"Shackled. Beaten. Starved. What the fuck?"

McCormack stepped back, stood off to the side of the whiteboard. He'd been mid-flow, briefing the new task force— his own unit and two others. Now he ceded the floor to Haddow. They had all seen that morning's *Record*:

TORTURE KILLING OF TOP TORY:
Ex-MP Butchered in Four-Day Ordeal.

"Details," Haddow said. "There are details in here beyond what was disclosed in the presser."

He slapped the paper against the nearest desk, like someone swatting a bluebottle. In the still, airless room it felt like a gunshot. Some of the detectives dropped their eyes and others truculently held his gaze as Haddow scanned the faces. He came to rest on McCormack's. "What the fuck kind of show are you running here?"

McCormack's tone when he answered was studiedly mild. "You took the words right out of my mouth, sir."

Haddow's smile showed a glint of incisor. "You want to explain that, Detective?"

"I'm saying, it's hard to run a tight ship when half of Glasgow CID is on board." He gestured vaguely round the crowded room. "You make the circle as big as this, don't be surprised when it's easy to break."

Haddow set the paper gently down on the desk. "That's about your measure, McCormack, isn't it? Maligning your fellow officers."

"Isn't that what you were doing?"

"Naw, son." Haddow advanced on him. "Just one of them. The one who thinks he's the Second Coming. We should strew palms in the bloody car park when you come to work in the mornings. Know something, McCormack? You better hope you clear this. Make some friends upstairs. Because I'll tell you this: you're gonnae need them."

He was off then, door banging, leaving McCormack to face the folded arms and dipped chins of the Serious Crime Squad.

McCormack looked round the sullen faces, trying to pick up the thread. Derek Goldie spoke up. "Never mind, boss. At least you're dressed for it."

McCormack was wearing a dark suit, white shirt and black tie. It was the funeral of the Tradeston fire victims that afternoon.

"Yes, thanks for that, Detective."

Goldie grinned. "I come to bury Duncan, not to praise him."

Later that morning, McCormack parked in Lorraine Road in the city's West End and strolled round into Great Western Terrace. Millionaire's Row. A secret street behind a screen of trees. A few yards away, buses groaned past on the city's western artery. Here, though, residents' cars were parked in gleaming isolation in the vacant spaces of the private driveway, and McCormack walked the flagstones of the broad, railed-off pavement, looking for Number Seven.

Or, rather, he was looking for Number VII, since each town-house had its Roman numeral in gold leaf on a central fanlight. Each house had its own pillared portico, with four Ionic columns bracing a massy entablature. Leading to each front door was a buttressed stone staircase flanked with wrought-iron lampposts showcasing globed glass lamps the size of beachballs. It was a far cry from the tenements of Crawford Street.

McCormack was still twenty or thirty yards away when he saw the man hurrying down the steps of one of the houses. He wasn't sure, at this distance, if the house was the one he was making for, but he quickened his pace.

The man came towards McCormack with his head down, pulling his raincoat closed over a pale green suit. As they neared each other, the man in the raincoat glanced up from under a twist of auburn curls and caught McCormack's eye. The look that passed between them lasted a fraction of a second but it was enough to stop McCormack in his tracks. Faced with the hostile concentration of McCormack's glare the man visibly quailed. That in itself wasn't what mattered, but as he cast his eyes down and as his tongue flicked out to wet his bottom lip, the look on the man's face was an unmistakable compound of guilt and fear.

McCormack looked up at the nearest house, scanning the fanlight for the numeral, but the gold leaf had flaked away. He hurried on, another fifteen yards, till he caught the glinting figures—a V and two IIs. When he turned, the man in the raincoat was already rounding the corner into Westbourne Gardens. From there he could vanish into one of the lanes or push on into the streets of Hyndland. No point giving chase.

McCormack sat on the top step.

What's the point in having instinct, he thought, if you don't act on it?

He lit a cigarette and replayed the incident. McCormack had seen the man coming down the stone steps. Had the man been inside the house, or had he just knocked the door and turned away when no one answered? McCormack closed his eyes. The man had come down the steps at a kind of tripping run, as if maybe he'd pulled the door shut on his way out and his momentum had carried him down the steps. When you knock on a door and no one answers, what do you do? You don't come dancing down the steps. You pause, you strain to hear, listening for footsteps approaching the door. And when you do decide to give up, you leave slowly, reluctantly, you descend the steps heavily, maybe pausing halfway down, maybe turning back for a final look.

He was sure of it. The man had been inside the house.

McCormack finished his cigarette. He was still sitting on the steps ten minutes later when Eileen Elliot pulled up in a metallic grey Jaguar XJ-S and clicked up the steps with a frown on her face.

"Am I late, Inspector? I do apologize."

"You're not late." McCormack rose, dusting the backside of his suit trousers. "I'm early."

He was always early. It was something he'd done for years. If he knew he was meeting someone he'd turn up with twenty minutes to spare, scope the place, try to glean whatever advantage he could.

Eileen Elliot scoured her handbag and produced a key. McCormack stepped in front of her as they reached the top step. "Actually: would you mind?" He took the latch-key from her, slotted it home and flicked his wrist. The door swung open.

McCormack stretched an arm out behind him, hand splayed, to stay Eileen Elliot. He wanted to savour the atmosphere of the house without adulteration from the woman beside him, her perfume, her hairspray, her breath coming in vexed little gasps.

He crossed the threshold. Was it imagination? He sensed an agitation in the darkened hallway, a swirl of molecules as if the passage of a body had set the air astir. This wasn't the lulled, stagnant air of a house that had lain vacant for three or four days. And that smell. He had no idea how Gavin Elliot smelled—at least how he smelled alive—but wasn't that spoor of maleness (cloth, tobacco, armpits, Brylcreem) too fresh to be Elliot's?

Eileen Elliot spoke softly. "What is it, Inspector?" A pause. "Do you think there's someone here?"

"No," McCormack said. "I think we just missed them." He told her about the man in the raincoat. The green suit. The reddish wavy hair.

"It doesn't," she said. "No. It's not ringing any bells."

"Miss Elliot, who has keys to your father's house?"

She frowned at him. In the darkened hallway she told it off on her fingers. "Me. Julia, my father's secretary." Again the trill of bitchiness on that last word. "And there's the housekeeper. He has a housekeeper who comes twice a week. Monday and Fridays."

"I'll need the details. And there's no one else he might have given a key to?"

"I wouldn't have thought so," she said. She laid three fingers on McCormack's wrist. "You should understand, Inspector. I wasn't terribly close to my father. I loved him, but I didn't always like him particularly." She gave a curt little smile. "I'm saying there may have been, let's say, relationships that I didn't know about."

McCormack remembered a line from the *Tribune*'s obit: *He kept his personal life out of the spotlight.*

"Did he have many of those? I mean relationships?"

"That's my point, Inspector. I wouldn't know."

McCormack nodded. He was on the point of saying, *You don't know much, do you?* But he bit it back. He told Eileen Elliot to stay behind him as they moved through the house. They started in the basement. An exercise room with a rowing machine, bench-press and barbells. A barrel-vaulted billiard room, wood-panelled and church-like in the stillness, the green baize like a manicured lawn in the light from the basement window. A utility room with washing machine and tumble dryer, big twin Belfast sinks. McCormack felt a light breeze and he turned to see the jimmied window, the bootprint on the sill. And, yes, the trampled flowerbed outside. The garden was empty. He drew the short CID truncheon from his pocket.

Back up on the ground floor was the drawing room, the dining room, the kitchen with its walk-in pantry. McCormack slapped the pantry's thick cream walls, felt the heavy coolness on his palm. Then he gripped the barley-sugar bannister and climbed to the first floor, past the stained-glass window on the landing. There were bedrooms here, four in a row, empty and innocent, a vast slate-tiled bathroom with both a sunken spa and a claw-foot bath. And then, at the corridor's end, under the broad eaves, through a half-open door: Elliot's study.

They could see the disorder from the corridor. Books in broken-backed heaps on the floor. The massive leather-top desk ransacked, its drawers tugged askew, pigeonholes rifled, papers scattered everywhere, fanned out on the carpet, hanging like tongues from the half-open drawers, the captain's chair toppled, a pen-set and paperweight on the floor beside the ashtray and a gold Dunhill lighter, a smashed goblet, its jagged scalloped bowl snagging the light from a skylight window.

McCormack crouched down to peer at the papers on the floor. Bills and invoices, it looked like. Company paperwork. Eileen Elliot reached out gingerly for the stem of the shattered glass and McCormack gripped her wrist.

"Prints," he cautioned her.

His knees cracked as he rose to his feet.

"Whatever it was," he said, glancing round at the blizzard of paper, the splayed mound of books, the denuded shelves, "we can be pretty sure they didn't find it."

He could smell the spilled whisky from the broken glass, a ghost of peatsmoke. They checked back through the other

rooms for items of value. An antique key-fob and a pair of platinum cufflinks glinting on the dresser in the master bedroom.
Gold-leaf plate on the dining room sideboard. Two Cadells
and a Fergusson on the walls.

Robbery wasn't the motive here. At least, not robbery as
commonly practised, for items of general value. Something
very particular had been sought here, something valuable in a
specific context. And it hadn't been found.

McCormack parted with Eileen Elliot on the front steps.

"Thanks for your time, Miss Elliot. The Forensics department will contact you to arrange access for fingerprinting."

She fished the keys from her handbag, held them out, jig-
gled them gently.

"Take these. I've a spare set at home."

"That's very helpful."

"Not at all." She snapped the handbag shut. "What were
they looking for, Inspector, do you imagine?"

"Hard to say." McCormack stowed the keys in his trouser
pocket. "A document, certainly. Maybe a letter. Something
sensitive, possibly incriminating. Best not to speculate. I'd like
to talk further, Miss Elliot, but I have somewhere to be."

She looked at the black tie. "Yes, I noticed. I didn't like to
ask. No one close, I hope."

"Thankfully, no. Miss Elliot, I want to give you my assur-
ance, once more, that we will find whoever killed your father.
We'll find them and we will put them away."

She leaned in, her eyes frankly scanning his face, and she
looked almost happy. "I don't doubt it, Inspector."

The priest himself gave the homily—the bereaved husband
and father looked too broken to do more than slump in his
pew—and the theme was not mercy but justice. The powerful
who prey on the weak must not escape judgement. Vengeance
must fall on the evildoers, no matter how powerful, no matter

how *well connected* they were. The cruel fires kindled in that Glasgow tenement will be as nothing to the fires the guilty will suffer in hell, but the fires of earthly justice must be kindled too, so that the terrible iniquity of this crime may be consumed in the flames of retribution.

McCormack and Goldie sat together near the back. McCormack could tell that Goldie was unsettled by being in a chapel. All that standing up and sitting down had shaken his Protestant soul and when McCormack filed out to receive, he'd had to place his hand on Goldie's shoulder to stop him following.

Across the sea of hats and the men's bald spots, McCormack watched the cropped fair head of the husband and father. The man who was here to bury his daughter, his estranged wife. Chisholm was the man's name. Gordon Chisholm. He sat a little apart from the others on his pew, in the transient celebrity of bereavement, a figure out of Shakespeare, his whole family extinguished at a stroke.

Then the organ started up and six pall-bearers shouldered the mother's coffin and carried it down the aisle. Chisholm rose and lifted the little girl's coffin on his own, holding it crosswise in his arms like some terrible offering, moving stiffly forward in the wake of his estranged wife. As the man came towards them McCormack's eye caught a flash of scarlet: Chisholm's socks, an incongruous, jaunty crimson.

Afterwards they queued with the others and took Chisholm's hand, told him they were sorry for his trouble. There was no bite to the man's handshake, it just slipped from your grasp.

Outside, the mourners gathered in little eddying groups beneath the linden trees. Women embraced. The men lit cigarettes and nodded at one another.

McCormack was leaning in to get a light from Goldie when he sensed a presence at his elbow.

A small man with a face like a clenched fist. He stood too close to McCormack and spoke in a murderous undertone. McCormack focused on the small hard knot of the man's tie.

"That cancerous bastard," the man was saying. "You gonnae let him walk? Or are you gonnae put him away?"

He could smell whisky on the man's breath.

"Do I know you?"

"You were down in London, weren't you?" He spoke it like an accusation. "Why did you even come back? If you do fuck all. Every person in that church. Every person in this fucking city knows who did it. And what do you do?"

An awareness was passing through the crowd, something in the man's stance, some charge in the air. People turned to stare. Hands came up to shield eyes from the sun. Cigarettes were stayed on their way to lips. One of the photographers started snapping some shots.

A woman appeared beside the angry man. "That's enough now, Bobby." She took his elbow, tried to steer him away but he shook her off and stepped back up to McCormack.

"You show up here in your fancy suit. With your Sunday face on, your fucking crocodile tears. Making out like you give a fuck. If you gave a fuck Walter Maitland would be in Barlinnie. If you gave a fuck that wee lassie and her maw would still be here." There was spittle on his lips; he wiped his hand across his mouth. "You have any idea what that man's been through? Gordon Chisholm. He watched his sergeant shot dead in the street. Over the water. Bled out in front of him. And now this? Why don't you show that man some common charity, eh? Why don't you do your fucking job?"

He was finished now, moving smartly off as if he had somewhere urgent to be. The woman started after him and then turned back. "Just so you know," she said to McCormack. "I agree with everything he said. Every word of it." Then she set off sadly in the small man's wake.

"The fuck was that all about?" Goldie jerked his head in the direction of the departing man and woman. "Who even was that?"

"No idea." McCormack dropped his cigarette and dragged his shoe across it. "Had my fucking number, though."

"Dunc. Dunc, come on. He's bang out of order. You're knocking your pan out trying to put Maitland away. We all are."

"Are we? Are we, Derek? We've been on Maitland's case for months. Is he any nearer the jail? Have we made the remotest difference?"

"You said it yourself, Dunc. It's a marathon, not a sprint. Come on. Let's get back to it."

McCormack followed Goldie to the car. His words to Shand came back to him. *He's not ruling the streets through fear; he's ruling them through favours.* That was true for certain people. There were others, though. People who got in the way. People who paid the price of Maitland's favours. The mourners were a congregation of these people, a gathering of Maitland's victims. And McCormack saw now that he shouldn't have come. The small man was right. His presence here wasn't a comfort to these people, to Gordon Chisholm and the rest. It was no kind of solace. An affront, rather. Empty bravado when what these people needed was action, a killer taken off the board.

The hearse slid away and the black Daimlers followed. Car doors were slamming in syncopation, engines catching. The mourners were preparing to drive out to Clydebank for the cremation. Goldie nosed the Velox into the traffic. They stayed in the convoy of mourners as it snaked along Dumbarton Road. Then Goldie flashed the indicator and hung a right and they were gone, free, off up the Crow Road in the direction of Temple.

They passed a billboard for Kestrel Lager ("It Bites") and McCormack thought, A Pint. I'll have earned a pint tonight.

15

D CI Haddow stood in the lounge of his Jordanhill villa and poured himself a brandy. He used one of the good crystal goblets. Now that Gillian was no longer there to stop him, he used the good crystal every night. He gave himself a little more than usual, in tribute to the kind of day he'd had. He carried the glass to the leather armchair and clicked it down on the little marble table. He lifted the *Tribune*. He hadn't had time to tackle the obits until now. Partly because half the bloody *Tribune* staff were camped outside Temple, looking for updates on the Elliot murder. He'd had meetings with the CC, the Deputy CC Crime, phone calls from the Lord Provost and the Secretary of bloody State. Everyone would be watching the progress on this one, which had better be good.

Well, fuck it. That was McCormack's lookout. He'd had Shand in the office earlier, reporting on the teuchter. According to Shand, McCormack was hell-for-leather all-guns-blazing on the Elliot case. Well, good. Shand himself was near wetting his breeks at the thought of working a big-time murder. He would find out soon enough that it wasn't all beer and skittles.

Haddow let a long slug of brandy slip down his gullet, land like a fireball in his belly. He felt the heat radiate outwards, searing his cheeks, tingling in his fingertips. There was a framed photograph on the marble table and he turned it to face him. Colin, on his graduation day. Wearing his academic robes and the hood with the purple trim, clutching the scarlet cardboard tube that contained his degree. He'd had hopes at one stage that Colin might follow him into the Force, but the smiling face in the photo seemed to mock that memory. Colin thought the police were a species of glorified bouncers, the state's hired thugs. He was down south, London, a social worker with Lambeth Council. Probably marking off the days until Haddow snuffed it and he could sell this place and all its fittings. Well, fuck it. Haddow turned the photograph back around. He wasn't dead yet. He opened the *Tribune* and found the obits, the one he'd been waiting to savour.

Sir Gavin Elliot

The former Conservative MP Sir Gavin Alexander Elliot, who has died aged 69, was the nearly man of Scottish politics, his fifteen-year Commons career spent principally on the back benches. Educated at Glasgow Academy, Elliot read law at the University of Glasgow before being called to the Scottish Bar. A successful legal career appeared to beckon, following a string of high-profile criminal defences in his native city. However, Elliot's true passion—outside the sphere of politics—turned out to be business. He discovered a talent for property speculation, quickly amassing an impressive portfolio of rental properties in Glasgow, before expanding into the hotel trade.

Elliot took the Glasgow Cathkin seat for the Conservatives in the 1951 general election. In the Commons, Elliot distinguished himself as a Tory traditionalist, not merely in his style of dress—he invariably sported a double-breasted pinstripe suit and a proudly anachronistic bowler hat—but in his uncompromising adherence to Conservative values and causes. An opponent of closer ties with Europe, he regarded the Common Market and later the European

Economic Community as a deadly threat to British sovereignty. He opposed sanctions on Rhodesia, following the Smith regime's unilateral declaration of independence in 1965.

A strict disciplinarian, Elliot advocated the return of both corporal and capital punishment, and regularly called for higher prison tariffs for crimes of a violent and sexual nature. He attempted to introduce a legal ban on criminals profiting from their published memoirs. As an elder in the Church of Scotland he opposed Sunday trading and the liberalizing of the law surrounding prostitution and homosexuality. His traditional views, however, did not prevent Elliot from capitalizing on his fellow man's moral frailties when he opened one of Glasgow's first casinos in 1965.

It was a surprise to many that Elliot never achieved the ministerial office to which his talents appeared to fit him and to which he himself undoubtedly aspired. It is understood that Sir Alec Douglas-Home promised Elliot the job of Scottish Secretary on the eve of the 1964 general election. The Tories' narrow loss to Harold Wilson's Labour came as a body blow to Elliot, who made no secret of his ambition to serve as Scottish Secretary. Disillusioned, Elliot stood down at the 1966 general election to concentrate on his business interests, which were by this time extensive, in both the construction and hospitality sectors.

The lure of politics, however, was not to be withstood. In a reversal of the more familiar career path, Elliot left the national political stage to take office at the local level, serving as a city councillor on the Glasgow Corporation from 1966 until he lost his seat in 1972. During his period in the City Chambers, Elliot's energies were focused on the city's ongoing redevelopment schemes, including the execution of the ring road and motorway system which he had championed as a Glasgow MP.

A fiercely private man, Elliot resented the increasing journalistic interest in politicians' personal lives, particularly in the wake of the Profumo scandal. Elliot kept his personal life out of the spotlight, and shunned publicity even for his regular charitable activities. In 1941 he married Patricia Burgess, a legal clerk, who died of cancer in 1968.

Gavin Elliot was knighted for services to politics, business and charity in 1969. He is survived by his daughter, Eileen, a businesswoman in Glasgow.

This could be the case, Haddow thought. The case that makes the difference between the back benches and ministerial office. If McCormack solved this promptly it would be money in the bank for Haddow when the CC came to retire. Equally, if the teuchter fucked it up, it would give him all the excuse he needed to move McCormack on, send him back into rotation in general CID, out in the bloody wilds somewhere, Easterhouse or Shettleston. Never have to suffer the sight of his self-righteous Highland puss again. It was an each-way bet he couldn't lose.

Alone in his big empty villa, Haddow hoisted his glass in a toast.

16

I t always struck McCormack as odd and rather reckless that darts was a diversion practised principally in pubs. To be hurling sharpened projectiles at a disc of sisal fibres while you and those around you tossed back whiskies seemed a warrantless tempting of fate. He caught the barman's eye and ordered two Macallans, flinching as another tungsten arrow passed within two hands-breadths of his head.

To the average Glasgow punter, the Park Bar on Argyle Street was just another teuchter pub, a place with fiddle music and sing-song accents. To the city's large population of Highlanders, it was a portal to home, a place where you could speak Gaelic and sing it, buy tickets to the Glasgow Skye Association's annual dance, squabble about shinty, arrange a lift to Ullapool, read the classifieds in the *West Highland Free Press*.

To Duncan McCormack, the Park Bar was where he met Greg Hislop every Thursday.

The Macallans landed on the bar-top. McCormack paid and ferried the drinks across to the corner table where Hislop was reading a book.

The old man took his glasses off and tucked them into his breast pocket.

"What's this you're reading?" McCormack asked.

"A novel." Hislop turned the book over so that the title was visible. It was Alistair MacLean's *The Guns of Navarone*. "A proper novel. He did this, they did that. He said, they said."

McCormack watered his whisky from the little ceramic jug on the table. "Killer plotline, Greg. Sounds a real page-turner."

"I mean it's in the past tense, you *gloic*. The story is over and done with, and someone's telling you what was important about it."

McCormack frowned. "As opposed to . . . ?"

"As opposed to all this present-tense *sgudal*. He walks to the door. He opens the door. He steps out into the street. Where everything's supposed to sound exciting whether it's important or not. He makes a cup of tea."

"It's supposed to make things more vivid," McCormack said. "Plus, that's what it's like, isn't it? Life, I mean. Something happens, you don't know if it's important or not."

"*Life?*" Hislop grimaced. "This is a novel. The writer should already know what matters. Otherwise he's just wasting your time."

Hislop's life was like a novel, McCormack thought. At least the part that everyone knew about; his wartime adventures in occupied France. Hislop was one of four Ballachulish men— all serving in the Argyll and Sutherland Highlanders—who'd missed being picked up at Dunkirk. All the British boats had flitted back to Blighty and the Balla boys were stranded. But they weren't quite finished yet. They headed south, pretending to be Russians, bamboozling the Germans by speaking Gaelic. They made it all the way to neutral Spain.

The story had a darker side, too. At one point on their journey, the Balla boys had killed someone—a priest, supposedly— who was threatening to expose them. In some versions of the story, the man who slit the padre's throat was Greg Hislop.

A cheer went up from the darts players in the corner. Handshakes all round and claps on the back: game over. The players crowded round the bar.

Everyone knew about Hislop's wartime trek down occupied France. Hislop had been dining out on the tale for thirty years. But there were other stories, too, stories from the early days, back before the war. Hislop had cut quite a figure in the Glasgow of the Thirties. A bad old cop for the bad old days. One of Sillitoe's Cossacks.

When Percy Sillitoe was brought up from Sheffield to be Glasgow's new Chief Constable at the start of the Thirties, his brief was to smash the city's gangs. He did this by recruiting scores of rough-arsed Highlanders, rangy six-footers, Argyllshire men for the most part. And he set them on the gangsters like a pack of dogs. They had carte blanche to do whatever it took. At the first sign of trouble the Cossacks piled out of the Black Marias, truncheons swinging, to knock seven bells out the Glasgow neds. Hislop had been pick of the bunch, brought down from Balla to crack Glaswegian skulls.

"So." Hislop's face had a slyish cast as he turned away to light a smoke. "How's tricks at Temple? How's your Elliot Ness impersonation coming along?"

"Oh Christ. Not you, too. Slowly, Greg. It's coming slowly."

"You know the problem, of course." Greg shook out the match, pulled the ashtray towards him. "Everyone took him too lightly. I'm talking about Maitland. And then it was too late. *You* took him too lightly. You thought he was just a thug, didn't you? Jumped-up bouncer. Truth is, he's smarter than most of us."

"You didn't need to outsmart them, though, did you?" McCormack said. "Back in the day. I'm talking about the Thirties."

Hislop squinted at him. "The Cossacks?" He shook his head. "Different times, Dochie. Different methods. That's all finished now. Good thing too."

"But was it as mental as they say? I mean, some of the old boys, the *seanairs*, they make it sound like the Wild bloody West."

Hislop pursed his lips. The big head tossed like a horse's as the memories scrolled behind his eyes. "Ach, who knows, son? They were bad times." He gripped his whisky glass, it disappeared in the massive fist. He shifted in his seat and hunched forward. "You know what the problem is, though, Duncan? With you fellows? Your generation?"

"You're sorting out the world's problems tonight, Greg."

"Do you want to hear this or not?"

"You mean I've got a choice? Sorry. On you go."

"You make it into a big dirty secret." Hislop shook his head in disgust. "You do it behind closed doors. Haul some *trustar* into the cells. Crowd in behind him so he doesn't know who's hitting him. That's no good." He tapped four fingers on the table. "We did it different. We walked into their fucking pubs and pulled them out into the street. We knocked the shite out of them with their mates and neighbours looking on. Took our time. Showed our faces." His own face was shining now, teeth bared in savage glee. "We stamped them back into the gutters, like the *radain* they are. You have to face it, Dochie." He swirled his whisky. "You're not cut out for that sort of thing."

McCormack stayed his glass, set it quietly down on the table. Was Hislop saying what he thought he was saying? Hislop sensed the sudden chill, looked up, gripped McCormack's forearm. "No, no, Dochie. Steady now. *Gabh air do shocair.* That's not what I meant at all. I meant you're not that kind of polis. That's all."

"O.K., Greg."

"That's all I meant. Now, I'll get them in. *Té bheag?*"

"Go on then."

Hislop crossed to the bar, returned with the whiskies. He talked on, about the old days, the Depression-era city. There was real reverence when he spoke about the *Sasannach*, Sillitoe. How he smartened up the Force, making changes to the uniform. It was Sillitoe who introduced the chequered hatband—

"Sillitoe Tartan"—modelled on the Highland regiments' Glengarries. Everyone—cops, neds, punters—got the message. This is a war. The Glasgow Polis are an army. Mess with us and we'll fuck you up. Quarter neither asked nor given.

But that was the Thirties. It was different now. The gangs had crept back in and nobody feared the polis anymore.

"This Partick thing," Hislop said finally. "You're working that?"

"The eminent Mr. Elliot. Aye. I think Haddow's trying to keep me away from Maitland."

"You know I met that fellow once."

"Elliot?"

"Back in the day, aye. It was a domestic. The neighbour called it in. She said it sounded like someone was being murdered. She could hear screaming through the walls."

"This is Great Western Terrace?"

"His big townhouse, aye. Anyway, I was in the area so I responded. He comes to the door in this silk robe. Like Noël fucking Coward. A thousand apologies, officer. I'll keep the noise down. Won't happen again. I told him I needed to check the house. Turns out there's a young thing parked on the living-room sofa wearing one of Elliot's shirts."

McCormack remembered Haddow's account of the rape accusation against Elliot. Supposedly malicious.

"How young's young?"

"Well that's the thing. Fifteen, I'd have said. But she fetches her handbag and her driver's licence says nineteen. I get her on her own and ask her if she's O.K. She says she's fine. What about the screams, I say. She says, Oh I get carried away. Can't help myself. I could show you if you'd like."

"Jesus Christ. What did you do?"

"I got off my mark, Dochie. I passed the information to the Women's Department at Stewart Street. Fuck knows what they did with it. Nothing, probably."

They drank in silence for a bit. The separate Women's Department no longer existed. It had been integrated into the general Force.

"You had no qualms, then?" Hislop said, out of the blue. "No doubts about coming back?"

Did he? It had taken him a while to feel home again. The truth was, it was coming here to the Park that made him feel properly home. Not the job. Not his name on a ribbed glass door at Temple cop shop.

"Should I have?" McCormack took a sip from his glass, clicked it down on the marble tabletop.

"Tsk, no." Hislop exhaled a blue cloud of smoke and it tumbled upwards in the evening sunlight of the half-frosted window. "Didn't Seamus a' Ghlinne find the negatives when he searched Levein's big house. Burnt them. That's all done with, Duncan."

Seamus a' Ghlinne. James MacInnes—James of the Glens—had been second-in-command of the Glasgow CID when his boss, Peter Levein, was tried and convicted of being accessory to the murders of three women. Levein had in his possession a number of photographs featuring D.I. Duncan McCormack in what the *Daily Record* would describe as "compromising poses".

"The rest's just gossip, Dochie, and sure you'd get that anywhere."

They sipped their whiskies for a bit. McCormack started to speak and then stopped. Eventually he set his glass down on the table. "Is it that obvious, Greg? I never knew it was obvious."

Hislop shrugged. "Well. Not obvious, but, you know."

"You're saying you knew beforehand? Before the Quaker?"

"Not knew. Guessed, maybe. Wondered. It's no business of mine, Dochie. It's no business of anyone's."

They drank in silence. Hislop had changed in the time McCormack had been away. His hair was finer. His ears looked bigger—old man's ears, paper thin. He was growing translucent, like a leaf.

"What's it been like then, being back? You getting much grief?"

"You mean about Levein?"

"He had plenty of friends, the same man."

That he did, McCormack thought. Though how many friends did he have when he hanged himself with a bedsheet in his cell at Peterhead?

"Tell me about it," he said. "I'm working for one of them."

"Not just Haddow I'm talking about. A lot of guys had hitched their wagon to Levein. When you took him out of the picture? Well. Let's say you burst a lot of coupons. Guys have long memories here. They've had plenty of time to think about what you've cost them."

"I did my job, Greg. I put away a dirty cop. Murdering scumbag."

"You think they should thank you for it?"

"I think they should count their blessings, Greg. Every day in life."

"Ah come on now, Dochie." Hislop was shaking his head, smiling. "You dropped a house on the Wicked Witch of the East. Find some Munchkins, they'll give you a fucking parade. Everyone else? They're waiting to stick the knife in. Your shout, fella."

McCormack lifted the empties and crossed to the bar.

17

I f you're looking for trouble in northwest Glasgow, then Maryhill's not a bad place to start. Even the Romans struggled here. They built a wall to keep the natives at bay and part of it straggles through Maryhill Park. Another wall—eight feet high and topped with jagged stones—was built around Maryhill Barracks. Thrown up in the 1870s to quell the threat of "riot and tumult" from the district's industrial workers, the barracks was home to the Highland Light Infantry, the British Army's Glasgow regiment, known as "the Glesga Keelies" or "Hell's Last Issue", famous for sewing razor blades in their caps to give them an edge in hand-to-hand combat.

But nothing lasts forever. They tore the barracks down in the Sixties and a housing scheme rose in its place. Tower blocks and maisonettes. White and bright and futuristic. But the barracks wall was left standing. Black and mossy and rough, it girdled almost the whole estate. So while the scheme might appear on the maps as the Wyndford Estate, everyone called it the Barracks. As for the soldiers, the Highland Light Infantry—now amalgamated into the Lowland Volunteers—flitted half a mile down the road to a split new barracks on Hotspur Street.

Between the civilian barracks and the military, the old barracks and the new, on a stretch of Garrioch Road lined with red sandstone tenements, stood the Barracks Bar. Hard men from the high flats and off-duty squaddies threw back their pints shoulder to shoulder in its spartan public bar. Whatever tensions may have obtained between the two groups were mostly kept in check, possibly due to the fact that the landlord was Walter Maitland's brother. If Hugh Maitland's presence explained the uneasy peace that reigned in the public bar, it also explained why D.C. Iain Shand was parked across the street that Thursday evening, at the entrance to Garrioch Quadrant.

Or at least, it explained why to the satisfaction of Iain Shand's boss, D.I. Duncan McCormack. Shand himself was having trouble working out what the hell he was doing here. He'd been watching the front door of the Barracks Bar for the past two hours and had seen nothing more promising than a drunk man pissing against the exterior wall and a Sally Army sergeant venturing in with a collection tin and some copies of *The War Cry*.

Shand shifted in his seat and used his handkerchief to mop a porthole in the condensation on the windscreen. Sitting in a car for two hours wasn't police work. It was dogwork, donkeywork, shitwork. Anyone could sit in a car. The Sally Army sergeant came through the double doors with a hangdog look. His stack of papers, folded over his forearm like a waiter's dishcloth, hadn't notably diminished. You're in the wrong army, Shand wanted to tell him. Between Maitland's soldiers and the Queen's, the Barracks Bar had things covered on the military front. You need to press ahead to other pastures, pal. Onward Christian Soldiers.

A big man came out of the pub. Six feet two or three. He stood there filling the pavement. Bald head, walrus 'tache. He made a big show of lighting a cigarette, not looking over at Shand. When he started to cross the road, still not looking at Shand, Shand felt the sudden thump in his chest and he scrambled up straight in the seat. The man was coming on and Shand speedily weighed it up: stay put or get out of the car? Getting out of the car would possibly escalate things but, fuck it, the size of this guy, there was no question: whatever was coming, better to be on your feet.

Shand got out of the car.

The big man pulled up about five feet away.

Shand pushed the Velox door with his fingertips and it only half closed, the mechanism meshing sloppily. The light stayed on in the car. Shand hitched his trousers and left his hands on his hips. Then he changed his mind and dropped them to his sides. His right hand opened and closed sporadically.

The big man nodded at the car. "Your door's not shut properly."

"I see that," Shand said.

"You needing some help?" The guy's tone was solicitous, patient.

Shand couldn't summon a smart remark. "What did you have in mind?" he managed.

"Well I don't know." The big man took a step forward. "You've been sitting there for two hours. If you're worried you'll get a knockback let me put your mind at ease. You'd pass for twenty-one. Well, in certain lights you would."

The man's jacket was hanging askew, something in the pocket breaking its lines. He had finished looking Shand over. He turned his attention to the car. Like all of the Force's unmarked cars the Velox had an extra aerial for the police radio. The big man frowned.

"You're not with the Quinns then?"

Shand could see the wheels turning, the big man refiguring the odds.

"My gang's a wee bit bigger than the Quinns." Shand stepped over and closed the car door properly. It was coming back to him now, the old Shand swagger.

"Right," the man said. "Anyway. You're welcome to come in, have a pint. It's Quiz Night tonight. Bell a couple of mates, get a team together. Could win a weekend in Blackpool. Crate of Bass."

Shand nodded. "That a composite prize? Need a crate of Bass to get through a weekend in Blackpool."

The big man kept his lips closed as he smiled. He turned to go.

"While you're here." Shand stepped forward a yard. The big man stopped. Shand took the headshot of Gavin Elliot from his wallet. "You ever see this guy?"

The big man didn't glance at the photo. "Naw, pal, see, you've got it wrong. I said it's Quiz Night in there. Not out here."

"Every night's Quiz Night," Shand said. "If I say it is." He held out the photo.

The man pursed his lips. "I don't know. It's a bad light," he said.

"The light's probably better in the station. Nice and bright in the interview rooms."

The man took the photo. "It's Jock Stein. It's Frank Sinatra. It's your auld faither. Hell would I know?"

Shand nodded. "Uh-huh. Gavin Elliot's his name. He worked with your boss."

The man pinched his bottom lip between finger and thumb, tugged on the lip, appeared to be thinking. "When you say 'worked': you mean he's moved on or he's dead?"

"You never read the papers?"

"Why would I read the papers? Pound's fucked. IRA bombs. The Middle East. You're better not knowing."

He passed the snapshot to Shand. "Sorry. Can't help you, son."

"The man's dead." Shand stowed the photo in his inside pocket. "Murdered. You've never seen him, though?"

The man shook his head.

"You know a woman called Yvonne Gray?"

"I know a lot of people. We could be here all night."

"Your choice, mate."

"Yvonne who?"

"Yvonne Gray."

"She dead too?"

"Missing. She worked as a pro. Sauna down Woodlands Road."

"Don't use saunas, mate. Never felt the need."

"Yvonne Gray," Shand repeated.

"You got a photo?"

"Just the name. She's early thirties, five-seven. Skinny, blonde. Worked there for two years. Healing Hands. It's one of Maitland's."

"You've got a photo of the dead grandad, no pic of the blonde slapper? You're missing a trick, son."

"That's a no?"

"Are we done here? I've a Quiz Night to run."

"Yeah. We're done. For now." Shand watched as the man waited for a break in the traffic to cross the road. "My name's Iain Shand, by the way," he said, half to himself. "I'll be seeing you around."

Shand went back to the Velox. He was about to turn the ignition key when he saw a figure slouching down from the direction of the Barracks estate. Early twenties, male, shoulder-length ginger hair in a centre parting, flared jeans, army surplus jacket. The man entered the lounge door of the Barracks Bar. Shand waited. Three minutes later the man emerged, zipping the army jacket, heading back up to the Barracks estate. Shand turned the key.

FRIDAY, 4 JULY 1975

18

O.K. What do we hear from the other forces? Anything with a similar MO? Torture. Bodies dumped in public."

"Nothing." Goldie knocked his knuckles on the desk. "Bugger all. Been in touch with all the divisions. The other Scottish forces. This guy's out on his own, Duncan. He's an original."

"Or they," McCormack said.

"Or she, come to that," Nicol added.

"Motive, then." McCormack crossed to the window, half-sat on the sill, folded his arms. "What do we think?"

"Unless it's some psychopath," Goldie said, "someone who just enjoys this stuff, then it's got to be revenge. It's got to be personal. Nothing else makes sense."

"What if he was trying to get information?" Nicol said.

Goldie spread his arms. "You think a sixty-nine-year-old man held out against torture? For four days? No chance. This was personal, Nicol. Whoever did this enjoyed it."

"Someone's still looking for information, though," McCormack said. "Whoever broke into Elliot's townhouse didn't find what they were after."

The techs had garnered no usable prints from Elliot's property, and a house-to-house on Great Western Terrace had thrown up nothing. The man with the green suit and the red hair had just been absorbed back into the city, swallowed up by some tenement close.

"O.K., I'm off to the Mitchell Library, sir. Look through the *Trib*, try to dig up more on Elliot's companies."

"Before you go, Nicol, did you hear back from Ullapool?"

He'd asked her to check in with Northern Constabulary regarding the Elliots' holiday home.

"I did, sir. They confirmed what the neighbour said. Mr. Urquhart. The Croft hadn't been used for weeks. The sergeant I spoke to said Elliot kept himself to himself. Might come into the village for a restaurant meal with his daughter from time to time, but that was the extent of it."

She was off. Goldie stood up and cleared his throat. McCormack looked at him. "What?"

"Actually. I've got to scoot off for an hour or two. I mean, is that all right?"

McCormack noticed for the first time the good suit, the tie in a pale blue silk. "You're looking uncharacteristically smart, Detective. What's the occasion?"

"My eldest." Goldie seemed suddenly lost for words. He looked up, grinned. "She's graduating. I mean, I know it's a murder inquiry, Dunc, but we've hit a bit of a lull. I'll make it up."

McCormack saw in his mind's eye a girl in a red coat and a white woolly hat with pom-poms, lifting a mittened hand as she skated past.

"The wee lassie at the ice-rink? She's graduating?"

"No!" Goldie laughed. "That's Debbie. Karen, this is. My eldest. She's a vet. Or she will be, in a couple of hours."

"Jesus, mate. That's outstanding." McCormack gripped Goldie's hand, drew him in for a clasp. "Give her my congratulations. And Debbie?"

"Eighteen," Goldie said. "Starting at Strathclyde after the summer."

"Christ Almighty. Where does it go, mate? On you go, then. Don't miss it."

Goldie turned at the door, pointed at McCormack. "I'll meet you back here at two."

"Dandy."

With Goldie gone, McCormack sat for a spell in the empty room. Where does it go? It wasn't hard to work out. It went to the job. The job ate it up, the time you might have spent with family. But the others, they at least had the semblance of a family life, happening offstage, a movie playing in another room. They might miss most of the day-to-day stuff, thanks to the job. The football practice, the chess club. But they checked in for the big stuff, the landmarks. Prize-givings, birthday parties, first communions, graduations. Soon it would be weddings. Christenings. The whole thing was passing him by. He'd always envisaged, growing up, that kids were in his future. Though he couldn't picture the rest of it—a girl, a bride, a table set for dinner—he somehow thought that he'd end up being a dad. Now he saw that for the fantasy it was.

Still. No point moping about the place with your face tripping you. There was work to be done. All the others were out and about. Shand was on surveillance outside Hugh Maitland's pub. Hugh Maitland was out of town, supposedly—down in London on business—but McCormack wanted Shand outside the Barracks Bar to verify. Plus, if he was honest, it kept Shand out of the way. McCormack had seen Shand slipping out of Haddow's office yesterday. He had known—or at least suspected—that Shand was Haddow's stoolie, but to have it confirmed was different. He felt a cold, almost impersonal rage at Shand's behaviour. You tried to mentor someone, teach them the basics of their trade, and they ran off to clype on you. Well, he hoped D.C. Shand had a taste for shitwork, liked spending long nights in his motor. Some people can't be told, McCormack reflected. They have to learn the hard way.

Fuck it, he thought. Let's go out and knock some doors. Go

back to Crawford Street and see if the lieges are feeling any chattier.

That evening, McCormack took the subway into town and nursed a couple of pints in the Horseshoe Bar. He hadn't been in the Horseshoe since he got back from London and he sat there at one end of the self-styled "longest bar in Europe", reading the paper and just enjoying the noise and the smoke and the burnt barley taste of the seventy shilling. As it turned out, the denizens of Crawford Street hadn't been any more gushing than they had been on Tuesday morning, but amid the Horseshoe's lovely hubbub that didn't seem to matter much.

Sauntering back to Buchanan Street subway in the evening sun, McCormack heard a sound on the wind that seemed like the tread of marching feet. At the junction with St. Vincent Street he pulled up short. He thought at first it was an Orange Parade but, no: marching down St. Vincent Street, six abreast, with the dipping sun at their backs, was a phalanx of soldiers in olive drab and foraging caps, sticks in their hands and a convoy of armoured vehicles in their midst. Was it some sort of invasion? A military coup? And then he remembered. The strike was over. The dustcart drivers had accepted terms and the army had been drafted in to clear the rubbish from the streets. The men passed McCormack in a kind of holiday cheer, grinning and swinging their spiked sticks, like an army of parkies. The armoured vehicles, McCormack saw now, were a trio of bin lorries.

On the subway back to Partick, McCormack caught the eye of a man sitting opposite. Early thirties, slim, in a dark suit and tie, top button of his shirt undone. The man looked slightly lit, as if he'd downed a couple of stiff ones in the pub after work. His skin was sallow—almost greenish under the white carriage lights. Dark hair sprouted from the gap at the vee of his shirt and along the backs of his hands. His shoulders rolled lazily with the jolting of the train. He was drumming the fingers of one hand on his knee. No ring.

McCormack lifted his eyes to the adverts over the man's head—*After Work You Need a Guinness*—but he was conscious of the lighthouse beam of the man's gaze passing over him every few seconds. As the train slowed, the man rose to his feet as a jolt tipped his balance and he reached out and gripped McCormack's knee to steady himself, righting himself with a push that included a barely perceptible twist. The man stood by the doors, holding on to the scuffed chrome pillar, turning to stare McCormack's way, but McCormack kept his gaze on the adverts till the doors shuddered open and the man stepped off down the platform. Then the doors hissed shut and the train plunged back into the dark.

McCormack shook out a smoke and lit up. There was a difference between taking a silly chance and deliberately flushing your career down the pan, but in McCormack's case the difference wasn't large. One could easily lead to the other.

Things had been better down in London. The city was huge, anonymous, there were places you could go, find yourself welcome. But even in London, with its daisy-chain of queer pubs and clubs, McCormack stuck to the old routines. Cruising. Cottaging. He never felt at home in the Black Cap in Camden or the King William up in Hampstead. All that forced camaraderie. All that determined belonging, with one eye on the door. McCormack was never ashamed. He was fine with who he was. But being gay, being queer, being bent: it wasn't a team sport. You were in this thing alone. A hurried coupling in a toilet stall, a quickie in a stand of trees didn't change that. An episode like that was just a match-flare in the darkness.

But some nights you could almost taste it, the electric thrill of risk. The gravitational pull of the familiar ritual.

Find a bus stop near a public toilet. Other folk are present—a woman with a dog, a gaggle of teens, a lone commuter—

but you find each other out. The sidelong glance. The second sidelong glance. The consciously neutral gaze. The gaze held just a shade too long. And then the flare of recognition, like laughter: message received. Flick your cigarette into the gutter, peel away from the bus stop and stroll to the Gents. Combing your hair in the cracked mirror you sense the dimming of the light, look up to see a man's frame blocking the entrance.

If any words are said, they are whispered, hissed: *Got somewhere to go?*

A shake of the head sends you jostling into a cubicle, all tugs and fumbling, shortness of breath, a face pressed hard against a door, and the rhythm, the silence, the ragged gasps, the sour smell of the other man, the thudding drum of your heart when you both hold your breath as somebody's heels rap smartly on the tiles.

But McCormack was done with all that. In the two months he'd been back in Glasgow he had kept his head down, got on with his work. He kept away from Kelvin Way, Queen's Park, Glasgow Green, the toilets at the corner of St. Vincent Street and Buchanan Street. There was a gay club now—Bennett's down on Glassford Street—and even the straight blokes were cavorting about in platform soles and glitter. It didn't matter. McCormack couldn't afford to be caught again. It just wasn't an option.

The train thundered out of the tunnel into Merkland Street station, juddered to a halt. McCormack hauled himself to his feet. Back in the flat he poured himself a Springbank and sat in the armchair by the window. The sound of a piano came through the wall. The wee boy next door had started learning. McCormack had seen him in the street, trailing after his mother. A boy of six or seven. Every night after tea he would pick haltingly through his repertoire of melodies. "Incey Wincey Spider", "Mary Had a Little Lamb", "Happy

Birthday to You". Tonight there was a new one: "You Are My Sunshine".

McCormack sipped his whisky and let his mind run through the details of the case. He thought about the man in the two-tone Volkswagen camper van. Something had bothered him when he heard the description. A little switch flicked in his mind. He hadn't known what it was at the time but now it came to him. Early thirties, smartly dressed, short fair hair neatly brushed to the side. Now who did that remind you of? He shook his head. All it needed was the overlapping teeth and the regimental tie. It was the bloody Quaker again. McCormack could picture the posters with the artist's impression, the face that had haunted the city for months, the face that watched their every move in the Murder Room at the old Marine. The Quaker.

And though McCormack himself had nailed the Quaker— or rather the two men who conspired in the murders—the face on the poster still spooked him. Even now, on his journeys through the city, he would come across a faded poster, pasted onto a brick wall, peeling from the Perspex pane of a bus shelter. The fair hair. The knowing smile. Was it all coming back? Gavin Elliot had been held somewhere, it seemed. He'd been tortured before being murdered and dumped. The degree of forethought and planning suggested the killer had done this before. Or would do it again. Could you stomach another of those? Another manhunt through the shattered city? McCormack drained the Springbank and smacked the glass down on the arm of his chair.

The boy through the wall was still murdering his tune. McCormack closed his eyes and tipped his head back onto the padded headrest. There was something soothing in the boy's persistence. The rhythm was all to pot but you could sense the boy's simple delight at being able to pick out a tune. What a revelation: you could move your fingers and capture the songs your mammy sang at bedtime.

That night in bed, McCormack had the wee boy's tune still running in his head: "You Are My Sunshine". He's right, McCormack thought. Stop trying to orchestrate a whole investigation. Do the simple things, one at a time. Pick out the melody.

UNSENT LETTERS #1

Flat 4c, 70 Craigpark
Glasgow
12 July 1969

Dear Chris,

I wanted to wait until things were better before I got in touch. I had it all worked out. You know? I'd be in a proper job—like a shop manageress, maybe a hotel receptionist. I'd be married. Weans. The full bit. Twin boys, was how I pictured it. Nice wee semi out in Clarkston or Bishopbriggs. We'd have you round for your tea, get to know each other again. Put the bad times where they belong—in the past. I can picture you with a boy on each knee, reading them stories. Walking them round to the park for a shot on the swings. We'd have Christmasses at ours. And sometimes you'd come round to do your washing and we'd sit and blether at the kitchen table while the twin-tub rumbled.

Wouldn't that have been something? I used to dream about it between clients, in the waiting room at Whitehill Street. Still do, sometimes. Aye, well. Kidding myself on, that's one thing I've always been good at, isn't it? I kept hoping, though; kept putting off writing my letter, putting it off and putting it off, and now I don't even know your address, Chris, or what it is I wanted to say.

You always pestered me to tell you things. What it was like when Da was still there and we were all together. Because I could remember and you couldn't. Holidays! Jesus, you would never stop asking about holidays. I could talk to you about that, if you'd like?

Me and you in the back seat of Uncle Billy's old Anglia, watching the raindrops racing on the windows. Off to Ardentinny or Carradale for a week by the sea. Soon as we arrived, Da would cart the suitcases in and we'd be off down the beach, him with his deckchair and a bag of cans. Ma with a picnic bag and a big red tartan blanket. She would plonk you on the blanket and settle down beside you with a Miss Marple.

And me? I'd be off, clambering over rocks, looking for pools. Whole afternoons I could spend, hunkered down, staring into rock pools. Sometimes a cloud would cover the sun and the pool would go suddenly clear and you could see it all, the green strands of algae waving in the water, the pink and red anemones, inch-long fish, the see-through shrimps waggling their feelers under the ledges of rock and maybe a crab creeping sideways out from its hidey-hole. There were limpets on the rocks like white stars and that seaweed with the bubbles you could pop. I always wanted to see a starfish but I don't think I ever did.

When the tide started to come in, Da would shout at me to come away but I never wanted to leave. A pool was its own wee universe, so special and complete and I wished it could stay that way forever, but finally the tide would come in and swamp it and it wouldn't even be a pool anymore, just another part of the sea.

Da started hitting her on one of these holidays. Carradale, it was. Maybe he'd done it before, but that was the first time I saw it. We were in the old holiday cottage up on the hillside and I remember the shock of it. I don't remember what they were fighting about but he hit her open-handed—not a slap, more of a cuff on the side of the head and he knocked her head onto a kitchen shelf. This ornamental plate fell down and smashed. Ma's head was all gashed and bleeding but she went down on her knees to pick up the pieces. We would have to pay for the plate, he said, and it made him even angrier and he stood over her for a second like he was planning on doing something worse, snorting like a bull, his fists flashing open and closed, but he turned and slammed out the door and was off down the hill to the pub. You were already asleep on the bottom bunk. Ma took me through and settled me in the top bunk and smoothed my hair and told me he didn't mean it, it was her fault, she provoked him. I was still awake when he came back from the pub. I could hear his voice, all low and pleading, like a mooing bull, and then the creak of the springs when they climbed into bed.

In the morning it all seemed forgotten. Da was up early cooking a fry-up and singing "Bye Bye Blackbird" while Ma sat on the wooden veranda looking down to the shore. There was a plaster on her head and her eye had come up all inky and bruised but she caked it over with make-up and wore a sunhat that day.

She took me aside that night and told me that Da had apologized. It would never happen again. He had promised. It was all finished, she said. But it wasn't finished. It was just the start. He kept it up on her when we got back to Glasgow. You were too wee to know what was happening but you sensed things were wrong, the way a dog does. You would go all quiet in the kitchen, running your cars across the lino. When you heard the change in his voice you would stop playing, sit there with a Matchbox car jammed in your mouth, sucking on the metal.

Ach, I'm sorry, Chris. What am I like? This was supposed to be a nice story about holidays, wasn't it? Happy families. The good old days. And in some ways they were. I mean I was glad when he left but then, bad as he was, she still loved him. And he was good for her, in some ways. As long as he was there, she had appearances to keep up. Keep us looking smart, get the sheets out on the line, take her turn at the stairs. Once he was gone, though, she just went to pieces. I tried to do what I could. I remember one day I was scrubbing the stairs, down on my knees with the pail and brush. It wasn't so bad. I was enjoying it, really, the rhythm of the thing, the wet scratch of the bristles, and then I heard the steps coming up the stairs and the shadow stopped and I knew, from the smell of carbolic and peppermint, I knew it was auld Mrs. Boyle from the top floor.

"Standing in for your mother again."

"My Ma's no well," I told her. "She's got a sore stomach."

I craned round. Mrs. Boyle looked down at me and I could tell what she was thinking as clear as if she'd said it. Do you think I'm soft in the head? Your mother's lying drunk on your living-room sofa. At half-past eleven in the forenoon. That's the kind of sore stomach she's got.

Mrs. Boyle looked at the pail of dirty water and the brush in my hand. She spoke almost under her breath before she climbed on up the stairs. Well, she said. It certainly suits you.

Her shoes scraped on up the stone stairs and I kidded on that I didn't know what she meant, but I knew straight away. She was calling me a scrubber. I got to my feet and I kicked that pail of dirty water down the stairs and went into the flat.

I know it was hard for you, Chris. To know what I did at Auldpark. What they made us do. It was hard. I know that. You were too wee to do anything about it. All the stuff that happened in the Home, at Auldpark, though: we never had any choice about that. We were made to do it. But out here, now, Chris, things are different. I get a lie-in every morning and most of the day to myself. I work for three or four hours a night. There's worse jobs, believe me. Most of the punters are lonely wee men. You feel sorry for them more than anything else.

McGlashan's guys come in, too, right enough. It's a perk for them, they get freebies. But it's not so bad. Some of them are nice, they treat us better than the punters do, bring us little gifts. There's one of them, guy called Walter, has taken a bit of a shine to me. Gave me a bottle of perfume the other day. Shalimar. Off the back of a lorry, probably, but still. You take what you can get, eh?

I keep thinking about your face, Chris. The day I left Auldpark. You looked so sad I almost laughed, God forgive me. Who stole your scone? I kept thinking. You looked as though all the smiles had been drained out of you and the line from Da's song came into my head: "No one here can love or understand me." And they couldn't, Chris, that was true. But I hope it's not true now. I hope you've found someone. I hope you've got a job and a house. I hope you're just ordinary, that's what I hope.

There's a lassie in the flat below, she's up half the night singing along to her records. She thinks she's gonnae be on Top of the Pops, like that wee lassie from Garfield Street. All these people with normal lives, Chris. They want to be special. Has no one told them they already are?

Your sister,

Isobel

19

The rain had eased, so at least he could stop turning the ignition every ninety seconds to work the windscreen wipers. Shand was back in Garrioch Quadrant, across from the Barracks Bar, slouched down in the red Velox. Disco lights—red, green and blue—were pulsing in sequence in the frosted glass windows of the pub. He could hear the low churning of a bass guitar and the snap of a snare drum from where he sat and jagged shards of guitar when the pub door was hauled open and laughing couples hurried inside.

He lit another cigarette and thought about the Goldberry Arms in Bank Street, Kilmarnock, how he waited outside for the old man on Friday nights, sitting on the wall of the Laigh Kirk. From time to time his father would come out with a packet of crisps and maybe one of those wee glass bottles of bitter lemon. But the night would wear on and the sky would darken and the boy on the wall would be forgotten. When the pub door opened briefly to the bright golden hubbub he would crane to try to spot his dad among the laughing, nodding faces. On nights like that the pub looked like a bright box of promise, a little corner of Christmas in the cold grey town.

Tonight, the Barracks Bar looked much the same. He glanced at his watch. Three hours to go. Three hours of watching the Barracks Bar on the off-chance that one of the Maitlands would show. It was a bullshit tasking but what the hell. You did the job you were detailed to do. You did it all the more thoroughly when you'd clocked that it was bollocks. McCormack had wanted him out of the road—that was the size of it. The teuchter didn't trust him.

A car was parked outside the pub, had been there since Shand's shift started. A Rover, dark reddish colour. Shand thought about the playground game: *Red Rover, Red Rover, let Shan-dy come over!* Or Bri-an or Bill-y or Gor-don. When your name was called you would leave your own side and charge across the playground to where the other team stood in a line, arms linked and swaying. If the line held firm then you joined the other side, but if you did manage to break through you got to take one of their players back to your own side. The game finished when everyone was on the same team.

A woman came out the door at a lick, settling her shoulder-bag, face like thunder. A man appeared immediately, stopping on the pavement, calling out after her, arms spread wide in appeal. When she carried on walking he threw up an arm and laughed to himself, shaking his head. He stayed on the pavement for a minute, rocking on his heels, looking around. Then he dug out his smokes, cupped a match to light his cigarette and swaggered back inside.

Then the ginger-haired guy from last night was back. Into the lounge bar, out three minutes later. Maybe it was a pissstop. Maybe the guy got caught short at the same spot every night. Shand smirked at his own little joke.

Shand looked at his watch again. Two hours fifty minutes. His stomach rumbled extravagantly, a long hollow spiral of sound, plaintive, low, like a wolf's howl. In two hours and fifty minutes he could go home and eat. He pictured the thick disc of fillet steak in bloodied butcher's paper on his fridge's top shelf, how he would set the pan to a high heat with the fat spurting, then that lovely noise, that burst of percussion when the meat hit the fat, pressing down with the spatula, searing the sides, blood oozing out, chopped onions next, crisping and charring, that heady smell, and fat halves of a pulpy tomato shrivelling under the grill.

A clack on the window roused him from his vision. He thought it was the woman from the pub at first but, no, it was bloody Nicol, leaning down with a silly grin and now hauling open the passenger door. She dropped into the seat and tossed a package wrapped in newsprint onto his lap.

"Chips," she said. "Wasn't sure if you were a pickled onion man or not, so I didn't bother. I, on the other hand . . ." She had unwrapped her own parcel and held the silvery globe of a pickled onion between finger and thumb. She popped it into her mouth, crunching ecstatically.

Shand didn't ask. He fell to, bolting the chips, cramming them into his mouth as smells of vinegar, fat, starch, damp newsprint clouded the car windows.

"I would say thanks," he said, wiping a porthole in the misted window with the ball of his fist. "But something tells me there's a quid pro quo coming here."

"No such thing as a free bag of chips. Aw, give over!" Nicol wrinkled her nose as he held up a greenish uncooked chip before leaning over to drop it in the ashtray. "No sign of the brother, then? Or Sir Walter himself?"

Shand looked across at the Barracks Bar. The Rover was still parked in front of it. He looked back at Nicol. "Liz: could you maybe tell me what the fuck's going on?"

Nicol pointed a chip at Shand. "The thing is, Iain: he knows. McCormack knows. We all do."

She bit into the chip. Shand frowned. "See, that's not answering my question, is it? Strictly speaking. Knows what, Nicol? What is it you all think you know?"

"A wee bit late, Iain, wouldn't you think? A wee bit late to be little boy lost. My advice—and I say this, you know, all bull-shit aside. My advice is go now. Before they launch an investi-gation. Maybe they'll even let you keep your pension."

Shand had finished his chips. He balled the wrapper thoughtfully, tossed it over his shoulder and worked the driver's window down. "You're not making much sense, Nicol, you know that?"

"Iain, stop. I checked your locker, mate. McCormack knows. Goldie knows. We all do."

The cool night air came in at the window. Shand looked over at the pub. A cat was sitting on the Rover's bonnet. Its eyes glowed green and hollow as it turned its head towards them.

"You're fucked," Nicol said. "Strictly speaking."

"It belongs to . . ." He rubbed his temples with his splayed right hand. "The gun belongs to one of Maitland's guys. All right? I'm talking one of the top men."

"O.K." Nicol nodded. "Now all we need to establish is what a shooter belonging to one of Maitland's goons is doing in a polisman's locker."

"And you're the detective? Why do you think it's there, Liz? I'm trying to turn him." He nodded. "I'm close, too."

"Oh, Iain." Nicol laughed. "Give us peace. Maitland's muscle's gonna be Shandy's tame tout? That's your explanation?"

Shand sighed, dug into his jacket pocket for his smokes. "You never hear of Ockham's Razor, Nicol?"

"I've stopped, thanks. But really? You reckon that's the simplest explanation?"

"And you don't?"

"I think there might be another school of thought, Iain. One that says you're the guy who tips off Maitland when a raid's on the cards. You keep him briefed, tell him the things he needs to worry about. The gun's a quid pro quo. Gives you something to prove you're not crooked, you've recovered a pistol from the bad guys. You just haven't had a chance to plant it yet."

"Kenny Hinshelwood." Shand craned round in his seat. "That name ring any bells, Detective?"

It did. Dimly, faintly, like a bell chiming under water in the church of a sunken village. But the face wouldn't come, nor the context. Just the nimbus around the name: Kenny Hinshelwood.

Shand wore a thin smile. "Guess there are limits to D.C. Nicol's omniscience after all. Two years back," he said. "Body in the stairwell of a Sighthill tenement. Junior Maitland player. Shot dead as he left a brothel."

"That was Hinshelwood?"

"That was Hinshelwood. Topped by my contact. Some sort of drugs beef, supposedly."

"You're saying that's the gun? The gun in your locker was used in a murder? And that's a good thing?"

"If you want to turn a gangster it's a good thing. It's a very good thing. Got my boy's dabs all over it."

"And Iain Shand's? Got any of his?"

"Jesus, Nicol. Credit me with some sense."

The ginger-haired youth was back again, loping down from the direction of the Barracks estate. Hands plunged in the pockets of his army surplus jacket. He ducked into the lounge bar.

"So how did you get the gun?"

"I got the gun, Nicol. I can't tell you how."

She shook her head. "It's too late for games, Iain. Anyway. You'll never turn him. One of Maitland's? He'll tell you to fuck off. Do his stint. Badge of honour for these guys."

"It's not just that," Shand said. "I think he wants out. He's had enough." Shand glanced at Nicol. "Something's happened. I know, I know. But I'm telling you. Something's changed, he's a different guy."

Nicol snorted. "One of Maitland's hoods has a crisis of conscience? Wouldn't you need a conscience to begin with? Or is it like one of these phantom itch things? Stab of pain in an amputated limb?"

"I'm serious, Nicol. It's something to do with the fire. He kept saying that the fire had changed things. The fire was too far."

"The fire?"

"I think he meant the Tradeston thing. You know, the warehouse? They set fire to Quinn's warehouse and the tenement next door goes up. Four dead."

"What is he, an idiot? You go around setting fire to things then people are liable to get hurt. That's the thing about fire, you know? It spreads. You can't control it."

"I don't know. He's not saying any more, but something about that fire got to him."

They sat in silence, thinking. Their breath clouded the windows.

"This Hinshelwood thing?" Nicol said. "McCormack takes this to Haddow and you're up the road. Not off the Force; up the road. You're in Barlinnie, chum. And not the Special Unit either, with the carpets and the art classes and the bloody ping-pong table. The nonce wing, where they shoot their load in your macaroni cheese."

"Aye, O.K., thanks for that, Nicol. But if we turn this guy." Shand squeezed right round to face her. "If we turn my guy, we've got Maitland. Think about it, Liz. We've got everything. You've got to tell McCormack. You've got to make him see."

Nicol was rooting in her handbag. "Sometimes, Iain, sometimes you think you're running a tout and then you realize the tout's running you. See what I'm saying?" She flipped down the sun-visor, fixed her lipstick in the little mirror. "Look. I'm heading back to Temple now. I'll talk to McCormack. See what I can do. He's not gonna like it, though. He's gonna come after you, would be my bet. I'll try to swing by later. Maybe bring McCormack if he doesn't threaten to rip your head off. Sit tight, Ian."

She clipped off into the night leaving a spoor of perfume

and a square of paper tissue bearing a lipstick kiss. Shand felt dirty, as if this had been some kind of assignation, as if he'd been used.

A gun in his locker.

A gun in his locker didn't mean anything. Or it meant what he said it meant. A lead. A breakthrough. The key to finally pinning shit on Maitland. He would meet his guy tomorrow and give him the ultimatum. Choose your side, buddy. Come over to the bright side or take your chances.

He sat there for another hour, thinking it through. People came and went from the Barracks Bar—couples and groups and single men—but the ginger-haired dealer never appeared. Shand lit his umpteenth cigarette. Was he kidding himself? Was it fantasy to think that his Maitland contact would flip? Maybe he himself should have gone over to Maitland's when he had the chance. Taken the money. The game stops when everyone's on the same side.

But the game never stops.

Shand flicked his smoke out of the open window.

The game never stops but the way it gets played can sometimes change. Things were going to be different. It was time to get back on the front foot.

He could start off by rousting the ginger-haired dealer in the lounge bar toilet.

Red Rover, Red Rover, let Shan-dy come over!

Shand climbed out of the Velox. The day had been fine and there was still a whisper of heat in the night-time breeze. Scents—the yeasty smell from the brewery, but also foreign, unnamable tinctures—seemed to hang in the air. Glasgow felt like Paris on nights like these, or what you imagined Paris felt like. Heady, magical, a place where anything might happen. The *Tribune*'s morgue came back to him then, all the lives brought together in those dusty files, all the city's souls. He took a deep breath, paid it out slowly. It was good just to stand here for a minute after the hours in the car. He was conscious of the strength in his thighs, the packed slabs of muscle across his chest, his biceps straining the lightweight fabric of his suit. The music from the pub pulsed faintly in the night.

He thought of the wee boy on the Laigh Kirk wall. The taste of bitter lemon. *Can we go now, Dad?*

He buttoned his jacket. This business with McCormack would sort itself out. He was young, he was fit, he stood six feet one in his stocking soles. He was a Serious Crime Squad detective in the Strathclyde Police CID. He was Iain Fucking Shand.

He stepped out onto the roadway. He was passing the Rover when the world went white.

II
In a Dark Wood

SATURDAY, 5 JULY 1975

20

You may never have experienced a bomb blast, but as soon as you hear one you know what it is. McCormack and Nicol had been driving down Maryhill Road. The sound was so loud and overpowering that McCormack wrenched the wheel and righted it just in time to evade an oncoming bus. "Jesus fuck," he said softly. Nicol said nothing. They both knew what it was. It couldn't have been anything else.

When they turned into Garrioch Road they could see the dust and smoke hanging whitely in the black sky above the rooftops. They came through the roundabout and turned the corner. It was like driving onto a battlefield.

There were bodies in the road. Figures stumbled blindly in the headlights, arms up as though to ward off blows. Some were running, swerving round the Velox as McCormack swung tight in to the kerb. Nicol grabbed the radio to call it in as McCormack tumbled out into the red glare and smoke. Already you could hear the throb of sirens.

The facade of the Barracks Bar was gone. It was just gone. The three floors of tenement flats above the pub had slumped in a kind of ragged V. Through the smoke and fires in the pub itself the ceiling beams were hanging askew.

The blast had blown people across the street. It stripped the clothes off people's backs, turned the world inside out. A couch lay in the roadway, beside three twisted barstools and a dented fridge. Inside the ruined pub was a car, charred and smoking, windows gone, the kind of thing you might see in a barricade on the TV news, the latest from war-torn Ulster. All the windows in a three-block radius had been pulverized—a slushy tide of glass that lashed across a hundred rooms, slashing at faces, pitting mirrors and wallpaper.

A passing motorcyclist had been slammed against a lamppost. His body and that of his bike were bent like staples.

McCormack and Nicol got to work, helping the wounded. They picked through the bricks and splintered beams with their bare hands and whatever implements they could improvise—McCormack used a crumpled beer-tray to shovel the rubble from a groaning man's trapped legs.

And all the while they looked for Iain Shand. And Iain Shand could not be found.

Reinforcements arrived—Derek Goldie among them. Residents from the nearby tenements and the Barracks flats came out to help, forming human chains to clear the rubble into smoking cairns by the roadside. The two-note sirens waxed and waned and Klieg lights threw thick columns of brightness into the night, creating a ghostly semblance of day. Ambulance men stepped over charred rafters, tilting their stretchers to keep their burdens level. McCormack worked till his nails were split and his knuckles skinned and his fingers flayed and torn and eventually Goldie led him away and folded him gently into the back of a squad car.

At eight o'clock the next morning, McCormack lay in his bed at 42 Caird Drive, staring up at the ceiling as the sun pierced a gap in the curtains. The alarm clock beside his head was ticking, ticking.

The events of the night before were running like a movie on the white of the ceiling, so he closed his eyes. The same events kept playing on the red of his closed eyelids, so he threw back the sheets and swung out of bed.

The sheets were stained with dust and soot. He'd been too

tired to shower when a squad car dropped him home in the small hours of the morning.

In the bathroom McCormack tugged the cord and the room exploded into light. His dead father stood there like a ghost.

McCormack took a step towards the mirror. It was dust. Caked in his eyebrows, layered in his hair. Filling the lines on his brow, the crowsfeet at his eyes. Dust from the bombing. He looked about eighty years old.

He took his index finger and tugged his lower eyelid down and the vivid crescent of red in the grey-white face flashed an image into his brain: *red flesh, white stump of bone.* He was suddenly sick, straight into the sink, a green bile that he sluiced away, dragging the back of his hand across his mouth.

He had slept in his clothes, crashing numbly onto the bed after shrugging out of his jacket and stepping out of his shoes. Now he worked the buttons on his shredded shirt and unhooked the belt of his ruined trousers. Naked, he stepped gratefully under the spray.

He ran the water as hot as he could stand, twisted his head beneath the spray and felt the grit dissolving. The water was a mercy. He jabbed his fingers into his hair and worked the dirt from the follicles, watched it swirl away down the plughole, sandy granules, flakes of dust and ash. Soot. Whatever else. More flashes, jagged shards: figures bending in the arc-lights, their shadows leaping; a woman with her hair burnt off on one side of her head; something charred and fleshy smoking in the roadway. He squeezed his eyes tight shut and focused on the water drumming on his skull.

He stepped from the shower as pink as a ham. The dirt and gunk that clogged his cuts was gone and he tracked watery blood across the living-room carpet.

He switched the radio on and *Cowards* he heard in Prime Minister Wilson's adenoidal Yorkshire: *despicable act . . .*

British people . . . way of life . . . continue as normal. He switched it off and wrapped the towel round his middle. He found a box of sticking plasters and patched up his fingers and barked knuckles.

Smell of smoke in his nostrils. He retrieved his trousers and shirt from the bathroom. He crossed to the bedroom, fished his jacket from the floor, emptied its pockets, pulled the bedspread free and bundled the clothes in it, wedged the whole mess in a black plastic binbag.

Normal, Wilson had said. *Continue as normal.* Breakfast was normal. McCormack dressed in his second-best suit and walked down the hill to a caff on Dumbarton Road.

He ordered a roll and square sausage and a pot of tea. He lit a Regal. The smoke batting into his lungs made him heave and he quickly crushed the Regal in the ashtray, flapped away the smoke. He closed his eyes.

And now the waitress brought McCormack his tea in its Pyrex cup and saucer, and a plate with his well-fired roll and sausage. He opened the roll and glugged a bolus of brown sauce onto the square sausage, slicked it across with his knife. Then he closed the roll and bit into it, smelled the charred, crisp edges and tasted the hot pink meat and suddenly he was scattering empty chairs as he bolted for the exit.

He made it just in time. The vomit came out in a hurtling rush, hissing on the pavement. McCormack caught his breath, bent double with his hands on his knees, his vision blurred with tears, as a figure strolled into his line of vision, tapping a rolled-up newspaper against a dungareed leg. "Big night, pal?" the man asked as he passed. "Ach well, better out than in." McCormack just grunted. His hair hung in strings, his throat was raw, the acid burned his sinuses like horseradish.

He straightened up and found a handkerchief, climbed up the hill to the flat. He was brushing his teeth for the second time that morning when a knock came to the door. No buzzer: some idiot had left the street door open again, was McCormack's first thought.

He spat the toothpaste into the sink, quickly rinsed. He was wiping his mouth with his handkerchief when he opened the door.

At first he failed to recognize the man in front of him. The figure was familiar, but out of context somehow. He had curly brown hair, good teeth, a smile that was starting to falter.

For a second he thought it was Shand, back from the dead, some wide-eyed revenant, pieced back together. A wraith demanding vengeance.

Then the green eyes crinkled and it all fell into place.

"Jesus Christ."

"Not quite. But I'll take away your sins if you let me come in."

McCormack stood aside. The man dropped his holdall and closed the door behind him, pulling McCormack towards him. They kissed, gingerly at first, then more urgently, teeth bumping lips, the man's hand on the base of McCormack's skull, pressing him close.

McCormack broke loose. "The fuck are you doing here, Victor?"

Victor took McCormack's hands in his. "Jesus. Your poor hands." He stroked the bandaged fingers. "How bad was it, Dunc? Was it hellish? The papers said you lost a man."

Vic had been a soldier. He'd seen combat. He knew what this moment was about, knew what McCormack was feeling before McCormack himself was sure. McCormack wanted to let himself go, lay his forehead on Victor's neck, talk it all out, but he drew his hands away and stepped back.

"But how did you get here so soon?"

Victor smiled. "I didn't *know*, Dunc. I took the sleeper. The guard got the papers at Carlisle. I found out then."

McCormack was shaking his head. "You can't be here, Vic.

It's too— I mean: fuck. This is a murder inquiry I'm in. A bloody bomb blast now. This is twelve-hour days. Seven-day weeks. You know this, Vic. You know how this works."

Victor gripped McCormack's biceps. "I can help, Dunc. I can look after things while you work. Look, I came up to make a go of this. To stop running away from the best thing I've had. To stop you running away. You wouldn't answer my fucking letters so I came up to tell you in person. But that doesn't matter. That can wait. You go and work. Sort this out. When it's over, we'll talk. That's all. All right?"

McCormack didn't trust himself to speak. He nodded, embraced Victor again, bumping shoulders, clapping backs.

"You fucking soft southern poofter."

"That's me."

"There's a spare set of keys in the bedside cabinet. Make yourself at home. I've, look, I've really got to go."

"Of course you do. Don't worry about me, Dunc. Just go. I'll be here when you get back."

21

B ad business." Haddow was shaking his head. "Bad business. Six dead. Iain Shand and Maitland's bloody brother among them."

They were in the DCI's office at Temple. McCormack stood, said nothing.

"I'm not going to lie, McCormack. I think Flett was wrong to bring you back. I think you should've stayed gone. You know that."

McCormack focused his gaze on the corkboard over Haddow's shoulder. It was a physical reaction, the urge to punch Haddow, to land a piledriver right between his eyes. If he squinted he could see the duty rosters pinned up on Haddow's board.

"But this goes beyond personalities," Haddow continued. "You've lost a man. We've all lost a man but it's your team. We're sorry for your loss."

If you're sorry, McCormack thought, why am I not sitting down? Would a cup of tea not be in order? Am I on the actual carpet here?

He squeezed out a single syllable. "Sir."

"But just for the record—and there *will* be a record, Detective, an inquiry will have to be held—what the hell was D.C. Shand doing outside the Barracks Bar?"

There was a square of greaseproof paper on Haddow's desk with the crusts of a sandwich on it. McCormack felt his stomach flutter. *Please God*, he thought; *don't be sick. Not here.*

"It was a surveillance op, sir. Connected to the Gavin Elliot investigation."

"Connected how?" The wooden chair complained as Haddow leaned back in it, smoothing his tie.

"Elliot was in a business partnership with Hugh Maitland. Or at least Hugh Maitland's wife. Property company. We're exploring the possibility that the Maitland connection might have a bearing on Elliot's murder."

"They were directors of the same company? So what? Doesn't mean they were close."

"No, sir. But the victim's daughter confirms that her father had regular contact with the Maitlands."

"Eileen Elliot said that?"

"She was very clear on the subject."

"Maitlands, plural?"

"Seems to me if you're doing business with Hugh, sir, Walter's going to know about it."

Haddow breathed through his nose, the thick tongue poking into one cheek then the other, then running over his bottom teeth. "Well, Hugh's done his last bit of business. But there's a link, then. Is that what you're saying? The murder of Gavin Elliot. The bombing last night."

"It's a possibility, sir. The two *men* were linked, certainly. Elliot and Hugh Maitland."

"O.K. Well, we bear that in mind, McCormack, see how it develops. Meantime, best guess is still terrorism. They've had their share of incendiary devices down south. We've escaped that up here until now, but it looks like that's changed."

McCormack shifted his feet. "IRA's on ceasefire, sir."

Haddow nodded. He folded the square of greaseproof paper over the remains of his sandwich, crunched it into a ball. "Aye. Well. I don't suppose they send out press releases when they decide to break a ceasefire." He leaned back to drop the crumpled wrapper into a wastepaper basket. "They probably, I don't know, just set a fucking bomb off."

McCormack felt the blood in his ears, a pressure on his eyeballs. He closed his eyes, massaged the lids with finger and thumb, breathing deeply. He opened his eyes. Haddow was looking at him closely. "Incidentally, you were en route to the Barracks Bar with D.C. Nicol when the explosion took place?"

"That's right, sir."

"Can I ask why?"

McCormack's eyes fluttered shut again. *Because*, the voice in his head intoned, *D.C. Shand has a non-service-issue firearm in his locker. A firearm we believe may have been used in a gang-related killing. We were planning to confront D.C. Shand about this but we were too late. He's not just a dead polis; he was a bent one.*

He opened his eyes and said, "We were following some intel on another case. Missing prostitute. Routine stuff."

Haddow held his gaze for a sceptical beat, then nodded. "Still," he said. "I suppose we should count our blessings. The bloody football season hasn't started yet."

The city's two football clubs, Catholic and Protestant, green and blue. Celtic, the team of the immigrant Irish, whose fans waved tricolours and rattled the old tin shed of their ramshackle stadium with rebel songs. And stolid, True Blue, Protestant Rangers in their redbrick citadel south of the Clyde.

"Well no, sir. But the marching season has."

"What? Oh fuck, McCormack. You're right."

Every year on the twelfth of July, the militant Prods of the Orange Order paraded through the city's streets. Men in Sunday suits and orange collarettes swaggered to the music from uniformed flute bands. They marched to celebrate the victory of Protestant King William III over forces loyal to the Catholic King James. At the River Boyne. In Ireland. In 1690. Glasgow: where 1690 was as fresh in people's minds as 1960. Fresher.

"Well, fuck it," Haddow said. "Can't be helped. Just means

we need to clear this all the quicker. Hamill's team'll be working this, Patterson's too. You use your guys however you want.
You'll get reinforcements as required. Just let me know."

"Sir."

"We have to assume," Haddow continued. "We have to
assume there's a cell at large in Glasgow. A safe house. Houses.
East End, probably. The Gallowgate. The Calton. I mean, Jesus,
one of the Balcombe Street gang was a lad from Toryglen. I want
you and your officers to draw up a list of republican sympathiz-
ers. Known subversives. MI5 have sent a man up. Chinless prick
in a double-breasted suit. Spence is his name, based at Turnbull
Street. He might have some ideas. Anyway, talk to him too."

"I'll do that, sir."

"Identify suspects. Bring them in. We've got seven days,
remember, under the Prevention of Terrorism Act, if we need
it. I want you to go in hard, but, McCormack—".

"Yes, sir?"

"There are sensitivities here. We don't want to inflame the
community. We don't want another Birmingham. I'm trusting
you to handle this. All right?" He looked at McCormack sig-
nificantly. "You're the man for this job."

"Understood, sir."

McCormack walked down the corridor shaking his head.
Bloody brilliant. First class. Now all he had to do was identify an
active service unit of the Irish Republican Army operating in the
East End of Glasgow, while not upsetting the locals. Which
would of course be a piece of piss since he, D.I. Duncan
McCormack, by virtue of his Roman Catholicism, was part of
"the community". The fact that he was Highland while "the
community" was Irish, didn't matter: he was a Catholic, a Fenian,
a tarrier, a Taig, a pape, a bead-rattler, a tim. He was one of them.

He popped his head into the Byre. Nicol and Goldie looked
up.

"Breath of air," he said. "Come on."

22

They walked north on Bearsden Road. The Forth and Clyde Canal passed under the road about fifty yards north of the station. McCormack led them down the ramp to the towpath.

It was a different world down here, away from the traffic. Tranquil, bucolic. Across the canal a stand of trees climbed a squat yellow hill. They felt the sun on their half-closed eyelids as they walked. This particular stretch of canal marked the northern edge of the city—beyond the trees were fields and moorland. They might have been deep in the country had it not been for the skeletal frames of twin gasometers that rose in the distance.

They walked in silence till they came to a bench. Nicol and Goldie sat. McCormack stood. He found his cigarettes, offered them round. A man came up the towpath, wheeling a bike, a black Pashley with a butcher's basket. They smoked till he passed.

"Suffering Jesus," McCormack said, shaking his head. He could have been commenting on the meeting with Haddow, Iain Shand's death, the whole situation with the bomb. Something seemed to strike him and he frowned suddenly at the two on the bench. "How are you bearing up, then? How are you both . . . coping?"

Nicol and Goldie exchanged a glance. "The old bedside manner could do with some work," Goldie said.

"Christ, I'm your bloody boss. I'm supposed to look out for you. Take an interest in your what-do-you-call-it. Welfare."

He looked off up the towpath. The man with the bike was glancing back at them.

"We're O.K., sir," Nicol said. "What about you?"

McCormack smoked. The fingers that raised the cigarette to his lips were ringed with sticking plasters. "You mean apart from the fact that I sent a colleague to his death last night? Dandy."

The man with the bike had stopped. He was looking back at them, studying them openly. McCormack looked away and then whipped round suddenly, feigning a lunge and stamping the gravel footpath, roaring. The man scrambled onto his bike and wobbled off, picking up speed as he rounded the bend.

They were quiet for a minute. "You weren't to know," Goldie said, finally. "It's not your fault. It was a legitimate tasking."

"It was a way of getting Shand out of the road," McCormack said. "I wanted shot of him. We all did."

Speaking the dead man's name seemed to change things. It felt like some acknowledgement was needed, some tribute due.

"He was a good cop," Nicol offered.

"Don't." McCormack held up his hand. "Don't embarrass us all. Let's be honest, Nicol. None of us liked him. He was a pain in the arse. But whatever he did, he's paid for it. And the job now is simple. We find whoever killed him. O.K.?"

Goldie nodded. "O.K., Dunc. We make it right."

"Can't make it right." McCormack snapped his cigarette into the canal. "A man's dead. We just try and make it a wee bit less wrong. We find who killed him. And we don't do that by rounding up Celtic fans in Gallowgate pubs."

"That's what he wants, is it?" Nicol asked. "Haddow?"

"He thinks we've got the Glasgow Brigade of the IRA in a flat on the Gallowgate."

"You don't think maybe he's got a point?" Goldie asked.

"The Provos bombing a Glasgow pub?" McCormack shook

his head. "Come on, Derek. They've got a policy. Scotland's off limits. No one wants to make Glasgow another Belfast."

"They *had* a policy," Goldie said. "Things can change."

McCormack shrugged. "They haven't claimed it, have they?"

"They never claimed Birmingham either."

This was true. The bombs in Birmingham last year. Two pubs. Twenty-one dead. They knew it was IRA but the call to claim it never came.

"But if the army's the target, why not just bomb the barracks? It's two hundred yards down the road."

"Softer target," Goldie said. "You get the off-duty squaddies. You also get civilians. Ramps up the terror. It's what they did in Birmingham."

"But this is different," McCormack said. "We've got the prior connection with Elliot."

"What's Gavin Elliot got to do with a bomb in the Barracks Bar?"

McCormack shook his head. "I haven't learned much in eighteen years," he said. "I've learned this, though. Once you start relying on coincidence to explain what happened, that's when you stop being a polis."

Goldie leaned forward and spat on the ground between his feet. "I don't buy it. You know how it works, Dunc. Everything looks different after a thing like this. A murder. A bomb. Everyone looks guilty. You start to see connections that don't exist."

"Come on." McCormack's mouth twisted in scorn. "Gavin Elliot turns up murdered. We find a link between Elliot and Hugh Maitland. Hugh Maitland's pub gets blown to bits, Hugh Maitland along with it. You know what a pattern of events is? Jesus."

"It's a squaddie pub," Goldie insisted. "Army barracks is just down the street."

"Bloody Barracks *estate* is closer, man. It's a Maitland pub before it's a squaddie pub."

"Look." Nicol held her hand up. "Can we just agree we don't know why the pub was bombed. Not yet. Can we just accept that?"

"Maitland's pub was bombed for the same reason Gavin Elliot was murdered," McCormack said. "We just don't know what that reason is."

The others were silent. A swan had drifted over and was pecking forlornly in the reeds. McCormack tugged at the knot of his tie. "What got Elliot killed was his connection with the Maitlands. That's got to be our working assumption. We need to find out more about this connection. What was Elliot doing with the Maitlands, beyond a bit of property speculation? And we need to come down like a ton of fucking bricks on the Quinns."

"You think it's the Quinns bombed the pub?"

"Well if it wasn't the Provos it was someone with a pretty big grudge against Maitland. And the balls to bomb his brother's pub."

Goldie rubbed his unshaved chin. "There's more than the Quinns got a grudge against Maitland. Plus, would they even have the know-how? Is it not a bit specialized?"

"It's an an-fo bomb," Nicol said. "You mix ammonium nitrate with fuel oil. Maybe add a bit of gelignite to give it a bigger kick. It's not too hard to pick up. Plus, they've got connections over the water, haven't they?"

"O.K., then." McCormack looked from one to the other. "We start with the Quinns. Derek: we need a Black Maria, three or four uniforms for nine o'clock. We're hitting their pub—we're hitting Dixon's tonight. Meantime, roust your touts—find out what they're saying about the Quinns."

"What about the gun?" Nicol asked. "We're going out on a limb for a guy who had a gangster's gun in his locker."

"Right. That's the other thing. You've still got the key to Shand's locker?"

Nicol nodded. "Should I give it to the techs? Get some latents?"

"Let's leave it for now," McCormack said. "I'm not sure we want to trust Haddow on this. But we need to find Shand's tout, his inside man in Maitland's crew. Put a list together, Nicol. We need to work out who it is. We'll only get one shot at it before they twig they've a rat in the camp. We need to get it right first time." He could taste the bile in his mouth from earlier. He cleared his throat and spat on the grass. "For once."

"So we're running our own investigation now?" Nicol asked. She glanced from McCormack to Goldie. She didn't look nervous; she just wanted to know where they stood.

"We always were." McCormack shrugged. "Only this time Haddow doesn't have an inside man."

A pair of ducks flapped noisily down to land on the water, tucked their wings in and glided off. "Not sure I'm entirely happy with that," Goldie said. "To be honest. Going behind Haddow's back."

"You're worried it might damage your career, Detective?" McCormack said. The tip of his tongue was visible through slightly parted lips. Goldie had been stuck at sergeant since before McCormack left for London.

"Aye. O.K., smartarse. And whose fault's that?"

"Insubordination, D.S. Goldie! You're implying that your perceived closeness to me has hampered your chances of promotion? I think you might be right. In which case, the sensible course of action should surely be: fuck it. In for a penny."

"Aye, O.K. And what are you doing, while I'm busy sabotaging my own career?"

"Me? I get the easy job. I get to go and talk to Iain Shand's fiancée."

He turned on his heel and started back up the towpath. The others rose from the bench and followed.

23

Millport, on the Isle of Cumbrae. The prom was thick with milling bodies. Pink clouds of candy floss. Short-sleeved shirts and summer dresses. A small boy was waddling towards him, picking bang-snaps out of a packet and sparking them off the pavement. Kidd remembered them from his own youth, little twists of paper filled with sand and explosives that snapped like gunfire when you dropped them. A Jack Russell was yapping at the boy's heels and Kidd stepped onto the roadway into the path of a clanging bicycle bell that made him jump back onto the pavement.

A woman laughed rudely in his face as she passed. Kidd wiped the sweat from his brow with a sodden hankie. He would never find Yvonne Gray in this melee. The man who came to his Maryhill flat was very clear; Kidd's job was to find Yvonne Gray and find her fast. Get the details of her whereabouts back to Maitland's boys. They'd done some digging, found out that she'd lived near Largs for a spell when she was younger. So Kidd spent the whole of Friday trailing up and down the streets of Largs, mooching in cafés, watching the waltzers at the seafront shows, looking for a face that matched the photo in his pocket. No joy. Today he'd had the bright idea of taking the short ferry ride over to the Isle of Cumbrae to try his luck in Millport. Now, though, he was starting to wish he'd stayed in Largs. He wanted away from the sun and the noise and the crowds and the smells. He was standing on the promenade and turned his back on the beach and looked up College

Street to where it dwindled in the green gloom of overhanging trees. It looked quiet and cool up there and Kidd plunged blindly across Glasgow Street in a kind of daze.

On College Street he passed low houses on one side and the Garrison wall on the other. Soon the dappled shade of the trees was playing on his face. He was barely a hundred yards from the prom but it felt like another world. He walked on and a grand stone archway opened up in the wall on his right. Through the arch was a path that dropped down between rows of tall trees whose crowns met in an arch of their own. It looked like the entrance to some enchanted castle but the sign on the wall said *Cathedral of the Isles: The Scottish Episcopal Church Welcomes You*, so he stepped down onto the path.

At the far end the path rose to a short flight of steps. Kidd climbed them and saw to his left the little cathedral sitting up on its grassy terrace, a doorway under the tall grey spire.

Inside, the church was somehow tiny and huge. There were only five or six narrow rows of wooden chairs on either side of the aisle but the ceiling seemed high as the sky, rising above the whitewashed walls in an intricate meshing of dark wooden rafters. There was something austere and kirk-like in the plain white walls but at the front of the church, up some stairs and through a grey marble arch was the gorgeousness of the altar, all rich green cloth and golden candlesticks.

It took Kidd back to his time at Auldpark. Every Sunday the kids from the Home got the option of church. The Catholics went off to Mass and a smaller number—Kidd and his sister Izzy among them—were driven in a minibus to the local Church of Scotland. It was a chance to get away from the Home, to do something normal for an hour. But it never really worked. The Auldpark kids sat together in two pews near the back. People knew the Auldparkers were poor souls, they didn't have much, and so they would bring little presents of sweets and comics and knitted gloves. It was kind, it was well meant, but it made you feel like an abandoned puppy, an object on which normal folk could exercise their pity. When you filed out for Sunday School in the cold church hall you could tell that the normal kids hated you, that they only hid their hate because they feared you as well. Kidd remembered one Christmas when Izzy was picked to play Mary in the nativity. She looked so happy and proud in her white robes, holding the Christ-child in her tartan shawl like it was her own wee baby. The hatred, though, from the other kids was almost nuclear. It was radioactive. How come an Auldparker gets to play Mary? Izzy told him later that when the play was over one of the angels spat in her face, a proper oyster that hung and dribbled in Izzy's hair.

Kidd took a seat at the back of the church. There was one other person, a woman, blond-haired, sitting near the front on the opposite side. Later, Kidd would come to think of this moment as something fey, a premonition, but he sensed right away that this woman was Yvonne Gray. The hair was the wrong colour, he could only see her back, but somehow he knew. And when, five minutes later, she rose and turned and came down the aisle he was sure: this was the face in the photograph he carried in the breast pocket of his shirt.

Kidd counted to ten before he got up from his seat. The woman was halfway down the avenue as he trotted down the cathedral steps. He dogged her down College Street, back to the noise and the glare. She turned into one of the seafront cafés, the skirt of her sundress flaring in a breeze. Kidd quickened his pace.

In the doorway of the café, Kidd paused, taking his bearings in the noise and smoke and chatter, but he spotted her at a far corner table, setting her sunhat on the chair beside her.

He edged and sidled through the crowded room and stopped with his fingertips touching the chair-back.

"Is this seat taken? Would you mind?"

She looked coolly up at him, then plucked her sunhat from the wickerwork seat and dropped it in her lap.

"You're a lifesaver," Kidd told her. He picked up a laminated menu, fanned himself with it. "Hot enough. Sheesh."

"Didn't I see you just now?" she said. "In the cathedral? Are you following me?"

"No! I mean"—Kidd grinned weakly—"I thought I knew you. You looked like someone I know."

He wanted to take the photograph out and hold it up next to her face, just to be sure.

"Right. This someone you know; does she like cream tea? Does she like scones?"

"What's that?"

The woman nodded to a space behind Kidd's shoulder and he craned round to see the waitress approaching.

"Oh. Right you are." He ordered coffee for himself and tea and cake for her and then he sat there smiling, casting around for something to say. "Are you religious?" he finally managed.

"What? No!"

"It's just, you looked like you were praying." He gestured over his shoulder with his thumb. "In the cathedral, I mean."

"Well if it comes to that, I was."

"But you're not religious?"

"I don't believe in God but sometimes I pray to him," she said. "I figure, play the odds. What's the harm?"

"How's that working out?"

"Honestly?" She smiled. "Not that great. But, you know, tomorrow's another day."

He laughed. "You here on holiday?" he asked her.

"You're full of questions," she said.

"I'm sorry. I do that. It's nerves. Why don't you ask me something?"

They'd told him that she was on the game. She didn't look like she was on the game. She worked in Maitland's sauna up the West End. Not a class joint, exactly, but a cut above the knocking-shops in the schemes.

Would she be a user? He glanced down at her forearms and she followed his gaze. He coloured, and then the waitress was back with a tray, setting down their things.

"Do you know the Barracks Bar?" Yvonne asked him, when the waitress had gone.

"What?" Kidd's cup rattled. He was thrown. Had she clocked him already? Pegged him for one of Maitland's crew?

"You said ask me something. I'm asking you, do you know the Barracks Bar? In Glasgow?"

"Do I . . . ? Yeah. I know it. Up Maryhill way. Why?"

Why is she asking about a Maitland pub? The fuck is she driving at?

"Oh did you not hear?" She looked at him sharply. "It got bombed."

Kidd looked around the café, back at Yvonne. "What you on about?"

Yvonne shook her head, gripping his forearm. "I'm not kidding. Honest to God. It got bombed. Look: what's your name?"

"Ah, Chris." He didn't have time to come up with a false one.

"Well, look, Chris." There was a rack of newspapers on the wall behind her, for the use of patrons. She fished one out and unfolded it in front of him: *INFERNO!* with a grainy shot of the blasted pub, its rafters ablaze.

He scanned through the story as Yvonne talked on.

"What a way to go, though, eh? Blown to bits while you're having a drink. One of the women, they're saying she was still alive—after the blast, like. Covered in flames. Can you imagine? One minute you're sipping a Sweetheart stout with your pals, next thing you're on bloody fire. They managed to put the flames out and they got her into an ambulance. But, aye, she died at the hospital."

Kidd gripped his coffee cup. He felt sick. He thought of the four folk in the Tradeston tenement, waiting for the flames to reach them. His four victims. And now this. Jesus Christ. But even as he shook his head and buried his nose in his teacup a part of him was thinking, *Denny Quinn. Fuck me! What a way to hit back. What a way to return the fucking serve.*

He pushed the paper away. Jesus Christ. It would be fun and games now. Maitland would come down on the Quinns like the wrath of God. A phrase from his schoolbooks came back to him. *Letters of fire and sword.* That's what the Quinns had coming. Letters of fire and sword. The paper was saying it might be the IRA but fuck that. It was the Quinns. He knew it in his bones.

And him? He was the fucking Angel of Death, wasn't he? Bringing misery wherever he went. Those poor souls in the tenement. This lassie here. Once he told them he had found her, they would hurt her too. Maybe do away with her.

He glanced up. She was spreading her scone, happy as Larry. The yellow butter and now the little carton of jam, raspberry, smearing it over the pale butter, clunking the knife down on her plate, all smeared with red.

"Are you O.K.?"

She was watching him with real concern, the scone poised at her lips. She set it down on her plate.

"You look terrible. You're white as a sheet."

"I'm fine," he told her. "I'm just. It's too close in here."

"Too close?" she scoffed. "Don't give us it. It's the story in the paper, isn't it? It's O.K. I think it's sweet. I'm Yvonne, by the way." So it was real names for her too. Real first names, anyway.

"So what is it you do, Chris?" She took a bite of her scone.

"Me?" Kidd shrugged. "I'm a painter and decorator."

She laughed, put her hand up to her mouth to keep the crumbs from falling. "Really?"

"Naw. I lied to make myself sound more glamorous."

She laughed again. "It's not that. It's just, well, you don't look like a painter and decorator."

"I'm sorry about that. I'll try harder."

"A painter and decorator's a wee old guy with white dungarees and a pot belly and wee flecks of paint on his specs."

"That's just when we're working. This is what we look like in civvies."

She took the last bite of scone, washed it down with tea. "What *are* you doing here, anyway?"

"Same as you," he said. "Getting out of the city for a bit of fun. Bit of a break. Speaking of which." He mugged a Cagney accent. "Let's blow this joint, doll-face."

"Let me finish my tea."

They queued for the ferry. Back in Largs he offered to walk her to her guesthouse. She told him she had some shopping to do in town. Maybe he could see her another day if he was planning to stay around. They arranged to meet in Nardini's café the following evening. Kidd walked back to his flat.

24

Nobody claimed it. Not the IRA. Not the INLA. Not the UDA. Not the UVF. Not the Tartan Army or the Army of the Provisional Government. Not the Red Army Faction or the Salvation Army or the Boys bloody Brigade.

On the evening after the Barracks Bar bomb, the atrocity was still unclaimed. Glasgow had no one to blame.

All day, the authorities waited for the culprits to identify themselves. The Home Secretary in London lifted the phone to call the Scottish Secretary in Edinburgh. The Scottish Secretary telephoned the Chief Constable. And the Chief Constable went on TV to pledge that his officers would bring the perpetrators to justice.

But nobody claimed it. There was no one to blame.

By late afternoon on the day after the bombing, Roy Jenkins, the Home Secretary, was touring the wreckage in a light rain, nodding and frowning with his hands clasped behind his back like a minor royal. When a reporter asked who he held responsible for the outrage, Jenkins declared his confidence in the police investigation.

The Glasgow papers were less circumspect.

IRA KILLERS BOMB CITY. BLOODY FRIDAY.
PROVISIONALS KILL SIX. ARMY PUB BLASTED
IN PROVO OUTRAGE.

It was later that afternoon when reports started filtering in, reports of chapels being attacked, windows broken. Someone daubed MURDERING SCUM in foot-high white letters on a Catholic school in Drumchapel.

A boy in a Celtic top got beaten by a mob on Sauchiehall Street; fractured skull, teeth kicked out of his head.

There were people to blame after all, it seemed.

The Archbishop of Glasgow demanded action from the police and the government. Were Catholic citizens to be harassed and harried, denied their rights as British subjects? Their places of worship desecrated? As six o'clock Mass started that night, groups of young male parishioners linked arms to guard the entrances to the city's Catholic churches.

A few hours later, another place of resort for young Catholic men on the city's South Side was left unguarded. That was an error. McCormack and his men made a lot of noise, pulling up in front of Dixon's Tavern on Victoria Road. A Black Maria and an unmarked car. The squeal of tyres. Doors banging open. Six uniforms piling out of the van. Boots on the pavement. Helmets, not flat caps. Something sinister in the flash of chin-straps.

McCormack and Goldie stepped out of the car, raincoats billowing.

A drunk man was sitting on the pavement, slumped against the pub wall, head between his knees. He seemed to start awake when he heard the commotion. He pushed his head back against the wall to focus on McCormack and the others, slurred some opaque malediction and spat on his own lapel.

Two of the uniforms took up position on either side of the pub doors. McCormack pushed through the double doors with the others at his back.

They had timed it for maximum effect. It was half-past nine, half an hour from closing time. The crowd was six-deep at the bar, packed tight and swaying, men bringing pints to their lips with little tilts of their forearms, no room to bend their elbows. At the front of the crowd disembodied arms thrust banknotes at the trio of barmen who scurried around, dodging each other, pulling beer taps with one hand while reaching back with the other to press tumblers against the whisky optics.

It took a moment for the presence of the polis to register but, once it did, silence rippled from the tables at the door to the booths at the back.

McCormack stepped forward, Goldie at his shoulder. The uniforms stood at the door, two on each side, truncheons drawn.

McCormack glanced towards the bar, but the duty manager a paunchy middle-aged man in a white shirt and black tie— wasn't the man in charge. There was a booth against the back wall that commanded a view down the length of the pub and a man stood up from that booth now, stood up and stretched like someone rising from bed, and stepped out onto the floor.

The drinkers shuffled back to give him space. He was young twenty-three, twenty-four—and just shy of six feet. His shoulders were squared and he wore a pinstripe, three-piece suit, black, with flared high-waisted trousers and a tightly buttoned waistcoat. The floppy collar of a turquoise silk shirt spread over the lapels of his jacket. He looked around the pub with a benign smile on his lips and then he spread his hands.

"You gonnae stand there all night, copper? Cat got your tongue?"

McCormack smiled. "We'd like a quick word."

"Would you?" The man took a draw of his cigarette and stubbed it out in the ashtray. "Would you now? Well, that's a shame. 'Cause I might be busy."

"Then again," McCormack said. "You might not."

He stepped unhurriedly through the parting crowd. The man in the turquoise shirt was still smiling when McCormack gave a short roll of his shoulders and punched him in the stomach. As the man buckled over, McCormack drew his truncheon from the poacher's pocket of his raincoat and stunned him on the base of the skull. The man dropped to the floor like a bundle of stair rods.

The silence thickened in the crowded pub.

The man's four companions had sprung to their feet when their leader was felled but they didn't move from the booth. They swayed stiffly, hemmed in by the table, half-standing, fists flashing open and closed, gunslingers who'd misplaced their guns. McCormack watched them mildly for a moment, arms at his sides, before turning slowly and strolling over to the bar. The drinkers pressed back as McCormack rested his truncheon crosswise on the bar-top and set off down the bar, dragging his truncheon behind him, sweeping all the drinks to the floor. The drinkers pressed back further to avoid the spillage and shattering glass.

When McCormack reached the end he flipped the hatch and stepped behind the bar. The bar staff retreated to the far end. McCormack paused for a second and then swung his truncheon at the nearest bottle—a Magnum of Famous Grouse—which shivered into pieces, the whisky spattering onto the soiled lino. Then he made his way down the line of optics, smashing each bottle in turn, finding his rhythm, thrashing the glass into slivers, a noise like shingle churning in the pounding surf. He stopped at the end to catch his breath.

Nobody spoke. There was a thin gurgling sound, as of a dozen little rivers. McCormack came out from behind the bar. He plucked a bar towel from the bar-top and wiped the mess from his truncheon. Then he nodded to the uniforms at the door and two of them sprang forward and took an arm each of the man on the floor, hauled him through the pub, his legs dragging behind him.

The leader's four henchmen were cuffed and marched out to the van. McCormack surveyed the scene, the smashed gantry, the cowed, resentful men. He stood there nodding, the right half of his raincoat slick with spirits. Then he turned and walked out of the pub.

An hour later he was back at Temple, sitting beside Goldie. Interview Room Number One. The man from Dixon's Tavern sat across from them, slumped in his seat, hands flat on the table. His turquoise shirt had been torn at the collar.

"Denny Quinn," McCormack said. "How's the head? You want a Disprin?"

"Fuck you, you fucking bent pig cunt."

"Very good." McCormack nodded amiably. "On the plus side, suddenly you're not too busy anymore. A window's opened up. We can have our wee chat."

"Want my solicitor. You've got fuck all to hold me. I'll be out that door in ten minutes."

McCormack had a Styrofoam cup of coffee in front of him. He prised off the plastic lid. He looked up at Quinn and smiled. He took a brown paper sachet of sugar and tore the end off, pouring the sugar into the coffee. He stirred it with a plastic spatula.

"Outside?" he said. "Really? You know you're safer in here than you are out there. You're lucky it was us who came for you. Not Wattie Maitland's boys."

Quinn said nothing.

"Right now, this is the only place that's safe for you. You know that? You're out on the streets, Maitland'll get you. You go to Barlinnie, Maitland'll get you. You hear what happened to your boy in D Wing? Eamon Fallon?"

"I heard."

"Someone hit him. The old cueball in a sock routine. Smashed his cheekbone. Fractured his eye-socket in three places."

"I said I heard."

"You can't even keep your soldiers safe. You're hanging by

a thread here, Denny. Maitland's gonnae finish you. I'd lay money that one of your crew is setting you up as we speak."

There was a lull in the cool bare room. Then Goldie spoke for the first time.

"Didn't you used to have a pub?"

Quinn stirred slightly in his seat. He was leaning back in the plastic chair, side-on to the interview desk, long legs crossed at the ankles, arms folded. He looked at Goldie from under his fringe.

"That supposed to mean something?"

Goldie had a stubby pencil in his hand, turning it through his fingers and rapping the blunt end on the scored, charred surface of the desk. "Dixon's Tavern on Allison Street?"

"Still got it, shithead. What's your point?"

"Really? You've still got the pub?" The pencil kept turning through Goldie's fingers, kept rapping on the desk. "Hate to break it to you. There was a little accident this evening, after you left. Those big frosted windows. Might take you some time to get back on your feet. And when you do, we'll oppose your licence. Here's the stop press, Denny: you're out of the hospitality game."

Denny Quinn swept the hair off his face, looked at Goldie with no expression.

"But I wouldn't worry too much." McCormack leaned forward, elbows on the table. "You're out of all the other games too. What did you think—you kill a polis and it's business as usual?"

The chair legs scraped on the grimed concrete. Quinn was sitting upright now, a hand raised as if in benediction. "Whoa. Hold the fuck on here. What the fuck?" He looked at Goldie and then back at McCormack. "Kill a polis? Who killed a polis? No one killed a polis."

McCormack jabbed a finger at the door. "There's an empty desk down the corridor there. Would you like to see it?"

Quinn pressed his palms onto the desktop, leaned forward.

"Look. Haud on a minute here. You think that was me? You think I bombed Walter Maitland's *pub*? Offed his fucking brother? You think I've got a death-wish?"

Goldie stopped twirling the pencil and jabbed it at Quinn. "Wrong answer, son. Walter Maitland is not your concern. Your concern is Detective Constable Iain Shand. Late of this parish. Let's focus on him."

"Kill a Maitland? Kill a fucking *cop*?" This was getting worse and worse for Denny Quinn. He drew the back of his hand under his nose. "I never did it. Never fucking did it, never planted a bomb. Denny Quinn!" Suddenly he was jabbing himself in the chest. "I'm Denny Quinn, from Cumberland Street. I'm not the fucking IRA."

There were footsteps in the corridor. Raucous voices. The other cops knew Denny Quinn was in here. Someone slapped the door of the interview room on his way past, a single juddering blow. The footsteps receded, the voices dwindled, a loud laugh made tinny by the corridor's acoustics.

Denny's head slumped onto his chest, as though he were sleeping. He spoke quietly now, brow furrowed, mumbling to the surface of the table, maybe to himself. "You've got it all wrong. Bomb a pub? Kill a polis? Where's the mileage in that?"

"You wanted to hit back at Maitland," McCormack told him. "After the Tradeston thing."

"Naw." There was a yelp of desperation in Quinn's voice. "Naw. That's not how it was."

"You didn't want to hit back? You let Maitland burn your warehouse down and you don't lift a finger? Big Bad Denny Quinn?"

"We were biding our time." Quinn was rubbing his palms up and down his thighs. He was shaking his head more quickly now, as if he could refuse to recognize the whole situation. "We were planning our move."

"Shite!" McCormack leaned forward. "That's shite, son.

You were gagging to hit back at Maitland. What's the softest target? The brother's pub. Leave the car bomb outside. Like the boys across the water. Proper little Provo. Boom! Blow the Orange fuckers into bits."

"Naw. You've got it wrong. I couldn't— It's not—"

Quinn's voice had assumed the jumpy, nasal tone of all the desperate men who had sat in that chair. McCormack could hear in it the whines and justifications that had echoed off the tiles of a hundred rooms like this.

Never heard of him.

I wasn't there.

It's all a lie.

She's making it up.

Don't know.

I can't remember.

It wasnae me.

You've got it wrong.

It wasnae me.

"Fuck up, son. Now D.C. Shand? Shand was just an accident. I'm prepared to accept that. Collateral damage. But that changes nothing. You killed a cop, son. You bombed a squaddie pub. Those boys in Birmingham?" McCormack shook his head. "The boys who did what you did, bombed a pub? If they're lucky, they'll get life. If they're *lucky*. 'Cause if they ever let them out, they'll last ten minutes."

Quinn was tugging at his collar, craning his neck, tossing his head like a skittish horse. "I need my lawyer."

"You think? Naw, son." McCormack was smiling. "You don't *get* a lawyer. You don't get anything till you tell me what happened. We've got seven days, Denny. You're here on your fucking holidays."

"What?"

"Prevention of Terror, Volunteer Quinn. You're mine for a week."

Quinn looked at the door. "No. That's not true. I need a lawyer."

"You need to start talking, Denny. That's what you need. Actually, you know what? Talk if you want. But if you don't talk? You and I are heading down the corridor to the cellblock and Iain Shand's colleagues, who are really keen to meet you, might pay us a wee visit. You want me to open that door?" McCormack held Quinn's gaze and raised his right hand to point at the door, thumb up, cocked pistol, *bang-bang-you're-dead*. "They'll use your fucking napper as a Lambeg drum. They'll kick you into paste, son. We will kill you. That's not even a threat. We'll kill you right now." McCormack looked calmly at Quinn, looked through him, like he was already dead. "You need to catch up with yourself, son. Your career as the John Dillinger of the South Side? That's finished. That's gone. The prize now is walking out of here. That's it. So. You got something to say to me, now would be a useful time." McCormack sat back and let his hands flop between his knees. "Or should we head on down that corridor and have ourselves a party?"

Quinn planted his elbows on the desk, dipped his head to run his fingers through his hair. Then he blew out a rasping sigh and tugged his smokes from his jacket pocket. McCormack pushed the ashtray towards him.

SUNDAY, 6 JULY 1975

25

McCormack was in the office early. The papers were full of the bombing outrage. Find these IRA scumbags. Bring back hanging. Headshot of the smiling victims beside pictures of the blasted pub. Eyewitness accounts. Fiery denunciations from local MPs. The Queen's expression of sympathy. Flags at half-mast. Scottish golfers to wear black armbands at the Open. Calls for calm from the Catholic Archbishop of Glasgow, the Grandmaster of the Orange Order.

McCormack was beginning to suspect that a bombing was the very worst crime to investigate. It was almost comically hopeless. The evidence was everywhere and nowhere. Whole streets could be affected, the bomber's handiwork plain as day, scattered over hundreds of yards. But the clues that mattered the dabs on the device or on the steering wheel, the fibres on the seat or in the footwell—were annihilated by the crime itself.

Usually this didn't matter, since bombers could be counted on to claim responsibility. But where a bombing wasn't claimed, what did you have to go on? Stupid questions, mainly.

Who could have packed explosives into a car boot, driven to Maryhill?

Anyone.

Who were your prime suspects?

People with cars.

Denny Quinn had spoken last night but it was all rubbish.

Complaints about Maitland encroaching on his turf, crossing the river to sell drugs in Quinn's pubs. He was still denying involvement in the bombing, wouldn't admit any links with the boys across the water. McCormack would hold him for another few days—the full week if needed. Maybe some incentive would be required—six CID men with sticks and steel-cappers—but one way or another Denny Quinn would tell them what he knew.

Otherwise, the only hope was that the bomber had done something odd or noteworthy when parking the car. Garrioch Road was a street of four-storey sandstone tenements. That was a lot of windows. Maybe someone had noticed the Rover being parked outside the Barracks Bar and maybe they remembered the driver.

Detectives from Temple and uniforms from across the city had climbed the tenement stairs, knocking doors and asking questions. The usual hostility to the polis seemed to have been fleetingly suspended—no one takes kindly to their local pub being blasted into next week, taking their own front windows with it—but the results of the canvass were patchy. The car parked in front of the Barracks Bar was a red Rover—all the witnesses agreed on that. It turned out to have been stolen in Greenock on Thursday morning. It seemed to have been left outside the Barracks Bar under cover of darkness on the Thursday night. A woman across the way, who had risen in the small hours to settle her crying baby, reported seeing a drunk man walking down a row of cars, trying the handles. He tried the Rover's door but the car was locked and he passed on down the street. Neither the woman with the baby nor anyone else had spotted the Rover's driver.

There was, however, one other piece of information that McCormack found intriguing. Two days before the bombing, a man in a third-floor flat had been standing at the bay window of his living room when a VW camper van pulled in and parked right below him, across from the pub. It was maybe four o'clock in the afternoon. The man—a former foreman at the Macdonald biscuit factory in Hillington—noticed the camper van because he always noticed camper vans. He had planned to buy one in his retirement and tour the Highlands with his wife. But the wife died of cancer a few years back and the idea lost its appeal. Still, he admired this particular Kombi—a two-tone affair, cream and olive green—as it manoeuvred into the parking space below him. The man waited for the driver to emerge, on some errand at the Barracks Bar, perhaps. Or for the passenger door to open in case he was dropping somebody off. Or maybe he was picking someone up. But nothing happened. The driver stayed put behind the wheel, though he turned the engine off. Nobody emerged from the tenements or the pub to approach the van. In five minutes or so the engine started up and the van pulled away.

"Did he get a look at the driver?" McCormack had asked the uniform who brought him this information.

"No. As I say, sir, the driver never left the vehicle, and the witness couldn't see his face from his window."

"The van itself. Did he get the registration?"

"He didn't. But he got a good look at the van. He's sure about the colours. Said it looked to be in pretty good nick. Oh, and it was split-screen."

"What does that mean, split-screen?"

"The windscreen, sir. Some of them have one big pane of glass. Others have a strut down the middle with the windscreen split in two."

McCormack thought about it. Witnesses had seen a camper van at Crawford Street when Elliot's body was being dumped. He already suspected that the two crimes were linked. If the man they were seeking was the driver of the camper van then the case looked a little less hopeless, though they'd been working through the list of VW camper van owners in the city for the past five days without success. And, of course, the whole point about a camper van was that you travelled in it. The killer could be based outside the city.

He rose and turned to stand at the window. Everything in his vision looked sharp and fresh: the little bubbles and imperfections on the brickwork of the window; the flaking green paint of the frame; the patterns and perforations on the greying lace curtain he was holding aside. He'd noticed this before, how a murder renewed things. Like the city after a shower of rain. Everything rinsed and expectant.

"Sir." Nicol was at the door.

McCormack dropped the curtain. "Come in, Nicol. Sit."

She didn't sit. "The gun's gone," she said, without preamble. Her cheeks were flushed and hectic, as if she'd been running. McCormack looked beyond her shoulder to the empty squad room and the door to the corridor. She reached behind her and closed his office door.

"When?"

"I don't know, sir. Now. I was getting his belongings together so that we could give them to the next of kin, the fiancée." Her hands lifted and fell in her lap. "It's gone. The gun's gone."

"Jesus Christ." Their eyes were locked when a knock came at the door and the desk sergeant poked his head in. "It's Spence, sir. The bloke up from London? Wants to see you now. He's using DCI Haddow's office."

"Thanks, Brian. I'll be there directly." The door swung shut. McCormack pointed at Nicol. "They're going to use this against us, you know that? Shand was one of ours. One of ours and a dirty cop."

"He's dead."

"Doesnae matter. He was still a bent cop."

"He was Haddow's responsibility. You said it yourself. It

was Haddow assigned him to the team. Haddow picked him, sir. Not you."

"He was dirty, Nicol. He was on our squad. We'll get the blame."

"You keep saying he was dirty. We don't know he was dirty."

"He was off freelancing. He was Haddow's nark. Suddenly he deserves the George Medal?"

"He was Haddow's nark! So what! He was an arsehole too. No argument. But he was still a good polis. You might have found that out if you'd trusted him even the tiniest bit. Maybe we'd be in a better place if you had. Maybe you wouldn't have to smash up pubs like a bloody bikers' gang to show how great a cop you are."

Nicol stopped abruptly. Her sudden rage had carried her over the cliff. Now she stood, wincing, waiting to hit the ground. McCormack took a step back, buttoned his jacket. "O.K., then. Well. It's nice to know where you stand."

"Sir, I shouldn't have said that. I overste—"

"Ho! Ho! Don't start back-tracking now, Nicol. You've said your piece. Stick to it. Doesnae bother me. We're all under pressure here. That's why we need to sort this out before anyone else does. Starting with the gun. We need to find Shand's inside man. But right now, we need to find that fucking gun."

He was off and down the corridor, through to the Big House. Haddow's door.

"Come!"

In Haddow's office a thin man sat behind Haddow's desk. He wore a pale grey pinstripe suit and a rich-looking cream-coloured shirt. College tie: blue, with red, white and brown stripes. He had a notepad and a mug of tea in front of him on the desk. His hair was the colour of chocolate.

"My name's Michael Spence. Please: sit down." He didn't

get up, didn't offer to shake hands. "Thanks for making the time, Detective."

McCormack said nothing, took his seat.

"I've spoken to DCI Haddow. Some of the uniforms who attended the scene. I think we have a pretty clear idea of what happened."

McCormack cuffed his left wrist in the finger and thumb of his right hand, started to twist, easing some stiffness in the joint. "Is that right?"

"The bomb was placed in a burgundy Rover saloon car, parked overnight in front of the Barracks Bar. It detonated at around 9:15 on Friday night, devastating the bar and the flat directly above, causing damage to property in a radius of five hundred yards. Twenty-nine injured. Five dead."

"It sounds very neat when you say it like that."

"I'm sorry?"

McCormack was massaging his other wrist. "It looked a bit messier on Friday night."

"Quite. Well, I'll leave you to fill in the local colour. I'm trying to establish the facts. Is there something wrong with your hands, Detective?"

"I spent Friday night digging through piles of bricks and rubble. Trying to find survivors. Bodies. Trying to find my colleague. Yes, as it happens. There's something wrong with my hands."

Spence looked at him neutrally. "I see. As I say, I'm looking to establish the facts. I'd like you tell me what happened, please. In your own words, Detective. Start from the start."

McCormack smiled. His eyes strayed to the board behind Spence's shoulder. Then he noticed that Spence wasn't smiling. "Oh fuck. You're *serious?*"

"You think I would joke at a time like this?"

"How would I know what happened? I was just there. Smoke. Dust. Lights. Fires. Screaming—lots of screaming.

Sirens. I tried to help. I tried to help people. You want to make a tidy story out of that? Three pars and a neat conclusion?"

"I want to make sense of it, Detective, yes. With your help, if you'll let me."

"Bits of people in the street. A woman with her face half off."

"I get the picture, Detective. It was a chaotic scene. You don't think your officer, D.C. Shand, could have been the target?"

McCormack came back slowly from the horrors of Garrioch Road. "What? Shand? No! No chance. I mean, how could they know he'd be there?"

"He'd been there the night before, hadn't he? On surveillance from—what was it?—6 P.M. to midnight. He'd even spoken to one of the doormen, as I understand it."

"But that was a one-off. I mean, as far as anyone else knew. It wasn't a pattern."

"How many people knew you were planning to deploy D.C. Shand on surveillance for a second consecutive night?"

"Oh no. Fuck you. Fuck *you*." McCormack was out of his seat. "You think one of my team would give up their mate to whoever planted that bomb? We lost a fucking colleague that night. We lost one of our own."

Spence looked mildly pained. "Try to compose yourself, Detective. Look, I understand. I get it. Shand was your buddy. I'm just asking questions. I just want to know what happened. Help us catch whoever did this."

McCormack eased back into his chair. "Shand was parked across the street anyway. If he hadn't been crossing the street, he might even still be alive. Plus, a *bomb*? You want to kill a polis, there's easier ways."

"Well, possibly not if you want to make it look like something else. Let's assume, though, that D.C. Shand wasn't the target. Who was? The army?"

McCormack thought about it. "Which one?"

Spence smiled, shook his head. "You're saying this is a gang thing?"

"I'm saying who the fuck knows? Maitland's been at war with the Quinns for three or four months. This would be a bit . . . ambitious for the Quinns, but who knows?"

"What do they say, the Quinns? Have you spoken to them?"

McCormack jabbed his thumb at the door behind him. "I've got Denny Quinn in cell number three. Ask him yourself."

"I'm asking you."

"He's got an alibi. He always has an alibi. He thinks we're in Maitland's pocket, we're out to fit him up."

"What do *you* think, Detective?"

McCormack smoothed his tie. "I try to keep an open mind."

Spence nodded. "You were down in the Met, weren't you, McCormack?"

"Six years."

"So you know how this works, then. Right? Bombs, bomb-scares. The disruption. The terror. What makes you think this is different?"

"Who said I do?"

"Haddow said. DCI Haddow said you do. Says you don't think it's the Irish."

McCormack shifted in his chair. "How would it benefit any-one? Turning Glasgow into another Belfast. I just don't see it."

Spence took a sip of his tea. "You're Roman Catholic, I believe, Detective McCormack."

"What's that got to do with the price of fish?"

"Not much, where I come from. Here, from what I gather, it's another matter. Being a Roman's a big deal up here, right? Being a Catholic po*lice* officer?"

"Except I'm not Irish, if that's what you're thinking. I'm a Highlander. It's a different thing entirely."

"Do the bigots see the difference? The guys who write 'Fuck the Pope' on toilet walls? Does it matter to them, that difference?"

The old joke came back to McCormack. *Why do people write "Fuck the Pope" on toilet walls? Because they can't be bothered writing "Fuck the Moderator of the General Assembly of the Church of Scotland".*

"Something's funny, Detective?"

"No. It's just, I don't even know what you're on about here."

"It's a question of allegiance, D.I. McCormack. Maybe you just don't want to think the IRA would bomb Glasgow because, well, maybe you sympathize a little. Understandably. I'm trying to take an objective view."

McCormack wiped a hand down his face. "Obviously. That makes sense. I mean, because you're betraying no fucking hint of bias whatsoever."

Spence smiled with his mouth shut. He set his pen down on the desk, aligned it with the edge of his notebook. "O.K. Look, D.I. McCormack. I know the last thing you need right now is someone swanning up from London to make your life more difficult."

McCormack thought of Victor, lying on the sofa at Caird Drive. *You don't know the fucking half of it,* he wanted to say.

"And you're right," Spence went on. "I'm out of my depth. I don't know the terrain, the lie of the land. So why don't you help me? Instead of sitting there sulking. Tell me what happened. Tell me about the murder you're working."

"What murder?"

"You think they're connected, don't you? That's what Haddow tells me. The bomb and the murder of this business-man." He looked at his notes. "This Graham Elliot."

"Gavin," McCormack said. "His name's Gavin Elliot. A former MP. It's just an idea. Just a theory."

"Based on what, though?"

McCormack sighed. "Based on Gavin Elliot was doing business with Hugh Maitland. The Barracks Bar was Maitland's pub."

"It's a squaddie pub, too, though."

"Like I said, it's a theory."

"Nothing else, then? Nothing else that ties them together? The bombing, the Elliot murder?"

McCormack thought about the camper van. Parked in Crawford Street. Parked in Garrioch Road. "Nothing. No. It just seemed like too much of a coincidence."

Spence nodded. "They happen," he said. "Coincidences. Keep us in the loop then, Detective. If something comes up, I'm first in line. Understood? You call me. Before anyone. Before Haddow." He bent his head to the papers on his desk. "A lot of people are watching this, McCormack. Waiting for a result. Powerful people."

McCormack stood up. "Really? There's people watching here, too. People whose fathers and brothers, sisters and sons went for a pint on Friday night and never came home. They're the people I'm paid to serve."

26

M cCormack needed some air. He stood on the low doorstep of Temple Police Station, watching the traffic flow down to the city. There was a horrible genius to it. The car bomb. Something as blandly ubiquitous as a parked car was now a weapon of war, might burst in jagged shards, shooting steel and shattered glass in all directions, punching through walls, shredding the flesh of nearby humans.

There was a car parked in front of the station on a double yellow line. An Austin Allegro. Beige. Tax disc displayed. Chrome trim glinting. As McCormack stood, taking drags on a cigarette, the car seemed to change before his eyes, seemed to squat like some kind of malevolent beast, preparing to spring.

He dropped his cigarette on the pavement, dragged his sole across it and sauntered across to the car. He walked right around it, stooping to study the short, sloping boot. Could a bomb be in there? Almost without thinking, he reached out and pushed the button with his thumb. It opened and the boot swung up. McCormack bent to look. There was a pair of woman's shoes, high heels, lying on their sides. A golf umbrella, red and white, tightly rolled. A spare wheel embedded in the wheel-well. Faint smell of creosote.

He closed the boot, walked round to the kerbside and bent to peer into the car's interior, his face pressed to the passenger window, his hands shading his eyes to kill the reflection.

"Here! Here! What the fuck!"

McCormack straightened up and turned. A man was striding towards him, a carrier bag in one hand, car keys swinging from the other fist. "The fuck you think you're doing?"

McCormack reached lazily into his inside pocket, flipped open his warrant card. "This your vehicle, sir?"

The man stiffened, reared back as if a force-field surrounded the card in McCormack's hand. "It is, aye. What's this about?"

"It's illegally parked."

"You're fucking kidding."

"You don't agree?"

"I was two minutes. Five, tops. I was getting some messages from round the corner." He hoisted the carrier bag in his left fist. "Couldnae get parked round there. So, you know, come on. Are you gonnae write me up?"

McCormack ignored the man's question. He nodded at the gutter, the two broad yellow stripes running next to the kerb. "What's that then?"

The man rubbed his thumb along his top lip. "You're a detective, right? All you boys in there. You're CID?"

"Detective Inspector," McCormack said.

"Right." The man looked off down the street, back at McCormack. "Business a bit slow today, is that it? You're bang up to date with all the robberies and rapes and murders? In-tray's lying empty?"

McCormack grinned. Not twelve yards away was a white-washed cell with soundproof walls, a sluice hole in a sloping floor. He felt the tension of the last few days draining out of him. He let his eyelids close.

"Sir!" The voice came from behind him, from the station doorway. McCormack opened his eyes.

"Sir. You'll want to hear this."

Nicol was on the doorstep. She looked at the man on the pavement and back at McCormack, a question in her eyes.

"Go on," he told her. "I'll be in directly."

"You park right outside a police station," McCormack said. "After what happened on Friday night?"

"I don't see. What does that— I mean, fuck. I'm buying fucking tatties." He held the plastic bag at eye-level, as though it was a lantern and he was studying McCormack by its light. "Tatties."

McCormack stepped towards the man, smiling, threw an arm round his shoulders and drew him in, drew his head close to McCormack's own, his lips almost touching the man's right ear. He spoke very softly. "Get to fuck," he told him.

He released the man and stalked back into the station.

Nicol was hovering in the corridor. "It's Quinn, sir. He's feeling the benefit of a good night's sleep. Made a remarkable recovery."

"You mean his memory seems to be returning?"

"Almost like magic," Nicol said.

Quinn was lying on his pallet when they opened his cell. "Did you bring a cup of tea at least?"

"You'll get your tea when you've earned it. Come on."

They took him along to the interview room. McCormack sat down at the desk like a man sitting down for his dinner. Nicol sat beside him. Quinn slid into the opposite chair and rubbed his jaw.

"Go on then," McCormack said briskly.

"I've got family," Quinn told them. "Over the water."

"Belfast?"

Quinn nodded.

"Addresses?"

"Look, I don't want them hassled."

"Too fucking late, son. I didn't want my mucker blown into tiny bits. Addresses."

He gave an address in the Short Strand area of the city.

"And what? Where do they come in?"

Quinn said they were connected. He said it was hard not to be connected in a place like that. He said the men they knew, in the Organization, they controlled a distillery in the Republic. They needed someone to get the whiskey to the mainland, supply the hotel and bar trade in London. Undercut the legitimate suppliers. The Quinns took care of that.

"For what?"

"For a taste." Quinn stuck his thumbs in the pockets of his suit waistcoat. He was still wearing the full suit, after a night in the cells. "Share of the profits."

"This is the warehouse that got torched? The Tradeston fire?"

Quinn nodded.

"You must have been popular."

Quinn turned to look at the blank tiled wall, as if there was a window in it. He lifted one shoulder, dropped it.

"I mean, what was it? A hundred barrels? More?"

"Aye." Quinn wiped his hands up and down his face. "Something like that," he said.

"And to be clear." McCormack pointed at Nicol's notebook, her pen poised over it. "This Organization we're talking about, this is the Irish Republican Army? The Provisionals?"

"If you tell them," Quinn said. "If they know I spoke to you, they'll kill me. I mean, you know that, right?"

"Well then." McCormack spread his hands. "It seems pretty clear what happened here, doesn't it? They asked you what the fuck was going on. You told them it was Maitland torched the warehouse. They sent someone over to even the score."

"Naw." Quinn shifted in his seat. "Naw. No one came over."

"You fingered the target. They did the op. That's how it works. Right?"

"They didnae do it. That's what I'm saying. It wasnae them."

Nicol spoke up, her voice high and clear in the tiled room. "How do you know?"

"How do I know?" Quinn looked at her. "They told me."

"Oh. O.K. then." McCormack nodded heavily. "I mean if they *told* you, that's that. Case closed."

Quinn smiled. Some of the tension seemed to have left his shoulders. He kept his gaze on Nicol but spoke to McCormack. "Why would they lie? It's not like they're embarrassed about it? Killing folk. That's their job. Bloody boast about it."

McCormack caught Nicol's eye. Quinn had a point. He leaned back, gestured for Nicol to take over.

Nicol looked down at the table for a second or two. "Can I get this straight?" She sighted down her pen at Quinn, as though it was a sabre. "Maitland burns down your warehouse. You don't lift a finger. It's IRA whiskey inside. *They* don't lift a finger. So who exactly, in your estimation, bombed the Barracks Bar?"

"You want to know where Lord Lucan is, too?" Quinn was shaking his head. "That's *your* fucking job, copper. *You* find the bad guys. I'm telling you who *didnae* do it."

"Right. I see." Nicol tapped the pen on her notebook. "You sound pretty close to them, though. I mean, you know what they did and didn't do, how they operate. And all you do is sell their whiskey? Wee errand boy for the Provos? Come on, Denny. You're in it deeper than that."

McCormack was nodding, hunched over the table.

"And you're up and down to London," Nicol said. "By your own admission. You wouldn't be helping them, Denny? With their little bombing campaign?"

"Aw, here it comes. Now you're gonnae frame me? Like youse are framing those boys in Birmingham? They didnae do it, either."

"Right. They told you, I suppose," Nicol said.

"The fucking 'Ra told me, matter of fact. The fucking 'Ra told me. Nobody in Belfast thinks these boys did it."

"So who did do it?" McCormack asked.

"Some other unit. I don't know. You think they'd tell me? Christ, you think I'd tell you if they did? Grassing on the Provos? Might as well do myself now. Get it over with."

He popped two fingers into his mouth, pistol-style, and mimed the shot, head jerking back.

"And that's all you did with them, Denny? Smuggle some booze? That's your line?"

"I swear to God. I mean, if someone needed a place to lie low, sometimes . . ."

"You provided safe houses. For the fucking IRA, Denny?"

"I gave some people a place to stay. I don't know if they were 'Ra or not. I never asked. They never told. I won't be fucking doing it again, thanks to you cunts and Maitland. Be lucky if they ever talk to me again."

"Oh I don't know, Denny. Those boys in Belfast. They might be giving *you* the safe house before you're done. Might want to think about relocating."

"Oh is that right? Go back to where I come from. That's the script, is it?"

"Not at all. I'm just thinking, if I was in your position, I'd take the guns and bombs of Belfast ahead of Walter Maitland. You about ready for the road?"

Quinn straightened up. "You letting me go?"

"I told you." McCormack took out his smokes, passed one to Quinn. "You're safer in here. Wouldn't last ten minutes out there. But if you're ready . . ."

"My funeral, right? Fucking watch me." Quinn was all bravado now. "I'll walk right down Maryhill Road on my way home. Have a quick half in the Duke."

"All right, Denny. Before you challenge the whole Northside to unarmed combat, one last thing. You know anyone who drives a camper van?"

"A what?" He was shooting his cuffs, tugging the points of his waistcoat. Was this a trick question?

"Volkswagen camper van. Like on *Scooby Doo*. You watch the cartoons, Denny? Green and white."

"What's this, a Celtic supporters' bus?"

"Just answer the question."

"Do I look like I drive a camper van? I drive a fucking MG, mate. Camper van!"

"Not you. Someone you know. An associate. Friend. Someone who works for you. Anyone."

Quinn started to shake his head, flinched, and gingerly patted the base of his skull. "Near cracked my fucking napper, so you did. Should sue the arse off you."

McCormack waited.

"No." Quinn looked at Nicol and back to McCormack. "I don't know anyone who drives a fucking camper van. Can I go now?"

"You better say a novena, Denny. Sacrifice a lamb and paint your door with its blood. Hope the wrath of Maitland passes you by."

"I'll paint my door with that cunt's blood if he tries anything. Tell him I said it."

They watched him swagger out past the charge bar.

Back in the Byre, Goldie was standing in front of the corkboard. The pictures were pinned there like some sort of creepy family tree. Walter Maitland at the top, his brother Hugh ("DECEASED" magic-markered below his name) to the right and slightly lower. Then beneath them in a row, like their four impossible adult kids, the truculent mugshots: Maitland's lieutenants.

"What do we reckon, then?" Goldie said. "Place your bets."

"Forget that just now." McCormack closed the door behind them. "This fucking gun, Nicol. What's the story?"

"Gun?" Goldie asked. "What gun?"

"She's only lost the fucking gun," McCormack said. "It's gone from the locker."

"The gun that Shand had? It's not gone." Goldie was laughing. "I took it."

"What are you talking about?"

"I knew they'd be looking for his things. To give to his fiancée, like. I borrowed Liz's key from her desk drawer. It's in there." He pointed to the filing cabinet. "Bottom drawer."

"Oh for fuck's sake, Derek. You couldn't have told us?"

"Haven't bloody seen you. I'm telling you now. Now, if we're all done throwing hissy fits, what about these jokers? Four-card monte: which one's the winner?"

They turned to study the snaps on the wall.

Maitland was smart enough to keep the circle small. He knew that the bigger the circle, the greater the chance it would break, that someone would go over to the cops or the Quinns. Apart from his brother, there were only four men he trusted. They all grew up in Maryhill, within three or four streets of the Maitland home in Fingal Street.

There was John McPhail, Maitland's first cousin, aged thirty-two. The family resemblance was clear in the cleft chin, the oddly neat ears and the widow's peak that had come down from Maitland's Highland grandfather. McPhail ran Maitland's brothels—the knocking-shops in Maryhill, Riddrie, Dennistoun, and the more upscale saunas in the West End and city centre. His ostensible job was owner-manager of a newsagent's in Maryhill. As family, McPhail had enjoyed a comparatively easy rise to the top. He'd done a stint of "hoosey"—juvenile detention at Polmont Young Offenders Institution—in his teens, but had never done time in an adult jail. He had the reputation of a wannabe hardman, riding his cousin's coattails.

Alex Kerr ran Maitland's rackets. Big, red-faced, forty-five. He drank whisky steadily, stoically, from morning till night, with no apparent impairment. He oversaw the money-lenders who did business in Maitland's Northside territories.

He collected the protection money from the shops and businesses in the same areas. He'd done serious time—twelve years
for armed robbery and he possessed the stillness and self-con-
tainment of a man who knew what boredom was. Kerr was a
born-again Christian, an elder in a Baptist tabernacle in
Possilpark. He sometimes carried a Bible on his rounds,
though the fear of God was rarely invoked. The fear of Walter
Maitland was generally enough.

The third photo showed a sneering Jackie Fleeting. All
streaked blond hair and capped incisors. The Nembutal stare.
Fleeting's beat was drugs and booze. He ran untaxed whisky
down to London's clubland—the very racket the Quinns
aimed to threaten with their Tradeston warehouse—and he
bossed the Maitlands' cannabis dealers. The Flamingo-print
Hawaiian shirt he was wearing was the quietest thing about
him. He drove a souped-up Cortina with a Dixie horn and
played bass in a pub-rock four-piece on weekends. In his late
teens he served three years in Barlinnie for assault with a
deadly weapon when he knifed his mother's boyfriend in the
neck.

The fourth face—a face you never wanted to see, when
opening your front door—was that of William "Bud" Hunter.
Maitland's muscle. Thirty-two, five feet ten: trim, fit, nasty.
Hunter worked across all of Maitland's businesses, sorting out
problems wherever they arose. Hunter had boxed for Scotland
at the 1970 Commonwealth Games in Edinburgh, taking wel-
terweight bronze against a Ghanaian southpaw. He wasn't big
for an enforcer but he was fast and hard and he had little trouble convincing people that he meant what he said.

They had to pick Shand's tout from this line-up and they
had to get it right. Bring in the wrong man and he'd go back
and tell Maitland there was a rat in the camp. Then Maitland
would identify and neutralize the tout before McCormack and
his crew even knew who it was. A high-stakes game, but they

were ready for it, there was a buzz in the Byre as they got down to business. It was like one of these riddles where one door leads to freedom and the other to a ravenous lion and you have to work out which was which.

"It could be the cousin," Goldie said, nodding at the mugshot of John McPhail. "Grows up in the shadow. Never gets the credit. Always second fiddle. Jealousy's a terrible thing."

"Jealousy's one thing," McCormack said. "Pig stupidity's something else. Think what he's got to lose, Derek. The others turn tout, all they're giving up's the gang. He's giving up his family too. They'd cut him off, the lot of them. McPhail's a mummy's boy. He's not cut out for that."

They mentally scored McPhail off the list. That left three: Kerr, Fleeting, Hunter.

"Let's think about the gun." McCormack said. "Whoever killed the dealer left his dabs on the gun. Now, whose job is it to dispose of rival drug dealers when the need arises?"

"Hunter."

"Hunter. So, if there was something personal here, if there was some kind of honour thing involved, then maybe Kerr or Fleeting pulled the trigger. But if it's purely business, then it's Hunter all the way. It's Hunter's job. He'd be pissed off if someone else got it."

"Hold on, though." Goldie tapped the photo of Hunter. "If Hunter's the professional, if he's the old hand, how come he leaves his dabs on the gun? He doesn't chuck it in the Clyde? Suddenly he's an amateur?"

"Who knows?" McCormack said. "He gets cocky. Starts thinking he's invincible. Or it's just carelessness. In any case, we play the percentages, Derek. It's all we can do. Let's assume that Hunter's the shooter."

"So it's Kerr or Fleeting who're setting him up. One of these two's the tout."

They stared at the photos, as if the guilty party might give himself away. As if the photos were the windows of an advent calendar and one of them hid the gold star.

"We need to find out who had a beef with Hunter," Goldie said. "One of these guys wants Hunter gone. Wants him gone bad enough to burn the whole house down."

"Get onto it, then," McCormack said. "Talk to your own touts. See if there's any word of Hunter falling out with either of these jokers."

Nicol had been quiet for a spell, sitting at her desk. She rose now and crossed to the corkboard. "Have either of these two lived outside Glasgow?" She tapped the photos of Kerr and Fleeting. "I mean, have they spent any length of time in a different city? Down south, maybe. Manchester, London."

"Not following you here." McCormack stood with his hands on his hips.

Goldie squinted at Nicol. "You're saying the tout was maybe working for a rival team? They were planning to muscle in?"

"No. I just mean, whoever was planning to shop Hunter, he knows he's finished in Glasgow. That probably means it's someone who knows there's a world outside this city. He knows he can make a life for himself someplace else. Because he's done it before."

"That's a thought, Nicol. Good. Look into it. Derek: get onto your touts. We need to move quickly with this, before Maitland finds out he's got a leaky boat. Kerr or Fleeting: let's aim to pick a winner tomorrow." He lifted his jacket.

"Bid for freedom?"

"I wish. Bid for my bloody bed. I'll be in a bit later tomorrow. Bloody Haddow wants me to talk to a Politics prof at the uni. Terrorism expert. Wild goose chase."

MONDAY, 7 JULY 1975

27

M cCormack followed the curve of University Gardens, enjoying the mid-morning sun on his face. Term was over and there was something secret and hopeful in the dormant campus, the flicker of the leaves on the lime trees, the sun-warmed stone of the buildings. Back home in Ballachulish, university had never seemed an option. Not to McCormack. You worked in the quarry or you joined the army. Maybe the polis, if you were feeling adventurous. But he wondered sometimes, when his job brought him up to Gilmorehill, what it might have been like to study here, to stroll these streets in earnest, hold court in the Beer Bar at the Union, drum your feet in lectures when the prof was deadly dull.

He passed the sign for Geography. Each of the houses in University Gardens contained a different department, as if each subject was a family. The House of History. The House of Archaeology.

He came to the junction with University Avenue. Off to his right were the glories of the quads and the cloisters and the Gothic clocktower but he turned left up the hill and cut down a lane to the ugliest structure on campus.

The Adam Smith Building was a concrete crate clad in roughcast panels the colour of rain clouds. A great square lift-shaft clamped to one end of the building had the look of an industrial incinerator. McCormack pushed through the double doors into the lobby and started up the stairs, past signs for Sociology, Economics and Anthropology.

On the third floor he found the Politics Department Office and asked for Professor Barclay. He followed the directions to the end of the west corridor. The door was slightly ajar, with a newspaper cartoon sellotaped to it: Richard Nixon, his arms outspread like a vulture's wings, his hands making V for victory signs. Above Nixon's right hand were the words "Foreign Policy Victories"; above the left, "Watergate Coverup". A voice boomed out from the room.

"You need to actually walk through the door. Otherwise I can't see you."

McCormack pushed the door with his fingertips. Professor John Barclay was sitting behind a large desk strewn with stacked folders, papers, curving towers of books. It looked like a kid had been building a play-fort out of solemn monographs on British foreign policy. The disorder of the desk was in sharp contrast to the man behind it. He wore a black pinstripe suit, bright white shirt and grey silk tie. More like a banker than a university don.

"Inspector McCormack." Barclay rose to shake McCormack's hand over the fortifications. "Take a seat. I understand you lost a colleague."

"That's right."

"I'm sorry to hear that. My condolences. Now, what is it you want to know, Inspector? You think this was our friends from across the water?"

"I want to know what *you* think." McCormack gestured at the shelves of books. "You're the expert."

"Well, it's certainly possible. But likely? I wouldn't have thought so. They haven't claimed it, have they?"

"They never claimed Birmingham."

"Birmingham was a mess, a complete fiasco. They mistimed the warning, didn't give the police a chance to clear the area. Who would want to claim that?" Barclay fiddled with a cufflink. "I take it there was no warning this time? No phone call to the police or papers? No codename?"

"Not as far as we know."

"Then it's probably not the Provisionals. That's a solid protocol. If they're hitting a civilian target—even a bar used by soldiers—they call in a warning."

McCormack nodded. "And if it's not the Provos?"

Barclay exhaled. "Well. Let's see. Who's been setting car bombs lately? Take your pick. Animal Liberation Front. The Angry Brigade. Up here you've got the Tartan Army. The Army of the Provisional Government. You know, the chaps who've been blowing up oil pipelines? But hitting a Glasgow pub? I can't see it. This pub, though. The papers are saying it's a local for squaddies. Is there anything else that makes it stand out?"

McCormack was distracted by the bookshelves. Rows and piles and columns of books. He wondered how many Barclay had read. "It's owned by the brother of a man we might describe as a person of interest," he said. "Plenty of interest."

"A gangster?" Barclay whistled. "Well there you are then. It's the rival gang, on the balance of probabilities. That explains why no one's claimed it. The message isn't aimed at you and me. It's aimed at your person of interest. And I imagine he got it. Loud and clear."

"Come on, though. Wannabe hardmen setting off bombs?"

"But that's the genius of it, Inspector. Don't you see? The car bomb's the ultimate equalizer. Anyone with half a brain and a jerrycan of fertilizer's got an army. You can be as powerful as you like, as well-protected as you like. The guy with the car bomb can get you. Think of the very first one. You know who invented the car bomb?"

"I'm assuming it wasn't the Irish."

"Italian-American anarchists. Sacco and Vanzetti's buddies. They parked a horse and cart in Wall Street. This is 1920. Gelignite in the wagon, outside J.P. Morgan and Co. Killed thirty-nine, injured hundreds. Dirt-poor Italian immigrants.

They shut down Wall Street. The Stock Exchange stopped trading for the first time ever."

"Barracks Bar in Maryhill's a far cry from Manhattan."

"Indeed, but the principle's the same." Barclay was getting into this now. He took two hands and pushed a stack of papers and books to the edge of the desk, freeing up space to gesticulate. "See, what you need to appreciate. On the one hand, the car bomb is a terrible thing. Horrible. It's devilish, really. But it's also, from the point of view of the bomber, a thing of beauty. A terrible beauty, but beauty nonetheless."

"'Too long a sacrifice can make a stone of the heart.'"

"You know your Irish poets, Inspector. Did you study here before joining the Force?"

"I didn't make it to university, no."

"Pity. Would have saved you from the misery of National Service. Jesus, what sadist invented that?"

"I didn't do National Service, either."

"No? Forgive me, you look old enough."

"I am old enough. I did a different kind of training. It didn't work out."

"Apprenticeship?"

"Something like that. You talked about beauty, Professor. There wasn't much beauty on Garrioch Road on Saturday night."

"No, no. I'm sorry. You're right. But look at it from the bomber's standpoint. Three things. One." Barclay jabbed his index finger at the ceiling. *Why do they always think and talk in threes?* McCormack wondered. "You can't escape a car bomb. Unless you're going to ban cars from cities—and we've just knocked down half of Glasgow to bring cars *into* the city—you can't isolate the threat. Any car on any street could be a bomb. Two. A car bomb is excellent publicity. You can't hide an explosion. You can't cover it up. Detonate a car bomb and you're on every front page. You're lead item on the news."

"And what's three?"

"You know what three is." Barclay smiled. "You've found out three this week. A car bomb destroys the very traces of the bomber. A group might claim it. But you can't pin it on an individual. All the traces are blown into dust. It's the perfect criminal device. It disposes of the evidence as it goes."

Barclay sat back. He seemed enormously pleased by his little recital. McCormack nodded and got to his feet. He had done what he'd been asked, jumped through Haddow's hoop. Time to go back and get on with his work. "Thanks for your time, Professor."

Barclay stayed sitting. He tapped his fingers against his lips. "What about this other thing? How's that progressing?"

McCormack buttoned his jacket. "What other thing?"

"Gavin Elliot."

"The Gavin Elliot investigation is receiving appropriate attention, Professor. Why the interest?"

Barclay took the silver pen from his breast pocket and bent to the papers on his desk. "Well," he said. "He never showed much patience in life. Nice to see someone making him wait a bit in death."

"You knew Gavin Elliot?" The door was open in McCormack's hand but he paused on the threshold.

"Knew him?" Barclay looked up, pointed the pen at McCormack. "You haven't done your homework, Inspector." He smiled. "I beat him."

"Beat him? How?"

"Took his seat off him in '72."

McCormack closed the door again. "You were a city councillor?"

"Still am. Some of us manage the practical side of the discipline, Inspector. Not just the theory."

McCormack sat back down at the desk. "Well, can you tell me about that? I mean, what was Elliot like? As a politician, did he have particular enemies?"

"You mean apart from me?" Barclay's jaw slackened waggishly. "Well, look, the thing is, we didn't overlap. By definition. But let's say Mr. Elliot cast a long shadow. A lot of people in George Square still talk about him. Not fondly."

"And why's that?"

"I think they feel he failed to measure up. There's an element of sacrifice involved in public service, Inspector. You have to give of yourself. Stand up and be counted. Otherwise, what's the point?"

"You're not on the stump," McCormack said. "You can practise that in your mirror, not on me."

Two lines appeared beside Barclay's mouth. "Corruption, Inspector. Is that blunt enough for you? Is that concise enough to hold your attention?"

"It is if you can stand it up."

"The Transport Committee," Barclay said. "The Housing Committee. You know what these committees did?"

"You're saying the names were a decoy?"

Barclay ignored this. "Roads, Inspector. They decided where the roads went. The course of the M8, specifically."

"So what?"

"'So what?'" he says. "Let's say you knew in advance where the motorway would go. How do you suppose you might use that information?"

"I suppose you might buy up properties in the relevant parts of the city. I also suppose that serving on these committees while sitting on the board of a property company might constitute a fairly obvious conflict of interest."

"Oh he came off the board," Barclay said. "He severed all connections with Wyndford Property. Supposedly. But if someone were to look at a map, they might find some interesting correspondences between Wyndford's portfolio and the course of the M8 motorway."

"They bought up buildings knowing that the Corporation

would have to acquire them through Compulsory Purchase."

Barclay shook his head. "Actually, it's worse than that. The Corporation *gave* some of its housing stock away. Handed it over to developers who promised to regenerate the areas. Then, when the course of the motorway gets decided, suddenly they have to buy it back. At market value."

"Elliot gave buildings to his company so that the Corporation could buy them back?"

"You have to admire the man's style, Inspector. The hidden hand."

McCormack jotted the names of the committees in his notebook. "And was there anyone in particular who seemed concerned at Elliot's conduct?"

"You're looking for suspects? In the city Corporation? 'Let Glasgow Flourish by the Wielding of the Sword?' I don't think so. Plenty of folk would have welcomed Gavin Elliot's demise. But do the deed themselves? That's not how we operate."

McCormack stood for the second time. He opened the door and then paused, as if confused about something.

"Is there something else, Inspector?"

"I don't know. It's just, you sit on this till now?"

Barclay's cufflinks winked as he held up his hands. "Elliot's money? Maitland's muscle? I'm not stupid, Inspector. That's not a fair fight."

"It's fair now? Only one of them's dead."

"Yes. Well, I'm counting on you to be discreet, Inspector. Keep my name in the background."

"Right. I forgot. Stand up and be counted," McCormack said. "Otherwise, what's the point?"

28

Kidd stood outside the bank on the Main Street of Largs and watched Yvonne walk away along Bath Street. He'd seen her twice since that time on the island, and each time they'd had more to talk about. He felt like he'd known her for months. He waited to see if she would turn around and when she did he grinned and returned her thumbs-up before setting off towards Gallowgate Street. They'd arranged to meet later, outside Nardini's. Have a fish tea, maybe stroll to the Pencil.

In the fine afternoon, with a bright stripe of sun on the firth and the cars queuing for the ferry, and the mild green hump of Cumbrae across the water, nothing seemed irretrievable. Maybe he could even talk them out of it, whatever they were planning for Yvonne. He had money in the bank with the Maitlands, surely. He'd killed four people for Walter Maitland. He could go to jail for Walter Maitland. He'd taken the war to the Quinns. Did that count for nothing?

At his own closemouth on Brisbane Road he stood for a spell on the pavement with the sun on his neck, breathing the salt air, sensing the vigour in his limbs, the pumping of his heart, the blood tingling in his fingertips. He pictured Yvonne's laughing face as he passed out of the sunshine into the cool gloom of the passageway. It would all work out.

He took the first flight of stairs in three lunging jumps, then he danced up the second in a quick sprint, touching each step, his feet a blur. He was inside the flat, standing at the sink drinking off a glass of water before he realized something was wrong.

A smell of cigarette smoke. Not his brand.

Glass still in hand he walked like a man in a dream to cross the hall and stand in front of the living-room door. It was slightly ajar. He put his fingertips to the door and pushed. The door swung open on a man sitting in the armchair by the window.

The man had been looking out of the window. He turned his head to look at Kidd without expression and then he turned back to the window. He took a deep drag on his cigarette and stubbed it out in an ashtray balanced on the arm of his chair.

Kidd still hadn't moved. The man looked at him again and jerked his head, a little spasm, to bring Kidd into the room.

He nodded at the sofa and Kidd dropped into it and water from the glass he carried slopped onto the thigh of his jeans. He brushed at it with his free hand.

"Christopher Kidd," the man said.

"Aye. That's me." Kidd nodded. The man studied him. Kidd swallowed. "Sorry, I'm just . . ." He waved a vague hand. "I'm a bit surprised."

"We were surprised too," the man said. "Just a bit."

"Right," Kidd said. "Right." He didn't need to ask who the *we* might be. He looked at the glass in his hand and raised it as if to take a drink, then decided against it.

"Would you like to know why?" the man was saying. "Would you like to know why we were surprised?"

Kidd half-shrugged. He shook his head, let some air escape from between his pursed lips. There must be words. Somewhere in his brain there must be words, somewhere in the universe, any words at all, but none would come.

"We were surprised because you were supposed to phone. That was the deal."

Kidd nodded. "I know. I mean I would have. I was about to phone."

"You were supposed to phone when you found the woman." The man lifted a mug from the windowsill and raised it to Kidd. "By the way, I made myself a cup of tea. I hope you don't mind." He drained the mug and set it back on the sill.

Kidd said nothing.

"You *did* find the woman?" With his raised eyebrows the man looked almost camp. "I mean, I'm assuming it's Yvonne Gray? The woman you've been seeing?"

Kidd understood that he knew. The man knew. There was no possibility of fudging this. "Well. I wanted to be sure," Kidd said. "Before I, you know, called."

"Before you called," the man said.

"Right. Like I said."

"You've got her photo," the man said. "You know what she looks like. How fucking sure do you need to be?"

"I didn't want to waste your time."

The man smiled thinly. "Bit late for that."

Kidd looked at the floor. The tension of the past few days was draining out of him. He almost felt relieved. It was a holiday he'd been on. A little break, a diversion. It wasn't reality. What did you think, it was happy ever after with a Woodlands Road scrubber in a seaside resort? You could just pack up your troubles and sail off into the sunset?

"Hey. Don't be so hard on yourself. You found her, didn't you? You did your job."

Kidd looked up at the man, nodded. "So what happens now?" he said.

"Aye." The man clicked his tongue. "Well. That's the question, isn't it?"

"I mean how much does she owe? How much money?"

He was looking at Kidd almost sadly. "Really? You want to take on her debt, too? You don't think maybe you're in deep enough, son. On your own account? Four folk dead."

"I'm asking how much she owes."

"Four people dead. A deliberate fire. And the fingers all pointing in one direction. To us. To Mr. Maitland. Maybe you should be thinking about that."

"I did what I was told," Kidd said. "I followed my instructions."

"Don't tell me," the man said. "You think I give a fuck? There's four folk deid. That's the bottom line. Your fault. Mr. Maitland's problem."

"But what's the figure? There has to be a figure."

The man shook his head. "Honestly? It's gone a bit beyond that, Christopher. It's gone beyond weekly fuckin payments."

Kidd looked out the window. He could hear the distant sound of the shows from the promenade, the music from the waltzers. People were out there laughing, enjoying themselves, stuffing candyfloss into their faces.

". . . and that's the position. O.K.?"

He turned back. The man was still speaking.

"You want to act the big man. You want to stand at the top boys' corner in the Duke. With your two-quid haircut and your fifty-quid suit. Comes at a price, son. This is the deal."

Kidd nodded. He'd known, as soon as he saw the man sitting in the chair, what the end would be. Maybe he'd known it all along. He had no particular desire, now, to lord it over the punters in the Duke of Perth. He didn't want to be one of the Maitland crew. But nor did he fancy a decade of slopping out in HMP Peterhead.

"So what did she do?" he asked. "At least tell me that. What did she do that was so bad?"

The man leaned forward and spoke softly. "That's none of your fucking business. That's Mr. Maitland's business. He's done his job, son. Do yours."

The man sat back, tugging the points of his waistcoat, brushing specks of dust from the sleeves of his suit. He grinned at Kidd. Kidd saw that he'd been asking himself the wrong question. The question wasn't what it feels like to kill. It was what it feels like to *force* a man to kill.

But even coercion comes at a price.

"Do it for what?" Kidd said. "Mr. Maitland's good opinion?"

The man raised his eyebrows, a kind of sardonic approval coating his eyes. "Well, now. We don't want to stop a fella getting ahead. What did you have in mind?"

"I'll do her for a grand."

The man cocked his head at Kidd. "A grand? That's a different picture, son. That's the main feature. You're the wee picture."

"You're paying for the job. Job's the same, whoever does it."

"Still, though. Five hundred's nearer the mark. Half now."

What choice did he have? "Let's see it, then."

The man dug into his hip pocket and drew out a folded wad. He thumbed tens onto the coffee table, counting as he went. He squared them off with his fingers, left them in a tidy stack.

"Look at you," the man said. "Proper button man. You've done four already, without even trying. Who knows what you could do if you put your mind to it?" He stood up and stretched. As he walked to the door he stopped beside Kidd's chair and clamped a hand on Kidd's shoulder. "Phone us when it's done, Christopher. Pick your moment. Just don't be too long about it. All right?"

He clapped Kidd's shoulder, twice, in a gesture of encouragement or condolence. Then he was gone, the door swinging free. Kidd sat on the sofa, hearing the footsteps echo on the stairs, a jaunty snatch of whistling in the closemouth. Then a car door closed, followed by an engine revving and dying away.

29

Victor was in the kitchen, just after five, chopping carrots with a kind of murderous determination. He glanced up and nodded as if McCormack was a distant acquaintance and bent to his task, his mouth as straight and hard as the knife. *Shunk. Shunk.* McCormack tossed his jacket on the armchair and started to roll up his sleeves. He wanted to cross to Victor and kiss him but something in the set of Victor's shoulders, the angle of his forearms, acted like a force-field.

"Smells good," McCormack said. There was mince browning in a pot on the stove. The scent of almost-singed meat filled the kitchen.

"Uh-huh."

Victor kept chopping. The sound of the knife hitting the board was alarmingly loud in the small room. McCormack crossed to the stove. He plucked a wooden spoon from the utensil drum and broke up the mince, clacking the spoon on the pot as he turned the crumbling meat. He found the lid and clamped it to the pot, drained the fat into the sink and put the pot back on the stove. He took the just-boiled kettle and tipped boiling water into the pot, stirred it through and turned down the heat. He wiped his hands on the dishtowel that hung from the chrome bar on the oven's door.

Victor still hadn't spoken. It's a good thing, McCormack thought wryly, it's a good thing there's a detective present. Someone to deduce that something's up. Victor was aggrieved about something and now, suddenly, McCormack was too. He was tired. He'd spent the past nine hours struggling to make sense of a brutal murder and a bombing that killed six. Victor had been making mince.

But then, just as it threatened to boil over, McCormack's anger died. The flame just dropped. Who knew what kind of day Victor had been having? He'd given up everything—his home, his job, family and friends—to come up here and make a go of it in Glasgow. He was entitled to the odd bad day. So, then, how to play it? Ask straight out what was wrong? Or talk around Vic's mood in the hope it might disperse on its own?

McCormack loosened his tie. He cast around for a neutral subject.

"Any mail?" he asked casually.

The question seemed to infuriate Victor. The knife wavered in the air like a dowsing rod.

"'Any mail?' says he. 'Any *mail?*'"

McCormack felt his anger bubbling back. "It's a simple question, Victor. A yes or no answer would usually do."

"Yes!" Victor pronounced the syllable with venomous clarity. "Yes, Duncan! There is mail. There is quite a lot of mail, in fact."

He looked up long enough to jerk his head at something across the room. McCormack followed Victor's gaze to the mantelpiece where he saw, his stomach clenching, a little stack of letters.

"Oh, Victor."

"What?" Victor stopped chopping and straightened up, the knife hanging loose at his side. His eyebrows climbed steeply. "What is it, Duncan? You were saving them up? I mean, not to answer them. O.K. That's one thing. But not to *read* the bloody things?"

He started chopping again, then tossed the knife down with

a sudden clatter and slumped where he stood, blotting an eye with the back of his hand.

McCormack crossed and held him, pulled him in tight. "Ah, Victor. Vic. Listen, I'm sorry. I'm sorry."

Victor's arms hung loose at his sides but he endured the hug. McCormack gripped all the tighter. "I couldn't face them, Vic. I couldn't do it. I didn't have the stomach. I knew what they would say and I didn't have any answers. I ran away. I'm sorry."

Victor's arms came gingerly up and held McCormack. "But why, Dunc? What made you go?"

For a minute, McCormack's laboured breathing was the only sound. "It's this . . . half-life, Vic," he said finally. "Caring, but not too much. Meeting up three times a week but not living together. Not risking too much. Watching your back. I could do it with the others. I didn't mind that. But not with you. It was easier to, easier to finish, than settle for that."

They stood there holding one another. An ice-cream van's chimes sounded tinny in the distance. McCormack let his forehead rest in the crook of Victor's neck. He could feel the breath from Victor's nostrils on his cheek. He felt the ache in his arms and chest and legs from digging through the rubble of the Barracks Bar bomb. He closed his eyes.

"It's the job, too," he said. "I can't do this job looking over my shoulder, Vic. I can't do it. It's hard enough without that."

Victor gripped him by the shoulders and held him off, scanning his face with a tragic earnestness. "But I can help. Don't you see that? I can make it easier. Take your troubles away. Not add to them. We can be careful, Dunc. I'll get a job. I'll get a place of my own. We can do this. We can do it."

And now he pulled McCormack close and they kissed, slow and deep, and then they stagger-stumbled like one unwieldy creature to the bedroom where Victor detached himself and pushed McCormack two-handed in the chest. McCormack fell back on the bed as Victor dropped to his knees, tugging at McCormack's belt and hauling down McCormack's trousers. His hands braced on the bed, on either side of McCormack's thighs, Victor lowered his head. McCormack lay back, arms above his head, and watched the ceiling and concentrated on making as little noise as he could. At times like these it felt to McCormack as though the flat was a cage of netting suspended in the middle of the building, its walls a porous membrane. He was alive to every creak and dunt, the thinness of the walls, as if the tenement block was a kind of aural panopticon that funnelled every sound to the other residents, let everyone eavesdrop on their business.

And then, just as suddenly, he didn't care, he was lost in the soft, insistent rhythm and he lay on his back with the backs of his hands gently batting the mattress. He lay like someone on the ocean floor, as though with every dip of his head Victor was drawing him to the surface, floating him up through the murky depths to the lighter, sunshot reaches and on towards the wavering surface whose skin he would shortly break.

And then, just at the bit, just as McCormack arched and buckled as Victor brought him off, somebody coughed.

It might have been a third occupant of the bed, it sounded so close. They froze, eyes locked in fear and shock. And then Victor's eyes widened in mock horror. Flopping down dramatically, he played dead and McCormack felt the laughter bubble up, a snitter, a snort. He clenched his fists, bit Victor's shoulder, but the laughter wouldn't be stemmed and it spouted out of him like a river, a torrent, the two of them gripping each other and shaking as the laughter poured through them.

They lay back, spent. A door slammed in next door's flat and McCormack's bandaged fingers found their way to

Victor's face, felt the sweat at his temples, his damp springy curls.

Later, after dinner, they held the letters over the sink and burned them, ceremonially, one by one. The letters were a liability, they could have fallen into the wrong hands. There was no point in taking silly risks.

30

L iz Nicol steered the Wolseley up Woodlands Road, glad to turn her back on the dismal five-lane valley of the new motorway. Weren't streets supposed to link things? The M8 had split the city in two, driving a tarmac trench between the city centre and the West End. Woodlands Road used to share something of the buzz of Sauchiehall Street; now it felt like the outer suburbs.

She turned up Lynedoch Street, climbing towards the triple towers of Trinity College, black against the night-time sky. There were bin bags sagging in heaps beside the college walls, glinting in the streetlights. She hung a right down Lynedoch Place, back down the hill into Woodlands Gate, rolling to a stop halfway down the slope.

She parked in the lee of an elm tree and killed the engine. From where she sat she could see a stretch of Woodlands Road that included the pink neon sign of Healing Hands and the doorway with the buzzer. She was less than fifty yards away, but up here on the slope she would be difficult to spot. A wedge of grassy banking to her left marked the outer edge of Kelvingrove Park. To her right was the shuttered bulk of St. Jude's Free Presbyterian Church.

Nicol reached behind her for the handles of a drawstring shopping bag. She drew out a tartan flask with a white plastic cup and propped it between the seats. Then she took out a package in greaseproof paper and opened it on the passenger seat. She lifted a sandwich and took a bite, chewing slowly. She

thought about Yvonne Gray. She had managed to get hold of
Yvonne Gray's neighbour, Carol Bissett, the woman who sometimes watched Yvonne's son. Bissett claimed that Yvonne had
left without warning, as if on the spur of the moment. As if she
was scared, Nicol thought. She took another bite of her sandwich. Maybe the fact that Yvonne Gray had worked in the
Barracks Bar was a coincidence, but Nicol didn't think so. Like
cops the world over, she didn't believe in coincidence. There was
no point in making another visit to the sauna, but if she could get
one of the women on their own, maybe she could find out more
about Yvonne. She wound down the window an inch or two to
let the night air in. Keeping the doorway of Healing Hands in
view, she felt for the mechanism at the side of the seat and gave
the knob a couple of twists, reclining the seat just a little.

She was in for the long haul.

As it turned out, she didn't have long to wait. Less than an
hour later she spotted a woman emerging from Healing
Hands. The woman walked with her head down, heading west,
and at first Nicol took her for a cleaner. She wore jeans and
training shoes, a dark anorak, and her hair was scraped back in
a ponytail. But she walked with the lithe, easy gait of a young
woman and she carried some sort of sports bag or holdall on
her shoulder.

Nicol was out of the car and across the street in seconds.
She fell into step with the woman as she turned down West
End Park Street.

The woman quickened her pace.

"Miss. A word, please. Miss!"

The woman turned, shaking her head. Her gaze took in
Nicol's warrant card and Nicol's face with the same disdain.
"Oh brilliant. They send the wee lassie to hassle the hoors."

Nicol stowed the card in her raincoat pocket. "Hold on,
here. Nobody 'sent' anyone. And less of the 'wee lassie':
Detective Constable, thanks very much."

"Right." The woman looked Nicol up and down. "It's a step up from making the tea, I suppose."

Nicol took a step towards her. She said quietly, "It's a step up from something."

"Oh really? Fuck you." The woman hitched her bag and turned to leave.

Nicol caught her arm. "You want a trip to Anniesland, that's fine. Nice cosy interview room in Temple cop shop. Makes no odds to me."

The woman glanced down to where Nicol's hand bunched the fabric of her anorak. Nicol released her grip. "It's up to you."

"You not got proper criminals to catch?"

"Let's see. Proper criminals?" Nicol folded her arms. "How about Walter Maitland? Does Walter Maitland count?"

Straight away, she wished she hadn't said it. The woman's sneering face just dropped. Shutters down, lights out. "Don't know about that," she said. She looked at the ground.

"Look, I don't care what you've been doing. Honest. I don't. I'm trying to find one of your colleagues. She's gone missing."

The woman glanced up, smirking again—at the word "colleagues", no doubt—and she hitched her holdall higher on her shoulder. "No one's gone missing."

"You're supposed to make eye-contact," Nicol said. "When you tell a lie. Means it's not so much of a giveaway. When I say someone's missing, I'm talking about Yvonne."

The woman said nothing.

"Yvonne Gray," Nicol said. "Know her well, did you? See her outside work, spend much time with her?"

"Oh for fuck sake. This is the plan, is it? This is how you fit in with the other cops. How you get the men to like you. Hassling other women? Asking stupid questions?"

"You think that's how you get men to like you? Jesus, you're in the wrong job, hen."

Despite herself, the woman smiled, her sealed lips splitting, the streetlight sliding over wet-look lip-gloss. She had changed her clothes but she hadn't taken off her make-up. Nicol smiled too. "It's just a few questions. It won't take long. Look, we can go to a caff, my car's up the street. Get you something to eat."

"Ah, fuck it." The woman nodded at a nearby flight of steps. "This is my close. We can talk in here. Come on."

Nicol followed the woman up the stairs. She could see something pointy—a high-heeled shoe, probably—pressing against the leather of her Gola holdall.

Inside the flat, the woman snapped on the lights, slung her holdall on the sofa, and motioned Nicol to an armchair. She stood with her hands on her hips. "I'm Rona, by the way. Rona Shaw. You want a coffee?"

Nicol undid the belt of her raincoat, worked the buttons. "That would be great, Rona. I'm Liz."

Rona disappeared into the little kitchenette and Nicol made a recce of the room. There was a navy leatherette sofa and two armchairs. In front of the darkened electric fire stood a wooden clothes horse draped with tights and underwear. On top of the sideboard was a glinting tray with a huddle of bottles—gin, Cinzano, the custard-yellow of Advocaat—beside a cut-glass decanter of whisky. Nicol wondered if Rona entertained in here, if there were clients who had struck up a private arrangement. She opened the top drawer of the sideboard and paused for a second or two; then she slid it shut.

Rona came back with two mugs of black coffee, a bottle of Bailey's Irish Cream wedged under her arm. The bottle was beaded with condensation.

Nicol took a seat in one of the armchairs. "You do know Yvonne Gray's left? We went to her place: she's gone. Flitted."

Rona knelt beside the coffee table, set the mugs down, a teaspoon clanking in her own mug. The bottle cap rasped as she unscrewed it and glugged some Bailey's into her mug, the spoon tinkling as she stirred.

"People move on," she said. "That's what happens. Just a matter of time with Yvonne. You want some of this?" She proffered the bottle.

"I'll take it black, thanks. What do you mean, a matter of time?"

Rona frowned. She settled back against the base of the sofa, her knees drawn up in front of her. She waved her mug in Nicol's direction. "You've seen her, right?"

Nicol nodded.

"Come on, then. She's mid-thirties if she's a day. I mean, Jesus, she was working for the *old* boss. The guy who got killed."

"John McGlashan?"

"She used to talk about him. Fuckin scary-sounding dude. No wonder somebody topped him."

Nicol nodded. The hierarchy of Glasgow hookers was unforgiving as the caste-system, but a little more fluid. Yvonne was on the slide. "You mean her days were numbered? At Healing Hands?"

Rona took a swig of her coffee, licked the cream off her top lip. "She'd have been back on Bothwell Street within the year. Or maybe one of the knocking-shops in Maryhill." She shook her head at the thought. She could afford to. Even in jeans and a black T-shirt—she'd ditched her anorak in the kitchenette Rona was worth looking at. Her slender arm tautened gracefully as she stretched to set her mug on the coffee table. She was all legs and cheekbones, green eyes with plenty of milky white, rimmed in kohl. It would be a long time before she needed to worry about Bothwell Street. She seemed to read Nicol's mind. "I'm not gloating," she said. "It'll come to us all."

"But Yvonne wasn't moving on," Nicol said. "She was running. She dropped everything and fled. You know she's got a kid?"

"She told me, aye. A wee boy. Running from what?"

"That's the question. She took the kid and left. We think she heard something. Maybe saw something." Nicol paused. "Look, Rona, it's natural to feel loyal to a friend—"

"I don't know what she saw. I don't know where she went. She wasnae my friend."

"Wasnae?"

Rona flapped a slim wrist. "Isnae. Whatever. You're the one saying she's gone." She reached for her mug, buried her nose in it.

"You want them to find her?" Nicol jerked her thumb at the door. "Is that what you want? Maitland's boys? 'Cause you can bet they're looking. Much better we find her first, Rona."

"And what? Set her up in a nice wee flat on the moon?" Nicol said nothing. Rona raised her eyebrows. "No? Because if it's somewhere on this particular planet, Walter Maitland'll find her. He'll find me, too, if I tell you anything. What's your name again? Liz something."

"Liz Nicol."

Rona grinned. "Lizzie Nicol! Wee Lizzie Nicol's gonnae save me from Walter Maitland." She raised her mug in a toast. "Full marks for humour, I'll give you that."

Nicol didn't smile. "Our gang's slightly bigger than his," she said. "If it comes to picking sides."

"Is that right? I'll take my chances."

"I don't fancy them. I could huckle you right now for what you've got in that top drawer."

Rona craned round slowly to look at the sideboard; she led with her jaw when she turned back to Nicol. "You fucking bitch."

"Yeah, yeah. Walter Maitland gonnae save you from Wee Lizzie Nicol? Let's hear it, Rona. Where's Yvonne Gray?"

Rona lunged forward and snatched the bottle, glaring at Nicol. The rasp of the screwtop flared like a hiss as she tipped another measure into her coffee. She smacked the bottle down on the coffee table and leaned back against the sofa. She reached up with one hand and tugged the scrunchy from her ponytail, shook loose her hair.

"She talked about getting away," she said.

"London?"

"Nah. Just to the coast. Ayrshire. She grew up there, from what she said."

"She grew up in a home, Rona. In Bishopbriggs. She was looked-after."

"Was she? Right. Well, maybe she was making it up. Like I said, I'm not her friend. I didnae know her that well."

Nicol watched her glug down some more of the fortified coffee. "So what did she say, then—about where she grew up?"

"She said it was on the coast. She talked about the Red House. How she'd go back to the Red House one day."

"What does that mean? Red roof? Red paint?"

"The Red House. I don't know. That's all she called it. And how you could see the boats out on the water. All the boats with their white sails. I don't know if she was making it up now, if you're saying she grew up in a home."

Nicol was writing this down. She looked up. "What else, Rona? Who lived in the Red House? Was it a holiday home? A bed and breakfast?"

"I don't know. But she said there was an island, too. You could see an island."

"From the Red House? What island was this? Was it Arran? Bute?"

"She never said. She had a name for it, though."

Nicol waited. She drew a line under her notes, rested the point of the pen on the paper. "What was the island, Rona?"

"She called it Crocodile Island."

Nicol wrote it down. It was like something out of Enid Blyton. The Famous Five. "You don't get crocodiles in the Firth of Clyde, Rona, not the last time I looked."

Rona shrugged. "That's what she called it."

Nicol closed her notebook, stowed it in her handbag. "You know she used to work in the Barracks Bar?"

"She mentioned it."

"Hugh Maitland's pub."

"I don't know about that."

"O.K. then, Rona." Nicol drained her coffee. "Thanks for your time."

Rona nursed her mug. She was half-smiling into it. She looked up. "You want to ask me then? What it's like. Go ahead. I don't mind."

Nicol clicked her ballpoint pen, clipped it to her inside pocket. She didn't meet Rona's eyes. "What what's like?"

"You know what. Six in the same night. Seven or eight sometimes."

"I'm not your priest, Rona. I'm not judging you."

"Right." She chewed her bottom lip. "You were my priest, I'd probably have fucked you. Your husband too. You got a husband?"

The question ambushed her. Nicol buried her chin in her chest. "No. I— Not anymore."

"You mean he's dead?"

Nicol clenched her right hand, unclenched. "He left," she said. "Ran off with some stupid wee—" She bit it back, the hard word, smiled at the floor, shaking her head. "He left. All right?"

"Some stupid wee hoor?" Rona said. "But you're not judging. Right."

Nicol looked up. "I'm *not* judging. It would have been better if she did what you did. More honest."

"There's hoors and there's hoors, is that it?"

"Something like that. Look, I don't want to fight, Rona. I want to find Yvonne. You're sure she didn't say anything else? About the place down the coast."

"The Red House. A view of the island. That was all. Crocodile Island."

"You'll let me know," Nicol set a card down on the coffee table, rose to her feet. "If you think of something else?"

Rona stayed sitting, cradling her mug of Bailey's-laced coffee. She nodded at the coffee, didn't raise her head as Nicol left.

31

Victor came in from the pub. After dinner he'd gone out for a couple of pints with his ex-army mates, guys he'd served with in Korea, guys who'd stayed with the regiment when the fighting stopped, when their National Service was over. They met up every few weeks in a bar in the city centre. When they found out Victor was coming to town, they'd invited him along.

"Roasted cheese?" Vic was rubbing his hands together briskly. He always had a hunger on him when he came in from the pub.

"Aye, great, Vic. Thanks." McCormack went back to his notebook. He was working on his speech. It was the funeral on Tuesday and Shand's fiancée had asked McCormack to say a few words. He was aware of Vic padding back and forth behind him in the walk-in kitchen. The rattle of the grill pan. The irregular *thunk* of the knife against breadboard as Vic shaved slices from the block of cheddar. Vic breathing through his nose like a trotting horse. The kettle bubbling up and clicking off, the chink and clatter of teaspoons.

"All right. Here we are! Get outside that."

Vic laid two plates of roasted cheese on the coffee table, went back for the mugs of tea. They sat across from each other, plates on their laps. The smell of melted cheese and slightly burnt toast seemed to spark McCormack's hunger. He bit greedily into a slice, the hot cheese nearly burning his gums. They ate in silence, slurping their tea.

"Christ, that was good." McCormack wiped his lips with a paper tissue, held out his mug to clink it with Vic's.

"Good night?" McCormack asked. Vic didn't answer. He set his plate down on the table. "That Gavin Elliot," he said.

McCormack reached for his smokes. "What about him?"

"You said his hands had been bashed."

McCormack did this sometimes, talked things through with Vic, picked his brains. Work stuff. He frowned. "You weren't discussing this with your mates?"

"Don't be stupid, Dunc. But the geezer's hands. They'd been knocked about?"

"Broken fingers." McCormack lit up, shook out the match. "Two on each hand."

"Feet and all?"

McCormack took a long drag on his cigarette, eyes narrowed against the smoke. He exhaled slowly, studying Vic. "Elliot's feet were badly bruised. Snapped metatarsals. One of the ankles was swollen to twice its natural size. The other ankle was chafed and raw. He'd lost two toenails on his right foot."

Vic nodded, breathed out heavily through his nose. He nodded again, gathered the plates and crossed to the sink. He ran the water and squirted some Fairy Liquid onto each plate in turn, wiped them with the scourer and rinsed them under the tap. He stacked the plates on the rack on the draining board and lifted a tea towel from the hook before McCormack lost his patience.

"You're not gonnae tell me then? What the fuck's going on here, Vic?"

Vic carried on drying the plates, his big shoulders moving under his checked shirt. When he'd stowed the plates in the cupboard he turned and leaned against the worktop with the dishtowel over one shoulder.

"And these injuries—how did he come by them? I mean, I assume there's a theory?"

McCormack shifted in his chair. "The pathologist believes the injuries to the feet are consistent with someone having stamped on him. Possibly in heavy boots. Also, he'd been shackled by one ankle. The fingers were struck with something hard, a pipe or baton. Length of hose maybe. He was tortured, Vic. They tortured him. That's the theory."

Vic nodded. "I think I know," he said. "I think I know what happened here, Dunc."

"What the hell are you talking about?"

"You can't bring me into it." Vic pointed at McCormack across the room. "I'm serious, Dunc. You can't say you got it from me. O.K.?"

"Got what, for Christ's sake? You haven't told me anything."

"I mean it."

"Yes, Vic! Jesus! I'll keep you out of it. What the fuck." McCormack was on his feet now. For some reason he felt he needed to be fully upright when he heard this.

There was a smile snagging the corner of Vic's mouth and then he was deadly earnest. "There's a guy in the group," he said. "Came out of the regiment a couple of years back. He said something tonight."

"I thought you didn't talk to them."

"Would you listen, for chrissake!"

McCormack waited. He studied the end of his cigarette, avoiding Vic's eyes.

"This is something he'd never tell anyone outside the group. I shouldn't even be telling you."

McCormack nodded. He smoked and studied the glowing fag-end.

Vic was folding the dishtowel, folding it in half and then half again. He set it on the countertop. "He served in Ulster, this guy. He said they ran some kind of experiment. The army and the RUC. Special Branch, I'm guessing."

McCormack felt the skin on the back of his neck tighten. "What kind of experiment?"

"They lifted Catholics. Civil Rights guys, mostly. Low-level nationalists. Choppered them off to some interrogation centre outside Belfast. But they flew them around a bit first. Made the flight seem longer. Told them they were in England when they landed."

"So what was the experiment?"

"Actually, before they landed—get this—they got the choppers to hover just six feet off the ground. Then they threw them out the door. The guys were hooded, they thought they were goners. Goodnight Vienna."

"And the experiment," McCormack said again. "What was the experiment?"

"Sensory deprivation, basically," Vic said. "They kept these guys hooded. Put them in boiler suits. Naked except for these boiler suits and hoods."

McCormack was quiet now, the cigarette forgotten in the ashtray.

"They used white noise," Vic continued. "Kept them in a stress position for two days and nights. You know what that is, a stress position?"

McCormack shook his head tightly. "Show me."

"You're facing a wall." Vic pushed off the sink and crossed to the little kitchenette wall, faced it, his voice muted now as he continued. "Legs apart. Leaning on the wall with your fingertips. All the weight of your body on your fingertips. Splayed."

McCormack wanted to try it. He turned to the living-room wall, moved an occasional table out of the way. He spread his legs and leaned onto the wall.

"Now try and hold it," Vic said.

He felt like a pianist with his fingers on the keys, waiting for inspiration, waiting for the music to start. And then it did.

After only a minute or two. The skin was white around his fingernails. His calves were tight and his fingers felt like hot points of light burning into the wall. But the wall stayed firm, seemed to push back against him.

"Now hold it there. Hold it there or I'll smash your fingers with this here truncheon," Vic said, mugging a thick Ulster accent. "Ya Fenian cunt. Ya shiftless fucking soapdodging Taig."

McCormack snorted. He wanted to laugh but the pain was too great. He held it for as long as he could.

"Fuck it." He collapsed his fingers into fists, rested his forehead on the wall. Vic mimed slamming a truncheon onto McCormack's fists. McCormack turned and slumped back against the wall, drawing Vic towards him.

"I've cracked," he told Vic. "I'll tell you everything." He was gripping Vic's collar in his fists, bunching the soft flannel. They kissed, briefly, awkwardly, foreheads bumping as McCormack resettled his weight. Vic pulled away, gently. "But that's the thing," he said. "They didn't actually want information. Most of the victims were civvies, or very low-ranking 'Ra. They knew nothing worth knowing."

"What then?" McCormack was flexing his throbbing fingers, bunching his fists, unbunching them. He could taste the beer from Victor's mouth. "What were they doing it for? What did they want?"

"They wanted to know how human beings coped with those levels of stress. What it would take to break a dozen healthy young men. It was an experiment. Like something with lab rats."

"Jesus." McCormack straightened up against the wall. He paced towards his phantom in the window, pressed his head against the cold black glass. "That's what he was doing, then? Whoever killed Elliot. He was putting him through the same experiment."

"The 'five techniques'," Vic said. "That's what they call it."
He told them off on his fingers. "Hooding, white noise, sleep
deprivation, stress position. What else? Oh, food: they didn't
give them food or drink."

Nothing in his stomach. The swollen bile duct. "Listen,
Vic." McCormack's tone had clenched. In a voice consciously
devoid of intimacy, he said, "I'm going to need the name. I
mean, you knew that before you told me, didn't you? I need to
know."

"You're not serious? You fucking *are* serious! Fuck off,
Dunc. No way. I told you at the start. No names, no fucking
pack-drill."

"Murder, Vic. This is a murder inquiry."

"I don't care if it's the fucking Quaker come back to life.
You're not getting the name, Duncan. That's not happening."
He crossed back to the sink, started mopping up the water
from the draining board. "I should never have opened my
fucking mouth."

And that was that. Vic went righteously to bed and
McCormack got the bottle of Grouse down from the cupboard
and smacked it onto the table.

If Vic kept shtum they were screwed. There was no way
McCormack could ferret out the names of soldiers who'd been
party to this kind of op. An op whose very existence would be
denied. An op that never happened.

He took a sip of whisky. But if he knew the name of Vic's
buddy he could quiz the guy discreetly, get him to think back.
Was there a man among the detail on that particular op who
stood out, who was a little wrong, a little out of true? A man
with a Glasgow background, maybe?

But there was no point badgering Vic. Two fights in one
day. Already McCormack had spotted the old withdrawal in
Victor, a tincture of distance, as if Vic was remembering how
things ended the first time round and was pondering whether

they'd be down this road again. There was no choice here, no room for debate: if he wanted to be with Vic he would have to let this drop.

He took his whisky glass and poured what was left down the sink and went through to the room.

Vic was lying on his side, his shoulder like a flank of beef beneath the covers. McCormack stripped to his boxers and slipped in beside him. He thought about pulling on Vic's shoulder, tugging that firm, broad body round towards him and he lay for a while imagining the precise warmth of Vic's skin beneath his hands. But he flopped back onto his own cool slice of the bed, folded his hands on his stomach, let his eyes adjust to the dark. He could make out the shape of his dark suit hanging on the wardrobe door, a white shirt bisected by a stripe of black tie.

The few times he'd been with women there had been moments like this, arctic silences when a green crevasse appeared to have split the bed in two. He'd thought then that being with a man would be different, they would be close enough or same enough to avoid these moments, but it wasn't true. He turned on his side and plumped the pillow and felt the echo of pain in his fingers. What did Gavin Elliot feel, standing for hours against a wall, his whole weight pressing on his trembling hands? Maybe that's what it came down to in the end. Not thoughts, not feelings, not resentment or betrayal or the absence of love. Just the dull burn of pain. How much pain could you stand? McCormack slapped the pillow and turned again, facing the blank wall.

UNSENT LETTERS #2

Flat 4c, 70 Craigpark
Glasgow
18 July 1969

Dear Chris,

You would have been proud of me today. Instead of slugging about in bed I got up for once and headed off on an adventure. Way out west, like Laurel and Hardy. I caught the bus into town and took the subway out to Kelvinbridge. When I climbed the steps to the pavement the sunshine felt tropical. More like South Pacific than Great Western Road.

I bought filled rolls and a fern cake in a baker's and went to eat them in Kelvingrove Park. The crowds had come out with the sun. Weans were playing in the fountain, filling Fairy Liquid bottles and scooshing big jets of water into the sky. Folk were picnicking everywhere, on the flat and up on the slopes, blankets spread out like towels on a beach. I found a corner of a bench just below Park Gardens. Two old boys were in possession but I just smiled brightly and they shuffled along, faces tripping them.

I ate my lunch and then I picked my way down the hill. The old folk were out in force on the bowling greens—you could hear their thin cheers and the clack of the bowls. I climbed the steps and went into the museum, through the big revolving door, nodding at the old commissionaire, sweltering in his dark green uniform. It was lovely and cool inside, all cold stone and marble floors and big vaulted ceilings. I wandered through the galleries looking at the paintings in their golden frames. There was one I liked, "A Lady in Black". This stuck-up looking wifey in a broad black hat, sitting in front of a table. She had one elbow propped on the back of the chair, the other hand in her lap. The table behind her was all carved and fancy and painted gold; on its black lacquered top there was a vase and two pink roses. She was wearing these golden gloves and a black fur coat with grey collar and cuffs. The way the light fell on the fabric you could feel the actual fur of the coat, you wanted to bunch it in your fists, bury your face in its folds.

I was still looking at this painting when I heard footsteps and I turned to see this family coming down the gallery—a mum and dad and their wee boy. There was something familiar about the dad. As he got closer I saw I knew him. He was one of my clients. He'd seen me too. He was starting to smile but there was a frown line between his eyes, you could practically see the cogs turning as he tried to work out where he knew me from. As he passed he gave me a nice big hello and I said hello right back. And then I kept watching as he walked on, and I counted to three or maybe four when he stopped dead in his tracks and turned to stare at me with this look of absolute horror on his face. I gave him a wink and he turned back and stumped on and I could see his wife drawing up close to hiss something in his ear and his hand coming up to bat away whatever she'd asked. That's your gas at a peep, Mister, I said to myself. Didn't look to bump into your hoor at the art gallery!

Anyway. Chris. Listen. I need to tell you something. I've been putting it off. Don't get mad, but I was there the night you came looking for me. At Whitehill Street. I was there. I'm sorry. Really I am.

I had a feeling you would come. Your pal Gavaghan had been in, a week or two earlier. I made out I didn't recognize him but I knew he'd clocked me. I sort of suspected he would tell you and that you would show up. I'd just finished with a client and Rose—she's the madam—told me somebody was asking for Isobel. We don't use our own names with the punters so I knew something was up. There's a spyhole in one of the panels of the waiting room and there you were, sitting straight-backed on the banquette, your clenched fists bunched on your knees. I told Rose you were an old boyfriend and she got one of the other girls to see to you.

Chris, I'm sorry. I miss you, I want to see you, but not like that, not in that place. I had this idea, like I said, that I'd be in my own house and settled down and we would have you round for your tea. Uncle Chris, you'd be. I couldn't do it the other way.

Anyway, back to today. All the way home I kept thinking, not about the punter in the Kelvingrove and what he'd say to his wife, but about the fur coat in the painting. It's like the painter knew, the way he painted the coat, he knew that clothes were important. You know what I did with my first earnings, when I started in Whitehill Street? I went straight down to Fraser's and bought myself some gear. My own stuff. Capri pants and a peasant blouse, wedge-heel sandals, pillar-box red. You remember the stuff they made us wear at Auldpark, Chris? Jesus. What frights we must have looked. Jumble-sale bargains and hand-me-downs. The only thing I liked was this coat I had. A navy-blue duffel with wooden toggles and a red tartan lining. God, I loved that coat. I looked like something out of the Famous Five. I wore it all the time.

I mind at church once, we were filing out for Sunday School and this wee bitch, Kirsty Baird was her name, she says to me, "That's my coat you're wearing." I didn't even know what she meant. "Naw it's no; it's mine," I told her. "It is so my coat," she says. "It's my cast-off." I didn't know what a cast-off was either. "Look, I can prove it. Take it off a minute." Everyone was watching now so I took off the coat and she pointed to the label where a squiggle of black pen had scored something out but you could still read what it was. Two letters: KB. "That's me," she said smugly. "That's my coat. My mammy gives our old things to the Auldparkers. When we're done with them." I felt as if someone had slapped me. My face was stinging, there was a ringing in my ears. I sat there through Sunday School and climbed back onto the bus like a zombie and I never wore the coat again.

Stupid, eh? Anyway, fuck her, the stuck-up bitch!!

I'll write again soon, Chris. That's if the Quaker doesnae get me! Only joking!! But those bloody posters would give you the willies, wouldn't they? Looking down at you with that creepy half-smile. You should see them in the work just now. The girls, they're all jumpy, it's all they can talk about. Quaker this, Quaker that. They're worried he's maybe a punter, maybe he'll follow them home one night. I tell them if you don't want the Quaker to get you, just lay off the dancing! That's where he gets them, isn't it? Picking them up at the Barrowland.

Walter, the bloke I told you about, he works there as a bouncer. Or, sorry, a "steward" he calls it! Anyway, he says he's seen the Quaker in the Barrowland. When he saw the picture, the artist's impression, he thought straight away, "I know that fella. He's a regular." The guy hasn't darkened the door in months, but if he does come in, Walter says he'll recognize him. That's why, you ask me, I think it's probably finished. I think the Quaker knows too many folk would recognize him now, it's too risky for him. Anyway, you know me, Chris, I was never much of a dancer anyway, I think I'm safe enough from his clutches!

By the way, speaking of Walter, he says he's going to find me something. Another job. I know, I know. I'm not daft, I know he's not about to sweep me off my feet or anything. But he likes me, I think. Says he knows of a job coming up, a friend of his is starting a new business. It's all a bit vague, but still. We'll see what happens. You take care, Chris, wherever you are.

Your sister,

Isobel

TUESDAY, 8 JULY 1975

32

S oldiers?" Goldie said. He said it once more as if he was learning the word in a foreign language. He waggled the pen between finger and thumb.

They were back in the office, still in their funeral blacks. The service had been hard. Shand's fiancée Joanna seemed to sleepwalk through the proceedings in a Mogadon glaze. His elderly parents leaned on one another in the front pew until the coffin was carried out, then limply wiped each mourner's hand with their own as the crowd filed out of the church.

"Maybe you should stick that thing in your ear," McCormack told him. "Get rid of the wax. Soldiers, Detective. We're looking for current or recently discharged army personnel. Served in Ulster within the past three years, or been discharged within the same timeframe. If currently serving, they were on leave between 27 June and 3 July. Home addresses within the city boundary. Got it? Get on to the MOD. Get the list. Get it done."

Goldie finished writing it down. "Any particular reason?"

McCormack took his glasses off. He rubbed a hand down his face and put his glasses back on. "Let's say I'm playing a hunch, Derek. If something comes of it, I'll let you know. Meantime, can we get this done? Nicol, a word."

He moved towards his office. At the doorway he turned. Nicol hadn't stirred. No one was going anywhere till he told them what was what.

McCormack's hands came to rest on his hips. He stood

there like some sort of gym instructor. He shook his head. "O.K. Look. I can't tell you where I got this. And it might be nothing anyway."

McCormack paused. The pair continued watching him like Labradors. "Go on then," Goldie said.

"There's a place outside Belfast." McCormack slipped his hands in his trouser pockets, perched on the edge of one of the desks. "Army installation. They take suspected Provos there. Or even just random Catholics. Lift them off the streets."

"Interrogation centre," Goldie said.

"Not quite." McCormack shrugged. "Torture centre, more like. They have this thing called the Five Techniques. They starve the prisoners. Keep them from sleep. Play loud noises. Make them stand against walls for hours at a time. And they hood them." McCormack nodded. "They put them in boiler suits and hood them."

Goldie and Nicol shared a look. Nicol glanced at the corkboard, where a photo of Gavin Elliot in a faded boiler suit was pinned next to a clipping from the *Record*. "You're saying it's a soldier?" she asked. "You think it's a soldier who killed Gavin Elliot and bombed the Barracks Bar?"

Now that she had said it, it seemed a larger thing than it had in McCormack's mind. No one said anything.

Goldie looked at McCormack and dropped his eyes to the desk. McCormack knew what he was thinking. Goldie was thinking about the Quaker. Chasing soldiers. One of the lines of inquiry had been that the Quaker was a soldier. The descriptions of the killer—short hair, clean shaven, regimental tie—suggested a service background. The team in the Murder Room at the Marine had gone through the lists of serving soldiers who'd been home on leave at the time of the murders. Now they'd have to do it all again. The army was going to wonder what they'd done to piss off the Glasgow CID.

"Well." McCormack slid off the desk and stood, his arms hanging loose by his sides. "We don't want to alarm anyone."

"A soldier bombing a squaddie pub?" Nicol chewed her lip. "In the marching season? You don't want to *alarm* anyone?"

"They think it's the Irish," Goldie said. "They think it's terrorism. You're going to go to Haddow and tell him it's a *soldier*?"

"No." McCormack looked from one to the other. "We're not telling anyone anything. If the MOD wants to know what we're doing, you tell them it's a routine assault in a Glasgow pub. Witness heard the assailant talk about returning to his regiment. You're following a line of inquiry, crossing the Ts. We work our way through the list. If we get a match, *then* we worry about telling Haddow."

"You mean we do this on the fly?"

"What choice have we got? We owe it to Iain, don't we? We owe it to Shand."

33

I t's just me!"
Nicol let herself in to her parents' house. She shut the front door, hung her raincoat on the hallstand and crossed the hall to her father's study. She paused before the heavy wooden panels, her fingers on the ridged brass doorknob. She could hear a blare of telly from the lounge, then a brief upheaval of voices and the volume falling.

"Elizabeth?"

"I'll be through in a minute," she called, twisting her wrist and stepping into the darkened room.

She closed the door behind her and leant against it, eyes shut, inhaling the familiar scent. Dad's Study. A compound of stagnant air, stale cigarette smoke, leather upholstery, brittle-paged, damp-speckled books, and a lemony edge of furniture polish. The blinds were drawn against the summer dusk and the whole room seemed to be holding its breath.

Her father loved old maps. He had Armstrong's Map of Ayrshire along one wall of the study. Six big napkin-sized sheets, spliced together and framed in a great square rigging of wood. As a girl, Nicol loved to let herself into the study. She would stand on a chair and lose herself in this ink-and-paper landscape. It wasn't a pictorial map, exactly, but it had little perspective drawings of all the Ayrshire hills, shaded on their eastern side, and rows of tiny trees around doll's-house sketches of the bigger estates. There were places that Nicol had never heard of—a little townland on the county's northern edge was labelled "Back of the World"—and some of the names had an old-fashioned twist. Crosshouse, where she'd gone to church-hall dances as a girl, appeared as "Corshouse", and the grim pit village of Hurlford bore the magical name of "Whirlfoord".

She opened her eyes and crossed to the far wall. She turned on the bracket lamp beside the map of Ayrshire. The map showed six islands in the waters of the Firth of Clyde. Great Cumbrae and Little Cumbrae nestled in close to the coast. Behind them was the rugged bulk of Bute. To the south lay the Isle of Arran and the little dot of Ailsa Craig, out on its own. And finally, almost blocking the mouth of Ardrossan Harbour, was the little rickle of rocks and grass known as Horse Isle.

A knock came at the study door and then her mother's voice. "Elizabeth? Your father's putting the kettle on. You'll stay for some supper?"

"Lovely. Thanks. I'll be out directly." She could sense her mother still hovering in the hallway.

"Is it do with your work, Elizabeth? What you're doing in there?"

"It is, Mum. Yes."

"Fine, then. Come out when you're ready."

The floorboards creaked as her mother retreated. Nicol took out her notebook. She jotted down the names of the six islands. She looked down the list and back at the map. Bute was out, she decided. The Isle of Bute. Too big, too far away. She put a line through it in her book. Arran? Too big and too far south. You'd want something that was small enough that you could imagine it was your island alone. Ailsa Craig was small, but it was too far out to sea, just a sort of scone-shaped blue outline on the horizon when you saw it from the coast. She drew a line through Arran and Ailsa Craig. It was Horse Isle or one of the Cumbraes.

She studied Great Cumbrae—or "Great Cumbra", as the

map had it. There wasn't much to it. Three hills in the northern part of the island, a "Kirktown" near the centre with a drawing of a church beside it, and a cluster of buildings in Millport. The rest was mainly the names of bays on the western side, but she felt a little jolt when she spotted a nubby peninsula on the island's southeast that bore the name "Red Castle". Could this be the Red House that Yvonne Gray mentioned to Rona? But of course the Red House had to be onshore—it was the Red House that gave a view of Crocodile Island.

Stuff it. She circled "Great Cumbrae", "Little Cumbrae" and "Horse Isle" in her notebook and stowed it in her jacket.

She found her parents in the kitchen, working side by side at the countertop. Her mum was buttering slices of toast— plain loaf, not pan—and her dad was shaving slices off a cheddar block with the steely concentration of a man defusing a bomb.

"Go on to the room, Lizzie," he told her, not taking his eyes from the cheese. "We'll bring it through."

She retreated to the lounge, where a gas fire burned weakly, its flames white and ghostly in the fading day. The house was a rambling, Arts and Crafts villa with a lodge-house by the gateposts of its gravelled drive. Since her "Separation"—the word her parents used for her husband having left her—Nicol had been living in the lodge, like some sort of skulking caretaker or security guard, keeping the city's badness at bay, stemming its tide of violence and crime. The lodge had been a playhouse for Nicol and her sister when they were small, and behind most cupboard doors was a frozen avalanche of badminton rackets, clothes-less dolls, *Bunty* annuals and board games.

Nicol had been living there for nearly seven months. She ate meals mainly on her own but she crunched up the driveway in the evenings, when her shifts allowed, to take supper with her parents. Sometimes she worked on her cases in her father's study, spreading her papers out across his big oak desk, while her parents watched telly in the lounge.

She had been embarrassed by this house as a girl. It was so much grander than the houses of her friends. She liked to tell herself that it wasn't anything special. But now, looking round the wood-panelled living room with its mullioned bay window, its marble fireplace, its acreage of rugs and polished parquet, she felt the old embarrassment anew. Most of Glasgow's citizens thought themselves lucky to be sardined into single-ends and two-room flats, and here was Lizzie Nicol with the run of a mansion like a cruise ship in a sea of barbered grass. But it was just temporary, she reminded herself, until she got her arse in gear and found a place of her own.

Her parents came through, bearing plates of toasted cheese and the tea things on a tray. They sat down at the table to eat. Her father turned on the TV news. There was something ceremonial in her parents' attitude to TV. They acquired one early—before the Coronation, even—but they hadn't grown up with it, like Nicol had. There was an item towards the end about the bombing, how the police were no closer to catching the perpetrators. There was footage of the Barracks Bar with safety barriers round it and then Shand's picture flashed up on the screen, his wedding photo, smiling—all freckles and crooked teeth.

Her mother cleared the plates away and took them to the kitchen. Nicol turned to her father. "I wanted to talk to you, Dad. If you've a minute."

"Is this work, Lizzie?" Her father was all business now, rising to turn down the telly, tugging the knees of his slacks to fix the creases as he sat back down and crossed his legs. He'd been a criminal lawyer and he took a vicarious delight in helping out with his daughter's cases. Between bites of toasted cheese, Nicol told him about Rona, the Red House, the view of Crocodile Island.

"There are eight hundred islands off the coast of Scotland, Lizzie," her father said, smiling. "Just so you know."

"Not Scotland," Nicol said. "This is just Ayrshire we're talking about."

"Well now, that makes a difference." Her father set his teacup down, wiped his hands with a linen napkin. "Though I don't think there's crocodiles on any of them. Even in Ayrshire."

"Shaped like one is what I'm thinking," Nicol said.

Her father nodded, his eyes pegging left and right as he mentally ran through the list. "Well, Arran's the Sleeping Warrior, isn't it? Five hills like a man in armour, lying on his back. The Cumbraes are just, I suppose, island-shaped. Or like whales, maybe. Not crocodiles. Ailsa Craig's like a currant bun. Horse Isle's too low to be shaped like anything, unless maybe from the air. What's left?"

Nicol consulted her notes. "The Isle of Bute. But you can't see the whole thing anyway, from the coast. The Cumbraes are always in front of it."

"Not Bute, then. I'm sorry, Precious. Your Crocodile Island remains a mystery." He took out his cigarettes and lit up. "Your mother has me down to five a day. Isn't that right, Alice? Now, is this to do with our friend across the river?"

"It might be," said Nicol. "We're not sure yet."

"She doesn't want to talk about that, John," Nicol's mother said. "Too much shop gets talked in this house already. Too much entirely."

Mr. Nicol raised his hands in mock surrender. "I'm taking an interest, woman. In our daughter's occupation. Anyway. I don't see you getting up to change the channel when that man comes on the news."

"That's different," her mother said.

They sat in silence for a bit, watching the weather report.

"You'll have been in town today, then, Mum?"

Nicol was looking at her notebook when she asked this, so it took her a moment to register the pause. Her mother always went into town on a Tuesday. She looked up sharply. Her mother was picking crumbs from the tablecloth and wouldn't meet her eye.

"Actually, no, I didn't bother," her mother said, risking a swift glance at her husband.

"You don't need to protect me, Mum," Nicol said. "You were meeting Moira and the boys. It's fine. Honestly. How are they keeping?"

Moira was Nicol's younger sister. She lived in a nice house in Clarkston with her husband Doug and their twin boys.

Nicol's mother closed her eyes. Her hands on the oilcloth had bunched into fists. "She wanted to tell you herself, Elizabeth," she said.

Nicol looked at her father and back to her mother. "She's pregnant?" Nicol asked. "Moira's pregnant?"

"It's early days yet," her mother said. "Ten weeks just. So, you know, keep it to yourself. Just in case."

"Ah that's great news," Nicol said. She heard her voice sounding brittle and thin, a wavering note of desperation. "She'll be delighted. I'll phone her tonight, congratulate her. Brilliant."

"Elizabeth." Her mother reached across and gripped Nicol's hand in hers. "Listen. Your time's not over. Your time will come."

"Mum."

"I'm just saying. What happened in the past is finished. It's over, Elizabeth. Don't give up, that's all."

Nicol pulled her hand away. Her father made a steadying gesture, pressing down with his palms on empty air.

"What?" Her mother swirled the teapot, tipped a steaming jet into her cup. "I'm just saying. I'm just telling the truth. It's not the end of the world. I had two between Lizzie and Moira."

Nicol stood abruptly, her knees catching the lip of the table, rattling the plates and cutlery. She dropped the napkin on her seat and stumbled blindly out to the bathroom. She washed her face at the sink and glared at herself in the mirror. *Get it together, Nicol. Screw the nut.*

She wanted to go back out and shout at her mother, *It wasn't a fucking miscarriage: how many times?* But she sat on the toilet seat and collected herself. She remembered sitting on this toilet seat, psyching herself up, on the night they told her parents. It was Christmas Eve, 1973. She got pregnant in November, so it was still early days, but they broke the news—she and Kenny—on Christmas Eve. There were whoops and exclamations, laughter and toasts; Buck's Fizz for herself and Mum; Glenfiddich and cigars for Kenny and Dad. By springtime she was starting to show, her dresses tightening, her breasts getting heavy. Men held doors for her; women felt her bump for luck. She was blooming in concert with the year, in step with the seasons. She felt the enchantment of it, the life inside her, the little heel that would poke whitely out from her belly's perfect curve.

And then, with the suddenness of a nightmare, when the baby was almost due, everything changed. She woke up one morning after a restless night and the baby seemed quiet. By lunchtime it still hadn't moved. She went to the hospital. They couldn't find a heartbeat. Suddenly the magical thing inside her was a grey weight, a cold anvil of flesh. She thought they would open her up, but no, they told her, there's less than two weeks to go. Her body would go into labour naturally. It was safer this way. Those eleven days were the longest of her life. She drifted around in a sick daze, sedated, inhabiting a shadowworld, a horrible parody of impending motherhood. Her closet full of maternity dresses. Her breasts filling with pointless milk. When the contractions started, Kenny helped her into the car. They drove to the Victoria in silence, without urgency.

Dead inside.

She had thought that was a metaphor. Now she knew it was real. When the time came she sweated and pushed and laboured and cried to bring forth her dead wee boy. She held him and kissed his hard little lips, his closed blue eyelids. She cupped the little marbles of his heels. But the death was still inside her. She knew it always would be. The enchantment was gone. It wasn't that life had ceased to hold any value, just that she knew how brittle it could be, what it might cost. A knot in the umbilical cord had cut off her son's life.

The experience changed her. Kenny struggled to deal with it. He wanted them to try again, put it behind them. She knew it would always be above and beyond, inside and out, behind her and before. It would colour everything. It was her element now. That's why they split up, though you needn't tell people that. You could blame it on the job, the terrible hours, you could say she'd sacrificed her marriage to the job and in a way that was even true. Because everything that had happened since that day in the maternity ward at the Victoria had made her a better polis. It had given her perspective, a patience in dealing with people's troubles. And when she stood above the body of the old man in Crawford Street she learned something else. She felt a kinship with the dead now, a sympathy. She looked into the ruined face of the murdered man and an almost tribal affinity stirred. She was this man's kin, she was halfway dead herself, she would do all she could to find his killer.

Back in the living room she hugged her mother and apologized.

"I better go, Mum. I've got work to do."

Her father came out of his study as she was wrestling into her raincoat. He was grinning widely, showing his neat little dentures. "Well it took me long enough," he was saying. "But I found your island."

He was holding an open book in his splayed right hand. Nicol knew the marbled blue leatherette cover from her child-hood—it was a family album of early holidays.

"I can't believe I didn't get it right away," her father said. "It came to me as I was drying the dishes. Now look at this."

Nicol took the book in her hands. There were a dozen photos on display, six to a page. Her dad tapped one of the snaps.

She hadn't seen this one in years, if ever. She had no memory of it being taken, nor of the moment that it framed.

It showed Nicol and her sister Moira aged six or seven, standing side by side on a long, low, rugged rock, grinning and holding hands. There was water behind them and a line of big villas in the distance, but what caught the eye was the rock beneath their feet. At one end, where the rock tapered and split, someone had painted two long rows of jagged teeth, brilliantly white, outlined with red and black lips beneath a red-rimmed white staring eye.

"Crocodile Rock!" her father exclaimed. "The beach at Millport. You must remember that, Lizzie!"

She shook her head, tracing the painted jaws with her finger. "Would you look at that," she said. She felt her face creasing in a smile till it matched her seven-year-old face in the photo. "Dad: you're a genius."

WEDNESDAY, 9 JULY 1975

34

The list provided by the MoD had close to a hundred names on it.

"O.K." McCormack handed the Xeroxed copy to Goldie. "Lot of squaddies in this town. But that's no surprise. We make a start. We're looking for alibis and we're looking to corroborate them. Start crossing these names off this list."

"That's the royal 'we', is it?" Goldie tugged the phone book from its shelf, slapped it down onto his desk. "You know Quinn's done a runner, don't you?"

"What's that?"

"Denny Quinn. He's left town. Word is he's over in Belfast. That's what my tout's saying anyway."

McCormack was shaking his head. "Come on, Derek. That doesn't mean Quinn did it. It just means Quinn thinks *Maitland* thinks he did it. Start working that list."

Nicol was preparing to drive down to Ayrshire on her search for the Red House.

"I'm sure D.C. Nicol here is heartbroken that she can't help you out, Derek."

"I'm slaving over a hot phone and she's off on a jolly to the coast. Doon the watter. Eating sliders on the prom."

Nicol turned at the door, blew Goldie a kiss. "I'll bring you back a stick of rock."

"Right. And I'll show you where to stick it."

It was mid-morning when Nicol reached Largs. The town looked neat and bright, with the sun warming the sandstone spires and glinting on the plate-glass windows of the ice-cream parlour.

She turned onto Gallowgate Street, past the tiny ferry terminal, and headed north beside the glittering firth, along a seafront street of detached villas.

If Yvonne Gray's Red House had a view of Cumbrae, then the odds were good that it was here.

But as she toured the long lateral avenues, and climbed the gentle inclines of the side-streets, Nicol began to lose heart. A lot of the houses had sandstone facades, the colour of cream of tomato soup. Others had red clay roof tiles. There were bungalows with arched doorways edged in red-and-white brick, fresh-painted trenches of crimson along the bottom of whitewashed gables. Even the council estates on the hill were roofed in fat terracotta tiles. Whole streets were patterned red and white, like a barber's pole. It gave the town a bright, sweetie-shop feel but it didn't make it any easier to identify the Red House.

Once, on the road north out of town, Nicol spotted a house whose upper storey was painted scarlet. She parked in the driveway and walked past the freshly mown lawn and the cabbage tree and the park bench under the picture window to ring the doorbell. She turned round to check the view. Cumbrae: low and green across the firth.

"May I help you?"

The woman was early forties, prematurely grey. She wore comfortable slacks and a short-sleeved polyester jumper patterned with tiny perforations. Nicol produced her warrant card and the photo of Yvonne Gray in quick succession. The woman studied them both.

"No. I'm sorry. I can't say I've seen her. A local lass, is she? Has she gone missing?"

"She's not exactly local." Nicol pressed the photo into the woman's hands. "We think she spent some time in Largs as a girl. She may have come back here recently. Take your time."

"I wish I could help." The woman handed the photo back. "Sorry."

"She described living somewhere called 'the Red House'. Do you know what that might mean? Is there a house in town that would fit that description?"

"Is that why you're here?" The woman's face brightened. "You think this is the house she meant?"

"Well we don't know. I'm just looking for a house that fits the bill."

The woman seemed disappointed that her own house wasn't the one.

Nicol drove back into town. She showed Yvonne's photo round the pubs and cafés. No one had seen her. It wasn't the clearest likeness, and anyway, Yvonne had probably dyed her hair by now, chopped and changed it. Nicol stopped for a bite of lunch in a tearoom on Main Street.

She ordered a ham salad and slumped at a table by the window.

They'd had months to come at Maitland. Were they any closer to nailing him? They'd tried every angle. Nicol counted them off.

There was the Tradeston fire that killed four people. This was Maitland sending a message to the Quinns, torching the upstarts' warehouse, but he wasn't daft. The job had been carried out at night, with no witnesses. Probably by some wee ned on the fringes of Maitland's outfit. There was nothing to tie the fire to Maitland, no way to link him to the deaths.

There was the murder of Gavin Elliot. Ex-MP, top city businessman, associate of Hugh Maitland. Elliot's demise spoke to bitter hatred, some fierce and personal enmity. A partnership gone sour? Revenge for some act of betrayal? Again, it was conjecture, speculation. Nobody knew who had killed Gavin Elliot.

And now Yvonne Gray. The longest shot of all. She acted

funny when they raided Healing Hands. And then she left town in a hurry. As though something had spooked her. She'd seen something—heard something—and now she wanted gone before Maitland found out. But who said it was something about Maitland that Yvonne Gray had discovered? She worked in one of Maitland's saunas. But so what? Plenty of women worked in Maitland's saunas.

But she'd worked in the Barracks Bar too, Nicol reflected. Hugh Maitland's pub. Where the bomb went off. What did McCormack always say? We're polis. We don't believe in coincidences. It's like Protestants and purgatory—we don't hold with it.

A shadow fell on the table. "Get you anything else?" The waitress hovered, eyebrows arched.

Nicol used her foot to push the chair opposite out from the table. "Have a seat."

The waitress looked over at the counter and back at Nicol. Her eyes dropped to the warrant card open on the table and she slid into the vacant seat. Nicol put her warrant card away, replaced it with the snapshot of Yvonne Gray. She used two fingers to slide it across to the waitress's side of the table. She told the story: a "Red House" with a view of an island.

"Never seen her in my life," the girl said. "She's not a regular in here, that's for sure."

"I'm beginning to wonder if she's ever set foot in Largs."

"What about Fairlie?" the waitress said.

Fairlie was a village just south of the town. Nicol shrugged, stirred her coffee. "Well, I drove through it."

"I know. Blink and you'll miss it. You didn't walk the beach, then?"

"The beach?" Nicol thought back to her drive through Fairlie. A single long street, it had seemed, with trees overhanging the narrow pavements. But no beach.

"Aye. You can't drive it. There's no road. A lot of big houses back onto it, though. Fairlie beach. You might get lucky there."

Nicol didn't feel lucky. She felt like the whole day—the whole job, maybe—was a waste of time. But she thanked the waitress and got in her car and headed south. She drove back through Fairlie, down the long main street, mature trees, no sign of a beach, she could have been miles inland. But at the southern edge of the village a shallow bay opened up on her right.

She parked the Velox. There was a path, she followed it past an abandoned hotel and, yes, here was the beach, curving round to a headland maybe a mile away.

There were views of Cumbrae. You could see houses on the island's shoreline. It looked swimmable.

The flagged path gave way to a path cut out of the sandstone rock. On Nicol's right as she walked was the sea wall— old, rough, high, she trailed her hand along its gritty skin—and behind it, up on higher ground, the backs of imposing villas. These would be the former holiday homes of Glasgow merchants, Nicol thought. Men who assuaged the cares of office with a paddle in the Firth of Clyde. She pictured them in shirt-sleeves and braces, Captains of Industry, jauntily hatted, their suit trousers rolled to the knees.

She passed an Italianate villa in honeyed stone, a white-washed mansion with a semicircular balcony.

And then she saw it.

It looked like a New England barn, looming over the beach, pushing out from a big timbered villa like some massive wooden conservatory. It was long and oblong but curved at the end, and a steep slated roof swept tightly round to follow the curve. On top was a weathervane: an arrow through a slim straight post below a cockerel's silhouette.

Above all, it was red. Not a cheerful pillar-box lipstick red. More a sombre oxblood. But red for all that. And Nicol knew.

She knew without needing to be told, without the slightest whisper of doubt, she knew that she'd found the place.

This was what she was looking for.

This was the Red House.

Nicol clambered over the rocks to the rough footpath hewn from the stone. There was a break in the seawall. A green lane, floored in overgrown grass and canopied with trees, led up the side of the Red House. Nicol set off along it.

35

They stood at the railing, sharing a Regal. Kidd had plenty of smokes but they liked it this way, passing the tab back and forth, a little pink beacon in the failing light.

"I've been here before," Yvonne said softly, almost to herself. "Years back. Or maybe not this place exactly, but somewhere like it. Somewhere on the coast." A breeze had got up and she pulled her bolero jacket tighter. She nodded at the horizon. "I mind the shape of the island out here. And I mind a big ship. We watched a white ship going past."

"Like a ferry?"

"I don't think so." She took the cigarette from Kidd and moistened her lips before taking a drag. "It had funnels, and these big wheels on the side."

"You mean the *Waverley*," Kidd said. "It's a famous paddlesteamer. They took us on it as weans. For a day out. We got to go down to the engine room and see all the pistons and things." He took the smoke back from Yvonne. He gripped it furtively, cupped in his hand, the glowing tip almost touching his palm. "I could have watched it all day. That engine. It was alive, almost. The way it moved."

He turned to kiss her and something blundered down between them, a bird—no, a bat, a little handkerchief of darkness. It flopped and tumbled off towards the trees.

They grinned at each other, soundless, and Yvonne gripped his lapels and pulled him down towards her.

That a kiss could be as satisfying as sex was something new

to Kidd. A kiss. The waxy surface of her lipsticked lips, the sudden hot intimacy of a mouth. Because kissing was what she held back, wasn't it? When she did her job. It's what the Others—he was thinking of them now as the Others, a shuffling line of faceless men—never got. Only Kidd got that.

But then, so what? What did that matter now? He saw how foolish he'd been. Making a life with Yvonne? What planet was he on? Maybe it was being down here—walking the beach, riding the waltzers, guzzling candyfloss. It wasn't real life. It was just a holiday and holidays came to an end.

They walked along the promenade and out of town by the coastal path. They came to the little grassy promontory where the Pencil stood, the monument to the Battle of Largs. The Scots had beaten the Vikings here, sending them back across the sea, ousting them forever from their Scottish possessions. A great stone obelisk rose to mark the spot, its top shaped like a sharpened pencil.

She had a wean. She'd told him about the wean while they lay in bed in the guesthouse. In the unguarded lull after sex. All fuzzy and numb and confiding. A wee boy of three. His name was David. The wean was living with her mum in Rutherglen. It made things messier but, really, what choice did he have?

Yvonne trailed a palm across the rough stone blocks as she circled the base.

"It's weird to think of it," she said, looking out across the firth. "You don't think of them as real people, do you? Just pictures in a history book, with silly horns sticking out of their helmets."

Kidd said nothing.

"I'm talking about Vikings," Yvonne said. "You know: the battle?"

You could do it here, Kidd thought. In the bushes or down by the rocks. It was late now, the sun sinking red behind

Cumbrae, the sky all pinks and yellows. The last dog walkers had whistled their Labs and Retrievers back along the path to Largs. No courting couples on the empty benches. He stepped towards her in the rising dark but she skipped off lightly, dancing down the grassy slope towards the rocks.

"Come on!" she shouted.

She was out on the rocks now, the jagged sandstone ridges, her figure black against the yellow sky so that her raised and beckoning arm gave her the look of a heraldic emblem.

Kidd picked his way down the grass and followed her onto the rocks. The tide was high and little inlets and pools glimmered amid the ridges. He stepped with care, feeling with his feet till he made it out to where Yvonne stood, on a big rock at the edge, above the swirling waves. He could hear the swell slapping and churning at their feet, the last light catching greasy straps of sea wrack that pulsed as the water rose and fell.

Yvonne reached behind her for his hand and drew him into her back, pulling his arms round her and fastening his hands like a belt, clamping her own hands on top of his. He dropped his chin onto her shoulder and nuzzled her neck.

A simple push, he thought. One push and she was gone.

Could you actually do it, though, he wondered. Kill someone? But then, he'd done it already. He'd killed four people in the Tradeston fire. If Hell existed he would go there when he died. He hadn't meant to kill those people but what did that matter? Four people were dead. Not killing this one wouldn't make things right.

She craned her head round for a kiss and he found her mouth. He could taste the vinegar from the chips they'd shared earlier, the bite of salt on her lips. He pulled his mouth away.

"What's the matter?" She reached round to clamp her palm on the back of his neck and pulled him down again and they kissed again, deeper this time, her fleshy tongue probing his cheek. "That's better," she said.

She pulled away and they stood looking out to sea.

"You said *they*," Yvonne said.

"Hmm?" He rested his hand on her back, he could feel the rigging of her bra beneath the jacket. Across the water, the Isle of Cumbrae stood out black against the sky, sinister now, no longer the friendly green dolphin of daytime but a humped beast, a dark Leviathan.

"When you said about the trip. You said *they*. 'They took us on a trip.' Who's *they*? Did you mean your parents?"

"Oh right. No. The staff from the home. Auldpark."

"You were looked-after?"

"Aye. You?"

"I can always tell," Yvonne said. "It's like a secret code or something."

Had anybody seen them on the path? A couple of dog walkers, no one else. And Kidd had pulled Yvonne close to him as they passed, their heads pressed together so that his face would be obscured.

Something moved in the water at their feet, five yards from the rocks. Light picked out a tiny glistening disc, another beside it; black; a pair of eyes. He drew a sharp breath, cut it short. The head turned in the water, sleek and round. A seal. He was about to point it out to Yvonne but it was gone. Was it an omen? Some kind of sign? Did it mean he should do it or that he shouldn't do it?

Beneath the clean smell of her hair he could smell his own fear—the nasty, brassy tang—and he supposed she could smell it too.

Behind them was the Pencil. He thought about the battle, all those centuries past. Were the Vikings scared? They had set up camp out there on the Isle of Cumbrae, that black hump in the darkness. Then they'd crossed the narrow firth, beaching their longboats and splashing up the sands to meet the Scots. You thought of them as the ultimate warriors, the Vikings, the real hard men, but the Scots had wasted them.

Hundreds of men had died here. Thousands, maybe. Right on this spot. What difference could another death make? The sea wouldn't bother, nor the rocks.

They'd been fighting over territory, hadn't they? The Vikings and the Scots. Like the Maitlands and the Quinns. This girl whose bony shoulder he could feel beneath his hand wasn't an invading army. But she was some kind of threat to Walter Maitland, and she had to go. And it was his job, as one of Maitland's soldiers, to see it through.

He looked behind him, scanning the path down which they had come, the patch of grass at their backs. The place looked deserted but it was too dark to tell. Was there someone out there, some meddling civilian?

He shuffled over behind her, wrapped his arms around her again.

You could swap places with her. Tumble into the water, feel the seaweed wrap itself round you, dragging you down.

But what good would that do? Someone else would be sent in your place. Somebody else would kill her.

The time for thinking like this was gone, if it ever existed. It was time for action.

A simple push, he thought. Disengage his arms and jab her sharply, two-handed, in the small of the back. To claw her way back onto the slick rocks would be beyond her. But she had to know why it was happening. He owed her that much. With his face still pressed against her own he spoke softly into the night.

"Yvonne." He spoke the word like a charm, a magic spell. "Yvonne Gray. I know who you are."

She didn't move. He felt her cheek bunching against his own in what had to be, of all things, a smile.

He spun her round to face him, gripping her shoulders, and

326 - LIAM McILVANNEY

her teeth were bared in a fantastic grin. Her white face was turned up towards him and her blond hair gleamed in the dark. A lot of whores got their blond from a bottle, but Yvonne's was real. Everything about her, he suddenly realized, was real.

"You know who I am, do you?"

She ought to be scared, Kidd thought. Why wasn't she scared, out here in the dark with a man who knew her secrets? A man who could snuff her out like a candle.

"Snap," she said. She was grinning still, he could see her teeth. "I know who you are too. Christopher Kidd." Her black eyes flashed in the failing light, scanning his bewildered face. "I knew your sister, Chris. I knew Isobel."

36

All Yvonne Gray ever knew about her father was his name and what he did for a living. Sam Gray was a merchant seaman who left shortly after his daughter was born. Her mother made a go of it for a couple of years, paying a neighbour to watch Yvonne while she went out to work as a hairdresser. But Sally Gray had married early—she was only eighteen when Yvonne was born—and her life, in the way of these things, began to feel cramped and unhappy. She saw her friends making good marriages to young men with trades. She saw her friends taking secretarial courses, moving down to London, spending money on clothes and parties. It hadn't escaped her mind that she was young enough to start again, so long as she acted in time. Sally Gray left Yvonne with the neighbour one day and just never came back. Yvonne was taken into care.

Growing up in care wasn't as grim as people thought. Yvonne made friends easily and there were always three or four girls you could chum about with, plaiting each other's hair and swapping lies about your families. But once, when she was turning thirteen, Yvonne had the chance of a foster placement with a family down in Ayrshire. Bob and Janet Wylie had been fostering kids for the best part of a decade, generally for five or six months at a time. Recently they had adopted one of their foster kids, a girl called Isobel. It seemed that Isobel was finding it hard to settle into her new life and the Wylies decided that having another child in the house—a girl Isobel's age, a girl from a similar background—might ease the transition. So they arranged for Yvonne to come down from Glasgow to stay, the way you might corral a docile mare with a mustang. Yvonne's role was to break Isobel in, domesticate her.

It was—though Yvonne didn't appreciate this at the time— an audition for the role of Isobel's sister, the role of Bob and Janet's second daughter.

It didn't work out. Yvonne liked Isobel and she was pretty sure that Isobel liked her. But she couldn't bring Isobel back from the brink. It was as if Isobel was determined not to be won over by her new life. As if this new life—where you had a bedroom of your own, a wardrobe of new clothes, a full fridge, chocolate biscuits for the asking, goodnight kisses—was a lie and it was Isobel's mission to expose it. She kept pushing things with her new parents, testing how far she could go, how much they would take. She stayed out late, smoked Mr. Wylie's cigarettes, came home with cider on her breath, her throat patched with lovebites like lurid brown roses. She got in with an older crowd who hung around the Amusements in Largs. She started bringing them back to the house, where items of Mrs. Wylie's jewellery began to go missing. When Mrs. Wylie confronted her with this, Isobel said that old rich people shouldn't hoard their wealth like misers but be glad to share it with those less fortunate. One of the missing items was an eternity ring that had been passed down from Mrs. Wylie's grandmother. That made no difference to Isobel.

Eventually, the police were called in, then the social workers, and finally, with a grim, knowing little smile, Isobel packed her few belongings in a suitcase and went back to Glasgow, back to Auldpark, though she kept the Wylies' name and remained their legal daughter. With Isobel gone, there was no reason for Yvonne to stay, and she left the Red House and the beach and the views of Cumbrae and went back into care.

And that was that. It was an episode in her life that seemed as self-contained and closed-off as a snow-globe. She never expected to see Isobel Wylie again. But on her second or third shift at the Dennistoun brothel on Alexandra Parade there was a girl with the same gait, the same slight overbite as Isobel. She smoked her cigarettes in the same manner, sucking the smoke in at one side of her mouth, blowing it out the other, and then holding the cigarette aloft in two fingers with her thumb extended, like a pope about to bestow a blessing. Yvonne bummed a cigarette from her and accepted a light and said, "Are you Isobel Wylie?"

She looked at Yvonne for a moment, frowning. "Do I know you?"

"Sort of." Yvonne bit back a nervous laugh. "I used to be your sister."

Isobel stared at her and then leaned over to clink her glass against Yvonne's. A smile spread across her face and the laughter bubbled up.

After that they were pals. They looked out for one another, kept close tabs when a dodgy punter was in the building. In due course Yvonne raised the topic of the Red House. What had gone wrong? What had made Isobel so determined to screw things up, get herself sent back into care? She wondered if maybe Mr. Wylie had been interfering with her? Nothing of the sort, said Isobel. It was to do with her brother. When the Wylies adopted Isobel they left her brother Christopher behind. They didn't want to adopt Chris. They just wanted a girl. Isobel couldn't bear it and so she did all she could to make them send her back. She didn't seem to appreciate that in ending the Red House experiment for herself, she had also ended it for Yvonne.

"And how's Chris, now?" Yvonne had asked, lounging on the green faux-leather banquette in the room where they waited for the clients.

"That's the thing," Isobel said, blowing smoke out the side of her mouth. "We lost touch."

"How? What happened?"

Isobel tucked her legs up underneath her. "I don't know. I was so glad to get away from Auldpark, I just never went back to see him. At first I was too scared to go back and then, well, it got too late. You know how it works."

Yvonne nodded. She did know how it worked. She had no siblings of her own but she had seen it happen with friends who'd been in care, how they drifted apart from their brothers, sisters. Once your parents had given up on the idea of family it wasn't easy to keep it going. Your heart wasn't in it.

They stayed friends, Yvonne and Isobel, sharing jokes and cigarettes in between clients at Alexandra Parade and sometimes going for a drink at the Shuna Bar, but they never spoke about the Red House again. Then things started going wrong for Isobel. She was drinking heavily. One night a punter complained that she was too drunk to respond properly. Another night she started slapping a punter who clamoured for anal and the bouncer had to restrain her. She missed a shift. She missed another. Then one night Yvonne came in to work and a new girl was sitting on the green banquette. Isobel was finished; she'd been let go.

And that was that. Yvonne was sorry to lose contact with her old acquaintance for a second time. She wondered for a while if maybe she was to blame. Maybe her presence, reminding Isobel of the past, of the life she might have led—they might *both* have led, if things had worked out differently; maybe that pushed Isobel over the edge. Yvonne looked in at the Shuna Bar a couple of times, and tried Isobel's phone number till it was disconnected. She assumed Isobel was now working the streets, standing in shop doorways in Bothwell Street, or up in Blythswood Square. Short skirt and gooseflesh. Trying to blunt the hangover with a wee wrap of speed. It was another snow-globe: sealed off, finished and done with. Then, six years later, she overheard a drunken conversation in the Healing Hands sauna.

This was the narrative she told Christopher Kidd, in her little box room in the seafront guest house in Largs, on the night he decided not to kill her. She had smuggled Kidd past the landlady's ground-floor bedroom, the two of them tiptoeing up the stairs, clutching each other's shoulder, and now they sat side by side on Yvonne's bed, talking in whispers, as the moon pushed a lozenge of cold blue light across the bedroom floor. They had still to decide what the plan was from here. First, though, Kidd needed to hear the rest. What had Yvonne Gray heard in the linen closet at Healing Hands?

Like other "saunas", Healing Hands went through a power of linen: bedsheets, towels, and the snap-button tunics of the girls. There was a small laundry room where the washing machine and tumble dryer swished and rumbled round the clock. At the far end of the laundry room was a walk-in closet where the freshly laundered linen was stored. This had been a pantry in a previous configuration of the building and it was beautifully cool and quiet. Yvonne liked to steal a few minutes alone in the linen closet, in between clients, wallowing in the silence and calm, the clean, baked aroma of folded laundry. She was in there one night, perched on the edge of one of the lower shelves, when she must have dozed off for a few minutes. She was wakened by a deep laugh that seemed to echo round the tiny room. She gasped and gripped tightly the edge of the shelf.

There was a small bar in Healing Hands, for the use of clients who had finished with the girls and wanted somewhere to wind down. Sometimes Maitland's goons used it to talk over bits of business. One of the bench seats was directly through the wall from the linen closet. What Yvonne heard now was the lugubrious voice of Alex Kerr, the man who ran Maitland's money-lending rackets.

"No, no. Glash was still in the big chair at that stage," Kerr was saying. "Walter was just the errand boy. He was still working the door at the Barrowland. Chucker-out. But that was his trick, see? He wanted folk to think he was just Glash's muscle. Brains in his fists. Well, you've seen how that worked out."

"McGlashan was the business, though, wasn't he?" The voice was younger than Kerr's and more nasal. Yvonne seemed to recognize it, though she couldn't quite place it. "I mean, we ruled the fucking city when Glash was in the chair."

Someone shifted his bulk against the thin boards separating the bar from the linen closet. "John McGlashan couldnae lace Walter Maitland's boots. That's the truth of it, son. You think the fucking Tims are a threat to Walter Maitland? Denny fucking Quinn? Turn it up. Walter knows what Quinn's gonnae do before Quinn does. Walter knows everything."

"He didn't know what Glash was up to, though, did he?" the other man said. The voice was so familiar: Yvonne closed her eyes and tried to match it to a face but nothing came.

"You mean he didn't know Glash was the Quaker? Aye he fuckin' did."

"But they'd have charged him, wouldn't they? As an accomplice, like."

"Couldnae get him." Someone set a glass down on a table. "He's too cute for them. I'll tell you how cute he is. You know the polis that went down over the Quaker thing? Peter Levein?"

"The porker in Glash's pocket?"

"Aye. Well, here's what happened. I found this out later, off of McPhail. Glash was getting paranoid, right? The whole Quaker thing, it was getting too big. It was gonnae come out. He was trying to clean things up. There was this lassie, Helen Thaney. Fucking ride. Fenian, but. Still, she was tidy. Glash used to see her. Then she hooked up with Levein. Glash got it into his head that she knew, right? That Helen Thaney knew he was the Quaker. Maybe Levein had let it slip. Pillow talk."

"So what did he do?"

"He told Levein that she had to go. I mean, *go*."

"And Levein topped her?"

"Naw. Well, I mean not directly. There was a slapper in the Dennistoun knocking-shop. On Alexandra Parade? She looked a bit like Helen Thaney. Same size and that. She wound up choked, in Helen Thaney's clothes, her hair dyed to match Thaney's. Made it look like the Quaker had done it."

"Fuck. And the cop did this?"

Naw, Billy. That's what I'm trying to tell you. Maitland did it. Maitland did it for Levein. Without turning a hair."

"Walter was working for the polis?"

"Jesus, son. Would you listen? The polis were working for *him*. Once Walter had done that for the cop, it was the *cop* that needed to worry, no him."

There was silence for a minute, the other man thinking this through. Yvonne could hear the tinkle of ice-cubes as the men tipped their glasses to drink.

"And who was the hoor?"

"What? Oh, some slapper. Izzy Something."

Yvonne felt the tiny room buckle and swim. It was as though the towers of sheets and towels swung out to topple onto her. She gripped the shelf even tighter. It was Isobel. It was Isobel Wylie they were talking about. That's why she'd disappeared. Walter Maitland had killed Isobel to help out a friend, put a cop even deeper into his pocket. She was just a hoor. Who would miss her? Who would even know for sure that she'd gone?

"Walter did that?" the younger man said.

"Walter did that. He did a lot more besides, that you're better off not knowing about. And that's why nobody'll move against Walter, not if they've wit enough to tie their own laces. Cos he'd be six steps ahead of you. He'd know you were turning rat before you did."

There was some more talk, which seemed to focus on a boxing match that one of them had attended. Yvonne was shaking. The stacked towels on the wall racks looked like the rungs of a ladder; Yvonne wanted to climb them to freedom—up and out of her life in Glasgow. But she didn't dare move. Finally, the two men finished their drinks and left. Yvonne held her breath as the footsteps passed in the corridor and she counted to a hundred, and then a hundred again, before venturing out. She headed straight for the toilet and puked, throwing her guts in the pan, retching and heaving. She looked such a mess when she went back to the lounge that the madam sent her home straight away.

Now she sat on the edge of the thin single bed in the guest house in Largs, wondering whether or not to reach out for Christopher's hand. Kidd was sitting with his elbows on his knees, head in his hands, his shoulders lifting and falling with what could be deep breaths or stifled sobs. Then he rose and crossed to the window, leaned his palms on the sill, his forehead resting on the glass. Beyond the window was the shingle and the black incessant waves of the firth, but the glass threw back just his fogged reflection. The springs whispered as Yvonne rose and joined him at the window, slipping her arms lightly round his waist, laying her cheek against the hard ridge of his back.

"They couldn't even kill her in her own right." His back heaved convulsively. "They couldn't even give her that."

Yvonne pressed tighter. "What are you going to do, Chris?"

She could hear Kidd's heart knocking in the rigging of his ribcage. He lifted his forehead and brought it back sharply onto the glass. The window quivered.

"Kill him," he said simply, softly. "Get close to Walter Maitland and kill him."

37

McCormack stopped for a pint at Tennent's Bar on Byres Road. He wanted to stand for a while at the long horseshoe countertop with the talk eddying round him, amid the clink of glasses and the shallow camaraderie of men getting drunk. He ordered a pint of Guinness and watched it settle. There was something simple and perfect about a pint of Guinness, the black body, the milk-white collar just cresting the rim of the glass. Leave it as long as you could, was McCormack's philosophy. Let's enjoy that pristine moment.

Was Shand his fault? Would Iain Shand be another angry ghost to add to his collection, jabbering on in the shades of his mind? He paid out his breath in a long, low sigh. He stood there not drinking Guinness. The job was simple: keep people safe. He hadn't done that. He couldn't even keep his own officers safe. A bad cop. But they were all bad cops. When you were a cop, failure was your element. Results—those occasions where you mustered all the evidence and stood it up in court— were the exception. That's why you celebrated them like birthdays. They did happen, though. Maybe you couldn't bring Shand back. You could still try to punish his killers.

But who would bomb a Glasgow pub? Haddow blamed the Irish, like it was Birmingham over again. The Provisionals. Or even the other lot, the Loyalists, they'd been busy with the fertilizer recently, setting off bombs in the Republic. Then you had the Scottish nationalists, the guys who'd been blowing up oil pipelines for the past two years. What did they call themselves? The Army of the Provisional Government. Only, did these guys not get jailed a few months back, after a string of bank jobs? Or it could be the Quinns: payback for the Tradeston fire. Tit for tat. Back and forth.

All the deaths. All the pointless deaths. He thought of Shand's funeral, the elderly father's outsize ears as he sat in the pew beside the young bewildered fiancée. Then an earlier funeral, the young mum and toddler from the Tradeston fire. The bottomless pathos of the half-size coffin. The toddler's dad in his Slater's suit, something not quite right about him, wasn't there? Something slightly off, McCormack couldn't place what.

Jesus, you could spend your life at funerals in this game. McCormack reached for his pint, sucked down three milky gulps. Smoke from an abandoned cigarette in an ashtray on the bar-top was nipping his eyes. He leaned across and folded the cigarette back on itself, crushing the embers under the filter.

"Hi!" The man beside him had turned elaborately round and was craning up at McCormack. He pushed his spectacles up on his nose. "Hi, Heid-the-baw! That was my smoke."

"That a fact?" McCormack nodded at the man's right hand, where it hung at his side. "I thought *that* was your cigarette."

The man brought his hand up, studying it as if he'd never seen it before, a smoking Regal between his fingers. He looked narrowly at McCormack, leaning back to find his focus, and then turned muttering to his pal.

But the spell was broken. McCormack reached for his pint and swallowed a couple of draughts, the black bitterness through the sweet white cream at his lips, and all he could hear was the whining voice of the drunk man beside him.

"These Fenians," the man was saying. "Blow up a squaddie pub. Can you credit it? Bold as you like. In the middle of Maryhill."

The man's companion said something and the man laughed shortly, a sound like crunching ice-cubes. "Oh aye. No doubt. They'll be fucking loving it. Bead-rattling cunts. Let them fuck off back to Dublin if they love it so much."

McCormack tapped the guy's shoulder. "It got bombed," he said. "Just so you know. Dublin got bombed."

The guy glanced over his shoulder then back to his friend. Then he craned back round to McCormack. "You say something to me?"

"I said Dublin got bombed. Maybe you heard? Last year. By Protestants. Thirty-three people died. Thirty-four, if you count the unborn child." McCormack twisted his pint on its beermat. "One of the dead was a pregnant woman."

"Do I know you?" The man's glasses flashed as he turned right round, squinted up at McCormack. "I'm talking to my friend here. This is a private conversation."

"Yeah. Well. It's a public house. You're talking kind of loud. It's hard not to hear. And you're talking shite."

The man rolled his shoulders, tilted his chin at McCormack. "Is that right? You'll be one of them, like?"

McCormack stayed the pint at his lips. He laughed. "You're asking if I'm a Catholic? Really?" He made a pistol with the first two fingers of his right hand and slowly pointed them at the man and drew the sign of the cross in the smoky air. "*An ainm an Athar, agus a Mhic, agus an Spioraid Naoimh.*"

The man nodded, like this was a dirty trick but one that he'd expected. He drew the back of his hand across his mouth, muttering something as he did.

McCormack could see the barman out of the corner of his eye, the bright slash of his scarlet tie, moving down towards them, stopping four feet away, arms folded, legs planted. The little charge in the air was communicating itself to the groups around them, men falling silent, stepping back a couple of paces.

The man had taken off his glasses and folded them into his pocket. He was facing McCormack with his hands hanging loose at his sides.

McCormack closed his eyes. You came in for a quiet pint and a speccy bigot was getting ready to hit you. How easy it would be, McCormack thought, to throw it all away. Brawling in a public house. Punching a civilian. He'd seen it happen. Joe Winton from C Div. Bounced down to sergeant, back in uniform, pension holed below the waterline. All for the pleasure of lamping a twat in the face.

He reached into his jacket pocket and a man behind him grabbed his arm. McCormack shook him off and pulled out his warrant card. He flipped it open and thrust it in the drunk man's face.

"Drunk and disorderly. Resisting arrest. Whatever the fuck else I can think of. I'm counting to five."

The man looked at McCormack with pure hatred. He took his glasses from his breast pocket, shook the legs open, put them on with slow dignity, pushed off from the bar and swayed towards the double doors, pushing through them without looking back.

McCormack lit a cigarette, tremor in his hand. Conversations started up again. The barman moved off down the bar to serve a customer. Most of the men in the pub were unaware that something had happened. And nothing *had* happened. Except that McCormack's pint now tasted sour and the laughter around him rang hard and false. He lifted his pint to skull what was left but suddenly the whole thing—the smell of smoke and spilled beer, the flat Glasgow voices, the chiming of the cash register, the clatter of glasses—was somehow too much. He set down his pint and walked into the night.

As McCormack strolled down towards Partick he noticed that one of his shoelaces was loose. He stopped outside one of the tenements on Highburgh Road and propped his foot on a low wall. He was knotting the lace when it came to him, what had bothered him about Gordon Chisholm, the estranged husband of the woman who died in the Tradeston fire. It was his socks. The husband wore a black funeral suit. White shirt and black tie. Black Oxfords polished to parade-ground gloss. But his socks were livid scarlet. And he remembered what Vic had told him, about soldiers who served in Northern Ireland. When they were drinking off-duty in Belfast, in the city-centre pubs, they wore civilian gear. But they also wore brightly coloured socks—reds and yellows and pinks. It was like a code, a way to identify your mates. Trouble was, it was a code that the Provos had cracked.

The three Scottish soldiers. Three teenage squaddies lured from Mooney's Bar in Belfast's Cornmarket by a group of young women who promised them a party. They were shot in the back of the head on a lonely hillside as they stood in a line while taking a piss.

Three young boys. Two brothers from Ayr and their buddy from Glasgow.

It was the colour of their socks that gave them away.

Ten minutes later McCormack was in the flat, shaking Vic by the shoulder.

"Vic! Vic!" Vic didn't stir. He was passed out on the sofa, three big bottles of Bass on the coffee table. Three dead soldiers. McCormack slapped him on the shoulder. "I've got it, Vic! I know who it is."

Vic grunted. He sat up suddenly, eyebrows climbing. He scratched his head with both hands.

"Christ. I was out for the count. What time is it?"

"Never mind, Vic. Listen. I know who he is. I've got it."

Vic reached out and waggled the bottle nearest him. There was a hollow splash and he tipped his head back and shook the dregs into his throat. He set the bottle back on the table, clinked it against its fellows.

McCormack was standing by the sofa, his hands grasping the empty air in front of him. "It's the fire, Vic. The fire in the warehouse. Remember? The tenement next door got burned down and four people died."

Vic blinked a couple of times. He worked his jaw and stretched his lips, like the Tin Man after the oil had been applied. "O.K. Right. The fire. Down in Tradeston."

"It was Gavin Elliot's building. Elliot was the landlord."

Vic rubbed his face with both palms, waited for McCormack to explain.

"And the building was a firetrap. I mean, they never charged him or anything but he was, well, you'd have to say he was culpable. Rubbish piled up in the close. Some of the windows were painted shut."

"What the hell are you saying, Duncan?"

"It's the husband," McCormack said. "The father. Gordon Chisholm. There was a mother and child who died. The dad wasn't living with them at that point. But listen, it just came to me: I remembered it from the funerals. The guy Chisholm was a soldier. The guy who lost his wife and wee girl in the fire. He was in the army, Vic. He was one of yours."

Victor was fully awake now. He sat nodding with his big hands hanging loose between his knees.

"And the Barracks Bar?"

"Same guy. He used a camper van to dump Gavin Elliot's body. A camper van was spotted near the Barracks. Casing the place, probably. It's him, Vic."

Victor rubbed his bottom lip with the ball of his thumb. "Uh-huh. Tell me this then, Duncan. Why the fuck's a soldier bombing the Barracks Bar?"

"For the very same reason! Revenge, Vic. It's the Maitlands who set the fire that killed his family. Has to have been. What's the quickest way to hit back?"

Victor nodded. He could see the logic. You bomb the

brother's pub. If you get lucky—and this man had—then the brother's among the victims. If you don't get lucky, well, you've made some noise. You've made your point.

McCormack crossed and clapped him on the shoulder again, this time with affection, reassurance. "You did it, Vic. We'd never have got the ident without you. You were right all along, this is all down to you."

Victor nodded. He reached for his cigarettes. He seemed less than thrilled at his achievement.

III
THE BITE IN THE APPLE

THURSDAY, 10 JULY 1975

38

McCormack rose early, all jangly with nerves. These are the days you live for, he thought. Days when it all comes together the legwork, the shitwork, the guess-work—and you set yourself up for the win. He skipped breakfast, couldn't stomach the prospect of peeling the cold, damp strips of Danish from the packet, laying them down in the sputtering pan.

He cut himself shaving, a deep nick that bloomed scarlet, turned his shaving foam to strawberries and cream.

He showered, slurped a half-mug of tea and was driving to Temple by quarter to eight. He drummed his fingers on the wheel, knocked his knuckle on the window in time to the beat of a pop song on the radio. He recognized the symptoms. There was an intoxication that gripped at this stage of a case, a giddiness when you'd identified your culprit and were planning the big move. The take-down.

A double-decker pulled away from a stop just ahead of him and McCormack pumped the gas and swung out to overtake, cutting back into lane as a navy Princess zipped past in a blare of horn. He thought about using the siren, clamping the flashing light to the roof of the car and tearing up the long straight seam of Great Western Road. But no: he breathed in deeply through his nose, paid it out slowly, forced himself to stay just a shade under thirty.

Take your time, son, he told himself. Think it all through.

The soldier's name was Chisholm. He'd been a Royal

Highland Fusilier. Maybe his regiment would have his last address, assuming he wasn't in the phone book or listed on the voter's roll. Chisholm had held Gavin Elliot for four or five days, tortured him, making plenty of noise. You would need somewhere isolated, somewhere private. A farmhouse on the city's edge, maybe a detached villa with a soundproofed basement. Somewhere big, at any rate. Which probably meant an inheritance, since Chisholm couldn't have bought a goodsized property on his army pay.

Anyway, now that they knew who he was, the arrest was only a matter of time.

McCormack swung into his parking space at Temple. As he walked round to the front entrance he spotted a car parked out front, sleek and flash, gunboat grey, a Jag, the driver busy with the sports pages of the *Record*, tipping his ash out of the barely opened window with a dainty flick of his thumb.

McCormack pushed through the main door to see the desk sergeant struggling to his feet, flipping the hatch, heading out to waylay him.

"Duncan! I tried to call. You'd already left."

He was oddly agitated, his hands flapping up in front of him like doves from a conjuror's hat.

McCormack nodded. "O.K. Well, I'm here now, Brian. What's the drama?"

"There's someone here to see you."

"Male someone?" McCormack kept walking, shrugging out of his mackintosh. "Female someone? Through the Big House, are they? Which interview room?"

Brian was trotting after him. "Room One, Dunc. But, Duncan. I was trying to tell you." He stopped, dropped his arms to his sides. "It's Walter Maitland."

McCormack came to a halt now, turned to face Brian. He folded his raincoat, draped it over his forearm. "Walter Maitland's in Room One?"

"I wanted to warn you."

"He's looking for me? Me specifically?"

Brian nodded manically, gestured helplessly, struggled for words.

"It's O.K., Brian. Calm down. Did he say what it was about?"

"That's the thing. Won't talk to anyone except you. They're all on tenterhooks through there."

"Well." McCormack clapped Brian on the shoulder. "I better go and see what the fella wants then, hadn't I?"

McCormack carried on to the Byre—neither Nicol nor Goldie were at their desks yet—and unlocked his office. He hung his mack on the coatrack in the corner and looked round the little room. The telephone on his desk looked the same. The dented filing cabinet was the same shade of green. Everything seemed normal, except that Walter Maitland had come to Temple Police Station and asked for him by name. He waited for this to make some kind of sense but it didn't, so he fixed his tie in the little mirror on the back of his door and set off down the corridor.

Walter Maitland spun round as McCormack pushed the handle and breezed into the interview room. Maitland's teeth were bared in anger. He faced McCormack in a boxer's crouch.

"Took your sweet fucking time," he spat.

McCormack crossed to the nailed-down desk and drew out one of the chairs. He sat down with his back to Maitland. He took out his notebook and set it on the desk. He fetched a pen from his inside pocket, clicked it a couple of times and set it beside his notebook.

"Why don't you sit down, Mr. Maitland?"

There was a brief moment when McCormack felt the prickles on the back of his neck and wondered if Maitland might be about to throw himself at him but he held his nerve and

Maitland's thick frame came swinging into his peripheral vision, pulling out a chair on the far side of the desk and slumping down into it.

Maitland wore a black shirt, neatly pressed. An immaculate midnight-blue suit. He was clean-shaven, his black hair swept carefully back and parted. When he hunched forward over the desk, his massive hands rested on the scarred wood surface in loosely bunched fists. A thin scent of cologne snaked out from his open collar.

McCormack looked up from his notebook and met the gangster's gaze. There was rage there in Maitland's eyes, and maybe something else that McCormack couldn't read. He shifted on his seat, consciously sharpened his focus.

There was no reason McCormack could think of for Walter Maitland being where he was. Under normal circumstances, Maitland would never darken a police station's door. You might say that, doing what he did, Maitland forfeited the protection of the police. Where Maitland confronted a problem, Maitland or his men would sort it out. Clearly, then, Maitland had encountered a problem that he couldn't solve. Either that, or he was trying to put something over on McCormack.

McCormack watched as Maitland seemed to wrestle with the weight of what he had come here to say. The big fists were still planted on the desk, rocking almost imperceptibly back and forth as Maitland's nostrils pinched and flared.

"It's my boy," he said finally, flatly. "My boy's been taken."

"Taken?" McCormack was struggling to envisage this.

Maitland nodded, ran a big paw across his swept-back hair. "Aye. Taken."

"You're saying your son's been kidnapped?"

"Catch on fast, don't you?"

McCormack grimaced, drew back his head. He had spent weeks and months waiting to get Walter Maitland on the other side of an interview desk and now that it was happening it felt like a dream, like everything was back to front and it was Maitland who was in control, not him. Surely no one who had brains enough to kidnap Maitland's kid would be stupid enough to do it?

"And they know it's him?" McCormack said. "I mean, they know it's your boy they've kidnapped?"

"Well since they sent me a letter telling me what they'd done, I'd have to say yes."

McCormack clamped his fingers to his jaw. He felt the scrap of tissue paper he'd used to staunch his shaving cut and peeled it off, flicked it to the floor. Neither Maitland nor McCormack had specified who "they" might be, but you didn't need a clairvoyant here, you didn't need a fucking paragnost. "They" could only be the Quinns. But Maitland hadn't hit back yet for the Barracks Bar bomb. The ball was still in Maitland's court. What were the Quinns doing running amok like this? There was something wrong here, something too desperate, even for the Quinns. Kidnapping a rival's son was a declaration of all-out war. It meant that nothing was out of bounds, no protocols or codes need be respected. It was back to a state of nature, a war of every man against every man.

But that wasn't what bothered him most. What bothered McCormack was this: if the Quinns had taken Walter Maitland's son, why had Walter Maitland come to the police?

"What did they say, the Quinns? In the letter, I mean."

"It's not the Quinns," Maitland said.

"It has to be the Quinns. You're saying someone else has got the balls to take your boy?"

"It's not the Quinns," he said again. Angry as he was, Maitland was finding it hard to open up to the Highland detective and McCormack saw now what it was, the other thing, beneath the anger. It was embarrassment. It had cost Maitland a lot to come here, as a civilian. A supplicant. It was hard not to enjoy it a little, hard not to want to make him suffer a little more.

"Is it a ransom they want?"

"No." A lock of Maitland's hair swung loose as he shook his head. "No ransom."

McCormack was struck again by the fantastical nature of the situation. Someone had formulated the idea of kidnapping Walter Maitland's son. And instead of burying it in the uttermost recesses of their consciousness and thanking the Lord for a narrow escape, they had gone ahead and done it.

"Sorry, Mr. Maitland. When did this happen? How did they do it? I mean, where was your son?"

"He lives with his mother," Maitland said. "Down in Ayrshire." As if this was an explanation. As if it couldn't have happened if the boy had been living in Glasgow.

"And, what, they just walked up and took him?"

He couldn't picture it; the whole thing seemed unlikely.

Maitland's lower jaw seemed to lengthen. "You think he gets ferried about in an armoured fucking car? He's an ordinary boy. His mum's not involved. He's not involved."

"He is now."

Maitland's hands were on the table and they flexed, just once, into fists. His breath came through a little ragged until it evened out again. "He's not the only one."

McCormack asked more questions. He noted down the details, the park where the boy was taken, the boy's address in Ayrshire, the mother's name and phone number, the boy's age (twelve), his name (Robert), the contact number for Maitland.

"Have you got the letter?"

"You'll get the letter. I want to know what you're gonnae do about it."

"Well, you can rest assured we will pursue all avenues, Mr. Maitland."

"The fuck does that even mean?"

"It means the best thing you can do right now is wait, Mr. Maitland. And maybe you could moderate your language."

"My *lang*uage? My boy's been kidnapped. You cunt. You're worried about a sweary word?"

McCormack closed his notebook, set his pen down on top of it. "You know, Mr. Maitland. You go around setting fire to buildings, you have people stabbed, shot. People are apt to get irritated. It riles them up."

"You think I deserve this? You think I had it coming?"

"It's not about you, Mr. Maitland. Do I think your son deserves it? That's the question. And no. He doesn't. He's just in the way. But you? You deserve everything that's coming to you. I just hope I'm there to see it."

"You're fucking enjoying this. What kind of person—"

"You, Mr. Maitland! You're the kind of person who enjoys it. Seeing people suffer. I don't. I'm sorry for your boy. I'm sorry this has happened."

"Don't apologize to me. Save your fucking pity for the prick who did it. He's the one who'll need it."

The two men looked at each other across three feet of scarred wood. "I understand your anger. However," McCormack tapped his biro on the desktop, "sad as it is, the world doesn't stop because your boy's gone missing. Look, we have a lead on the Barracks Bar bombing. We know who killed your brother, Mr. Maitland. And Gavin Elliot, too. We know who did it."

Maitland sat back, nodding. He was calmer now, it was almost sardonic, the look he gave to McCormack as he crossed one leg onto a knee, gripping his ankle in a splayed hand. McCormack registered the glint of Maitland's wedding band, the sharp diamonds on his patterned socks.

"Oh course, that information is confidential for the moment," McCormack continued. "We can't give out the man's identity, but rest assured that we will be—is something *funny*?"

Maitland's tight smile slackened. "You don't need to tell me the name, polis. I know the fucking name."

McCormack looked up at the clock on the wall, as if it was important to register the time at this juncture, as if he would be asked to account for this detail at a later date. He had a brief dizzy wash of clairvoyance, he knew in some part of his brain what Maitland was about to say, the counters were dropping but just not quickly enough to forestall the gangster's voice.

"I know the name because it's the same fucking guy. The guy who topped Elliot, the guy who blasted the Barracks Bar, the guy who killed Hughie. It's the guy who took my boy. His name is Gordon Chisholm."

And now Maitland reached into his inside pocket and set it down on the desk, gently, an opened letter, its top edge shucked and ragged. McCormack glanced at him and reached for the envelope.

It bore a circular postmark: "Bearsden, Glasgow" round the edges, and "2 P.M., 8 July 1975" in the middle. So it was posted yesterday. Inside it was an A4 sheet, folded in three. As McCormack unfolded it a square of black card, edged in white, slipped out and landed on the desk. It was a Polaroid photograph. McCormack took out his handkerchief and flipped it over.

It showed a boy of twelve or thirteen from the chest and shoulders up, standing against a wall of concrete blocks. There was nothing to date the photograph, no newspaper in the boy's hands, and the backdrop was completely anonymous. It looked like some sort of outbuilding or industrial unit, just a wall of breezeblocks joined with thick strips of cement. It was an interior wall; the camera flash had bleached the boy's features, reddened his pupils. The boy himself seemed sombre, not obviously distressed or scared, despite the open gash on the bridge of his nose. His adolescent features were still too big for his face, but he would have his father's slightly banal, square-jawed good looks.

If he survived to inherit them.

McCormack turned to the letter. He flattened it out with the ball of his fist. It was handwritten in black biro on a plain white sheet of paper. Cursive script. No attempt to disguise the handwriting with block letters:

> Mr. Maitland,
>   The fire you set in Tradeston last month killed my wife and my only daughter. My daughter's name was Kirsty. She was four years old. You cannot know the pain of losing a child in this way. But you will. I have no demands. I seek no ransom. I am simply doing you the courtesy of giving you time to come to terms with your loss, which will not be long in coming.
>   Yours sincerely,
>   Gordon Chisholm

McCormack read the letter again. He turned the sheet over to check the back and held it up to the light for a watermark: nothing.

"That's an up-to-date picture of your lad?"

"That's Robert, aye. And that's the T-shirt he was wearing."

"What happened to his face?"

Maitland shrugged. "I'm assuming he put up a fight."

McCormack put the letter back on the table. "No phone calls? No other communication?"

"Just the letter."

"O.K. Well, we wait and see. What his next move is. He'll be back in touch, Mr. Maitland. Nothing surer. Meantime, we'll have Chisholm's photo in every newspaper, on the evening news. We'll find Gordon Chisholm. If we can, we'll find your boy."

Maitland stood up and buttoned his jacket. He walked past McCormack like a man wading through water.

39

We know who did it," McCormack said. "We know the name of the man who murdered Gavin Elliot. The man who bombed the Barracks Bar. Killed Iain Shand and the others."

This time at least his listeners didn't nod, didn't smirk back knowingly. They exchanged a look and said nothing.

"Walter Maitland knows it, too. Knew it without me having to tell him. He was in this morning, before you arrived."

This they did know. The whole station had been buzzing with the news that Walter Maitland hadcometosee McCormack. While McCormack was giving Haddow a debrief on the meeting, most of the station was crammed into the Byre, quizzing Goldie and Nicol about their boss's connection with Maitland.

"The man we're looking for," McCormack said, "is Gordon Chisholm."

He waited for the name to register. Nicol had her eyes shut, running the name through her mental database. Goldie looked blank. Eventually Nicol opened her eyes, shook her head. "I know the name, sir. I just can't place it."

"The Tradeston fire," McCormack told them. "Chisholm's the estranged husband of the woman who died. The wee girl's father. He served in Ulster with the Royal Highland Fusiliers in '71."

Goldie rubbed his thumb across his corrugated brow. "I still don't get it, Duncan. A soldier bombs the Barracks Bar? A squaddie pub? A guy who's served in Ulster?"

"He wasn't bombing a squaddie pub," McCormack said. "He was bombing a Maitland pub."

"He was taking revenge for the fire, sir, wasn't he?"

"We think so, Nicol. We know Maitland ordered the Tradeston fire. Chisholm blames him for his family's death."

Goldie stood up from his desk, hitched his trousers. "But why Elliot? I can see the Barracks Bar. He blames the Maitlands for setting the fire. It's the Maitlands who've killed his wife and wee lassie. He pays it back on a Maitland pub. But what's Elliot got to do with it? He kills Elliot—tortures the guy—because he did a bit of business with Hugh Maitland? They owned a couple of buildings together? It makes no sense, Dunc."

"He owned one building in particular," McCormack said. "Remember?"

Goldie looked at Nicol, back to McCormack. "The Tradeston tenement? Gavin Elliot was the landlord?"

"That's right. I'm thinking Chisholm blamed Elliot for the building's condition. Rubbish in the communal areas. Old furniture stacked in the back-close. Place was a firetrap."

"But there's something else," Nicol said. "Something you're not telling us."

"There is," McCormack said.

"Otherwise you'd be cock-a-hoop at having ID'd Chisholm. What's happened, sir?"

"He's taken Maitland's boy." A pause followed this statement. McCormack took his glasses off and rubbed a hand down his face. He put his glasses back on. "Gordon Chisholm has kidnapped Walter Maitland's son," he said, enunciating each syllable.

"Fucking hell," Goldie said. "Do we know where he is? Has he said what he wants?"

McCormack plucked the letter from his inside pocket, smoothed it out on Nicol's desk. "He doesn't want anything.

Just wants Maitland to know he's going to kill the boy. Wants him to suffer."

Goldie crossed to Nicol's desk, bent to read the note over her shoulder. "Well that's that." Goldie straightened up. "Boy's a goner. What age is he?"

"Twelve."

"You think he's dead already?" Nicol asked.

"I don't know. But whatever happens now, Chisholm's a dead man."

"That's for sure," Goldie said. "Snatching Maitland's kid? Jesus Christ. Even if he gives the boy back, Maitland's gonnae kill him. He probably figures, fuck it: may as well go through with it."

"He took the boy on Monday night," McCormack said lightly.

"Nearly two days." Goldie shook his head.

"Look, we know how these things work." McCormack lifted the letter and folded it, slid it back into his pocket. "The longer they go on, the greater the chance that the victim gets killed. Still. It's only two days. We proceed on the assumption the boy's still alive."

"How did he take him?" Nicol asked.

"Snatched him from a public park near the mum's house. Down in Ayrshire. West Kilbride. The postmark on the letter's Bearsden. Posted yesterday. I'm assuming Bearsden's a decoy, but maybe someone spotted him while he was there, saw where he was headed."

Nicol's fists were clenched, her eyes pressed shut. Then her eyes flashed open. "Sir. The camper van!"

"What's that?"

"There was a camper van spotted at Crawford Street on the night Elliot's body was dumped. It was spotted outside the Barracks Bar too. Chisholm drives a camper van. We've got the list of camper van owners, haven't we? Gordon Chisholm will be on it."

"He'll be on it if it's registered in Glasgow or if he bought the thing here," Goldie said. "Not if he bought it elsewhere."

"Can you find the list, Derek? If Chisholm's on it, we've got his address."

Nicol was frowning. "What if he doesn't have an address? That's kinda the whole point, sir, isn't it? Of a camper van. You go where you please."

"He held Gavin Elliot for five days, Nicol. He's holding Walter Maitland's boy. He's not doing that in a camper van. Of course he's got an address."

Goldie had found the list. It was stapled together, multiple sheets. He strolled towards them, leafing through it. They watched him as his eyes tracked back and forth, shaking his head as he flicked each page. He tossed it on the desk.

"Nup. Nothing."

"O.K. Keep the heid. We'll get him, Derek. Get one of the uniforms to go down to the DVLA office on Bothwell Street. Check the records. Every VW camper van bought in Scotland, registered in Scotland. Past ten years. We want him going through every card looking for Chisholm. We don't want to see his face till he's got an address for Gordon Chisholm. Understood?"

"Got it."

"Meantime, you get on to the MoD, Derek. We want Chisholm's full record. Names of mates, close associates. We want every address the army's ever had for him. Nicol?"

"Sir."

"Chisholm's family. We want the names of aunts, uncles, older relatives. Anyone who might have died and left him a house. We need to know who died, when, the contents of their will. Chisholm's holed up somewhere big or somewhere isolated. Probably both. He's in a farmhouse, maybe, a moorland cottage. Something like that. We need the address, we need it quick. What else?" McCormack had fetched his raincoat from behind his office door and was wrestling into it. "A photo. We need a recent photo. Headshot. The army must have one. We need Chisholm's description, photograph in all the papers, starting with today's *Evening Times*. Helpline number to this office—get a uniform manning a desk in here."

"Sir. Won't the papers have a photo? I mean from the funeral?"

McCormack stopped, his arm half into his raincoat sleeve, stared at Nicol. "They might, at that. But it needs to be clear, close-up. O.K.? By the way, how'd you get on down in Ayrshire? I forgot to ask."

"The Red House? Oh I found it all right, sir. Bloke called Wylie. A widower. He and his wife used to foster kids. They had Yvonne Gray for a year or two in the Fifties. Yvonne and another lassie. But it didn't work out. Says he hasn't seen Yvonne since she was a teenager."

"O.K. Well, we keep looking, Nicol. She'll turn up. Meantime, source a decent photo of Chisholm. Give Fiona Morrison at the *Record* a ring—tell her I'll send her some quotes later if she gives the Chisholm photo a show."

"On it, sir."

McCormack had his hand on the door.

"Hold on a minute, Duncan." Goldie had thought of something. "Chisholm sends a letter to Maitland. Not a ransom note or anything, he just wants Maitland to know why he's being punished."

"That's right."

"So how come he doesn't send anything to the Elliots?"

McCormack thought about this. He straightened his raincoat, turned down the collar. "Maybe he figured he'd tell Elliot in person. You know, while he was torturing him to death over four days."

"Aye, but then the knowledge would die with Elliot. He'd want other people to know, wouldn't he? Elliot's family?"

"O.K. Maybe." McCormack seemed weighed down by the light raincoat. He squared his shoulders with an effort. "Well, we bear it in mind, Derek. I'm off to Ingram Street."

"What for?"

"Meet the fire investigator. This whole thing seems to have started with the Tradeston fire. It's the fire that set Chisholm off. It's the fire that's got Shand's mystery tout all lathered up. I think the fire's the key. One of the keys. And we're missing something about it. O.K. We'll catch up later. In town. You know Varani's caff on the Gallowgate? Under the viaduct? I'll meet you both there. Two o'clock. I'll be the one downing triple whiskies."

Two minutes after McCormack left, Haddow came through to the Byre. He must have been watching, Nicol thought; picking his moment. He was nodding, shifty-looking, moving among the desks like a schoolmaster, pausing to glance at their work. Nicol caught Goldie's eye: what the hell are we getting now?

"I wanted to tell you," Haddow said. He had come to rest by the whiteboard. "I told McCormack earlier but I wanted to say it in person. This is fine police work. The CC's pleased, too."

Well, that's the main thing, Nicol thought. As long as the CC's off your back.

"We've had our moments," Haddow was saying. "D.I. McCormack and me. But this? This is a result. No question."

"Thanks, sir." Goldie spoke guardedly. "I mean, we've still got to catch him, though."

"Oh, you'll catch him all right." Haddow dismissed the very suggestion of failure with a flap of his hand. "There's no doubt about that, Detective."

It looked like confidence, Nicol thought, but really it was relief. Relief that it wasn't the Irish. They didn't have to deal with a terrorist threat. Or a gang war either, since it wasn't the

Quinns. And with those scenarios off the table, Haddow was happy. The boy who'd been kidnapped was the son of a gangster, not real people. They'd identified the culprit; they had a name and a face for the *Record*'s front page, and that was what mattered. The rest was just mopping up, and somebody else would do that as usual.

"And if *we* don't," Haddow said. "Walter Maitland sure as hell will."

On his way out the door, Haddow paused. "I'll be putting in a word for the pair of you, of course, when the time comes. Promotion, I mean."

They muttered their thanks. And then, as if something had just occurred to him, Haddow came back in and closed the door behind him.

"Listen, though. I know it hasn't been easy. Working with McCormack. I mean, he's not a team player. We all know that. Marches to his own bloody drum. So if there's anything troubling you. Anything I need to know about. My door's always open. O.K.? Strictest confidence. I'll say no more."

And he was gone, down the corridor, his high and tuneful whistling bouncing off the cold stone walls.

40

Gordon Chisholm woke up like a drowning man. Flailing, thrashing, lashed with sweat. He'd forgotten how it felt to start the day normally, to stretch your arms and step from your bed. The rattle of cornflakes in a bowl. The morning paper. The happy orange brightness of a glass of juice.

Every night his mind played endlessly a version of the same movie. It was playing it now, as he pulled back the covers and sprawled on the twisted sheets, and Chisholm endured it, actor and spectator, both inside and outside of the action.

Four soldiers move through the central streets. Four men in camo, ten yards apart. Boots and rifles. Glengarries with red touries. The man at the end facing backwards. When the man at the front stops, all stop, maintaining the distance between them. Then, at a signal, the patrol starts up again. The shoppers on Belfast's Royal Avenue go about their business with never a glance at the soldiers. It's as if a war is happening in a different dimension to everyday life. Or maybe this is a ghost column, a patrol from some long-forgotten conflict, and they will walk right through the red sandstone wall of the *Telegraph* building and disappear back to the past.

The man at the end is Gordon Chisholm. He flexes his fingers on his rifle. His palms are slick with sweat. He wants to wipe them on his combat trousers but he can't afford to let his attention slip. He's the eyes in the back of the head of the green beast that is snaking its way through the lunchtime crowds. He's watching for trouble, for the glint of a sniper's scope on a rooftop, the whirling arm of a youth stepping out of a doorway to launch a cobblestone or a milk bottle of petrol stoppered with a flaming rag. He has to keep glancing back to check for obstacles at his feet and to keep in visual contact with his comrades.

He cranes round to see the backpack on the third man and then turns back to the street. It's a cold day, overcast, the sky low and sagging with purple clouds. A small brown-and-white dog trots across the street, oblivious to the braking cars. A mother yanks the arm of her dawdling toddler. Two men lean in to light their cigarettes off the same match. Chisholm runs his tongue across his upper gums to ease the dryness in his mouth. He feels invisible. He wants someone to catch his eye, someone to admit that he exists, that he is here in this street at this moment. He feels invisible but his skin prickles with danger. *Look at me*, he wills them. *Look at me, for fuck's sake.*

And then somebody does.

A man leaning on the wall of the Central Library, close to the entrance. Denim jacket and long black hair. He looks up slyly from under his fringe and catches Chisholm's eye. There's a gleam of something that Chisholm can't read and then the man pushes off from the wall and starts to cross the street. Chisholm has time to grasp that something is happening when he hears the revs of an engine and the shriek of brakes and turns to see a van barrelling out of a side street and stopping dead in front of him. The rest of the patrol are on the other side of the van and now the driver's door swings open and the driver is crossing Royal Avenue at a run, knees pumping. Chisholm flexes his hands on the rifle and thinks about dropping to one knee but the driver is already lost amid the milling shoppers and this is when something snaps at Chisholm's shoulder and he's sitting down on the pavement with his rifle across his knees.

Time has slowed to almost to a stop by now and he takes in soundlessly the shine on his toecaps, a shucked half-orange in the gutter and the faces of shoppers, watching him now, all round eyes and open mouths, chewing the air, before the world sucks back up to speed and there is shouting and screams and he scrambles to his feet in a scrape of boots and lunges for the sidestreet.

The others are there too and they throw themselves behind the van, gripping their rifles, breathing. Chisholm pats himself down, flexes his shoulder, looking for the wound. He hasn't been hit; the bullet struck his pack, knocking him down. He's grinning, still heaving for breath, when he sees Mitchell's contorted face. Mitch thumbs at the van and mouths "Bomb!" and they clatter off down the sidestreet for thirty yards and collapse in a doorway. And it's only now, with Mitch radioing for backup and the siren whoops filling the air, it's only now that the three of them see it in each other's stricken faces. *The sergeant. Where's the fucking sergeant?*

And now they're back up the sidestreet, past the van with its open driver's door and round the corner to where a small crowd is gathered round a woman in a headscarf kneeling on the ground. Beside her are the soles of the sergeant's boots and his splayed knees in camouflage and now his white face, oddly peaceful, and the blood pooling behind his head.

They worked it out later. How it had happened. Two snipers. When the van burst out of Kent Street, the first sniper had taken his shot at Chisholm. The rest of the patrol saw that Chisholm had been cut off and they turned back to find him. That was when the second sniper shot Sergeant Skilling in the back of the head. They found two unfurnished top-floor flats, rented under false names, rent paid in advance. No prints, no casings. Just the net curtains blowing at the open sash windows.

After Sergeant Skilling's death, Chisholm became a kind of talisman to the other Fusiliers. Everyone wanted Chisholm on their patrol. Nothing would befall you if Chisholm was there, the man who shrugged off a sniper's bullet. He himself grew brutal and reckless. When they rumbled into the Short Strand or the streets around the Falls, looking for weapons, Chisholm would go berserk, ransacking the tiny houses, smashing the plaster saints. In the first house they raided after Skilling's death, Chisholm saw Jesus pointing mournfully at his exposed heart and he smashed the frame with his rifle butt. Jesus was there in every home they raided, catching Chisholm's eyes, and it got so that the first thing Chisholm did, as soon as they burst through a Fenian front door, was to seek out the picture of the Sacred Heart and smash it, trample it under his boots. *Fuck you, Fenian Jesus.*

They used his fury, the bosses did. Deployed him on a secret op, interrogating Fenians at a barracks north of Belfast. The Five Techniques. Torture. But he already knew. He was finished. He had to get out. He was unravelling. He couldn't see the red tourie on a Glengarry without picturing the bullet striking Sergeant Skilling's head, the blood spouting.

So he came home. To Glasgow. To Denise and wee Kirsty. To the scabby flat in Tradeston. But it felt like he was still over there. Denise was Catholic. There was a Sacred Heart in the hallway of the flat and whenever he passed it Chisholm was back in Belfast. One night he came in from the pub and took a hammer to the picture, smashed it to smithereens and just kept going, trashing the flat. When the police arrived they found him crying in the little kitchen on his knees amid the broken chairs, Denise stroking his hair and shushing him. They didn't charge him, just gave him a caution, but Denise had reached her limit.

And so, in his own way, had Chisholm. He remembered as a child—it was his earliest memory, sometimes he thought it was his only memory—his father, drunk and raging, crashing about in their room-and-kitchen, the plates on the dresser tottering, smashing. His father's sneering mouth beneath its gold moustache. The cruel shoulders bulging from the khaki braces.

Before he was three or four, Chisholm could tell by the sound of the key in the lock precisely how drunk his father was, how scared he needed to be. And after his father died, throughout all the years in the Home, Chisholm made the vow that they all made. He would be different. He wouldn't put his family through that. And yet, stop fucking press, here he was. Another drunken squaddie like his worthless da.

He moved out. Just till he could get himself sorted. He couldn't think of anywhere else to go, so he travelled down to Sergeant Skilling's house in Ayrshire, where he'd paid his respects when he first came home. Mrs. Skilling was a widow, she lived on her own—she was delighted to take Chisholm in. Just for a few weeks, he told her. Denise and he would be getting back together. Everything was going to be all right.

And then it happened.

The fire.

He saw it in the *Record*, a picture of the firemen's ladders and the blackened building and he recognized it straight off. He wondered if the fire was somehow punishment for his own profanation of the little homes of Belfast. He kept picturing the fire catching alight, the wee red tourie of flame appearing and blossoming into a flower and then a bush and then a spreading tree of fire. It seemed like an Act of God, or maybe an Act of Jesus and he thought of the orange tongues of flame around the glowing Sacred Heart. And then it came out that the fire had been started on purpose. Someone had set the fire and who could that be but the Maitlands? The warehouse belonged to the Quinns; it had to be the Maitlands who torched it. And now, like the answer to a prayer he hadn't made, here was the road to redemption. The fire was an act of terrorism, an act of war. Fine. Let's answer in kind. Elliot first, the slumlord with the firetrap rookeries. The Five Techniques once more. And when it was over, chuck him into the rubbish of Crawford Street. The Maitlands next, car bomb on a Friday night. He'd shared his bomb-making know-how with the Loyalists in Belfast, trained up four or five Blacknecks. Let's give the Maitlands a taste of that. And now this. The finale. Walter Maitland's boy. An eye for an eye and a tooth for a tooth. The boy was game, you had to give him that. He'd put up a fight when Chisholm snatched him. Had to slam the butt of a pistol in the boy's face, break his nose. A good kid, you'd say, but fuck it, so was Kirsty. What did Walter Maitland care about that?

Chisholm rose from the bed where he lay smoking. It was time to check on the boy, he hadn't seen him for four or five hours. He came down the stairs from the little attic room and paused in the flagged passageway. He could hear Mrs. Skilling clattering pans in the kitchen. She had taken to calling him Malcolm, as if Chisholm was her son, as if her poor murdered boy had stumbled back to thump on her door, like something out of *The Monkey's Paw*.

He stepped out of the cottage into the day. It was all sky and silence and the woody smell of heather. The moor rolled away to the horizon in all directions, except downhill where the little ribbon of road passed the whitewashed farmhouse, with the reservoir beyond. A whaup flapped up with its liquid, rising cry and he found himself wheeling round in a dizziness of blue as he tried to follow its flight. Maybe it would have been different. Maybe if they'd settled here when he came back from Belfast, and not a Tradeston tenement, they would still be together and Denise and wee Kirsty would still be alive. He stretched out his arms and breathed in the moorland air. Then he crossed towards the outbuilding. It was the perfect place to hold someone. There was little chance of discovery, no fear of being overheard. The boy was chained to a bracket in the wall. Hooded. Gagged. He could shout from now till the Day of Judgement. Nobody would hear him. Nobody would come.

41

Nicol nearly didn't hear the phone. She was chatting to the desk sergeant in the corridor. His wife had just given birth to their first child in the Southern General, a boy, nine pounds two ounces, named Michael after his grandad and possessor of a full head of jet-black hair (unlike his father, Nicol reflected, whose thinning locks were combed hopefully back over a spreading bald spot). Life went on, even in the midst of a murder inquiry. She was listening to the tale of young Michael's prowess as a sleeper ("Right through the night, from eight to eight, not a bother on him") when she caught the tinny pulse through the open door.

"Sorry, Brian: is that—"

She made it before the phone rang off.

"Is this Liz Nicol?"

The voice was tentative, sceptical. It sounded as if it was breaking up, drifting off.

Nicol made her own tones harder and more emphatic, as if to compensate. "This is D.C. Nicol, yes."

"It's me," the voice said, and then, when Nicol failed to respond: "Rona."

Rona? Nicol closed her eyes to concentrate. Do I know a Rona?

"From the sauna," the voice said testily. "Healing Hands."

"Oh, *Rona*. Of course. Sorry. You've got something to tell me, Rona?"

"Not on the phone."

They arranged to meet in fifteen minutes, in Kelvingrove Park, by the monument to Lord Roberts.

Nicol found a space on Park Terrace and hurried over to the park gates. The Lord Roberts statue—a man in a feathered helmet astride a prancing charger—stood just beyond the gates on the park's highest hill. Across the valley you could see the towers and spires of the university. Nicol stood at the railings in the shadow of the massive plinth and read the inscriptions: INDIAN MUTINY, UMBEYLA, ABYSSINIA, LUSHAI, AFGHANISTAN, BURMAH, SOUTH AFRICA.

She heard footsteps and saw Rona climbing the path towards her. She was dressed much the same as when Nicol had last seen her—jeans and a fitted check shirt, no make-up, hair scraped back in a scrunchy—but the frown line between her eyes was visible from thirty yards.

She greeted Nicol with a nod and the pair of them set off down the path towards the river.

"She phoned me," Rona said. "This morning."

"You mean the woman you're not pally with. The woman you barely know. That woman?"

"Aye, O.K." Rona's voice tightened a couple of notches. "So we're closer than I let on. But the rest was true. I didn't know what had happened. I didn't know where she was."

"But you do now?"

Rona folded her arms across her body, tucked her chin into her chest, as if she was facing into a wind. "Yvonne's in trouble, Liz. She thinks I am too. I think maybe she's right."

There was a wood pigeon in one of the trees; Nicol couldn't see it, but its forlorn call—low and foreboding, like an oboe came hooting down to them.

"How come you're in trouble?"

Rona ignored Nicol's question. "She's scared, Liz. She heard something in the sauna. There's a wee laundry room through the wall from the bar. She heard two of Maitland's boys talking."

"I knew it! That's what I told—look; never mind. What did she hear?"

"They were talking about a woman who was killed a few years back. When the Quaker stuff was happening. They said someone was trying to fake the death of a woman called Helen Thaney. So they killed this other woman. Well, Walter Maitland did. Made her look like this Helen Thaney."

"The fourth victim," Nicol said. "Jesus."

"What?"

"The fourth victim of the Quaker. It was made to look like a Quaker murder but it wasn't. The woman was wrongly identified as Helen Thaney. It even says Helen Thaney on her headstone. But it wasn't Helen Thaney. Does Yvonne know who the woman was?"

Rona folded her arms more tightly, hugging herself. "It was a girl who worked in the Dennistoun place. That's why she thinks I'm in danger too. We're all in danger. If they can wipe someone out as easy as that, just for looking like someone else."

"Who was it, Rona? Who did they kill?"

Rona was looking away across the park. She turned to look at Nicol. "It was Isobel Wylie."

"The wee girl that the Wylies adopted, down in Ayrshire."

Rona nodded. "So you found the Red House, then?"

"Oh I found it all right. It's in Fairlie, outside Largs. I spoke to the guy who fostered Yvonne and Isobel in the Fifties. But I never found Yvonne."

They had reached the memorial fountain now, and they turned down the path towards the river.

"Aye, but *they* did."

Nicol stopped. "Maitland found her?"

"They sent a guy down from Glasgow. And, aye, he found

her. But get this. As she's talking to him, Yvonne works out that she knows who he is."

"Maitland's guy?"

"It's Isobel's brother. Christopher Kidd. That was Isobel's name before the Wylies adopted her: Isobel Kidd. He was hanging round the Maitland crew, doing wee jobs for them. He knew Izzy had worked in a Maitland brothel and he was trying to find out what happened to her. On the fly, like."

"So Yvonne Gray told him."

"She says he went mental. She thinks he's planning to do something. You know: something stupid."

Going after Walter Maitland would certainly qualify as stupid. Someone had chalked a love-heart on the path, complete with arrow and initials, and Nicol drew the sole of her shoe across the outline as she stood there thinking. Whoever Christopher Kidd was, he wouldn't be a match for Maitland and his crew. He wouldn't get near Walter Maitland. They would take his knife or gun off him and break him into little pieces.

"She thinks they'll kill him," Rona was saying as if she was reading Nicol's thoughts. "Like they killed his sister."

"They'll do worse than that," Nicol said. "They'll force him to tell them where Yvonne is."

They walked on, slower, not speaking. They could hear the river, the Kelvin, and now they could see it, flashing and sparkling through the trees. It was green and shady down here and Nicol trailed her hand along the railings as she walked and waited for Rona to make her decision.

"She told me in confidence." Rona shook her head. "It wouldnae be right."

"Rona." Nicol stopped and gripped the woman's arm. "You're not thinking straight, Rona. Use your head. How did they find her down in Largs? Eh?"

Rona fumbled in her shirt pocket, pulled out a crumpled

roll-up. Picked some lint from the end, found a lighter in her jeans.

"They've got better intel than we've got, that's why," Nicol said. "How long you think it'll take them to find her now? Even without Christopher Kidd to lean on?"

They had stopped by the Highland Light Infantry memorial, opposite the Prince of Wales Bridge. An infantryman sat perched on a plinth of jagged rocks, in pith helmet and puttees, a hand resting on one knee, a knapsack slung over his shoulder. He looked as if he was about to swing his legs round and push himself off from the plinth, landing two-footed and striding off into the trees. As if all the wars were over.

Rona took a pull on her cigarette. She looked across the bridge at Kelvin Way and then back to Nicol. "You never heard this from me," she said.

42

Richard Boyd, the fire investigator, was a short man, pot-bellied in a grey polo shirt, with the serene, collected air of a man who knows the things you don't.

"Thanks for seeing me," McCormack said.

"That's all right." Boyd gestured for McCormack to sit. "I spoke to D.I. McCoy at Cumberland Street. He has my report."

They were in Boyd's office in the Central Fire Station on Ingram Street. A lime-green metal desk with a hooded type-writer. There was a public info poster behind Boyd's head: *Electricity Can Kill: Don't Take Chances.*

"I know that. I thought it would be quicker to hear it from the horse's mouth. I'm grateful for your time, Mr. Boyd."

"Fine, then. Floor's yours."

McCormack had his notebook out. "First of all, I under-stand that the fire was started deliberately. You're sure about that?"

"Sure as I can be."

"How do you know?"

Boyd stood up. "Let's take things in order, shall we?" He crossed to a large desk in the corner of the office, beckoned McCormack to follow. There were plans of the warehouse and the adjacent tenement spread out on the desk, and glossy black-and-white photos of the gutted buildings. "At first, to be honest, the fire looked accidental. Best guess for the source was a wall heater on the east wall of the first floor. Just here." He tapped the plan.

"Electrical fault?"

"It looked that way. There seems to have been a table or a desk under the heater. I surmised that there was paper on the desk. Box files, paper towels, toilet rolls, something like that."

"Paper?"

"It's a powerful accelerant, Inspector. People always think of petrol or bleach; paper does the job just as well. Better sometimes."

"You say the desk was under the heater?"

"That's right."

"So, wouldn't the flames rise?"

"Mostly, but not always. There's a rule of thumb: a fire burns seventy per cent up, thirty per cent down. More, if there's something flammable underneath it."

McCormack nodded. He spun one of the glossies till it was the right way round. The stark frame of the warehouse, charred rafters tilting down. Everything blurred and askew. It looked like a snapshot of Dresden.

"And then the whisky catches fire and it's Goodnight Vienna."

"Well, yes. But not just whisky. The warehouse was a woolstore for most of its existence. It stored bales of wool for the textile mills. You've got decades of lanolin impregnating that wooden floor."

"Lanolin?" McCormack cocked his head.

"An oil from wool, Inspector. Highly flammable. They told me you were a Highlander."

"Different kind of Highlander. So there's no need to reach for foul play?"

"That's what I thought. But look." Boyd tapped his forefinger onto three photographs in turn. "You'll see from these that not much was left of the warehouse. However, some of the flooring survives, from that first storey. I got them to take it up. Give me a minute." Boyd strode across to an inner door, punched the code into the entry system. He emerged a few seconds later in latex gloves with what looked like a plank of wood balanced on his palms. "Tongue and groove, Inspector. Tongue and groove. Smell this."

Boyd was smiling. He held his arms out to McCormack. It was a couple of floorboards, seamed in the middle, one end ragged and charred. McCormack bent towards the charred end.

"No, no, Inspector. The join. Smell the join."

As soon as he bent his head he caught the hit: heady, chemical, unmistakable.

"Petrol," he said.

Boyd smiled in triumph. He toted the floorboards to the evidence locker and came back, peeling off the latex gloves, almost gleeful. "It was the purest luck, Inspector. Pure luck that these floorboards survived. We've got two more of them back there. Now. My reading of the evidence? Whoever did this set up his combustible materials under the desk, beneath the wall heater." Again Boyd tapped the plan. "Then," he held up a finger; "then he's splashed a trail of water from the desk to the doorway." Boyd drew his finger across the plan.

"Water?" McCormack frowned.

"Bear with me, Inspector. You lay a thick trail of water. *Then* you lay a thinner trail of petrol on top of it. The petrol sits on top of the water. You light it at the doorway and it zips along to the desk. Boom! Undetectable, unless you're out of luck and it's a T & G floor and some of the petrol soaks into the grooves *and* some of the flooring survives. The floorboards were taken up here and here"—Boyd was tapping the plan again—" in a direct line between the desk and the doorway."

He stood up from the desk and crossed his arms, his head tipped smugly to one side.

McCormack was nodding. "That's impressive work, Mr. Boyd. Someone set the fire to make it look like an accident."

"If you're thinking insurance," Boyd said. "I'd say you're on the right lines."

Boyd walked him down to the street. They shook hands on the pavement.

"Just to be clear, though," McCormack said. "The warehouse was deliberate, but the tenement was accidental, right? I mean, whoever set the warehouse fire, they didn't expect the tenement to go up too? They didn't know the fire would spread?"

The Dennistoun bus was grinding past and Boyd waited till it turned the corner onto High Street. "Well, strictly speaking," he said, "the fire didn't spread."

McCormack blinked. Was this man's entire aim in life to make you feel stupid? And did you have to make it so easy for him? "Come again?"

"I mean, what you have to appreciate: the flames don't actually need to reach the next building. Once the heat gets sufficiently intense, net curtains will ignite through glass. That's what we think happened in this case."

"Jesus."

"The third-floor flat nearest the warehouse went up first. Then the flames spread to the flat above, and the top-floor single-end. No one had much of a chance. To escape, I mean."

"But whoever did this couldn't have known for certain that the curtains would ignite?"

"No. It's just bad luck for the arsonist." He grimaced. "Not great luck for the poor souls in the tenement, either. I hope you find whoever did this, Inspector."

McCormack shook Boyd's hand, thanked him for his time.

Outside, the clouds had cleared, the sky was Manchester City blue and the sun was dicing Ingram Street into zones of light and shadow. McCormack crossed to the sunny side and stood for a moment, his face tilted upwards, feeling the sun on his eyelids. Unlocking the Velox, he decided to take a detour on the way back to Temple and swung the car across the river on King George V Bridge. Cutting under the arch of the railway viaduct and heading east along Bedford street, he approached the Gorbals.

So much of the city's bad rep had stemmed from this cluster of streets. A scurrilous novel of the Thirties had made the area notorious and the press had blathered endlessly about box beds and razor gangs, electric soup, coal gas bubbled into milk, brothels and mass brawls, The Cumbie and the Tongs. Now, the streets were mostly cleared and the Hutchie C flats rose like the hull of ship above the last of the ramshackle tenements.

F Div's Gorbals sub-division was on Cumberland Street. McCormack parked outside St. Francis Catholic Church—let's give the motor a fighting chance of survival—and walked the few blocks to the station.

"Looking for McCoy." McCormack addressed the bent heads in the CID room. A woman with hoop earrings and a tight blond perm glanced up from her typewriter. "He's round the corner. Mercy dash for Empire biscuits."

The Silver Spoon café was quiet. McCoy was in a booth with a pot of tea and a fern cake in front of him, that day's *Tribune* open on the table. McCormack ordered coffee and slid in across from him.

McCoy turned the page, carried on reading. "It's customary to ask," he said, not looking up.

"Ask what?"

"Whether a seat is taken or not. It's called manners."

McCormack glanced round the empty café. He cleared his throat. "Excuse me. Is this seat taken?"

"It is, as a matter of fact. Sorry."

"Right. Well I won't be long. I'm Duncan McCormack, Serious Crime Squad."

McCoy looked up. He had deep-set eyes and heavy lids; a

thin sliver of fierce pale blue glinted out between slits. The effect was of a blade, partly unsheathed.

"You put Peter Levein away."

Fucking Levein, McCormack thought. Would he ever stop running into folk whose careers had been stymied by Levein's downfall.

"And he was your fairy godfather and I'm the big bad wolf."

"Far from it." McCoy smiled. "Peter Levein was a cunt of the first water. Hated my guts. Fucking delighted he's gone. Fair play to you."

McCormack grinned, explained about their interest in the Tradeston fire.

"You were OIC on it?" he asked. "The Tradeston fire?"

"Nah, mate. I just helped out for a bit. Frank Clarke was in charge. He's in court today, though, otherwise you could have asked him. You spoke to your man Boyd, though?"

"The fire guy? Yeah. Someone set it, he's adamant about that. Reckons it's an insurance job."

"Could be." McCoy was chewing a big chunk of fern cake; he sluiced it down with a swig of tea. "Could well be. But I've a tout down there. He says the Quinns are blaming Maitland. They're fucking raging, according to him. You think the Barracks Bar was the Quinns?"

McCormack leaned back as his coffee arrived. He didn't want word about Chisholm getting out too soon. When the waitress had gone he stirred his coffee. "Maybe. Why are the Quinns so sure the fire was Maitland?"

McCoy said, "Well, it would be classic Maitland, wouldn't it? I mean, it's reckless as fuck but it's kinda careful too. He burns down their warehouse, but makes it look like an accident. And if it turns out the fire was set deliberately; well; everyone's gonna blame the Quinns for an insurance job."

McCormack was unpeeling a little packet of sugar cubes. "I

don't know, Harry. I hear he's big on statements, is Maitland. What kind of statement is that: *I torched your place but I'm too feart to admit it*? That's his statement?" He popped a sugar cube into his mouth.

"It's all he needs," McCoy said. "The Quinns know—I mean they know in their *bones* it's Maitland who's done it, but there's this wee shred of doubt. Stops them going all out for revenge. It's cute."

"And Maitland would go to all this bother for a few crates of booze in a warehouse?"

"Mate. C'mon. It's Walter Maitland. He'd spend a pound to stop someone else making fifty pee."

McCormack crunched down on the sugar cube. The cheap sweetness flooded his mouth and he grimaced as he swallowed it down.

McCoy was still on about Maitland. "Because there's no consequence for him, is there? Four people died. Fine. He gave the order? So what? It's civilian casualties. He's like a politician. He's Spiro fucking Agnew."

He walked back with McCoy to look at the file on the Tradeston fire. They gave him a desk in an empty interview room. Somebody brought him a mug of milky tea along with the file.

There wasn't much to look at. The fire investigator's report and a sheaf of witness statements. Clarke's team had interviewed everyone in the tenements overlooking the warehouse. Three separate witnesses had seen the flames rising into the black sky. One witness reported spotting an unfamiliar vehicle parked on Centre Street on the night of the blaze. A dark-coloured Morris Minor van. But no one had spotted the perpetrator. And with no descriptions to go on, and no dabs or fibres at the scene, there wasn't much for the cops to do. Either the Quinns had set the fire as a botched insurance job, or, more likely, Maitland had torched the place to put them out of business. Either way, no one was lining up to tell the cops any-thing.

McCormack copied the names and addresses of the witnesses into his notebook and left his milky tea untouched. He waved to Harry McCoy on his way out.

43

Ten minutes later he was parking the car beside the ruined warehouse.

The day was overcast, the sky like a sheet of gauze. It looked as if the army had still to get around to clearing the rubbish from these streets. Or maybe this was how they always looked.

He walked around Tradeston, checking the addresses in his notebook against the buildings still standing on the streets. There were gapsites and half-demolished tenements but it was clear, after fifteen minutes of wandering around and climbing tenement stairs and craning out of landing windows, that the door-to-door team had successfully canvassed all of the buildings with a view of the warehouse. What they hadn't done, so far as McCormack could tell, was visit all of the buildings with a view of the tenement that caught on fire.

In McCormack's estimation there were two blocks that gave a view of the burned-out tenement but not of the warehouse. Both blocks were condemned. The nearer one had shattered windows on all four storeys, but the second block, on Kingston Street, showed signs of life. Yellow corkboard had replaced the ground-floor windows and slogans were daubed in white paint round the entrance, but the glass was intact on the upper floors and a pot-plant sat forlornly in a third-floor window.

McCormack crossed to the entrance. A set of goalposts had been painted on a nearby wall; "CELTIC FC" in thick white brushstrokes over the crossbar. A boy of three or four sat on the pavement, legs splayed, playing with a jagged hunk of rock, knocking it against the ground, scraping its pointed end to leave white scores on the cracked flagstones. He played with utter absorption, oblivious to the broken windows, the painted names and gang acronyms on the walls, the cans and bottles strewn about the street. He was happy. He was home.

McCormack stepped over the boy's outstretched leg and entered the close.

The stench of rubbish, burnt wood and urine was vinegar-sharp. McCormack found his handkerchief and pressed it to his nose as he climbed the stairs. On the third floor a name-plate on a door said "SWEENEY". He knocked and heard the barking of a dog, a harsh yap. Jack Russell, he guessed.

He heard the mortice lock turn. Two bolts clunked back, then the Yale was unsnibbed.

A figure stood in the gloom, a man, two hard shining eyes in a seamed and grizzled face. McCormack heard a low growl-ing sound and dropped his eyes to where a carpet-slippered foot kept a scuffling Westie at bay.

"Misty!" the man shouted. "Back, girl! Back, lass! What can I do for you, son?"

McCormack had his warrant card in his hand. "Detective Inspector Duncan McCormack. I'd like to come in, if I may."

"Is it about the fire?" the man said. "You took your bloody time."

The living room was a time-capsule, not unlike McCormack's own. A large, red Paisley-patterned rug—expensive but thread-bare—made an island on the lino. A white marble mantelpiece enclosed a green-tiled fireplace. There was a bright copper coal-scuttle brimming with coal, and a polished brass fire-set— tongs, spade and poker. The pot-plant on the windowsill was a signal to the vandals: *Somebody lives here; don't smash the win-dows.* But it told the authorities the same thing. It stopped them knocking the place down around his ears.

"You're Mr. Sweeney?" McCormack jerked his thumb in the direction of the front door as he took a seat in one of the two leather armchairs facing the fire.

"Aye, that's me. Frank Sweeney." The old man took the other armchair. There was a basket beside it for the dog. After sniffing McCormack's shoes, the dog retreated to its basket and curled up for a nap.

"And you saw the fire, Mr. Sweeney?"

"Aye. Well, I didn't see it start. But I saw it all right, of course I did. That poor wee lassie and her mammy. And the old boy on the floor below. Jim Stewart. I used to see him in the bookies, back and forward."

"And the fourth victim, too."

"Aye, right enough. That was some luck for him. The bloke who moved in."

McCormack paused. "Why bad luck for him, particularly?"

The old man waved his hand impatiently. "Well, I mean he'd just moved in. The day before."

"You're saying you saw this man move in?"

"Now, now." Sweeney shook his finger. "I never said that, did I?"

"Then how do you know?"

"The curtains!" The man was having fun schooling McCormack. "The day before the fire, net curtains went up in that third-floor window."

The words of Boyd, the little fire investigator, came back to McCormack. *When heat gets sufficiently intense, net curtains will ignite through glass.*

"You're sure about that?" McCormack craned round in his seat, looking out on the ruins.

"Son." The old man was laughing. "I've sat in this chair looking out on that building for fourteen year. You think I wouldn't notice something?"

"And you never told anyone? You never told the police?"

"Nobody asked," the old man said. "You're the first one to knock on my door. I'm telling *you.*"

"Did you see who put them up?"

"I think they did it in the night. I came through that morning and there they were. Large as life. Sounds like a little thing but I'll tell you, they fair cheered me up."

The dog woke then, raised its head to take a long look at McCormack, and settled back down to doze. McCormack turned back to the old man. "And on the night of the fire—did you see anyone coming and going?"

"I don't know." The old man rubbed his sparse bristles. "People come and go. It's hard to tell." He reached down to pet the dog.

"People?" McCormack asked.

The old man grimaced. "Men. The woman on the third floor, son. She sometimes had visitors."

"She was on the game?" McCormack thought about Yvonne Gray, the missing pro from the Woodlands Road sauna.

"Well, no. I don't think so. Nothing as clear-cut as that. Guys came to see her from time to time. I think maybe they helped her out." He showed his palms. "Look, there's no luck in it, son. Speaking ill of the dead."

"I understand. But on the night of the fire. Did the woman have visitors then?"

The old man looked down. He busied himself plucking dog-hairs from his trousers, straightening his creases. He looked up. "Three," he said. "Three men. One of them was a wee bit the worse for wear."

"Drunk?"

"The other two were helping him into the close. He was sort of slumped between them."

"What time was this?"

"I'm not sure. Midnight, maybe. I was on my way through to bed."

"So you didn't see them leave?"

"I went to my bed, son. Maybe twenty minutes later. The next thing I knew was when I woke up and the place was ablaze. But they must have got out before it started. I mean, obviously."

McCormack craned round to the window again. The ruined tenement stood stark against the sky. "How many people lived there, Mr. Sweeney?"

"I told you. The three of them. The woman and her wee girl. And the old boy on the second floor."

"And the guy who moved in. Who was he?"

"Well they never found out, did they? He'd be some poor sod looking for a hoose. Some of they landlords, well, they'll sell the keys to a flat for a few quid, even though they know it's condemned. There's some unscrupulous bastards out there, son."

As if it had heard him, the dog roused itself from the basket and trotted over to the window. It put its front paws up on the sill, scanning the street, tail wagging.

"Back to the three men," McCormack said. "Did you notice anything about them? The drunk man or the other two. Anything distinctive. Anything at all."

The old man cocked his head, replaying it in his mind, running through the brain's footage. "I don't know, son. It was three guys. Not young—maybe fifties, all three of them. I wasn't really paying attention. Tell you what I *did* notice, though." He wagged a finger in the air. "They arrived in a taxi, a black cab. But here's the thing. The taxi didn't pull away. I mean, when the three went into the close."

"You mean the taxi waited for them, meter running?"

"Well no. It was just parked there. Lights out. Engine off."

"Was the driver still at the wheel?"

He cocked his head again, closed his eyes. He tugged his lower lip between finger and thumb. After a bit he shook his head, bared his dentures at McCormack in a weak smile. "Ach, I'm sorry, son. I couldn't say. I'd just be guessing, ye know?"

"That's all right. And the taxi—how long was it there for?"

"Like I said, I went to bed. The taxi was still there when I went ben the room."

"And this was when? I mean, how long after it arrived?"

"Maybe twenty minutes," he said. "I had a wee nip before I went through. Half an hour, tops."

The dog left its post at the window and trotted back to its wicker basket. It gripped its pink flannel blanket in its teeth and tugged it into place before flopping down, its head hooked over the rim of the basket, eyebrows twitching.

"Would you have a smoke at all, son? I don't like to ask."

McCormack brought out his packet of Benson & Hedges, offered one and took one himself. He dug into his trouser pocket for a fiver, tucked it into the cigarette packet and set it down on the arm of the old man's chair. They lit up.

"Ye're a gentleman, son. Fair play to you."

They smoked in silence for a bit.

"Where will you go?" McCormack gestured round the shabby room. "When you have to leave."

The old man reached down to pat the dog. "The Necropolis, hopefully. I'm aiming to see out my time here, son. Me and Misty, here."

"And if you don't?"

"My daughter's out in Easterhouse. But, Jesus. Two buses to get back to civilization. The Necropolis is handier. Livelier, too." He laughed mirthlessly.

"You've been very helpful, Mr. Sweeney." McCormack stood to go. "I'll come back if there's anything else I need to ask."

"Just don't leave it too long, eh? I'm booked to go, son. Bound for glory, as they call it."

"Ah come on now, look at you. Strong as a bull. You'll see us all in a box."

The old man laughed. The dog walked with them to the door. McCormack could hear the bolts sliding home, the mortice lock turning, as he clumped down the echoing stairwell.

The wee boy playing on the pavement had gone. Crossing to the car, McCormack nudged a loose half-brick with his foot. He spun round, dribbled the half-brick between two puddles and booted it towards the daubed goal. It smacked home in the bottom right corner. One-nil! He turned back to the Velox, one arm raised like Denis Law to milk the acclaim of the crowd.

44

Nicol watched the late-morning foot-traffic on the Gallowgate. Shopworkers nipping out for an early lunch, a drunk man in a grey suit leaving handprints on the windows as he staggered east. Two boys playing kick-the-can.

A young mum parked her pram—a big Silver Cross with sparkling chrome chassis—on the pavement and crouched down to apply the brake. She pulled the hood forward to screen her baby from the sun before hauling open the café door and flopping at a table with a view of the street. Nicol caught the woman's eye and smiled. The woman dropped her shoulders theatrically and puffed the hair out of her eyes.

Nicol checked her watch. She was ten minutes early for McCormack and Goldie.

This had been her local when she worked in Central. All the waitresses knew her by name. Now she was a blow-in. A total nobody.

It seemed, somehow, an injustice. Central had been her first posting after training college. All the girls in her cohort at Tulliallan had been jealous. Central, right out the gate. Central was where it happened. Murders. Armed robberies. Prostitution. Central housed the Force HQ, the control room for the whole city. She remembered passing the head of CID in the corridor, how you never dared speak unless he spoke to you first.

Then she had applied for CID herself. They only took three

new recruits a year but Liz Nicol was one of them. She was posted out to E Div in Shettleston. The East End. Proper cops and robbers stuff. Housebreakings. Wages-van hijackings. Stick-up men waving sawn-offs in sub-post offices. There was a real camaraderie in Chester Street, it was them-and-us and Nicol was accepted straight away, one of the boys, sinking lagers in the Shieling Bar, taking her turn for whatever came in, on the book like anyone else.

All fun and games, till one day she was posted to the Scottish Crime Squad out in Airdrie.

Airdrie.

The cancered arsehole of Lanarkshire, a town so bleak and grey and barren that its very name was a defeated sigh. *Airdrie*. Where on her very first day Nicol found that her allotted desk had been commandeered by a fat D.C. called Wade who told her to take a running fuck to herself when she tried to claim it back. She waited till he was off on a break and then swept his belongings—notebook, pens, folders, framed photo of his missus, copy of the *Daily Express*—into a wastepaper basket before drizzling the two inches of cold milky tea from his mug all over his stuff. She placed the empty mug on top. The shift commander later told her why he didn't intervene; he wanted to see how she handled the situation. That afternoon they were called out to assist at a bank job in Wishaw. Nicol got into the passenger seat of an unmarked Austin 1100 and the sergeant at the wheel just sat there breathing through his nose, drumming his fingers on the wheel, till she got the message and unbuckled her seat belt and took her place in the back, letting Wade sit in the front. That's what it was like. For nearly three years.

Nicol dipped a finger of shortbread into her coffee, bit off the end. She felt, as she sometimes did, that the last six years had been a mistake and that everything would be fine if she could go back to being a WPC at Central. She glanced at the waitress, who stood by the counter, hand resting on the cash register, idly biting one of her nails. She had a sudden urge to let the waitress know she was a cop, to flash her card in the waitress's face and quiz her pugnaciously about a fictitious break-in at the hosiery outlet next door.

She was fingering her warrant card in her pocket when McCormack came off the street.

He was frowning, the big features compressed in concentration, the shoulders hunched. He shrugged out of his jacket and draped it over the back of a chair. The waitress appeared with a menu which he waved away, ordering two bacon rolls and a pot of tea. He lit a cigarette.

"It was deliberate, Nicol." He held her eye and nodded fiercely. "The tenement fire. It was deliberate."

Nicol frowned. "But we know that already, sir. They set fire to the warehouse. The fire spread to the tenement."

"It didn't spread. They torched the warehouse. Then they torched the tenement. Two fires, Nicol. Two different fires. They made it look like the fire spread, but it didn't."

He told her about the net curtains appearing in the window on the night before the conflagration, the drunk man being helped into the building.

"You're saying Maitland's boys set the fire to kill the drunk guy?"

"Drunk, drugged. Maybe he was dead already and they were just getting rid of the body."

Nicol shook her head. She was doing a sum that didn't add up. "But the other casualties, sir. What about them?"

"Collateral damage." McCormack shrugged. "Or maybe they thought the building was empty. Point is, this wasn't an accidental fire. It was a fire that was started to cover a murder."

Nicol straightened up in her seat. "But why go to all that trouble? It doesn't add up. Why not just kill him? Plant him in the Bluebell Woods or out on the Fenwick Moor?"

The waitress arrived with McCormack's tea in its glass cup

and saucer. He waited until she had set it down and walked away, then he leant forward, planting his elbows on the table. "It's less work to burn a body than to bury it. Plus, there's always the chance a buried body could turn up later. This was someone Maitland wanted gone. Badly. But he couldn't risk the body turning up in a shallow grave, stabbed or shot or strangled. It had to look like an accident."

A metallic splash sounded beside them. The baby at the next table was playing with a bunch of keys on the tray of her high chair and had dashed them to the floor. McCormack bent to retrieve them, jiggling them in front of the little chubby grasping hands before dropping them onto the tray of the high chair.

"What do you say?" the mother asked the baby.

The baby dunked the keys on the tray of the high chair, said nothing.

"So who the hell is it?" Nicol asked simply.

"Aye. Well." McCormack leaned back. "Ask me an easy one, can't you? It was someone who knew a lot more than was good for him. Beyond that, there's not much to go on."

"The body was burnt beyond recognition, sir, wasn't it? They couldn't identify it."

"Right. But nobody was trying too hard, were they? If you think your stiff's a vagrant, no fixed abode, you're not gonnae waste much time on the ident. No one's about to miss them. Nobody knows they're gone."

Nicol stirred her coffee. It was one of the basic rules of police work. Don't tie a Windsor when a simple knot will do. Crime is endless. Time is short. The waitress was back with McCormack's bacon rolls. He opened them both, thumped the HP sauce bottle with the heel of his hand until the brown goop glugged out in two big dollops that he spread across the bacon with his knife.

He tore a bite out of one of the rolls, waved the half-eaten roll in his hand. "Plus, everyone's minds are on what happens next. Do the Quinns hit back once their warehouse gets torched? Are we looking at another gang war? The tenement gets forgotten. It's a tragic accident. Too bad folk died, but come on. Tenement fires are like buses in this town. There'll be another along in a minute. You want a bite of this?" McCormack nodded at the other roll.

"I'm fine thanks, no. It's perfect, though, isn't it, sir? You kill your guy. You don't need to worry about the body."

"Just leave it in plain sight. When the tenement burns, our lot assume it's the body of a vagrant. Joe Bloggs, no fixed abode."

"And even if the guy you've killed is missed, well, nobody's ever gonna find the body."

"Exactly. So what about you?" McCormack started on the second roll. "How'd you get on with tracing Chisholm's family?"

"Easy. He hasn't got any."

McCormack put the roll down. "Chisholm's an orphan?"

"He was brought up in care. Different homes around the city. Nobody left him a house, that's for sure. There's no one to leave him anything, far as we know."

"So where the hell's he hiding? It's not some abandoned warehouse or vacant tenement. It's a private house and it's secure. Has to be."

They were staring pensively in the direction of the café door when Derek Goldie walked through it. "What?" Goldie glanced behind him as he advanced on the table. "My bloody flies undone? What you gawping at?"

He sat down and ordered tea and they brought him up to speed.

"So what do we do now?"

"We look for a missing person, Derek."

"But wait a minute: how would they know?" Goldie tapped

the table with his finger. "You're assuming that Maitland would know about the net curtains? How they can ignite from just the heat of a nearby fire."

"Derek. He's got touts in the polis. What's to stop him having touts in the Fire Service? It's Maitland's business to know this kind of stuff. Anyway, Mr. Camper-Van Man. Play a song for me."

"Wish I could, Dunc. There's no record of a van bought by Chisholm. The uniform drew a blank at the DVLA. I, on the other hand, took a trip into SCRO and dug around in the card index. And I didn't draw a blank."

"Chisholm's got a record?"

"Not exactly." Goldie looked at his notes. "He and his wife separated late last year. Prior to that, though, there were some incidents. B Div were called out twice. Domestic disturbances. Neighbours called it in. The second time the wife was in pretty bad shape. Burst lip. Swollen jaw. She wouldn't press charges, though."

"Well that figures. Treated them like shit when they were alive. Now that they're dead, he's the great avenger."

The waitress arrived with Goldie's tea.

"How do you mean, Dunc?"

"He's trying to show what a good husband and father he was by punishing anyone connected with the fire. Should look in the mirror if he wants someone to take it out on. Did you talk to the MoD?"

"Just what we already know. He was discharged in '72. Exemplary record."

"You ask about his time across the water? The Five Techniques?"

Goldie shook his head. "No joy. Can't provide details of operational deployments. Official Secrets. Blah-di-blah."

"Not even to the good old City of Glasgow Police? You surprise me."

"Strathclyde, Duncan. Strathclyde. Get with the programme."

McCormack had never got used to the Force's reorganization. "Did you get addresses?"

"Just the one we've got: Nelson Street in Tradeston. They had an earlier address for him, from when he first joined up, but it was the Gorbals. Florence Street. It's gone. Demolished."

You could start to take it personally, McCormack thought. Every building of interest has been flattened by the wrecking ball.

"Brilliant. Another dead end. O.K. Keep working the list, then. Guys he served with. Guys he was close to. Someone knows where Gordon Chisholm would hole up. We need to find that someone."

Goldie tipped his fingers to his temple in a mock salute. "Aye, aye, skip."

"Nicol. Get round to Central and check the Missing Persons. All divisions—just the city for the moment, not Strathclyde. Adult male. The fire was, what, the twenty-second? Let's look for men going missing on the twenty-second and right through the following week."

"What if they held him for a few days, though, sir? Like Elliot?"

McCormack looked at her. "You're right. Good point, Nicol. He was probably dead when they took him into the building. O.K. Adult males, then, citywide, second half of June."

"On it, boss. I'll get cracking now."

She lifted her bag and left, giving a little hand-flash wave to the baby in the high chair.

Goldie and McCormack drank their tea.

45

There's a man in a room with a hood on his head, in a circle of men, getting jostled and spun by the shoulders. It might be a game of blind man's buff until the first punch lands. A cheer goes up. More punches are thrown. A shuddering blow to the side of the head drops the man to his knees. A kick to the shoulder sends him toppling to the concrete where he bucks and writhes to dodge the swarming boots that jab at his kidneys, ribs, stomach, groin. His hands are cuffed behind his back. The boiler suit they have given him is three or four sizes too large and it slips down on one of his shoulders as he twists.

Then the kicking stops and the men step back, wiping their mouths with the backs of their hands. One of them places a finger to his lips as he walks across to the door where a black box stands on a table. The others jostle lazily, all wide eyes and silent grins, hands resting on one another's shoulders and backs. The man on the floor doesn't groan or scream; that will come later. For now he simply breathes, and his head twists round, craning for the slightest sound. The only sound in the room is the man's ragged breath. Now the man by the door hits a button on the box and the noise of a siren, thumpingly loud, floods the room. The men clap their hands to their ears and the man on the floor starts writhing again, as if the sounds coming from the black box are blows. The men file out and close the door, leaving the man on the floor with the noise and his pain.

Gordon Chisholm woke up in the bare room, sweating,

heart pounding. In the dream, somehow, Chisholm was the hooded man, whereas in reality he had been one of the tormentors, one of the grinning bad guys.

He pulled on his trousers, stuck the Glock in the waistband at the back and headed down to check on the boy.

In the kitchen he filled a tin mug with water and lifted two Mars Bars from a bowl on the table and stepped out into the yard.

Two days the boy had been with Chisholm, locked in one of the outbuildings. What was two days? Two days was nothing. He would let Maitland sweat, let the fears and the dread fester in his mind for another day. Then he would make the call. Tell Walter Maitland the precise time when his son would be killed.

Outside it was a blustery day, an edge of wet in the tumbling wind. Chisholm stood for a minute in the yard, his T-shirt snapping, filling his lungs with hilltop air. The moor stretched away in all directions. To the south was the grey bowl of the reservoir, its surface shirred. Apart from Blairpark Farm, down on the main road, there was no human dwelling in sight.

He crossed the yard, slid the bolts on the heavy white door, turned the big key.

Daylight flooded the outbuilding. The boy scrambled up to a sitting position, back against the wall. His left hand was cuffed to a rusting bracket set in one of the concrete blocks. His head in the black canvas hood twisted and jerked as Chisholm's boots scraped on the concrete floor.

There was a paraffin road lamp on the floor just inside the doorway. Chisholm knelt and set down the mug of water and the Mars Bars. He fumbled for his matches. He opened the lamp and lit the wick. When the lamp was burning he pulled the door closed behind him and locked it with the brown cast-iron key.

In the red glare of the lamp he crossed and set the mug and the chocolate bars down beside the boy. He took the hood by the corners and tugged it free of the boy's sweaty head, undid the soiled cotton gag. The boy's face was flushed. The gash on the bridge of his nose was healing but the nose itself was still swollen. A green track of snot had hardened on his upper lip.

Chisholm loosened the ties that bound the boy's hands and stood back against the far wall.

The boy ate greedily, watching Chisholm through lank strands of hair.

Chisholm lit a cigarette. He could smell the contents of the zinc bucket, could isolate the citrusy tang of urine, the earthy fecal fug under the chlorine burn of disinfectant.

"You know what he did?" Chisholm leaned against the wall, looking down his nose at the hunkered boy. "Your famous old man?"

The boy said nothing, chewed the chocolate bars. His animal eyes tracked the crazy man with the shaved head.

"No guesses? He killed my family." Chisholm studied his cigarette end. He seemed to feel the shock anew as he spoke the words. He spoke them again. "He killed my family. My wife. My wee girl."

The boy said something now, mumbling into his chin. Chisholm whipped round. "What was that? You got something to say?"

The boy swallowed down a chunk of Mars Bar, cleared his throat. "I said, he killed mine too."

Chisholm laughed. "You think it's a joke? You think this is funny?"

"There's more than one way to kill a family," the boy said. He took another bite and nodded at Chisholm, chewing.

"The fuck are you talking about?" Chisholm threw his arms up, cast around the empty room. "You're still here!"

"The family's not, though," the boy said quietly. "The family's gone. I see him every second Saturday. My mum hates me because I remind her of him. My sister and my mum fight all the time. Jane cannae wait to leave. Everyone blames everyone else for what's happened."

"That isn't—that's not the fucking issue," Chisholm said. "Nobody gives a shit about that."

The boy shrugged, as if to say, *If you don't like the answer, don't ask the question.*

Chisholm tried again. "Anyway. He'll get a taste of it now. He'll know what it feels like."

"He knows it already," the boy said. "He *knows* what it's like. If he gave a shit he wouldn't have done it."

Chisholm coughed, spat on the floor. He couldn't shake the feeling that he was still in the dream, still in the wrong role. It was he who should be calling the shots, making the plays. So why did he feel like the man in the boiler suit, hood on his head, being spun round by the laughing, jeering crowd?

"He won't give you it," the boy was saying now.

"Won't give what?"

"Whatever it is you've asked for. The ransom." The boy's tone was almost cheery. "You've no idea who you're dealing with, pal. You don't have a fucking scooby."

The boy had finished eating. He gulped down the last of the water in the tin mug. Chisholm knelt to reattach the boy's gag, fasten his hands. He dropped the hood over the boy's head, and leaned forward till his lips almost touched the black canvas.

He said softly, almost absent-mindedly, "I haven't asked for a ransom."

UNSENT LETTERS #3

Flat 4c, 70 Craigpark
Glasgow
25 July 1969

Dear Chris,

In case you want to picture me, I'm sitting here at the table in my living room with a glass of whisky and soda at my elbow, looking out over the city. Well, I say looking out over the city. I can see across the Wills cigarette factory to the Necropolis. What a classy Glasgow view! I'm on the top floor of a Dennistoun tenement. There's a church across the road called Our Lady of Good Counsel, which makes me smile. Maybe I should have listened to her. Is it too late now, do you think?

I'm getting a dab hand at this letter writing. It helps a lot. There's things I can put down here. Things I couldn't tell you face to face. I can't tell you about the Friends and what they did, Chris. Not yet. Maybe someday. But I can tell you about other stuff. I never really talked about the Red House. To you. Or anyone, really. About the Wylies, and why I kept the name. I put it all away and tried to forget about it, like the whole thing happened to someone else. And in a way it did. All the while I was down there in Ayrshire, in that big house by the sea, I felt like I was living someone else's life. Does that make sense?

Partly it was the house itself. Big, and bloody empty, and all echoey. All these rooms lying chilly and still. High ceilings. Sash windows. You walked the floors on tiptoe, scared to breathe. You felt like a ghost. And the house was so clean. Honest to God. She had a woman come in twice a week to clean and dust and you wondered what that woman found to do, the house was like a bloody show home.

I'm not complaining, mind. I had it good. I had a room to myself. My own wardrobe. My own clothes. My own toilet, if you can believe that, Chris—an ensuite! At Auldpark there was always a queue or someone banging to get in. But down at the Red House I could sit there like a Queen on my throne. And baths! I would lie in this big tub of bubbles, dozing off, topping up the hot from time to time, and when I was finished Mrs. Wylie—call me Margaret, she would tell me, but I never did—would ask me what I wanted for supper. Like it was a country club or something.

But the best thing was the sea, Chris, the beach. Once a year, if we were lucky, at home or Auldpark, we'd get taken to the beach. Now, every day, I could step out the back door onto the shore. White yachts in the firth and the green island beyond them. It was like living in a storybook. The Wylies had a wooden extension built out onto the rocks and when the tide was in you were surrounded on three sides by water. I used to pretend it was a boat, I would sail her up the west coast to pick you up and we'd set off on an adventure, Ireland or Spain or America. Hah!

Instead, I went back to Auldpark. Some adventure.

I want to explain something, Chris. When I left to go to the Wylies' in the first place, I wasn't running out on you. I just needed to get away. Because of the Friends. That old vulture Elliot and his cronies. Jenny, the social worker who set it up, I think she had an idea of what was going on. I was escaping, Chris. And it was great for a while, down there. It really was. But after a few months it just started to turn. It all went sour. It was like I stopped believing in it. The Wylies. The whole set-up. The beach at the back door.

The Wylies had fostered kids before, but this was different. They wanted so much to be a proper mum and dad, they wanted so much to have a kid of their own. And it got too much. You know how it works, Chris. How it starts, the doubt, how it eats away at you. Your own ma and da, the very folk who're supposed to love you, cause they don't have an option, you're their own flesh and blood: they don't love you. But suddenly this pair of strangers over here? Who don't know the first thing about you? They love you? You're like: Naw. I'm not buying it. They love the idea of having a kid. That's what they love. It's not the same thing.

So I started acting up. Little things at first. Leaving the milk out to spoil. Forgetting to switch the immerser off. Trailing dogshit on my trainers through the front room plush. On I went. From bad to worse. Lifting singles from Mr. Wylie's pack of Rothmans. Pilfering quids from Mrs. Wylie's purse. Getting drunk. Staying out. Getting in with a dodgy crowd. The police were called when a ring went missing from Mrs. Wylie's jewellery box. They thought it was one of my mates. It was me. I kept pushing it and pushing it to see when it would break. And before I knew it, as though I had wanted it all along, I was in a car heading back to Glasgow.

It wasn't the Wylies, though. They never wavered. They were all for seeing it through, loving me for who I was—the wee shite that I was—whatever I did. The Wylies were good people.

No.

It was something else that happened, that took me back to Auldpark. I'll tell you about it. Sometime. When you come round for your tea, eh? Deal?

The worse part about in was the other lassie. They brought this other girl down from Glasgow, another looked-after kid. To try to help me fit in, give me someone I could relate to. And when I went back to Auldpark, poor Yvonne got sent back to her place too, somewhere on the South Side. Her chance at a new life was over, too. Still, that's another story.

But I will say this.

Though my heart dropped and my stomach clenched and the bile climbed my thrapple when the dirty Auldpark stones came crunching under the tyres, I was pleased about one thing. I was pleased I would see you again. And that's the truth.

Ach, would you listen to me, Chris. I'm doing it again, amn't I? Bringing us down, I'm a pure drag. But hey, look, it's not all bad. In fact, wait till I tell you. This Walter I've been on about? He took me out last night to this restaurant. Talk about fancy! There were waiters in red tartan tuxes and champagne in these glasses shaped like bowls. I felt like Princess Margaret. It was out in the wilds, some sort of country house near Drymen. Anyway, it was a foursome we were on. This other couple—Peter and Helen they're called—were with us and what a night we made of it. The speciality of the place was lobster. You had to look down into the tank and point at the lobster you wanted. I felt so sorry for them, crawling over each other with their claws taped shut, poor things. They had no idea they were on the menu.

It turns out that Peter—he's a bit older than the rest of us, mid-fifties maybe—is opening a restaurant in the city centre later this year. He's looking for a hostess—someone to greet the diners and show them to their tables—and Walter thought I'd be perfect. So, I suppose as well as a night out this was sort of a job interview as well. I think I did O.K. but I suppose we'll find out! Walter thinks I'm a shoo-in. We'll see. Peter was in good form, certainly. I got the feeling they were celebrating something, maybe some business deal, something hush-hush. We were starting on a second bottle of champagne and I said about the glasses and Peter told me that this type of champagne glass was modelled on the left breast of Marie Antoinette. I felt quite the sophisticate, Chris, drinking out of the French Queen's tit!

And Helen. This sounds funny but, if you saw her—no kidding—you'd almost think she was me. She's like my double. She's like me if I had blond hair and plenty of cash! I'm joking, but she was dressed to the absolute nines. Diamond earrings. This black crepe dress. But her jacket? Bear with me here, Chris. She had this gorgeous houndstooth jacket—cashmere, with black vinyl edging at the pockets. Beautifully cut and fitted, two buttons, and a Peter Pan collar. Oh I know that doesn't mean anything to you, Chris, but it was gorgeous. O.K.? And when I pointed this out to her, she was all, "Oh, you must try it on." And then I did, and they all oohed-and-aahed at how it fitted me like a glove, like a dream. And it did. We could be twins, Helen and me. And then she said, "Look, Isobel, it's so much better on you. You should keep it. Please." And she *wouldn't take no for an answer. And it wasn't till I got it home that I saw the label. Pierre Cardin! Even you must've heard of Pierre Cardin, Chris. Beats Kirsty Baird's blue duffelcoat, that's for sure! We're going out again next week, the four of us. Walter's even booked me a hair appointment. You won't recognize me, when you see me again!*

Things are on the up, Chris. And listen: you're going to see me again. I'm making it my mission to root you out of whatever grotty flat you're hiding in. I'm getting Walter to help. He knows people, he can ask around. I'm going to find you, and when I do I can give you this letter in person. And then we can get back to normal. We'll be family again. You'll come to visit me. You'll bring flowers.

Your sister,

Isobel

FRIDAY, 11 JULY 1975

46

It felt strange, pushing through the doors at Central. Like going back to your old school, Nicol thought. Everything familiar and slightly weird. Dayshift uniforms milled around, never giving her a second glance. She felt like a ghost. The desk sergeant sent her up to the second floor where a constable from Missing Persons showed her into an empty cubicle and brought the files to her desk.

"You want the other divisions, too? We get them from the whole Force area now."

"Just Glasgow is fine for the moment, thanks."

He hovered in the doorway. "We've got telex files from all the UK forces, too. And if it's something really recent you could try the Sally Army. We get a lot of our info from them."

He was young, barely a year or two out of Tulliallan. A slight lad, strawberry blond; he watched Nicol hopefully through white eyelashes. This probably wasn't the posting he'd envisaged when he joined up.

Nicol smiled at him. "What's your name, Constable?"

"Yuill, ma'am. Robert Yuill."

"O.K., Robert Yuill. This is a murder inquiry I'm working. A multiple. So I appreciate your help here. Could be really important."

Yuill nodded sombrely. He flexed his hands where they hung by his sides. "Right. Well. I'm your man."

"It's also thirsty work," Nicol continued, turning back to the desk. "Two sugars, Robert. No milk. There's a good lad."

As Yuill slunk out, Nicol shuffled her chair round to the corner of the desk to check the view from the window. The room was on the Turnbull Street side of the building and there, looking slightly self-conscious in a shaft of afternoon sun, was the church, St. Andrew's in the Square, a little miracle of Enlightenment geometry in the tangled heart of the city. It used to amaze her, as she worked the stabbings and rapes and robberies, to look out onto these porticoes and columns, the tall slender spire with the dome at the top, a scene from some Age-of-Reason dreamworld, a place where crime was unknown, where order and beauty and harmony reigned.

She smiled to herself, bent her head to her work.

Two hours later she was back at the Byre.

"How was Central?" McCormack hovered in his doorway. "Any joy?"

"I think so." She drew her notebook out of her jacket pocket, flipped to the relevant page.

As Nicol had learned from further discussion with Constable Yuill, people go missing in the city of Glasgow at the rate of two hundred per month. In the second half of June, ninety-seven people were reported missing. Of these, around two thirds were children, many absconding from care homes or foster parents. A further dozen were repeat absconders. Of the remaining nineteen, eight were women. That left eleven. Of these, eight had been traced or returned within twenty-four hours.

"There's basically three," Nicol told him. "That's adult males who went missing in the second half of June and remain unaccounted for. Donald Naismith, twenty-seven, unemployed labourer. Campbell Sneddon, sixty-six, taxi driver for Clyde Cabs. George Maloney, fifty-two, painter and decorator."

"A cabbie?" McCormack came into the room, took the chair opposite Nicol. "There was a taxi outside the building on the night of the fire. Who reported him missing?"

Nicol checked her notes. "Next-door neighbour. Pints of

milk piling up on the step. Over in Knightswood. Monksbridge Avenue."

"O.K. Good. Check the cabbie first. Talk to the neighbour. Then the other two. We're looking for any connections to Maitland, no matter how slight."

"Got it."

McCormack went back through to his office. Nicol cursed herself. She'd just been at Central. She should have thought to look in on the hacks while she was there. She picked up the phone.

The Hackney Carriage Branch was a small unit staffed mainly by older officers, guys who were easing into retirement by overseeing the city's fleet of hackney cabs. All the hacks in Glasgow were registered with the city council. The job of the Hackney Carriage Branch was to vet potential drivers, rooting out those with convictions. They also tried to make sure the taxi firms adhered to at least some of the council's regulations. And they generally looked out for the drivers.

"Hackney Branch. Ritchie."

Bingo, thought Nicol. She'd worked with Malcolm Ritchie in her early days at Central. He was a tall, lugubrious south-sider with an atrocious comb-over.

"Malcolm, it's Liz. Liz Nicol."

"Lizzie Nic! Don't you guys have personal assistants to make your phone calls while you're off foiling assassination plots or bagging international diamond thieves?"

"Gave mine the day off," Nicol said. "He's taking the Bentley for its service."

"What can I do for you?"

"It's a long shot, Malcolm. Couple of weeks back. Twenty-second of June. Night of the big warehouse fire in Tradeston. A taxi was seen at the tenement next door. The one that caught fire. This is Nelson Street in Tradeston."

"Time?"

"Eleven-thirty, twelve midnight."

"And this is a drop-off we're talking about?"

"No, that's the thing. The taxi's there for about twenty minutes. Maybe more. Engine off. We've a witness who sees two guys helping a drunk guy. They oxter him into the building."

"And you think one of these guys is the driver?"

"That's the theory."

Ritchie exhaled, a sceptical noise. "I can check it out. I can find out which black hacks were in the vicinity at the time. But, Liz. If the guy's there for twenty minutes with his sign out, he's not on duty. If he's up to no good in that tenement, he's not running a meter."

"O.K., Malc. Do what you can. Appreciate it. Also, one other thing. Guy called Campbell Sneddon. Drove for Clyde Cabs until a couple of weeks back. Anything you can find on him. Thanks a million, Malc."

She could hear the little kiss of Ritchie dragging on a cigarette. "You want to tell me what we're dealing with here, Lizzie?"

Nicol glanced through the open door of the inner office, where McCormack sat hunched over a folder, his forehead cupped in his hand, elbow propped on the desk, and she made a decision. Malcolm Ritchie was a good polis. The more he knew, the better chance he had of helping her. "I can't go into details, Malc, but the drunk being helped into the building may have been killed in the fire."

"The unidentified body? That's Campbell Sneddon?"

"We don't know, Malc. It may be. And the driver? The guy who oxters the drunk guy into the building? We think maybe he's working for Walter Maitland."

"O.K. Well, Maitland's got cops. We all know that. Why wouldn't he have cabbies? I'll ask around. Maybe you can give me a hurl in the Bentley one day, when you're in the vicinity. Slumming it."

She gave Ritchie her number at Temple and rang off. Half an hour later she came back from the toilet to a ringing phone.

"Nicol? Jesus Christ, were you taking a bath?"

"Police work, Malcolm." Nicol pulled her chair out one-handed, sat, fished her notebook from her inside pocket, slapped it onto the desk. "That stuff you do in the outside world, where you have to take your feet off the desk. Remember it?"

"Fuck you, Lizzie Nicol. Wear out more leather in a shift on the beat than you plainer cunts do in a month."

"Sprinting for the canteen queue, Malc? Doesnae count."

"You want to hear this or not?"

"I'm all ears. Breathless with anticipation."

"O.K. Drivers who're cosy with Maitland. No one's got form: that's the first thing. Might be different with the mini-cabs. But no one driving a hackney's got form."

Ritchie's tone was hardening as he spoke. He was defending the honour of the Hackney Carriage Branch. But Nicol knew all this anyway. A conviction of any kind precluded you from landing a city council licence.

"Understood, Malcolm."

"That said, I asked around. Consensus is, there's two or three guys around Maryhill who might be close to Maitland."

Nicol clicked her pen, drew a circle in her notebook. She wrote "Maryhill" in the circle and drew three straight lines leading out from the circumference like spokes, like the rays of the sun. "Close meaning what?"

"Meaning they see something, maybe they hear a conversation in the back of the cab, they report it back. It's an eyes and ears thing. Touts, basically, except they're touting for the bad guys instead of us."

"You got names?"

Ritchie read out the details and Nicol took them down.

Maryhill addresses. Three names that meant nothing to her. Andrew Greig. Tom McLennan. Michael Weir.

"Working on the twenty-second, were they?"

"Two of them. Both working the West End, Partick, during the timeframe. Never crossed the river."

"And the third?"

"Off-duty. That's McLennan. Drives for Clyde Cabs."

Nicol circled McLennan's name. "Got it. Now what about the actual night, Malcolm? Many fares to Nelson Street?"

"Nada. No drop-offs or pick-ups in Nelson Street the whole night. Couple skirting the area in the relevant timeframe. I checked them out; they didn't see anything. Can give you their details if you want."

"That's all right, Malc. Listen—appreciate your help."

"Well. We got to look out for the rock stars."

Nicol phoned the taxi company, Clyde Cabs, told them she wanted to see Tom McLennan straight away. No: not in half an hour, not at the end of his shift. Now. When he drops his next fare, send him straight to Temple Police Station.

Fifteen minutes later the desk sergeant hovered in the doorway behind a tall man in his mid-twenties who fixed Nicol in a blowtorch gaze, tossing a bunch of keys in one hand.

"Thanks, Brian." Nicol got to her feet, stretched. "Room One's free, is it?"

"Should be." The desk sergeant was already retreating to his lair.

The man had long, shoulder-length hair. He stood there throwing glances round the shabby room.

"If you'll come with me, Mr. McLennan." Nicol ushered him out of the office, led him down the corridor. He kept shooting glances at her, shaking his head.

"A liberty," he was saying. "You know what this is? A bloody liberty. I missed an airport fare for this. You're picking my pocket."

They had reached Interview Room One. Nicol held the door open with an outstretched arm. "We'll have you out of here just as soon as we can, Mr. McLennan. Take a seat."

She watched him stalk to the desk, still bouncing his keys. He wore a short leather jerkin, elasticated at waist and cuffs, tight Wranglers that flared out over calfskin boots with Cuban heels.

He tossed his keys onto the desk, thumped down into the plastic bucket seat, paddled his hands on the desk; drumroll.

"You get paid by the hour, do you?" He tipped his chin at Nicol, watching her take her seat.

Nicol said nothing. She looked neutrally at McLennan as she took her notebook out, her Bic pen, set them on the desk.

McLennan rubbed the bristles on his jaw. "Say you got paid by the interview. You're just about to start on me and someone comes through that door, takes you out to fix my engine. You'd like that, would you? You'd just accept it?"

Nicol straightened her notebook, aligned it with the corner of the desk. She looked up at McLennan and tapped herself on the breastbone. "Me," she said. "I'm the polis. I do the questions. Your bit's the answers."

McLennan put his hands up to the back of his neck and used them to flip his long hair over his collar. "You'd want compensation," he said. "You'd want recompensed for lost earnings."

The scrape of Nicol's chair legs was loud and sudden. McLennan squinted up at her, as though blinking into the sun.

"Come with me, Mr. McLennan." Nicol snatched up her notebook, her pen, strode to the door. "I need to show you something."

They were back down the corridor, McLennan's bootheels knocking and clacking. Down a step and into the cellblock.

McLennan turned to face her. They stood on the greasy roughcast floor that sloped down to a drainage hole. Along one side of the room were the cells: three thick narrow doors standing ajar; three gloomy tiled interiors.

"They're all vacant." Nicol waved an arm at the row of doors. "They're all free. You can take your pick. This is a murder inquiry. People are dead. Several people. You're worried about a taxi fare?"

McLennan stole a glance at the cell doors. He rubbed a yellow finger under his nose. "You've got to look at it from my perspective," he said.

"Really? I'm looking at it from the perspective of, I don't know, four people who burned to death in a Tradeston tenement. A man who was tortured and beaten and thrown on a rubbish dump in Partick."

McLennan's eyes closed. He nodded.

"All right then. I'm sorry," he said. "We'll go back through. I'll answer your questions."

He started forward but Nicol placed her hand flat on his chest, held him at bay. "No. We do it here. Pick a cell."

McLennan turned, confronted the three doors as if they posed a riddle. Then he lunged for the middle one, hauled it open.

"Sit."

The only place to sit was the bare thin mattress in its concrete alcove. McLennan folded himself into the space. Nicol stood over him.

"Mr. McLennan. You work for Walter Maitland. What is it you do for him, exactly?"

McLennan's voice jumped half an octave. "Maitland? I work for Clyde Cabs! I'm a driver!"

"You know him, though?"

"Walter Maitland? No, I don't know him."

"You don't know who Walter Maitland is?"

"I live in Maryhill, hen. Not the moon. But I don't work for him."

"That's 'Detective' to you. You drive a cab. You're on Maitland's turf. But you've got nothing to do with him?"

McLennan grimaced. "Not really. We're supposed to, I don't know, report back. If we see things. You know?"

"You're talking about casing places for Maitland?"

"No! Nothing like that. Just if we come across something useful. I don't know. Maybe someone owes money. The word goes out. We see them, we're supposed to call it in. That's it. That's all."

He craned up hopefully, sagging smile. Nicol folded her arms. "You do other things for him? You ever transport things for Walter Maitland? People?" She paused. "Bodies?"

McLennan glanced at the cell door. "What the fuck are you talking about? You trying to scare me? Fucking job done, all right? *Bodies*?"

Nicol took a step towards him. "The night of June twenty-second. A Sunday. You were working that night?"

McLennan shook his head. "No. Definitely not. I was home with my girlfriend."

"What, you don't need to check? You remember it straight off?"

"You're saying it's a Sunday. I don't work Sundays."

"You know what happened that night, though?"

"Twenty-second of June? Well I'm guessing it's the fire. The big fire at Tradeston."

"Four people dead. Did you know it was going to happen, Mr. McLennan? Did you have advance warning?"

"Whoa, what the fuck? Suddenly I'm Walter Maitland's righthand man? Why would anyone tell me?"

"So it *was* Walter Maitland who did it? He gave the order?"

"No! I mean, how would I know? I'm just assuming. You keep mentioning Maitland."

"There was a taxi in the area, Mr. McLennan. Outside the tenement on Nelson Street. On the night of the fire. With one of Maitland's men, we think."

McLennan said nothing.

"Were you the driver, Mr. McLennan?"

"Me? No. I was home. I fuckin told you."

"Do you know Campbell Sneddon?"

"Campbell—aye. I drive beside him at Clyde. Or anyroads I did. He chucked it, couple of weeks back."

"Why did he quit?"

"Ask Campbell. How would I know?"

"Who would the driver be? That night in Tradeston."

"The fuck would I know? Could be anyone."

"We need a name, Mr. McLennan. Otherwise I may need to have a word with my colleagues at the Hackney Carriage Branch. Pretty hard to drive a hack without a licence."

"Pretty hard to drive a hack with broken fingers," McLennan said. "Pretty hard to drive when you're deid."

"You've been threatened, then? You've been threatened directly by Walter Maitland?"

"You think I'm gonnae shop Walter Maitland? On anything? I'll say it again, since you seem to be a wee bit slow here: I live in Maryhill. You want to relocate me and my family to Borneo, I'm happy to talk. Outer Mongolia. The Kalafuckinghari. Until then? I think I'll pass."

She let him go. She let him go and she took the Wolseley and drove out to Knightswood looking for Campbell Sneddon's neighbour.

McCormack sat at his desk in Temple in front of a big pile of newspapers. The papers carried a photo of Gordon Chisholm, plus a description, and the number of Temple Police Station. *Wanted in connection with the Barracks Bar bombing and the murder of Gavin Elliot.* Hopefully the coverage would produce some actual sightings, among the fake ones concocted by timewasters. It should also, McCormack reflected, put a dampener on the little bonfires of sectarian tension that had been flaring across the city. "Chisholm" wasn't a Catholic name.

Or at least it wasn't an Irish name, which was really the point here. And this particular Chisholm—as the papers had spelled out in headlines and opening pars—had been a soldier, a corporal in the British Army. And though the MoD had contrived to provide a photograph of Chisholm in civvies (open-necked shirt, dark pullover), his haircut and squared shoulders carried a distinctly military stamp. Whatever else might be the case, therefore, Glasgow was not at the mercy of an Active Service Unit of the Irish Republican Army. And the annual Orange Walk, due to take place in two days' time, would not now be seen as an ominous muster of loyalist strength. It would revert to being the usual dreary carnival of ignorance and bigotry.

His phone was ringing.

"Sir? It's Nicol."

He could tell from her voice, from its tightness and tone: she'd found something. He glanced through the half-open door of his office to where Goldie's feet—crossed at the ankles and sheathed in homely-looking, scuffed brown brogues—were propped on a desk.

"What have you got?"

"The taxi driver. Campbell Sneddon?"

"What about him?"

"I spoke to the neighbour. Know what Sneddon did before he was a cabbie?"

McCormack shrugged as if Nicol was in the room with him. His mind went back to a "People Who Help Us" poster on the wall of the classroom at Ballachulish Primary: postman, doctor, fireman, nurse.

"He waited tables at the Albany Hotel. He was the Governor of the Bank of England. I've no idea, Nicol."

"He was a caretaker," she said.

Through the doorway, Goldie uncrossed his feet, re-crossed them. There was an off-white ellipse of chewing gum on the sole of his left shoe. "Nicol, I don't see—"

"At a children's home, sir."

He saw it now. "Auldpark?"

"Auldpark."

"Ah, right. Nice work, Nicol. Looks like we've found our man. Dental records'll confirm it, but this looks good. You still over there? In Knightswood?"

"Yep. I'm in a phone box on Knightswood Road, sir. You want me to go back?"

"Talk to the other neighbours, Nicol. If there's a pub nearby, a bookie's, ask about him there. I'll check in with the taxi firm. See you back at the ranch."

47

Clyde Cabs was on the Broomielaw, in the twilit gloom beneath the railway bridge. McCormack felt the chill and damp as he stepped out of the sunlight into the shade of the girders. A train was passing overhead, clanking and shunting. The viaduct walls were glazed with white tiles, like a public urinal.

Dubious businesses—a shoe-repair shop, a bookmaker—had established themselves in the arches of the viaduct. The third arch was home to Clyde Cabs. McCormack showed his card to the girl at the front desk and was taken through to a small rear office.

There was a desk heaped with directories and littered with Styrofoam cups. Behind it a little fat man wore a short-sleeved shirt in a putrid green—chartreuse, maybe. Possibly snot. His paper was open to the sports section. It was close season, there was no sport worth the name, just the golf, maybe Wimbledon. But he'd found something. He looked up at McCormack.

"You see the draw, then? Piece of cake for the pair of them."

The draw for European football competitions had been announced that day. Rangers had drawn Bohemians of Dublin in the European Cup first round; Celtic would face Valur Reykjavik in the Cup Winners' Cup.

"Glamour ties," McCormack said, taking a seat. "D.I. Duncan McCormack. You are?"

"Eddie Irvine."

"You own the company?"

"Bought and paid for."

"It's about one of your drivers. Campbell Sneddon."

"*Ex*-drivers." Irvine held up a finger. "Sneddon hasn't darkened that door in weeks."

"Two weeks," McCormack said. "He disappeared two weeks and three days ago."

"There you are then."

A train shunted overhead and McCormack had to wait until it passed. "But you didn't report him missing. Why was that, Mr. Irvine?"

"He wasn't missing. He gave in his resignation."

"You mean he told you himself? He worked his notice?"

Irvine shrugged. "I didn't take the call personally. As I understand it, someone phoned in for him. There were plenty of drivers ready to work those shifts. I didn't lose much sleep over it."

"Do you have a record of who made that call?"

"Look, chief. I run a business here. We got a message. He wasnae coming back. What does it matter who told us?"

"O.K." McCormack loosened his tie, flipped his shirt's top button. "You hire Sneddon yourself?"

"What?"

"I mean, you personally. Did you interview Mr. Sneddon before you hired him?"

"Well, aye. I vet everyone that drives for me. He had a clean licence. He had good references. One of them from a city councillor, if I remember. He was polite. Neat. There was no reason not to hire him. If he's done something, if he's involved in something, that's got nothing to do with us."

McCormack heard laughter from somewhere else in the building. "What would he be involved in?"

"I'm just saying, you're obviously here because he's . . . I don't know. Something's happened and you think he's

involved. He drove for four years here. Never a single complaint. Either from him or against him. That's all I'm saying."

McCormack nodded. Irvine smiled hopefully. Behind him
was a Pirelli calendar for 1974, a black woman on a beach, her
face almost wholly in shadow, just the bright glossy red of her
lipsticked lips, slightly parted, catching the sun. "You mentioned references," McCormack said.

"Aye."

"I'll need to see them. In fact, I'll need to see his whole file.
Can you get it now, please?"

Irvine lifted his phone to dial and then dropped the receiver
back in its cradle. He took a breath and shouted *Sandra!* and the
girl poked her head through an adjoining door. "Sandra, can you
get Cammie Sneddon's file, please, for this gentleman here?"

The file was thin, just a copy of Sneddon's contract with his
home address listed, and carbon copies of letters detailing
minor changes to his terms of employment. There were also
two references—one from the director of Auldpark Children's
Home in Bishopbriggs, describing Sneddon's fifteen years of
faithful service as caretaker, and the other from Gavin Elliot.
In a brusque testimonial on Glasgow Corporation notepaper,
Elliot claimed to have known Campbell Sneddon for several
years in his capacity as patron of the Auldpark Children's
Home and to have observed Sneddon to be diligent and capa-
ble in the performance of his duties.

McCormack took out his notebook and scribbled down
Sneddon's home address. He stood to go. "O.K. Thanks for
your assistance."

Irvine made no move to get up, see him to the door. "So
what's he done?" he asked, a little bubble of laughter in his
voice. "Has he robbed a bank? Strangled his missus?"

McCormack paused on the threshold. "So far as we can tell,
Mr. Irvine, he got himself burned to death in a fire. Enjoy your
day."

McCormack pulled Irvine's door shut behind him. Instead of turning left to return to the street, he moved further into the building. There was a door at the end of the short corridor and he opened it without knocking.

Three men sat at a table playing cards, a pile of long cook's matches in front of one of them, smaller piles in front of the others. *Pontoons*, McCormack noted. A fourth man was standing off to the left, beside the sink, spouting water from a kettle into a cluster of mugs. A fifth man sat at a separate table, bending the unread portion of a paperback book, peering at McCormack over his reading glasses. All five wore light blue short-sleeved shirts and dark ties. A radio was playing softly in the background, a hit from a couple of years back: "Sunday Morning Symphony".

"Sorry to disturb you, gentlemen." McCormack had his warrant card out. "I need to ask you some questions."

"If it's about Lord Lucan," one of the card players said, "it wasnae me. I was on back-shift that night."

The others smirked. McCormack pulled out a chair from the book-reader's table and placed it in the middle of the room. He sat down. "It's about Campbell Sneddon," he said. "I want to know when you last saw him. What you talked about. What his mood was like."

There was a perceptible stiffening in the room, as though the temperature had dropped. The card players sat up straighter in their seats, placing their cards face down on the table. The man at the sink put the kettle gently back on the Formica. The reader took his glasses off and set them on the table. "What's he supposed to have done?" he said.

"Campbell Sneddon? He hasn't done anything. That we know of."

"Then how come you're looking for him?"

"We're not looking for him," McCormack said. "Quite the opposite. We think we've found him."

The significance of McCormack's words seemed to spread out and fill the little room.

"Cammie's dead?" the reader said softly.

"If it's him then, yes, I'm afraid he is."

"How?"

"I can't go into that at the moment. I need to know if there was anything in the weeks before he left, if he said anything or did anything that was out of the ordinary, that might give us some idea of his state of mind."

"State of mind?" One of the card players spoke up, the man with the biggest pile of matches, the banker. "You're saying Cammie killed himself?"

"No, no. I'm not saying that at all. We think he was involved in something, that maybe he got out of his depth."

"Jesus."

The man at the sink was putting milk and sugars in the teas. He carried three mugs across to the card players, came back for the other two. "You want one?" He held out a mug to McCormack.

"I'm fine, thanks. Did you know him well? Any of you?"

The banker lifted his mug, fished the teabag out with his fingers, dropped it in the ashtray. "I don't think anyone knew Cammie well. He kept to himself, you know? Some of the drivers, they play in the darts team, or they come on the golf trips. Cammie was never like that. He just did his shift, maybe stopped in here for a brew. That was it."

"So when he left," McCormack looked round the five faces, "it was right out of the blue?"

The card players exchanged glances. "Well. Being honest," the youngest one—skinny, ginger, with long hair and impressive sideburns—shot a glance at the banker. "It wasn't that much of a shock."

"You mean he'd spoken about leaving?"

"Not so much that. It's just, he kept dropping hints. Ye

know? His ship was gonnae come in. That sort of thing. Everything was gonnae be different."

"Did he say what it was?"

The young one shook his head. "Kept it close to his chest. I thought it was maybe an inheritance. Some auld auntie was about to croak. Something like that. But he never said."

"What about the rest of you? You hear anything like this?"

A few nods, mutterings. "It was just something he banged on about," the tea-maker offered. "No one paid it much attention. Until, you know, he went."

"O.K., guys." McCormack stood up. "Sorry to interrupt your break." He took a few business cards from his wallet and dropped them down beside the playing cards, like a fourth hand. "You remember something else, you call that number, O.K.? See you later."

He was back on the Broomielaw, heading past the Custom House, when he heard the clatter of feet. He spun round, side-stepping to the Custom House wall, dukes up ready. It was always on your mind, walking the city, that you might encounter someone you'd helped put away, someone who laid his ten-stretch in Saughton or Perth or Peterhead directly at your door. Whenever a man strode your way on a lonely street, whenever someone crossed a road towards you at a jog, you wondered if your number was up. So you hear the footsteps, you spin round with your fists up.

The other man had his hands up too, but with open palms, backing off with his eyes wide. "I'm sorry! I'm sorry! It's me!"

It was the young driver, the boy with the sideburns. McCormack dropped his hands. "Sorry, pal. Thought you might have been an unsatisfied customer. Kind of an occupational hazard. Is there something you've remembered?"

The driver shot a look behind him. "I should've told someone before now. I just never, I never got the chance."

A taxi passed them slowly, the driver craning round to scope them.

"Come on." McCormack took the young driver's sleeve. "Let's go for a walk."

They crossed Clyde Street. There was a walkway along the river and they started east along it, heading in the direction of Glasgow Green.

"I'm Alan Russell, by the way." The driver had his hand out and McCormack shook it.

"Pleased to meet you, Alan. My name's Duncan. What's on your mind?"

"It was last year," Russell said. "Around this time, in fact. We do a big outing to Troon. All the drivers, I mean. It's a charity thing. We take underprivileged kids down the coast for the day. Get the cabs decked out in streamers and what have you."

"I know it," said McCormack. "I've seen it in the paper."

"Well. We go down in this big convoy. I mean it's like all the drivers in the city, not just our lot. It looks amazin. Far as the eye can see, it's just black hacks."

Across the river, McCormack could see the elegant terraces of Carlton Place, shining in classical symmetry behind their intermittent screen of poplars. It looked like another country. Another century.

"So we get there last year," Russell was saying. "And it's a cracking day. Really scorching. And the kids are having a ball. There's adult helpers but the drivers help out, too. You buy the kids ice-cream, give them money for the rides at the shows. Anyway, I had three kids with me—two wee lassies and a wee boy—and I'm taking them to the putting green. And we start playing and I notice that one of the lassies is sort of hanging back, ye know?"

McCormack nodded. He sidestepped to let a cyclist pass them on the footpath.

"She was sort of hiding behind my legs. I thought it was a

joke at first, but then I saw. There was two boys playing the hole in front of us, with their driver. And the driver was Campbell Sneddon. It was Cammie she was scared of. Whenever he turned round she got really upset, you know. Agitated. And then, well, she had an accident."

"What do you mean—she tripped over?"

"No, she—well. She wet herself, O.K.? Right there on the putting green."

"O.K. So what happened?"

"I took her to get cleaned up. A waitress in a café helped her out. And I took her to a shop on the main street, got her some new gear. She just kinda shut down, you know? Stopped speaking. I thought it was just that she was, like, disturbed. A disturbed kid. Or maybe Cammie reminded her of someone. But now I'm thinking that maybe she knew him."

They came to a stop then, just before the low arches of the Victoria Bridge. They had come far enough, it was time to turn back.

"Do you remember where she was from? I mean where you picked her up?"

"Aye, it was a Home out in Bishopbriggs. Longpark. Or Parklands? Something like that."

"Auldpark?"

"That was it. How come you know . . . ?"

"Sneddon worked there. He was caretaker at Auldpark for fifteen years."

"Jesus. So the wee lassie knew him. Was it because of this that he . . . that somebody killed him?"

"We don't know, Alan." They walked on a little. McCormack took out his cigarettes, offered them. "You remember her name, the wee lassie?"

Russell shook his head. "Sorry, I don't." He leaned in to use the flame on McCormack's lighter. They walked on. Russell kicked a loose stone on the footpath—it clanged against the railings by the riverbank. "Maybe the Home would have a record. You know, who went in what taxi?"

"Auldpark closed last year," McCormack said. "The Council seems to have misplaced the records."

They were back where they started, adjacent to the Custom House. Russell scratched under his jawline. "I just wish I'd said. You know, earlier. Maybe it would've saved it happening to anyone else."

"You did the right thing, Alan. Don't worry about it. We appreciate your help."

He watched Russell cross the street, dodging neatly between oncoming buses. As he turned to go, McCormack noticed the little statue up on a plinth beside the steps. It was new—he hadn't spotted it before. It looked like a nun, up on a tall, narrow plinth, a woman in a long tunic—arms up in triumph, feet planted apart. She looked like the letter X, like a St. Andrew's cross. He moved closer. It was a monument to Dolores Ibarruri, heroine of the Spanish Civil War.

The plinth carried a quotation: "Better to die on your feet than live forever on your knees".

McCormack walked off towards Jamaica Street. Dying on your feet? he thought. Got that covered. Been doing that all summer.

48

K idd sat at the little table in the Duke of Perth, watching the door. He thought of it as "his" table, though this was only the second time he'd sat there. The same knot of top boys held the corner of the bar, though tonight they wore casual clothes—jeans and denim jackets, polo shirts, Adidas trainers—instead of the usual suits. Kidd wondered if they phoned each other in advance, like schoolgirls going to the disco: what are you wearing tonight?

He'd arranged to meet McPhail at seven o'clock. He took a sup of his pint and glanced at the big clock behind the bar: quarter past. He still had his nose in his pint when the door rattled. He set his drink down on the table and a shadow fell over it: McPhail.

"Bring your pint—come on."

McPhail set off up the pub. Kidd thought at first that he was taking him to join the circle of top boys but he passed them with a nod and carried on to a door marked "Private". He held it open for Kidd.

Inside was a function room, done out in the same wallpaper as the room they'd just left, the same dark wooden tables and chairs, the same metal ashtrays. A smaller, private version of the pub.

"Have a seat."

Kidd pulled out a wooden chair at the nearest table; McPhail sat on the padded bench seat, his back to the wall.

"You want another drink?"

"I'm fine."

"I'm gonnae have one. I mean, I take it we're celebrating?"

He pressed a buzzer on the wall beside him and the barman appeared at the door.

"Grouse, please, Harry, and another pint for my friend."

McPhail watched Kidd steadily, silently, both arms extended along the bench seat. He seemed cheerful, almost upbeat. Kidd looked around the room, fiddled with his drink. If this was some sort of game, if McPhail was waiting for him to speak first, he would have to wait.

"I heard you met Bud," McPhail said eventually.

So that was Bud Hunter, Kidd thought. The man in his flat at Largs. The man who told him to kill Yvonne, without actually saying the words.

"Right," Kidd said.

"He said you were taking your time."

The door opened just then and the barman came through carrying a tray. He set down McPhail's whisky and a little jug of water. He set down a fresh pint of heavy in front of Kidd. He studied the arrangement of the drinks and then nodded, leaving with the tray hanging down by his side.

"I didn't think it was a race," Kidd said. "I thought it was a question of getting the job done. Did I kill her or didn't I?"

McPhail tipped a little water into his whisky. "Well, now that you bring it up."

"Fuck off. You think I'm lying?"

"It's an honest question." McPhail swirled his glass to mix the water, took a sip of whisky. "Bud Hunter gave you two hundred and fifty quid. Who's to say you didnae give that to Yvonne Gray, send her on her merry way? Bud thought you looked pretty tight, you two. Pretty friendly, he said."

Kidd wasn't frightened of giving himself away. He'd been pretending all his life. Pretending was how you survived Auldpark. Pretending you'd done things. Pretending you hadn't. Pretending you were hard. Pretending you didn't care. Pretending wasn't a problem for Kidd. His only concern was that someone had spotted Yvonne as she left on the train. She'd taken the train to Ardrossan and caught a bus to Kilmarnock. At Kilmarnock she took the Carlisle train and changed there for Manchester. A friend in Manchester had agreed to put her up. She would wait there until things were sorted out back home. One way or another.

But Yvonne had left the guesthouse in Largs through the rear garden and a back alley, with her hair dyed black, in a headscarf and shades, wearing a jacket she'd bought from the landlady's daughter. There was no way that she'd been clocked.

Kidd drained his old pint, set it aside. Shifted the new one onto the beermat. "I needed to get to know her," he told McPhail. "Build up trust."

"Right enough. Trust's what it's all about," McPhail said. "Why don't you tell me how you done it, Christopher? Put my mind at ease."

"Easy," Kidd said. "I choked her. Took her out of town on the coastal path. They've got a monument there, the Pencil—"

"The Viking thing. Aye, that's right. On you go."

"Well. I did it there. Down by the rocks."

"Then what?"

Kidd could hear laughter from the other side of the door. He looked at McPhail. "I borrowed a rowing boat."

"You dumped her in the firth?"

"Aye."

"Whereabouts exactly? The Fairlie Roads? Next low tide you'll have wee kids wi' buckets and spades tripping over her."

"Naw." Kidd shook his head. "Dropped her in the channel. Over by Cumbrae. It's sixty feet deep. Weighted her down. She's safe enough."

"You better hope so."

It was always best, Kidd knew, to go on the offensive when you had something to hide. To feign indignation. He sat back now, lit a cigarette without offering, tossed the match in the ashtray. "I know what you're doing here, McPhail, by the way. Don't think I don't."

McPhail looked sharply at him. "Oh aye? What am I doing?"

"You're gonnae use this as an excuse, aren't you? Oh ye didnae bring photographic evidence of Yvonne Gray lying dead on the floor of a fucking rowing boat, so I'm no payin you. That's your chat, is it?"

"Naw. That's not—"

"Sitting there in your fucking fifty-quid suit. Ordering whiskies at the push of a button. A dirty welshing bastard. I took a big fucking risk—"

"Chris! Chris!" McPhail's hands were up. "Wait a fucking minute here." He fumbled in the inside pocket of his jacket, tossed something down on the table.

Kidd looked at the object on the table, back at McPhail with no change of expression. He reached out. It was a folded roll of notes, an elastic band round it.

"It's counted. It's there. No one was planning to stiff you, Chris. Jesus Christ. Keep the fucking heid, mate."

Kidd stowed the money in the pocket of his leather jerkin. "Fine, then."

"You know the guys out there?" McPhail jerked his thumb at the door. "Burgess and the rest of them?"

Kidd shrugged. "Know them to look at."

"Come on." McPhail stood up. "I'll introduce you."

Kidd stood, drained his pint. "Fine. You know who I'd rather meet, though."

McPhail laughed. "Time enough for that, Chris. He's grateful, if that's what you're worried about. He appreciates all you done. Believe me."

SATURDAY, 12 JULY 1975

49

Knock, knock."
Goldie stood in McCormack's open doorway, knuckling the ribbed glass panel. McCormack looked up from his files. "Got something, Derek?"

"I'm not sure. Maybe."

McCormack followed him through. One of the Ordnance Survey maps was spread on Goldie's desk. McCormack noticed the sickle-shaped coastline of Ayrshire, Argyll's fraying fringe of islands and peninsulas.

"I checked the names the MoD gave me. Chisholm's regimental buddies." Goldie pursed his lips. "Nothing doing. No one knows anything."

"You told me."

"Right. But then I checked for fatalities. Soldiers killed in action from Chisholm's company."

Goldie was leaning over, palms planted on the desk, scanning the map as if the story he was telling was coded in its contour lines and B-roads.

"On you go."

"Well. There's a guy called Malcolm Skilling. A sergeant. Did a couple of tours with in Ulster with Chisholm. He was killed in '72 by the Provisionals. Single shot to the head. Out on patrol in Belfast."

Goldie had lifted a corner of the map, started sifting through a sheaf of papers. He found a Xeroxed newspaper clipping. "Here."

It showed a dark-eyed young man in dress uniform—Glengarry, diced cap-band—gazing obliquely past the camera. "Fusilier Slain by IRA Bullet" was the headline.

"And Chisholm knew him?"

"Well I think he'd have to, wouldn't he? But here's the thing." Goldie nodded at the clipping in McCormack's hands. "You'll see there, he was the only child of Mrs. Martha Skilling, widow, aged sixty-three—she must have had him late—who resides at Howcraig Cottage, outside Largs."

Goldie turned back to the map, tapping it with one finger. McCormack bent to look.

The road from Largs to Glasgow snakes east across high moorland. Uphill from Muirhead Reservoir is a lonely farm called Blairpark. Climbing north from Blairpark, directly uphill into a bare patch of moor, taking a sharp dog-leg before pushing north once more, is a road that simply stops, peters out maybe half a mile from the Glasgow road. At the top of this moorland track McCormack could see a smallish structure, an old farmhouse, maybe an isolated cottage. It wasn't named but this, presumably, was Howcraig Cottage. There were outbuildings of some kind, little oblongs across from the main structure.

"Have you checked with the local polis? Got them to scope the place?"

Goldie shook his head. "Not yet. No point spooking him. If it even *is* him."

McCormack drew his finger in a circle round Howcraig Cottage. "O.K., Derek. Well, the location's interesting. It makes sense."

"What makes sense?" Nicol had appeared in the Byre. She slipped out of her jacket, hung it on the back of her chair, pinched the shoulders to straighten it. Goldie explained the situation, pointed out the locus on the map. Nicol pushed her hair back with two hands, held it in place in one fist and twisted a band round it.

"It's handy for West Kilbride, certainly," she said. West Kilbride was where Maitland's estranged wife lived. "Could've spied on them pretty easily from there. Plus," Nicol drew her finger up the coastline on the map. "The bus from Largs to Glasgow passes through Greenock."

"Where Chisholm stole the Rover."

Nicol nodded. "So what do we do?"

"Do?" McCormack grinned. "We're off on our holidays. Pack your buckets and spades, troops. We're heading Doon the Watter!"

Ninety minutes later the three of them were driving past Paisley in an unmarked Wolseley 1100, heading for Ayrshire. Since this was just a reconnaissance trip, and there was no hard intel placing Chisholm at the locus, Haddow hadn't sanctioned an armed escort. But he did agree to revolvers for the three of them, so McCormack, Nicol and Goldie had signed out Webley 38s from the armoury at Stewart Street.

As they passed Lochwinnoch the land began to change. The bare moor spread and swelled into ridges. Cloud shadows rippled over flanks of hills. Clumps of tussock-grass switched to and fro in the breeze and the odd tree, hunched and stunted, signalled the prevailing wind.

At Kilbirnie they stopped at a baker's for filled rolls which they ate in the car, slurping sweet tea from Styrofoam cups.

They drove on, every rise in the road lifting their sightline clear of the drystone dykes along the roadside, gifting glimpses of the firth and the islands, the blue peaks of Arran. As they passed Muirhead Reservoir on their left, McCormack leaned forward. "Slow down," he said to Nicol. "It's coming up. There!"

They saw the gateposts of Blairpark Farm looming on their right. Nicol signalled, turned into the driveway, crunched to a stop in the broad farm courtyard. A black-and-white collie dog came bouncing out of nowhere and flattened its chin against the ground, waggling its raised hindquarters.

They all got out of the car and a woman appeared in a doorway, drying her hands on a dishcloth. McCormack gave his hand to the dog and squatted down to ruffle its ears. Then he set off towards the farmhouse, flipping open his warrant card.

"D.I. Duncan McCormack," he told her. "This is D.S. Goldie and D.C. Nicol."

The woman nodded, unsmiling, "And what'll be your business with us?"

"It's more with your neighbour up the hill," McCormack said. "A Mrs. Skilling?"

The woman looked at Nicol and Goldie in turn. She craned her head to look at the Wolseley parked in the courtyard.

"You'll be after the lodger, then. The soldier."

"We might well be, Mrs. . . . . ?"

"I'm Anna Blackie. My man farms this hillside. You better come in."

Mrs. Blackie brought them into a low-ceilinged kitchen that smelled of cabbage and Brasso. It was cool after the heat of the day, with its stone flags and its big twin jaw-box sink. The kettle was rattling on its hob and, without a word, Mrs. Blackie set out mugs and sugar bowl and a milk jug, clinking teaspoons into the mugs. The three detectives eased into the chairs around the kitchen table.

"You mentioned a lodger, Mrs. Blackie." McCormack lifted a ceramic salt-shaker in the shape of a bird—a sparrow or maybe a wagtail. "How do you know he's a soldier?"

"She told me." Mrs. Blackie used the kettle to fill a green china teapot. "She said he was a friend of Malcolm. Her son. He was killed a few years back, over in Ireland."

"Right. And why would you assume we were here to see him, though? The soldier."

"You've never met him, have you?" She had broken veins on her cheeks, jagged pink zig-zags, but she looked almost young when she glanced slyly up at McCormack with a closed-lip smile.

"Gordon Chisholm?" McCormack set the salt-shaker down. "No, we've never met him."

That wasn't strictly true, McCormack thought. He had stood in a line to shake Chisholm's hand at the funerals of Chisholm's wife and daughter. But that hardly counted as meeting.

"Because you would know," Mrs. Blackie said. She lifted the tea-tray, brought it across, set it down on the kitchen table. "You would know, if you'd met him. He's not right. You can see it in his eyes. He's done things. Or maybe he's seen things. I wouldn't want to be behind those eyes. Not if you paid me."

She gripped the teapot by the handle and swirled it, tipping the liquid into four mugs in turn, the tendon in her forearm straining.

McCormack waited until she was sitting down, then he produced the flyer with Chisholm's face on it. "Is that him, Mrs. Blackie? Is that the lodger?"

"That's him." She took the flyer in both hands. "He's cut his hair. Stopped shaving too. But aye, that's your man."

The three detectives exchanged looks. "Is he up there now?" Nicol asked.

"I don't think so. I heard his van going down the lane this morning. Just after ten."

Goldie spoke softly. "And what kind of van does he drive?"

"One of those camper van things. Two colours. Pale green and cream. What is it he's done?"

McCormack seemed not to have heard the question. "Mrs. Blackie. I need you to tell me about the buildings up there. The layout."

Mrs. Blackie sipped her tea. "Not much to tell. There's a farmhouse. Single storey. More of a cottage, really. Couple of outbuildings. That's it."

"And if he does turn out to be home, will he see us coming up the track?"

"He'll *hear* you," Mrs. Blackie said. "It's not exactly the M8 out there."

"But if we leave the car here?"

Mrs. Blackie cupped her mug in both hands, stared out of the window. "Well. It's a steep enough track. You'd be covered by the high ground, I'd say, till you got to yon wee stand of trees. From the trees onward you'd be exposed, but the house faces east, looks out over the moor. The gable's blind. There's no window overlooking the track."

"And the woman? Mrs. Skilling?"

"She'll not see you coming." Mrs. Blackie was smiling into her tea. "You're safe enough there."

They left Mrs. Blackie in her kitchen and started up the slope on foot, McCormack pushing ahead, long lunging strides eating up the track. Nicol was shaking her head, trotting to keep pace. "Shouldn't we call it in, sir. Wait here for backup?"

"No time." McCormack climbed on, never breaking his stride.

"But we told DCI Haddow. I mean, that's the protocol, sir."

McCormack stopped, turned round abruptly. He reached under his jacket to adjust his shoulder-holster. "Nicol. The chances are that Chisholm's out. If the boy's being held at this address then we've got every chance of finding and freeing him before Chisholm returns. No fuss. No risk. We wait for backup we could miss that chance."

"Shouldn't we at least let them know what we're doing?"

McCormack looked at Goldie, only now arriving, flushed, panting. Goldie cleared his throat. "That could be rule number one of detective work," he told her. "You're doing something you shouldn't be doing, don't give the brass the chance to stop you."

They walked on, strung out in single file along the rising track. McCormack, Nicol, Goldie. The track was stony with a grassy camber up the middle. The sun passed behind a cloud and the atmosphere thickened and blued. McCormack kept his stride long and steady. In truth, he felt less certain than he'd made out to Nicol. From the start McCormack had felt wrong-footed by the kidnapping. Usually, with an abduction, you flooded the area with uniforms, blitzed the door-to-door, collated descriptions of strangers and vehicles, maybe landed partial digits from a number plate, hoped to identify the snatcher before the victim was harmed. None of that had been needed here. The first the police learned of the kidnapping was when Walter Maitland fronted up at Temple Police Station to say his boy had been taken. He already knew who the kidnapper was. Chisholm had had time to mail a bloody letter—complete with Polaroid photo—to Maitland before the police knew what had happened.

It left McCormack feeling that they were playing catch-up, like Chisholm knew their next move before they did. Which explained—or so McCormack hoped—the queasy feeling of déjà vu that now hit him like a dizzy spell as he led Nicol and Goldie up the stony track. Off to the right a green hill rose to a conic point and a hawk floated out of the sun, spiralling down through the thermals. The thin complaining bleats of sheep rose in the empty air. McCormack felt the sweat bloom between his shoulder blades, slide in runnels down his ribs.

At the stand of trees McCormack stopped, let the others catch up. The branches met overhead in a kind of bower and the three cops stood in the shade and studied the roughcast gable of the cottage, maybe fifty yards on up the hill.

"There are outbuildings in back of the cottage." McCormack turned to Goldie. "You search those, Derek. We'll keep the old woman busy. Shout out if you find anything. The boy. Or Chisholm for that matter."

They climbed the final yards in silence. Goldie slipped round the side of the cottage as McCormack and Nicol took the path.

When the woman opened the door she frowned helplessly out at McCormack and Nicol, her head twisting like a dog trying to sniff the wind. Her eyes were cloudy and white, like windows filmed in frost. "Mrs. Blackie? Is that you, Mrs. Blackie?"

McCormack folded his warrant card and put it away. "Mrs. Skilling?"

"Yes? Yes?"

"Mrs. Skilling, I'm a police officer. My name is Detective Inspector Duncan McCormack. This is Detective Constable Elizabeth Nicol. May we come in, please?"

"Police?" The woman's head was tossing, her lank hair swinging across her face. "Nobody called the police. You've got it wrong."

"There's nothing wrong, Mrs. Skilling. Nothing to worry about. We just need to ask you some questions." There was a pause. "Can we maybe come in?"

The woman's head jerked and her mouth slewed open and she turned and bumped off down the hallway, her thin brown hand slapping the wall. Ten feet or so down she swung her hip out to clear an ugly black bureau that was flush against the wall and disappeared through a white panelled door. McCormack caught the door before it swung shut. Mrs. Skilling was settling into an armchair facing twin windows. Her knitting rested on the arm of the chair and she drew it to her now, her fingers spidering over the bunched wool before the needles started clicking.

McCormack and Nicol settled into the floral-print sofa, their backs to the window.

"Mrs. Skilling," McCormack began. "You have a lodger staying with you at the minute. Is that correct?"

"A lodger?" The head tossed and the needles flashed. "What would I want with a lodger?"

McCormack caught Nicol's eye and jerked his head at the old woman. Nicol leaned forward. "Mrs. Skilling. There's a man's pair of Wellington boots in the hallway."

The woman laughed. "You'd want him to go out on the hill in his carpet slippers, would you?"

"Who, Mrs. Skilling?"

"Malcolm! My son Malcolm!" She slumped forward a little, shaking her head, her slack wrists holding the needles crossed. Then she sat up straight, her needles clicking again. "Who did you think it would be?"

"You have more than one son, Mrs. Skilling?" Maybe she had two sons, McCormack thought. Maybe she was mixing them up.

"We *want*ed more. Or anyway *he* did. But you take what you're given. God's will be done. I never complained. Not even when my sight failed."

"Mrs. Skilling." McCormack felt the skin tightening on his skull. "Your son is dead. He was killed in Ireland. The IRA shot him."

She didn't even pause in her knitting, just bared her dentures in a dainty grin. "You don't fool me, mister. No, you don't. They tried to tell me my son was gone. But he came back just the same. Came back to look after his mammy."

She nodded to herself. Her head lifted in something like triumph. "Do you think I don't know my own flesh and blood. You think I can't—well! Why don't you see for yourself?"

Maybe her sightloss had sharpened her other senses, but they heard now what the woman had caught—the faint rumble of a truck or van, the modulated whine of someone dropping down the gears to meet the slope.

Nicol braced herself to stand but McCormack gripped her sleeve, shook his head. He did, though, draw his Webley from its holster and drop his arm down by the side of the sofa, the tip of the Webley just nudging the carpet. They heard the gravel spurting from tyres and then the light dimmed as the camper van rolled to a stop in front of the windows.

The crisp clunk of a door closing; footsteps on gravel; the scratch of a key in the lock.

50

There was a pause and then muffled thumps as though
someone was unloading a bag of groceries on a
kitchen table and stowing them in a cupboard. Then
the steps came clumping down the hallway and the door was
swinging open.

Gordon Chisholm had been growing a beard. He wore
Polaroid sunglasses with a graded tint. But it was him all right.
He stood in the doorway in denim jacket and jeans, taking it
in, the cops on the sofa, his mouth opening as though time
had slowed and the film of the world was now running half-
speed. Before he could get a word out, Mrs. Skilling was craning forward.

"Malcolm! Malcolm, this is—well, I've forgotten the
names. But they're police officers! They wanted to see you."

Chisholm half-turned his head, as if her words were a hook
that had snagged his cheek, tugging him round, but he kept his
eyes on McCormack and Nicol.

"Fine," he said slowly. "Just got to get something from the
van." As he spoke the last words he was already lurching for
the hallway, the door clacking shut behind him, Nicol and
McCormack rising as one. The crash from the hallway suggested that Chisholm had collided with the wooden bureau
but when McCormack shouldered the door it wouldn't give
and he knew that Chisholm had slid the big bureau in front of
it. McCormack stepped back and charged the door again and
the door flexed like a diving board but stayed shut. The wood

was too flimsy. McCormack turned, leaned his back against the door and slid down onto his haunches, feet apart, and started to push. The bureau began to move, he heard the legs scraping on the stone-flagged floor and he strained his thighs once more and felt the bureau lurch again and he turned and squeezed through the gap and ran, Nicol at his heels.

He was halfway down the hallway when he heard the shot, a flat, cracking sound like a stick snapping neatly in half. He burst out into the daylight, spinning with his gun-arm extended, the scene rushing at him in blurred shards—a hill, the green camper van, a whitewashed wall, a flare of sun on the reservoir. He could hear running feet, a man's cries, and rounding the van he saw Goldie on the ground and then a shower of ice lashed his face. Chisholm was sprinting off up the hill, a flourish of blue against the dancing green. Goldie was trying to sit up, jacking forwards like a man performing sit-ups, his arms extended, his splay-fingered palms quivering either side of his left knee. A ragged hole had been blown in the trouser-leg and a white nub of bone shone out from a sump of black blood and pulped flesh.

He looked round for Nicol, waving the Webley. "Tie it up, Liz!" He was already turning to sprint after Chisholm. "Call it in!"

He saw her kneeling to Goldie as he turned and ran. He had fucked it up. Should've listened to Nicol, should've called it in, let the heavy mob handle it. Now he had a man down and was lugging his guts up a hillside in pursuit of an armed killer. Like the prize fucking eejit he was.

Fuck it.

Nothing for it now but to see the thing through.

Ice was dropping from his hair as he ran, tinkling onto his shoulders. Not ice: glass. Chisholm must have squeezed off a shot as McCormack rounded the camper van, shivering a window, showering McCormack in splinters. The hillside was steep, he felt his legs getting heavy, bones jarring, his thigh-muscles clenching. He reached a little plateau on the hillside and stopped, chest tight, heart booming. He cast around for a glimpse of Chisholm's blue denim: nothing. He jack-knifed over, hands on thighs, the Webley's barrel digging into his knee, biting great lungfuls of air, feeling the blood rushing up to his brain.

"Hey, polis!"

The voice snapped him upright. He gripped the Webley and jerked it around, covering the empty hillside.

"Down here, polis. This way."

McCormack saw the faint yellow path, peppered with sheep droppings, off to the right, along a narrow shelf of land. He started down it, following the barrel of the Webley.

"That's right. Keep it coming."

McCormack rounded a bush and Chisholm reared up out of nowhere, a grinning scarecrow, his arm wrapped matily round the boy's shoulders, a pistol jammed against the boy's temple. McCormack staggered back, almost toppled over the edge, slammed his left foot down to keep his balance and felt it give on the spongy, tussocky ground, a sprain or a break. He dropped to one knee but wrenched himself upright straight away, grimacing, gasping for his inhaler.

"Steady now, copper. Keep the heid, there."

McCormack stood shakily, favouring his right leg. There was a black hole in the hillside behind the two figures, a low, shallow cave, and McCormack could see the blue nylon sheath of a sleeping bag, the charred remnants of a fire.

"Robert! Robert Maitland!" He fixed the boy with his gaze, keeping the Webley trained on Chisholm. His voice sounded heightened, deranged, like a street preacher. He swallowed. "Robert, are you all right?"

It was a ridiculous question. The boy was shivering, pale, dressed in a thin white T-shirt and jeans, his face streaked with dirt and blood, a killer's pistol pressed to his head.

The boy nodded. He couldn't elaborate on the nod because a dirty grey rag was gagging his mouth. His ankles were bound in some sort of twine and his arms seemed pinned behind his back.

But he was alive.

McCormack took a breath, paid it out. Another. He stood on the hillside with the blood trilling in his veins. Nicol would be calling it in, getting backup. Help was on its way—squad cars from Largs, probably a chopper for Goldie. All he had to do was wait. Chisholm wasn't going anywhere. Neither was he.

"Gordon Chisholm," he said. "*Corporal* Chisholm."

"I'm no a Jock anymore."

McCormack was finding his breath now, his voice relaxing to its normal tone. "Ah, come on now. Look at you. You're in the field. You've engaged the enemy. You're holding a handgun at somebody's head."

Chisholm said nothing.

"And Gavin Elliot. That was a soldierly thing to do, wasn't it? Not strictly the Geneva Convention. But then, you didn't really worry about things like that, did you? Over there, I mean."

"Over where?"

"I'm talking about the Five Techniques, Gordon. I'm talking about Ulster."

"You were a Jock?" Chisholm's eyes were narrowed.

"Not me, pal. Someone I know." McCormack's ankle was throbbing, he wanted to sit down, take the weight off his leg altogether. "But Gavin Elliot wasn't some nameless Taig from the Falls or the Short Strand, was he? He was an ex-MP. Fucking Knight of the Realm. A decorated soldier. And you torture him for, what, four days? Keep him in his own shit? What would your COs think of that?"

"They'd think I did the right thing. If they knew what I

know. It was too good for him, what he got. What I gave him. If I coulda made him last longer I would've."

"Gives you a thrill, does it? Torturing innocent people?"

Chisholm hooked his elbow tighter round the boy's neck, jammed the barrel harder to his temple. "You mean over there? What would you know about it? There's a fucking war on, polisman. That woman down there? They shot her boy like a dog in the street. I had three mates. Provos honeytrapped them. One to the head while they were taking a piss at the side of the road. Left in a heap with their cocks hanging out."

"That wasn't the guys you tortured, though, was it? It wasn't Provos you picked up. It was innocent Catholics."

Chisholm sneered. "No such animal."

"Oh right. A Taig's a Taig. Like your Taig wife, eh? Like your Taig daughter."

"Leave them out of it, polis."

"Why? So you can kid on you're the good guy? You bombed a squaddie pub! In Glasgow! Even the Provos never did that. You're a traitor, mate. Fucking heretic, that's what you are."

Chisholm twisted his head as if the words were blows. "No! That's a lie. It was Maitland's pub."

"Because why? Because he set a fire that killed your wife and wee lassie? At least he didn't set out to hurt them. Can you say the same, Chisholm? Can you?"

He could see Chisholm's nostrils flare and he took a step forward, blanking the pain in his ankle.

"She had to call the polis on you. Twice. To protect herself. Protect her daughter from her own daddy."

"That's a fucking lie! That's not true!"

"I've read the files, though. You hurt them. Hurt your own. And now, what? You make it all better by killing that boy there? The hell did he ever do?"

"That's Maitland's lookout. He shoulda thought of that before he did what he did."

McCormack could hear it now, faintly at first, a gentle folding of the air. His mouth was suddenly dry but he managed to swallow, flexed his gun-arm to ease the burn in his bicep.

"Great. Then you'll be the same as him. Worse. You think he gives a shit about that boy? Walter Maitland gives a shit about Walter Maitland. Full stop. You want to hurt Walter Maitland? Hurt Walter Maitland. That's the only way. And you've just blown it. You'll never get near him."

Chisholm's mouth opened as if to speak but McCormack's gaze was climbing, high over Chisholm's shoulder. And now it shuddered into view, the chopper, clearing the hilltop, a clattering black metal beast, and Chisholm craned up to see, his gun pulling loose from the boy's head and tilting skywards and McCormack took his chance. A vermilion rose bloomed on Chisholm's exposed throat and he pitched forward, a second shot plucking a twist of smoke from the edge of his skull as he fell. McCormack moved smartly across, arm extended, firing as he went, and the body jumped on the grass as the bullets slammed home.

The boy was twisting and bucking, wide-eyed, as if the gag was choking him. McCormack dug into his pocket for his penknife and freed the blade, slicing through the gag. The boy sputtered and gasped, like someone surfacing from a deep dive. He lay on the grass as McCormack hacked through the cords binding his arms and feet. The boy struggled to his knees, fingers black with congested blood. He leaned forward with his hands on his knees and spat on the grass.

"It's O.K." McCormack clapped the boy on the back as the blades of the chopper flattened the grass and swallowed his words. "You did well, son. You did well."

IV
THE DOVE DESCENDING

SUNDAY, 13 JULY 1975

51

He woke before dawn in a strange room. Pale glow from a nightlight. Jug of water on a nightstand. He couldn't move. His arms and legs were pinned tight by hospital sheets and for a second it came back to him, after nearly twenty years, the sick fear he felt in 1956, when the women of the village would mouth a word they were scared to say out loud. *Polio.* Most of the victims were kids but it was still possible for a man of nineteen—as McCormack was then—to catch it. He had never known what fear was till that summer. Everyone was afraid. Everyone had a theory as to how you caught the virus. You could catch it from being out in the sun too long. Or from sharing someone's towel at the beach. Or from midgie bites. The saliva of cats. He used to lie awake at night in his single bed in West Laroch, imagining that he couldn't move, he was trapped in an Iron Lung. Even those words—Iron Lung—made him clench and sweat.

He tried to flex his foot and couldn't and he saw now, raising his head on the banked pillows, that the tightness wasn't just a question of bedsheets. His left foot, propped on a pillow and protruding from the pulled back sheets and blankets, was cased in plaster to the ankle.

He dozed off and when he woke again a man was outlined against the high window, two yards from McCormack's bed.

"Jesus, Vic. Who let you in?"

"What? They're gonna keep your cousin away? Your English cousin up from London?"

McCormack grinned. "Family first, cuz."

Victor sat down on the bed, pulling the sheets even tighter. He looked older in the light from the big windows, little filaments of silver in the two-day growth on his chin. "How you holding up, then?"

McCormack frowned. He was struggling to place what had brought him to a hospital. Then he remembered, in a rush. *It's O.K., son. You did well.* The whirr of the chopper blades. The red rose on Chisholm's stretched throat. The bile climbed his gullet.

He closed his eyes and swallowed. Then he opened them again. "I've got a broken ankle, Vic. I think I'll live."

"That's not what I meant."

"I know that's not what you meant."

McCormack lay back, turned his head to the window. Up here on the fifth floor you looked out over the blackened spire of the Cathedral to the slopes of the Necropolis, where John Knox on his sandstone column held court above his city of the dead. You could see the hills of Ayrshire from up here and McCormack pictured it again, the green hillside, Chisholm pitching forward, and the Maitland boy, eyes wide with terror. He felt the kick of the gun in the bones of his wrist. He closed his eyes. He didn't want to go into it. Even if he had wanted to talk about it he wouldn't have known where to start.

"You saved a life, Duncan. That's how you've got to look at it. Maybe two."

"You think he'd have killed himself?"

"I think he'd have killed you, Duncan."

McCormack leaned across to get the water jug. Victor was on his feet. "Here, let me." He poured a glass, passed it to McCormack, watched him drink.

"I just worry," Victor said. "This case. This city."

"Says the man who joined the army."

"The man who *left* the army."

"You think I should resign? And do what?"

"That's not what I said. I think you should step back from this one, though."

"Well that's easy. I fired my gun, Vic. I'm suspended till they clear me. *If* they clear me."

"Clear you? They'll give you a medal."

A nurse came in to check on McCormack, flashing a tight smile at Victor. She refilled the water jug at the big Belfast sink. Then she lifted the clipboard from its hook at the end of his bed and scribbled something on it. When she'd gone, McCormack frowned. "Vic, look. If we're gonna do this properly . . ."

"What?"

"People don't set up house with their 'cousins', Vic." McCormack sipped his water. "Not in Partick tenements."

Victor nodded. He rose and walked to the window, stood looking down at the hillside studded with tombs and mausoleums. "Not the most inspiring view, is it? I mean if you're lying here trying to get better. It's not too uplifting."

"This is Glasgow," McCormack said. "We don't do uplifting."

Victor was still facing the window. "Did you mean that? What you said?"

"Mean what?"

"About doing this properly."

"I wouldn't say it, Vic. Not if I didn't mean it."

Victor turned from the window. He took the empty glass from McCormack and set it back on the bedside cabinet. "I heard from Ross Holland," he said. "Last night."

McCormack shrugged.

"My mate from the regiment! He said there's a job going at the warehouse he works at. If I want it. Gave me the number to phone."

"Good. That's good, Vic."

"And I'll see about getting a flat. Somewhere out west. I want this to work, Dunc. For real this time. Anyway, look. I'll let you rest. You'll be home this afternoon, right?"

"Aye. Unless they amputate."

Victor grinned. He glanced at the door and then took McCormack's hand. He seemed unsure whether to risk something more. He was bending forward when the door opened and Nicol was standing there clutching a bottle of Lucozade to her chest like a driver on the podium at Silverstone.

"Nicol! Jesus." McCormack shuffled up in bed. "This is my cousin Victor. Victor, this is D.C. Liz Nicol."

Victor was stepping smartly round the bed with his hand extended. "You're the one who gets him into all this trouble, are you?"

"Oh I think he can manage that all by himself." Nicol was smiling. She gripped the bottle in her left hand and looked Victor in the eye as they shook.

"I don't doubt it. Good to meet you, D.C. Nicol. Duncan: keep in touch."

And he was off, the door banging, his tuneless whistle sounding a little self-conscious to McCormack's ears.

Nicol took a step forward into the room. She made a big show of studying Victor's departure, and turning to McCormack, head tilted.

"What?"

"Your cousin," she said, no tone.

"I can't have a cousin?"

"One of the, what, Cockney McCormacks? East End branch of the clan? How you feeling anyway, sir?"

"I'll live. I think my career as the champion miler of Partickhill may be over, though. Goldie?"

She grimaced. "Not great, sir. He's in the Western. They can save the leg, but he'll need a stick. He'll walk with a limp for the rest of his days."

"Desk job," McCormack said. "Bloody waste. Christ, Nicol. You're the last man standing. Woman."

"Rubbish, sir. You'll be up and about in no time."

"Aye, with no warrant card. I'm out the game till the inquiry happens."

"Have you seen the papers?"

"It's not always that simple, Nicol. Brass might take a different view. Stranger things have happened."

"You're a shoo-in, sir. Don't worry about it."

"How's the boy?"

"Maitland's son? He's fine. Bit dehydrated, bit shaken. Chisholm broke his nose when he snatched him; pistol-whipped him. But he's a big strong boy. He'll be right as rain, sir. Just like you."

"Well, if this bloody doctor ever does his rounds, we'll find out. Listen, thanks for stopping by, Nicol. Keep us posted, all right? Till I'm back in the saddle."

But before the doctor did his rounds, McCormack had one last visitor. Walter Maitland turned up to thank McCormack for saving his son.

"I saved you, too," McCormack told him. "Chisholm was coming for you."

Maitland crossed to the window, stood with his back to the room. "That's a nice thought. You any idea how many people want me dead, McCormack?"

"And they're all soldiers, are they? Trained killers?"

"Well his training wasn't too clever, was it? As things turned out."

"You mean because I killed him? You think I got lucky?"

Maitland turned from the window. "I'm sure you're very good at what you do, Inspector."

"Aye? Well maybe you'll find out." McCormack struggled up straighter in bed. "Maybe you'll wish I'd let Chisholm get to you after all. When you're seeing out your days in a six-by-eight cell in Peterhead."

"O.K., Inspector." Maitland nodded. "I've said what I came here to say, get well soon."

"Oh I will. But I've got something more to say to you. Chisholm might be gone, but I'm not. I'm coming after you too, Maitland. And I'm a sight more fucking dangerous than Gordon Chisholm ever was."

"Ach, you're getting all excited now, Detective. Let me call the nurse."

The door rattled shut behind him.

McCormack flopped back on the bed, hearing the knock of Maitland's heels dwindling in the distance as though the corridor was hollow.

52

It was late morning when McCormack was released. He emerged into the sunshine of Castle Street like Lazarus, leaving the cold corridors and blackened stone walls of the Infirmary behind him and heading back into the light. They'd given him crutches to support his ankle. Wary at first, he soon found that he enjoyed them. The rubberized ends bit pleasingly into the pavement and the little boost as you launched forward onto the sticks made it seem like a childhood game. He swung down Cathedral Street to the city centre, past the modernist blocks of the Strathclyde University campus. On the bridge across the railway tracks, passing the glass semicircle of Queen Street Station's gable, which peeked up over the balustrade like the top of a great glass clock, McCormack was stopped by a small man in a rumpled blue suit, who held up a blackened hand like a grimy traffic policeman and tilted forward from his ankles as though he was faring into a stiff wind.

"I'm an alcoholic, son. Have ye the price o' a half?"

McCormack smiled. He had braced his arms on his crutches, ready for some baroque, extravagant narrative that would lead him through various scrapes and adventures to land at last on the punchline request for a fifty-pence piece. Impressed by the small man's directness, and feeling that he had materialized like some storybook troll, collecting the toll for the bridge back to wellness, McCormack balanced one of his crutches against the balustrade, pulled his wad from his trouser pocket and peeled off a crisp green note.

The small man took the pound note from McCormack, held it above his head in two hands like the world's smallest football scarf, kissed it, tucked it into his breast pocket, clasped McCormack's hands in both of his, called for God to bless him, and strode off in the direction of the nearest pub— Sammy Dow's on Dundas Street, most probably.

At Buchanan Street, McCormack took the subway to Partick. He bought an armful of papers at a newsagent on Dumbarton Road and struggled up the hill to his flat.

Over a cup of tea and a smoke, with his leg propped on a kitchen chair, he caught up with the news. Nicol was right; the press was purring. *Hillside of Death. Hero Cop Shoots Bomber. Crack Marksman McCormack Dispatches Rogue Soldier.* Fiona Morrison in the *Record* was calling him "Strathclyde's top detective". He knew that the Force's official statement would have strictly maintained his anonymity, pending the inquiry into the shooting, so someone had obviously leaked his name. Not that it mattered. If the inquiry hadn't already been a formality, it surely was now.

The telephone rang. It was one of the DIs from Temple, passing on his good wishes. The phone rang every few minutes with colleagues congratulating him. Nothing like a fatal shooting to make a man popular. Haddow, it was true, hadn't been among the callers, but you couldn't expect miracles. The phone rang again and McCormack reached for it, thinking maybe this would be Haddow. Maybe miracles did happen.

It was Nicol. "There's someone who wants to see you," she said. "Get something off his chest."

"About what? I'm suspended, Nicol. I can't be taking statements."

"I know. But he's heard of you from Maitland's crew. It's you he wants to talk to."

McCormack glanced at the mantelpiece clock. "When?"

"He said he'd meet you in Kelvingrove Museum at two."

At five to two, McCormack got out of a taxi at the west end of Argyle Street and hobbled up the steps to the great red sandstone building. Pushing on the brass rail of the revolving door he had the sense of passing into another world: the museum hush, the chill of the marble tiles, the woody municipal smell.

He found Christopher Kidd on the first floor, standing in front of the Dalí. As McCormack approached down the long narrow balcony the painting struck him anew. The crucified Christ, waxy and yellow on a black background, viewed from above, just the top of the slumped head visible, the beautiful bow of the outstretched arms. And the cross itself, just hanging in the air, as if ready to drop like a dagger into the mundane landscape at the painting's foot, a daytime lake, two fishermen busy with their nets.

The young man turned as McCormack neared.

"Christopher?" McCormack held out his hand. "I'm Duncan McCormack."

Kidd looked at McCormack's hand, kept his own in the pockets of his army surplus jacket.

"There's no nails," he said.

"What's that?"

Kidd jerked his head at the painting. "There's no nails in his hands. What's holding him up there?"

McCormack looked. There was no crown of thorns either. "Will power?" he said. "Some people don't need much help to crucify themselves."

The light changed subtly. An attendant on his rounds had paused at the far end of the balcony. He was looking down towards them. Kidd plunged his hands ever deeper in his jacket pockets. His shoulders climbed.

"This place gives me the creeps."

"We can talk outside," McCormack said. "Take a walk in the park. Come on."

Outside, the sun beat down pleasantly on their heads. They headed past the bowling greens, towards Kelvin Way, Kidd taking it slow so that McCormack could keep up.

"I don't even know why I'm here," Kidd said. "I just came because Yvonne . . ." His sentence dwindled into nothing, as if it couldn't survive the cheerful atmosphere of the park. McCormack watched an elderly man in white slacks and a short-sleeved shirt drop into a crouch to release his bowl, then rise on his tiptoes to track its slow parabola.

"Yvonne spoke to D.C. Nicol," McCormack said. "D.C. Nicol suggested that I might be able to help. Help us get to the truth."

Kidd snorted. "A liar's gonnae help me get to the truth? That's a good one."

There was a rasp of gravel as McCormack stopped. "What makes you think I'm a liar?"

"You're a polis, aren't you?"

The question was rhetorical. Kidd stopped too when McCormack answered it.

"Not at this moment, no."

"But I thought. Yvonne said—"

"I've been suspended from duty," McCormack told him. "Pending an investigation."

Kidd smiled bleakly. His hands were still plunged in the pockets of his army surplus jacket and he spread them now, exposing the jacket's lining. "What, did you break your truncheon on somebody's skull? Push someone down a flight of stairs?"

"Something like that," McCormack said. "So long as we're telling the truth."

Kidd looked at him sidelong, as if seeing him for the first time. He nodded, and they set off again, slightly slower than before. "What happened to your leg?" Kidd asked him. "Was that to do with how you got suspended?"

McCormack shook his head. "Hiking accident. Listen, why don't you tell me what you came here to say?"

They walked on in silence. Kidd cleared his throat. "I did a favour for someone."

"This is Walter Maitland we're talking about?"

"She told you."

"D.C. Nicol told me that Maitland comes into the picture. She didn't say how."

Kidd swept a hand through his long hair, pushing it out of his eyes. "That's one way of putting it," he said. "He comes into the picture all right."

But it was a picture he didn't seem sure how to paint. There was a bench ahead of them, up the slope a little, and they climbed towards it. Kidd slipped his jacket off before he sat down. He looked out over the sunbathers, hunched forward on the bench, elbows on his knees. There was a home-made tattoo on his right wrist: FLEET in blue-green dots, unevenly spaced. His skin looked unhealthily white.

"Why don't you start from the beginning?" McCormack said.

"I wouldn't even know where that was."

"Well, you could tell me what the favour was."

Kidd ran both hands through his hair, sat up straighter on the bench.

"You got family?" he asked McCormack.

"Family? No. Not any more."

Kidd nodded. "I have a sister. *Had*. Isobel." He delivered the next words in a kind of flat monotone, like someone reciting the liturgy in church. "We lived in Maryhill. Oran Street. My old man left when I was six. Izzy was ten. My ma couldnae cope. She'd been ill. Izzy and me went into a home. We were looked-after."

It seemed an odd expression. They hadn't been looked after, not by the people whose job that was.

"You were both in Auldpark?"

"For a while, aye. But Izzy got the chance to leave. There was a couple down in Ayrshire. Near Largs, I think. They wanted to adopt her."

"But not you."

Kidd was watching a toddler stumping around on the grass, moving with that rocking, stiff-legged gait. The boy's mother followed a yard behind, arms spread to catch him if he fell. "They wanted a girl. Izzy had stayed with them before. They used to take in kids from the Home. For weekends, like. Seaside breaks. Anyway, it didn't work out."

"Why not?"

"Izzy was too much for them, I suppose." He smiled, remembering. "She could be wild. I used to think she did it to get back to the Home, like. Back to me."

"But you don't think that anymore."

The toddler came careening towards them. His momentum carried him up to the bench and Kidd put a hand out to steady him. The boy bumped to a halt against Kidd's knees and gripped Kidd's jeans. He smiled up, all eyes and shining gums.

"Oh, I'm sorry." The mum pushed her hair out of her eyes. "This one. Honest to God. He's got me run ragged."

"He's fine." Kidd dug into his pocket for a ten-pence piece. The boy closed his little fist over it.

"Oh now what do you say, Callum? Say thank you to the nice man? Say ta?"

She scooped him up and carried him back to his stroller, the boy twisting round to keep Kidd in his sights.

"When I was a wee boy," Kidd said. "Before."

There was no trailing pause after this word, and McCormack realized how cleanly Kidd's past was divided in two. "Before" was an era, a world in itself. There was the world before his father left, before his mother "couldnae cope", before he was taken into care. And there was everything after. The fallen world of now.

"On you go," McCormack said.

"We used to play in the backcourts." He looked at McCormack as if McCormack might not know what a back-court was. McCormack nodded. "The railings between the courts had been taken away. In the war, like. And some of the walls had been knocked through. It meant you could go from one end of our street to the other without leaving the back-courts. It was like a secret street."

Kidd was smiling at the memory. McCormack knew from his file that Kidd had gone into care in 1954. He couldn't have been more than six or seven when this was happening.

"I know," McCormack told him. "Neds used to use the courts as getaways. You'd be chasing some chancer down a street and he'd duck into a close. By the time you reached the backcourt he'd be gone. Along the backs and into another building before you could blink."

Kidd was grinning. "That's right. The bigger boys did that. But we just used it for fun. The bit I remember is, there were people who would ignore you if you passed them on the street, but in the backcourts? They'd say hello, maybe slip you a tanner. It got so I never wanted to go anywhere you couldn't get to by the secret street."

"It must have been hard," McCormack said.

"You mean when I left? Well that's the thing. The Home was kinda the same deal. There was the world outside and there was the world of the Home."

"The secret street."

"And I missed that. Bad as it was, I missed the Home, you know? When I left. It sounds stupid."

"Bad how?"

Kidd looked at the ground between his feet. "How do you think? The usual. But at least you were all in the same boat.

The normals hated you. You went to school in a special bus. You weren't a real person to them. You were like a Mongol or something. A tink. Worse. But inside the Home you were all the same."

"And you thought, what? That being in Maitland's crew would give you the same fuzzy feeling inside."

"Fuck you. You're in a gang, too, polis. Don't kid yourself."

"My gang doesn't go around setting buildings on fire. Burning people to death."

"Naw, you just throw them down the stairs. It's quicker. You worked in the Met, didn't you? Fascist bastards."

The suddenness of their anger surprised them both. They sat in silence for a minute. Kidd found his cigarettes, offered. They both lit up. Kidd sucked his smoke to a scorching orange, blew it out slowly. "I'm sorry. I shouldn't have said that. I killed four people. You didn't kill four people."

"Neither did you."

"Naw, it was me. I set the fire. It's my fault those people died. I'm going to hell." His smile was wolfish. "If they'll have me."

"No you're not. No you didn't."

"But that's what I'm telling you, polis." The edge was creeping back into Kidd's voice. "It was me that set the fire. I'm fucking bursting to it. I'm confessing."

McCormack shook his head. "Sorry, no."

Kidd swung round to face him. "What the fuck are you talking about?"

McCormack held out two hands, like a set of scales, balancing nothing. "There were two fires, Christopher. Two separate fires. You set the warehouse alight. And then someone else took advantage of that to start a fire in the tenement."

Kidd's right hand found his face. He dragged his fingers back and forth across his lips. His voice when it came was small and tight. "The fuck are you on about? Why would they do that?"

"Two men were seen carrying another man into the tenement on the night of the fire. We think they were disposing of a body. They wanted to make it look like an accident."

Kidd's eyes flickered as he processed this. "And the other folk in the tenement? What about them?"

"What about them? Collateral damage. Who gives a fuck about them? That's what we're dealing with, son. That's what we're up against."

"Fuck!" Kidd had his head in his hands. He stood up from the bench, walked a few yards, turned back, raised his leg and kicked the bench with the sole of his boot. "Fuck!" He turned to McCormack. His hands were on the back of his head, fingers laced, elbows high. The yellow Christ in Dalí's painting flashed into McCormack's mind. Kidd dropped his arms to his sides. "How come you're only finding out now?"

"No one thought to question it till now. It seemed obvious that the fire had spread from the warehouse. We didn't bother trying to confirm it. You don't waste time second-guessing what you already know. *Think* you know."

"Fuck. Do you know who he is?"

"The body in the tenement? Aye. We think it's Campbell Sneddon."

"From Auldpark? Wee Cammy?" The tension seemed to leave Kidd's shoulders. He frowned. "Why would they want to kill Wee Cammy?"

McCormack looked at him. Finally he said, "I think you probably know the answer to that. Better than I do. Why don't you sit down, Christopher?"

53

Kidd slumped down beside him on the bench. There were times, McCormack knew, when the best thing was to say nothing, leave the silence to be filled. There were times, too, when a nudge was needed.

"Isobel," McCormack said. "Your sister Isobel. Tell me about her, Christopher."

Kidd lifted his jacket from the seat and wrestled into it. The day was warm as ever but he wrapped the jacket tightly round him, turned up the collar, folded his arms.

"It only started when she came back," he said. "From Ayrshire, like. With her new name."

"What started?"

"When the Friends came. Some of the kids got told to come. Izzy was one of them."

Kidd was already retreating into the past, hunching into himself, staring at the ground. Even the cigarette was hidden, cupped in his hand, just a thin rim of filter visible.

"Come where, Christopher? Who were the Friends?"

Kidd looked up. "It was a charity thing. Friends of Auldpark. Businessmen. City councillors. Fancy lawyers. We didn't know who they were at the time, we just knew they were important. Big shots. They were our benefactors." He smiled. "I thought it meant maybe that they were our bosses. I didn't know what the word meant, *benefactors*."

"And what did they do?"

Kidd shrugged. "They held boxing events, you know?

Smokers. Charity dinners. Raise money for the Home. Gym equipment. Trips to the Highlands. That sort of thing. Every month or so they'd come by for a fancy dinner at Auldpark. Some of the girls got to go. Boys, too, sometimes. To say thanks." Kidd shook his head, spat on the ground. "It was like a special treat. But then, the ones who got to go, they never spoke about it afterwards. They just kept their heads down, changed the subject if you asked them about it."

"They wouldn't say what happened to them?"

"Well, we guessed. There was rumours, like. I mean, what else could it be?"

"And what about Izzy?"

"What about her? They were breaking her in. That's what they did. Get them used to it. Then they would put them to work in Glash's brothels when they left Auldpark."

"And Campbell Sneddon? He knew about all this?"

"He was the jannie. He couldnae not know. He wasnae involved, not that I ever heard. But aye, he must have known."

McCormack thought back to the Clyde Cabs canteen. Campbell Sneddon had told his colleagues that his ship was coming in. The good ship *Blackmail*. After years of silence he was threatening to tell what he'd seen at Auldpark. But who had he threatened? Not Maitland, surely. Possibly Elliot or one of the other "Friends". Politicians. Businessmen. Whoever it was, they'd contacted Maitland and Maitland had taken things in hand.

Kidd was looking out over the park but what he was seeing was the past. "I used to think we were in it together. Babes in the wood or something. But, I don't know. I think I just reminded her."

"What do you mean?"

"Of all the bad times, like. At home. At Auldpark. I was always there, watching, doing nothing."

"What could you have done?"

He tugged on his nose. "I don't know. More than I did. Something." He turned to McCormack. "I was weak, ye know? I was feart."

The Scots word took McCormack back to his childhood, when you were feart of everything. You were feart of the dark. You were feart of the old woman in Sutherland's shop. You were feart of God. You were feart of the black water that gathered in the quarry bottom. You were feart of dying in your sleep (*If I should die before I wake*). Above all, you were feart of men. Mr. Rankin's leather strap, split at the end like a snake's tongue. Your old man after his seventh drink. Father McGee in the confession box.

"You were a boy, Christopher."

Kidd shook his head and it came to McCormack that the man beside him hadn't ever been a boy, not properly. Ever since he could think, Kidd had been on his own, responsible for himself.

He was almost talking to himself now, going back over the story he'd been pondering for years.

"We sorta lost touch when Izzy left. Well. She stopped coming back, is what happened. I don't blame her."

"And when you got out—did you look for her then?"

Kidd's eyes narrowed, as if he was watching something at a great distance, as if he could see right through the crowd of people on the grassy slope to the past he shared with his dead sister.

"I knew she never really wanted to see me," he said. "So I thought, fuck you then. I'll stay away. Let you stew in it. And every month that went by I thought I was hurting her more. But the truth was, she didnae give a fuck. She couldnae care less if I left her alone. And then I was away for a while and I started thinking, maybe she's better off. Ye know? Without me. What use was I to her? What use had I ever been?"

"You were her brother, Chris. That's what use you were."

Kidd shook his head. "That's how you think, though. That's how we all thought. And that's what they counted on. With Izzy, you know? You think you're worthless, that nobody gives a fuck aboot ye. Ye're nothing. Not quoted. And that's how they get you."

"So what were you planning to do?"

Kidd's jaw muscles bulged and he shook his head tightly, eyes on the ground.

"Oh no, Chris. Have a go at Maitland? Take him out?"

Kidd rubbed his bottom lip with the ball of his thumb. "You think I couldnae do it?"

"Naw, son. It's too easy. You want a life sentence, not a death sentence. You want Maitland doing twenty up in Peterhead. A nobody. A number. A wee man in a blue suit in a room like a whitewashed shoebox."

Kidd looked at McCormack with a face as smooth and empty as a child's. "Why should he live and Isobel didn't?"

"That's not the point, son. There's people all over this city—you're one of them—who'll live with what Maitland's done for the rest of their lives. He should do the same. He should live with the consequences. Every day. Death's too easy."

Kidd spoke softly. "Not the way I've planned it, it's not."

"No, son. You want to hurt Walter Maitland? You want to get revenge for Izzy? This is how you do it. Get close to Maitland. Find out his secrets. Help us put him away."

"A *tout*?" There was a whole culture of contempt in Kidd's syllable. "Get revenge for Izzy by grassing to the polis?"

"Are ye wise, son?" His anger took McCormack by surprise, compressed his voice to a whispered hiss. "Grassing who? This is the cunt that killed your sister. Yvonne told you what she heard, right? Walter Maitland killed your sister. You get the goods on him, that's not grassing. That's standing up. Maybe it's about time you tried it."

He wondered for a second if he'd gone too far, if Kidd would tell him to get to fuck, stump off down the slope through the knots of sunbathers, amid the tinny din of transistors. But something else happened. Kidd slumped. All the fight went out of him. His hands hung loose between his knees and his head drooped onto his chest.

His voice sounded hollow when he spoke. "So how do we do this? Tell me what I need to do."

54

They decided to build on what Kidd had already done. He'd already told McPhail that he wanted more work, that he wanted to meet with Maitland, become a proper member of the crew. They agreed that Kidd should drop by the Duke again, hang with the top boys at the corner spot, catch McPhail alone and tell him he had information for Walter.

Meantime, McCormack had the small matter of a career that needed saving. At three o'clock that afternoon he found himself in an interview room at Central. Detective Superintendent Bob Skelton of C Div sat across the table, his notebook open.

"You want something before we start, Detective? Cup of tea? Water?"

"I'm fine, sir."

"And you're O.K. to do this now? We can give you more time, that's not a problem."

"I'm fine."

Skelton nodded. He looked at the clock on the wall, jotted something in his book.

"And you don't need a rep?"

"Well, you tell me, sir. I wouldn't have thought so."

"O.K. Good. Let's get started. You know why we're here, D.I. McCormack. It's to discuss the fatal shooting of Gordon Chisholm on Saturday, 12 July 1975 at Howcraig Cottage outside Largs, Ayrshire. Why don't you walk me through what happened, Detective."

McCormack shuffled back in his plastic bucket seat and

told the story, from their arrival at Howcraig Cottage to the shooting of Gordon Chisholm. Skelton stayed silent throughout, nodding occasionally, writing in his notebook.

"Thank you, Detective. Now, when Gordon Chisholm arrived at Howcraig Cottage, he entered the living room. Is that correct?"

"Not exactly. He poked his head in the door, basically. He registered the presence of myself and D.C. Nicol. Then he ran."

"But you ascertained that he was armed?"

"No. I did not."

"And yet you drew your weapon as you gave chase, before you determined that Chisholm was armed?"

"No. I heard a shot as I ran down the hallway. I drew my weapon then."

"I see. And then you gave chase to Mr. Chisholm as he fled up the hillside and confronted him outside what you describe as a low cave."

"That's right."

Skelton nodded. "Did you shout 'Armed Police' when you confronted Mr. Chisholm?"

"I don't remember. I was pointing a gun at his head. He knew who I was. I'm guessing he could put two and two together."

"Don't be smart, Detective. Did you advise him to drop his weapon, put his hands in the air?"

"I told him to release the boy."

"And his response?"

"He declined my invitation. He was getting agitated. He was gripping the boy's neck tighter. It was my judgement that he was about to shoot the boy."

"So you killed him?"

"The chopper appeared and I took my chance."

Skelton bent his head to his notebook and wrote for a minute. When he looked up he said, "Your DCI, Alan

Haddow. He tells me that you've been spending a lot of time building a case against Walter Maitland."

"Maitland's a major criminal. I'm a detective in the Serious Crime Squad."

"No doubt. Is it possible, though, that you might have been more inclined to shoot Gordon Chisholm because of this connection?"

"I don't follow."

"I mean, you kill the man who's holding Maitland's son. Gives you some kind of leverage over Maitland, doesn't it?"

"He was holding a gun to the boy's head. My concern was for the boy's safety. Not who his father was."

"O.K." Skelton pointed the blunt end of the pen at McCormack. "Back to DCI Haddow. How would you describe your relationship with your commanding officer?"

McCormack shifted in his seat. "I don't see the relevance of the question."

"Well. DCI Haddow seems to think that you don't see the relevance of him, to be blunt."

"I think that feeling's probably mutual."

"You're saying that your station commander doesn't support you in your police work?"

"I'm saying he hates my fucking guts."

"Because . . . ?"

"Because of what happened with Peter Levein. He thinks I ratted out a fellow polis."

"And what do you think?"

"I think I put a bad guy in jail. That's the job, last time I looked."

"And how do you know, though? That DCI Haddow thinks you're a rat?"

"It was when he used the word 'rat'. That was the giveaway."

"O.K., Detective." Skelton pulled a handkerchief from his

pocket. He took his glasses off and started cleaning them. "Your preoccupation with Walter Maitland. Would obsession be too strong a word?"

"I'm focused on putting him away. That's what I plan to do. In spite of DCI Haddow. In spite of you, if need be."

Skelton put his glasses back on. "You're not putting anyone away, Detective—you're not doing anything at all, until I say so. Are we clear?"

"You're the man on the right side of the desk."

"And expressing defiance and disrespect towards your unit commander is not the best way to demonstrate your fitness to return to active duty."

McCormack's ankle was throbbing. He could sense the thickened tissue under the tight strapping. If you flexed the joint a little the pain seemed to inflate the ligament, squeezing out all thoughts of the smart remarks you might otherwise be disposed to make.

Skelton had finished writing. He closed his notebook and laid his pen down on top of it.

"Is there anything else you'd like to say, D.I. McCormack? In mitigation?"

McCormack shook his head. "Well there you go. I don't think what I did needs mitigating. I shot a man who had a gun to the head of a twelve-year-old boy. A man who tortured and killed an elderly man, murdered six in a bomb attack, including one of my colleagues. I'm proud of what I did. I'd do it again. I'd do it right now."

"O.K., Detective. Thanks for your cooperation. I think I have everything I need. I'll make my recommendation in writing to the CC. You should hear before long."

He half-rose out of his seat to shake McCormack's hand.

McCormack hobbled out onto Turnbull Street in the afternoon sun. He replayed the interview, thought of all the things he could have said. He should have agreed with Skelton, showed himself properly penitent, made the right noises. And then what? Have the joy of reporting to Haddow again. Fuck it. The Empire Bar was round the corner. He would have a quick pint and give Nicol a call.

55

It was a clipping from the *Tribune*'s "City News" page dated 8 September 1967: "Church Rises from the Ashes". The report told how the Alexander Peden Memorial Church in Saracen Street, Possilpark, which burned down two years ago in an accidental fire, had reopened in newly built premises on the same site. A local businessman and parishioner had fronted the money for the building.

The picture showed a smiling minister in black gown and white Geneva bands flanked by dark-suited elders. Alex Kerr was among them, but what caught Nicol's eye was the church itself. A plain brick preaching-box with a pitched roof and portico'd porch.

It was the church she'd visited last week for Iain Shand's funeral.

Back at Temple she was at her desk when McCormack called.

"Ah, Jesus, Nicol. Kerr was an elder in Iain Shand's church? That's the connection?" She could hear the groan in McCormack's voice.

"I know, sir. How did we miss it?"

"All right. Don't fret about that. It's what you do now that counts. What are your thoughts?"

"Bring him in?"

"Aye. But not just him. Lift all four of them. Kerr, Fleeting, Hunter, McPhail. Same time, different nicks."

Nicol saw the logic. Keep them apart, leave no scope for the coordination of stories. "How do I play it then, sir?"

"With Kerr? Play it how you want, Nicol. This is your gig now. Trust your judgement."

"Maybe confront him with the gun? If he was willing to talk to Shand, maybe he'll talk to me."

"Right. Give him a reason to talk. It's worth a shot, Nicol. Keep us posted."

They lifted all four of Maitland's lieutenants that evening. The others were taken to different nicks: Stewart Street, Central, the old Marine in Partick. Kerr was brought to Temple.

"I know you." Kerr leaned forward as Nicol entered the interview room. He kicked the chair out at Nicol's side of the table, an act—she supposed—of courtesy. "You were at Iain's funeral."

"I was." Nicol sat down and looked at Kerr and immediately looked away. She had only seen photos of Kerr but she could tell at a glance the great change that had come over him. His cheeks had sunk. The bridge of his nose glistened white through the skin. The hair had thinned almost to nothing on the angry pink of his scalp. It was as if the skull was asserting itself, pushing through ahead of time.

"It's all right," he told her. "I've got a mirror. I know what I look like."

She looked up and smiled, her lips pressed tight. She didn't know what to say. She set her notebook on the table, pen beside it. Already the interview was slipping from her grasp, losing the shape she'd envisaged.

"Cancer," Kerr said decisively, as if in answer to a question Nicol had posed. "The lung. They opened me up six weeks ago to take half of the lung but the cancer had spread. They took the whole thing."

He spoke with a queer detachment, as if discussing the ailments of a third party.

"I'm sorry to hear that," Nicol said. And then almost apologetically, as if she knew that the moment for introductions had passed but she wanted to make hers anyway. "I'm Detective Constable Nicol."

"Are you a Roman?" Kerr asked her.

"I'm sorry, what?"

His face was a ruin—seamed and abraded and raw—but the eyes were still young. Pale, fierce, acetylene blue, they held Nicol in their beams. "A Roman Catholic." He pronounced the words with fastidious distaste.

She looked at him. "I'm Church of Scotland. What does it matter?"

"I always wondered," he said. "Whether it made it easier or not. I'm talking about confession, D.C. Nicol. You spend your life confessing to a priest. Does that mean you can't help confessing when you're sat across a desk from a polis? Or maybe it means you know all the tricks, the ways to keep things hidden?"

"You're saying you've got something you want to confess?"

Kerr pursed his lips. "Let's call it a trial run."

"Oh no." Nicol tugged on her lapels to settle her jacket, shot the cuffs of her blouse. She was conscious of her health, her youth, her beauty as a kind of affront to the man before her. "We don't play games here, Mr. Kerr. You've got something you want to get off your chest, let's hear it. Otherwise I've got some questions for you and you can sit there till you answer them."

Kerr's laugh was a wheeze from a broken bellows, a gust of dead air. "You cannae threaten me. Wee lassie, I'll be deid in a fortnight. Month at the outside. Play games? You've no fuckin idea."

Nicol watched him with the cold fascination of the well for the sick.

Kerr licked his cracked lips. "What I'm saying is, I'm gonnae have to account for myself at a higher bar than this. Before too long."

Nicol understood, a hardness came into her eyes and she

suppressed a smile. "And you think a confession here's going to help you there?"

Kerr's hands were resting on the table. Nicol noticed the wedding band loose on his finger, girdling the gnarled planet of his knuckle. He spread his hands. "Oh, I'm going to hell, Detective. If there's any justice. Nothing surer. Only, that's not how it works. We're not saved by our earthly deeds. It's the grace of our Lord Jesus Christ, freely given, with no regard for merit, that brings salvation."

"Well that's convenient. But what I don't get is, if you think you're already saved, why are you confessing?

"You never hear of hedging your bets?" The lips drew back over yellow tombstone teeth in what might have been a grin. "But listen. You said you had questions."

Nicol paused. She knew the art of interrogating a suspect. Get them to tell their version of events. Get them to keep telling it. Pick it apart, probe it, take the events out of sequence. Find an inconsistency and crowbar it open, question by question, till you get to the truth.

None of that applied to Kerr. He wasn't here to answer for a particular crime. Nicol's only objective was to find out whether Kerr was Iain Shand's tout. She had one card to play, one way to play it.

The gun was in a holdall at her feet. She drew it out in its plastic evidence bag and clapped it down on the table.

"Do you know what that is?" she asked Kerr.

"Do you?"

"It's the gun that killed a drug dealer called Kenny Hinshelwood two years back. It was passed to D.C. Shand by someone close to Walter Maitland. I think that someone was you. You knew Iain Shand through church. You knew you could trust him."

Kerr didn't even glance at the gun. "He told you that? Iain? He told you that was the piece that offed Hinshelwood?"

"You're saying it's not?"

Kerr spoke softly, as if explaining something to a child. "That's the gun that killed John McGlashan."

Nicol felt a ringing in her ears. The room seemed to shrink around them, contracting to the two chairs, the table, the black object on the table, the light pooling and sliding along the contours of the plastic bag.

The next question didn't need to be spoken. Nicol just looked at Kerr, raised her eyebrows slightly.

Kerr raised his chin, squared his shoulders. He'd been a handsome man, Nicol realized—strong jaw, good bones— before cancer ruined him. She felt his fierce blue eyes. He blinked slowly.

"Walter Maitland," he said. "Walter Maitland pulled the trigger."

Nicol kept her tone flat and neutral. "And how do you know that?"

"I was the driver," Kerr said. "I was parked across the street when he did it. He gave me the gun. That was always my job. Get rid of the piece."

"Except you didn't this time."

"I thought I might need some insurance," he said.

Nicol wanted to rush from the room, get McCormack on the phone. *We've done it, sir. We've nailed Maitland.*

Except they hadn't. Not yet.

Nicol spoke softly, her words edging out towards Kerr like someone on the verge of a frozen lake, venturing onto the ice.

"And you'll testify? You'll say all this in court?"

"Testify? I'll be dead, Detective. I'll be six feet under before this gets near a court. Anyway, you've got the gun, haven't you? Maitland's dabs all over it."

"But you'll sign a statement at least? You'll do that?"

Kerr looked at the floor between his knees. Then he looked up, avoided Nicol's gaze.

"You want something," Nicol stated. "What is it you want?"

"I had an understanding," Kerr said. "With young Iain. At least, it was a proposal. He was planning to take it to the higher-ups, see what they made of it."

"I can do that." Nicol was nodding smartly. "That's no problem. Tell me what you told Shand."

All the time, she was thinking, What can we give him? He'll be dead within the month. What can he possibly want?

"It's my boy," Kerr said. "Young Alex."

"He's in trouble?"

"Drugs. Dealing. He's looking at four years, the lawyer says. With me gone, well, it'll kill the missus to see the wee man inside."

"And you'll sign the statement if we get the charges dropped?"

"That was the deal."

"O.K. I mean, I'll need to clear it with my boss but, yeah, I can't see a problem."

"Good." Kerr tightened the knot of his tie. "That's fine, then. I'll give you Maitland."

"Can I ask, though." Nicol had the pen in her fingers and she wagged it at Kerr. "Was this an ongoing arrangement with D.C. Shand? You were planning to tout for him?"

Kerr smiled down at the table, shaking his head. "Ongoing? *I'm* not ongoing, for fuck's sake. Let me explain something to you, D.C. Nicol. When I passed that gun to Iain Shand, I did it on a patch of waste ground at Possilpark. But I've got a mate, see. He's in the camera club. He's very keen. He's got one of them big telephoto lenses."

"You were planning to blackmail D.C. Shand?"

"I know how it works, Detective. You bring in anything— drugs, cash, ammo—from a source, it needs to be recorded. Iain wasnae declaring that gun. I knew that. Plus, those photos? They don't look good. Not for someone like Iain."

"I knew it." Nicol tapped the pen on the table. "He wasn't running you. You were running him."

"To be fair, it would've worked both ways. We'd have helped him out, he'd have looked out for us. He was going far, was Iain. Could've worked out well."

"Us?"

"Well I wasnae gonnae be around, was I? I thought my boy could use him. Alex and he could work together when I'm gone. But then, you cannae legislate for bombs, can you?"

Something struck Nicol. "And had he started already? Iain, I mean. Was he helping you already?"

They had all noticed it. For months. How Maitland's crew seemed to know in advance when a raid was in the offing.

"Let's say Iain had established his bona fides," Kerr said. "Let's put it like that."

It came back to her, then, how Shand had egged McCormack on, urged him to keep after Maitland, even when Haddow had told them to stop. Shand needed McCormack on Maitland's case because he needed information to feed to Kerr.

Nicol knew she should leave it there, shake on this deal before Kerr changed his mind, but she heard herself saying, "And Auldpark? We need to know about Auldpark, too."

Kerr leaned back in his seat. He drew his hand across his scalp as if the hair was still there.

"You know what I do, Detective?"

"What you do?"

"My *job*, missy."

"You're a debt collector."

"That's right. Someone takes out a loan," Kerr said. "Or they run up a tab at the bookies. They've got to pay it back. Otherwise everything's out of whack. It's simple, really. Credit and debit, profit and loss. You're moving things from one column to the other."

"Restoring the balance," Nicol said.

"That's it. And sometimes you get a person who, well, they get in too deep. They make themselves a problem. And sometimes they have to go. And that's O.K. That's a debt, too. They're paying what's owed. Just not in money. But that's O.K. They knew what they were putting up. It's just business. Campbell Sneddon knew what he was getting into. But the others? The wee lassie and her mammy? The old boy on the floor below?" Kerr shook his head. "They were civilians. That weren't part of it at all."

"You're talking about the Tradeston fire?"

"They weren't involved. They shouldn't have been bothered."

"But Walter Maitland didn't see it like that."

"Walter didn't give a fuck. He just took it on himself. Who got to live. Who would die."

She saw now what troubled Kerr. The rackets and the hoors and the drugs and the murders. That was business. But the torching of the tenement and the deaths of the mother and child and the harmless old man? That was Walter Maitland playing God. That was heresy. That was blasphemy.

"So what about Auldpark?"

"Now understand," Kerr said. "There were sides to Walter's business that I had nothing to do with. Nothing at all." He looked steadily at Nicol, as if practising for that sterner test that would face him before long. "Though I maybe know others who did."

MONDAY, 14 JULY 1975

56

C hristopher Kidd put the used towel in the basket. He blessed himself as he put on his clothes, spoke to Isobel in his head. *Not long now.* He had shaved with special care as if this was a wedding he was going to. A first communion.

You'll enjoy it, he told her. *No kiddin. Watch for his face when he knows it gonnae happen.*

He pulled the tight T-shirt over his skinny ribs. His jeans were flared at the cuff, enough to nearly cover his Cuban-heeled boots. He lifted the army surplus jacket from its hook.

Coming down the tenement stairs he let his legs go loose, as always, dancing down to each landing like a slumping puppet, as though it was the stairs rapping against his feet and not the other way round. On the ground floor he passed through the cool gloom of the close towards the oblong of yellow sunlight.

He felt oddly normal, except his ears had that underwater muffle as though they needed to pop. He worked his jaw a couple of times but nothing happened and the sounds of the street—the gulls squabbling over a discarded sausage roll, two boys whooping past, the pneumatic hiss of the Number 12's brakes—all reached him as if from a distance.

On the bus he climbed to the top deck and sat at the front, placing his jacket on the seat beside him.

Here we go, Izzy. No stopping us now.

The cops had nearly managed to stop him. Once he'd set up the meet with Maitland, he was supposed to call the CID man,

McCormack. He didn't bother, but the woman polis, Nicol, had phoned Yvonne. Where's the meet? she was asking. Has he set up the meet yet? Yvonne saw her chance to pull a fast one. Aye, she told them. He's set it up. She gave them the proper time but she said the meeting was at Maitland's place in Bearsden. By the time the polis realized they'd been diddled, it would be too late.

The streets spooled past. He jumped down from the bus on Maryhill Road and pushed through the doors of the Duke.

He seemed to absorb it at once, the whole tableau, the barman raising his head from the sports page, sunlight from the half-frosted glass passing in shafts through the twisting smoke, the old man and woman dressed in overcoats despite the heat, lifting their drinks in unison from the round wooden table, the top boys hogging their corner spot, McPhail's arm raised in greeting.

Apart from Maitland's boys in their corner, the pub was quiet.

"He's in the back," McPhail said as Kidd approached the corner. "You'll have a drink."

"Pint of heavy," Kidd said, and McPhail turned to signal the barman.

It was real, now. It was happening, but Kidd couldn't shake his curious underwater feeling. The air was too viscous. His hearing was dulled. Even his eyesight seemed fogged.

"They lifted us yesterday. Did you hear?"

"What?"

"The polis." McPhail told it off on a thumb and three fingers: "Me. Alex Kerr. Bud Hunter. Fleeting. Held us overnight, the bastards. They're fucking planning something, Walter reckons. Think they can take us down. Let those bastard Quinns horn in."

The pint was brimming. Kidd took a gulp. "The Quinns?"

"Let them come ahead, though, eh?" McPhail leaned in

towards Kidd and held his jacket open. "Here's ma wee welcoming committee."

Kidd looked down. The lining of McPhail's jacket had been adapted. On both sides, long narrow poacher's pockets, taped handles protruding from each.

"Speaking of which." McPhail let his jacket fall shut and reached out to pat Kidd down. He patted Kidd's shoulders, frisked his underarms, ran his thumbs right around Kidd's belt, mashed the pockets of his army jacket.

"All right, mate. On ye go." McPhail was holding the door open with his outstretched arm. Kidd ducked under it.

Walter Maitland sat at a table in a white open-necked shirt with the cuffs turned up to the elbow. There were papers scattered at the table, a bundle of banknotes, an open ledger. A cigar burning in a smoked glass ashtray. A big brown bottle of Bass stood at Maitland's elbow, a glass tumbler next to it.

He didn't stand or offer his hand but he looked at Kidd over his reading glasses and waved him to a chair.

He took the reading glasses off and tossed them on the table.

"You know Bud," he said.

Kidd looked across the room as he eased himself into the chair and nodded at the man in the blue suit. The man who had paid him a visit in Largs.

Bud Hunter nodded back, sitting side-on to a table on which a tall glass of something fizzy stood untouched. It looked like soda water and lime.

Maitland leaned forward. "Christopher, is it?"

Kidd nodded. "That's right, Mr. Maitland. Christopher Kidd."

"Mr. Hunter tells me you did well. That thing down the coast. The thing across the river, too."

Kidd shifted in his seat. He had no experience of dealing with compliments.

"And now I hear you've got some news for us. Real stop-press stuff."

"Right." Kidd took a gulp of heavy. "Right. It's the Quinns."

"The Quinns? You're a proper fucking authority on the Quinns, aren't you? Someone might think you had an inside line on the Quinns. What's the Quinns, Christopher?"

"They're preparing a move. Not here. At your house. They've got someone over from Ireland. Put a bomb under your car. Mercury tilt. Sometime this week, probably."

Maitland and Hunter exchanged a look and Kidd saw, too late, what was wrong. It was too good. It was too specific. If it didn't come from the Quinns themselves, it could only have come from the cops.

Maitland tipped some beer into his tumbler, swirled the brown liquid, "Well, now. They told us you were the boy for the inside scoops. They weren't wrong."

Kidd tried to smile, glancing desperately from Maitland to Hunter. The dead eyes. Stony faces.

"But there's the thing." Maitland drained the inch of beer, tipped another two inches into the tumbler. "I knew a lassie once. Not *knew* knew. To work with, like. Isobel Wylie was her name."

He caught Kidd's gaze and held it. Kidd said nothing.

"And it turns out . . ." Maitland screwed his eyes shut and shook his head, a hand held up as if he was in pain and was waiting till the spasm passed. "It turns out this lassie's your sister."

Kidd deadpanned it, stared glassily back at Maitland. *He's got no idea, Izzy: He doesn't have a fucking clue.*

"She's your fucking *sister*?"

Still nothing from Kidd.

"You think you're the only one with intel, son? What, did you just forget to tell us?"

Kidd cleared his throat. "I was waiting."

"For what?"

"I don't know. The right time. I thought you might know what happened. To Izzy, I mean. I thought you could maybe tell me."

"You don't know what happened to your sister?"

"I lost touch with her. The last I knew she was working in a—she was working in Dennistoun. For John McGlashan. I figured . . ." he raised a hand helplessly.

"You figured what, son?"

"I figured maybe if something had happened to her. If she'd gone away, maybe. You would know about it."

Maitland lifted his cigar from the ashtray. He tapped it so that an inch of ash, a perfect grey-white cylinder, dropped noiselessly off. He pointed the glowing tip at Kidd.

"Your sister was a hoor, son. A tuppeny-hapenny hoor. Why exactly would I be keeping track of her?"

Kidd felt his scalp tighten. He reached into the pocket of his army surplus jacket and Bud Hunter was suddenly springing from his chair.

"It's my smokes!" Kidd held it aloft, the black packet of John Player Special, a box of Swan Vesta clamped by his thumb.

Hunter subsided.

"You shouldn't call her that." Kidd tugged on the leg of his jeans, the left one, bringing the hem up an inch or two. He pulled a cigarette from the packet, fumbled it into his mouth.

"Did I hurt your feelings?" Maitland said. "That's too bad. I must work on the old bedside manner."

Kidd tugged his jeans again, exposing the top of his left boot, which gaped a little. Something black and shiny winked up from the aperture. He took out a match. His hands were shaking and the match snapped. He fumbled for another and the box spilled from his grasp, dropped to the floor, matches scattering.

"Shit."

Kidd bent down and came up straight away with a Glock pistol in his hand.

There was no tremor now; his hand was cold and hard as the gun.

He stood up, the chair overturning behind him, and swung his arm to cover Hunter.

"You move an eyebrow and I'll fucking plug you."

Hunter raised his hands, a bulge in his jaw, a sullen burn in his eyes, and Kidd shot him in the chest, shot him again, Hunter's head snapping back like whiplash before he fell to the side, his skull cracking onto the table, his drink spilling.

And now the sound came rushing back to Kidd, as though his ears had finally popped. He could hear the thin hiss of Hunter's drink pattering onto the lino as Maitland struggled upright in his seat, his mouth yawing open like his jaw had come unhinged. Maitland's hands were held high, just as Hunter's had been, and he seemed to realize this connection and dropped them to the table, palms upward in a show of supplication.

"Christopher. Chris. Now, listen—"

There were noises from the outer bar and Kidd covered the door with the Glock, but the door stayed shut. Kidd could picture the top boys stiffening at the sound of gunfire, clutching fistfuls of each other's collars, all spooked-horse eyes and flared nostrils, turning in horror to the inner room. But no one was volunteering to get their head blown off by poking it round the door. Not yet anyway.

Kidd stood over Maitland. He had pictured this moment so often that it felt like déjà vu. The man sat at the table with his papers in front of him, his torso thick with middle age, his eyes red and pouchy. There was grey among the black of his slicked-back hair, twin furrows on his nose from where his glasses had rested. There was nothing that needed saying. Maitland knew who he was, why he was here. When Kidd spoke, it wasn't to the man in front of him.

"Here it comes, Izzy."

He watched the hope leave Maitland's eyes, the shoulders droop, a general subsidence enter the frame. The pupils narrowed in impotent defiance and the top lip twitched.

Kidd squeezed his finger. The bullet smashed through Maitland's teeth, cut the tongue, pulped the gullet. Blood was flooding from the ruined mouth as Maitland pitched forward onto the table.

Kidd felt oddly calm. Maitland's quiff had flopped, exposing a bald spot, a glistening disc of skin. The man was dead but Kidd aimed the gun once more and a light mist sprayed his cheeks like a cool smirr of rain.

He was swamped with tiredness, then, and almost sat down but he smacked the heel of his hand against his forehead and slammed out of the room. The rest happened in slow motion. It must have taken a second or two but to Kidd it seemed like he had all the time in the world. Moving into the bar he was conscious of a kind of silvery flash in his peripheral vision and he turned to see McPhail leaping forward with his arms aloft and twin machetes, his mouth a roaring hole. Kidd leaned back calmly. The first bullet, in the centre of McPhail's chest, didn't stop his momentum but the headshot dropped him. The rest of the top boys quailed back in their corner and Kidd turned and stumped off down the pub. As he passed the barman he threw out his hand, aiming without looking, and saw from the tail of his eye the man's arms jerking up. The old couple in their overcoats never stirred. They might have been set in concrete.

Outside on Maryhill Road he stopped to tuck the pistol into his waistband. He gulped down a lungful of air. The breeze seemed to revive him. He felt as if he could run through walls, jump over buildings, but when a parked car across the street flashed its lights he waited for a break in the traffic and jogged across the road.

In the passenger seat he plucked the handkerchief from the woman's hand, pulled down the visor with its little oblong mirror and wiped the spray of blood from his face. He craned round to smile at the wee boy strapped into the back seat beside a bulky suitcase.

Yvonne Gray glanced in the rearview, indicated conscientiously, and pulled out smartly into the lunchtime traffic.

57

When McCormack and Nicol turned onto Maryhill Road the circus had already started. An ambulance, double-parked in front of the Duke, a uniform directing traffic round it. Squad cars up on the pavement, the gawping knot of onlookers.

A uniform hoisted the red-and-white tape and they ducked under, McCormack favouring his good leg, and showed their warrant cards.

McCormack scanned the pub. The waxy wallpaper, nicotine yellow; the dark panelling. There were two empty wine glasses on a table to his left, three abandoned pints on the bar. A man in a white shirt and a grubby grey waistcoat was sitting at a table with his head in his hands. Barman, thought McCormack. The only man who couldn't leave his post.

The uniform standing by the inner door held it open as they approached. McCormack could see the Kleig lights' glare, the snapper stepping backwards into view, his elbow cocked above his head as he angled for the shot.

It looked like the aftermath of an epic debauch; two men slumped forward on their tables. Except for the smear of red and grey on the flocked wallpaper behind Walter Maitland, the blood puddling in Bud Hunter's lap.

A CID man stood in the centre of the room, hands on hips. He pursed his lips as he caught sight of McCormack and Nicol.

"D.I. McCormack." McCormack jerked his head towards Nicol. "D.C. Nicol. Serious Crime Squad."

"Anderson. F Div. What's your interest?"

"We know who did this."

Anderson mugged astonishment. "Really? Wow. I can see why you guys made the grade. High fucking flyers. You'll be telling me it was the Quinns next."

"It wasn't the Quinns."

"Naw. It was probably a bad pint. Two bad pints."

"The killer's name is Christopher Kidd. Double D. He was on the fringes of Maitland's crew. A regular in here. But, hey. You've got it covered. You're hunky fucking dory. We'll leave you to it."

Outside, McCormack paused on the pavement to light a cigarette. Kidd would be on the road by now, heading for the border if he'd any sense. *O young Lochinvar is come out of the west, / Through all the wide Border his steed was the best.* The lines from another poem came into McCormack's head, something they'd studied in Oban High:

And they are gone: aye, ages long ago
These lovers fled away into the storm.

A storm was coming. A storm was coming for Christopher Kidd. That was certain. Maitland's men would chase him down. Him and Yvonne Gray. Except, would they? Who was left? Maitland was dead—both Maitlands. McPhail and Hunter, too. Kerr was wracked with cancer. Fleeting was a lightweight. The hangers-on would scatter. Maitland's grubby little empire was finished.

"She must have known," Nicol was saying. "Yvonne. When she sent us to the house. She must have known that the meeting was here."

"Of course she did." McCormack dropped his smoke in the gutter as they crossed Maryhill Road. "She'd have been waiting on him here. Bloody getaway driver. Bonnie and Clyde."

"You think?"

"Ah, fuck it. Good luck to them."

McCormack climbed into the passenger seat. Nicol clicked her seat belt and tapped her hands on the wheel.

"Back to the ranch, sir?"

McCormack tapped the dashboard. "Actually, I think we've got one further errand to run, Detective, do we not?"

"You mean we notify Maitland's boy? The estranged wife?"

"Not at all. F Div will sort that out. The charming Detective Anderson."

"What, then?"

McCormack smiled.

It was the girl who answered the door—the teenager both had mistaken for Eileen Elliot's daughter. She led them through to a sunroom at the back of the house where Elliot sat in a wicker armchair, a book in her lap.

"You!" Her book closed with a smart clap. "What's the matter with you people? Haven't you caused enough pain?"

McCormack sat unbidden on a rattan sofa. Nicol followed suit. McCormack leaned forward, resting his arms on his knees. "I could ask you the same question, Miss Elliot."

The girl still hovered in the doorway.

"Tea, Sarah," Eileen said testily. Even during moments of trial the little rituals of hospitality had to be observed.

With the girl gone, Eileen Elliot stared at her visitors with naked contempt. She wore a denim shirt dress, cinched at the waist with a broad leather belt. Her hair was tied back in a garish headscarf. There was a scent in the room that McCormack couldn't place. Something bitter, sharp.

"Something that's troubled me," McCormack said. "Your father. When I told you about his injuries you seemed almost relieved. I couldn't understand it. Now I know why. You thought I'd found out. You thought I was there to tell you about Auldpark. About his 'charitable' work."

Eileen Elliot set the book down on a glass-topped table beside her chair and folded her hands in her lap. She looked at McCormack expectantly and said nothing.

"The thing I don't understand," McCormack said, "is why did you protect him?"

"Why wouldn't I?" Her nostrils flared. "I'm his daughter."

"Wasn't that his job, though? To protect you?"

Eileen Elliot laughed. "You didn't know my father, Inspector, did you?"

"Not in life, no."

"He was a child. That's what he was. If he saw something he wanted, he grabbed it. If he couldn't have what he wanted, he broke things. He needed protecting."

"By 'things' you mean 'people'? Young girls?"

Eileen Elliot's chin tilted belligerently. "My father laboured night and day for those girls. The charity work he did. You've no idea. And break them? Those girls were broken before they set foot in Auldpark. That's why they were there. My father helped them."

"*Helped* them?" McCormack's hands flew up. "Raped them? Fucked them? Passed them round his rich friends?"

"These weren't girl guides, Inspector. They came from broken homes. Their mothers were alcoholics. My father was being realistic. Setting them up for a life outside the Home."

"As *prostitutes*? Can you hear yourself?"

"This way they'd be productive members of society. Providing a service. Getting paid for it. What's wrong with that? It's how the world works."

McCormack closed his eyes. He was beyond anger. What could lead a person—a woman—to think that putting young girls through this was an act of charity?

Nicol spoke up. "But the girls were abused. They were interfered with. Wee lassies of nine and ten."

"They were getting attention."

"Attention!" Now he was angry, almost choking on the words. "The hell does that mean?"

The girl was back. She set the tray down and left. As the girl passed her chair, Eileen Elliot reached out almost absently and stroked her arm. She lifted the bone china teapot and swirled it. "I'll be mother, shall I?" She tipped tea into all three cups, added milk to her own from a little jug. "You've never suffered neglect," she said, looking down at the hand stirring the teaspoon. "Either of you. That's very evident." She looked up brightly. "I have."

"What are you talking about?"

"The literature is very clear on this, Inspector. A child will take negative attention—even to the extent of what an outsider might think of as abuse—in preference to neglect. It's neglect that the child cannot bear."

The child she was talking about was herself. But what right did she have to make this choice for the girls at Auldpark?

Beside him, Nicol cleared her throat. Her words came out crisply, icily. "And Isobel Wylie? Couldn't you have neglected her?"

Eileen Elliot's teaspoon clinked on her cup. "Isobel . . . I'm sorry, who? I don't know who you mean."

The eyes, below the scarlet flash of the headscarf, disagreed. The eyes knew exactly who Isobel Wylie was.

"Isobel Wylie. Isobel Kidd, as was. Before her adoption. Wee blonde girl. You don't remember? She was a special project of yours, you might say."

Eileen Elliot buried her nose in her teacup. She held the teacup in both hands.

"What about Bob Wylie? Remember him? He remembers you. I went to see him the other day. Down in Fairlie. The red house on the beach."

Eileen Elliot set the teacup down slowly. She sat with her hands in her lap, head bent.

McCormack spoke softly. "Was it your father, Eileen? Did your father want her back?"

She sat stock still for what felt like an age. Then she nodded, once. She didn't look up.

"And, what, you went down there to fetch her? Jesus Christ. She had a chance at a different life, a life outside the Home. And you dragged her back. You paid the Wylies to let her go."

"You don't understand. She was his favourite. He needed his special girls. If he couldn't get his special girls—" She stopped abruptly. She was hunched over now, her hands completely covering her face.

"Then what, Eileen?" Nicol's voice was a predator padding through the undergrowth, a big cat on soft paws. "If he couldn't get his special girls, then what?"

She took her hands away from her face and looked up. She couldn't speak but she didn't need to speak. Her face told the story.

"Ah, Jesus." McCormack looked away and shook his head. "And Sarah? Is Sarah . . . ?"

Eileen Elliot's head dropped again. They watched the headscarf. It dipped and rose, once.

"Oh Christ."

He had guessed it when he saw Eileen stroke the lassie's arm, but even so, the knowledge still winded him.

"I'm sorry." Eileen smudged her mascara with the heel of her hand. "I didn't know what to do. I just knew I couldn't take it. Not again. If he was busy with someone else then he wasn't coming for me. That's how I saw it. I'm sorry. I know it's no excuse."

They sat in the airy, sunlit room and no one knew what to say. McCormack caught the scent again and leaned over to glance in the wastepaper basket beside the sofa: an orange peel lay coiled like a snake.

"I should have been better," Eileen was saying. "I should've saved that poor girl. I was a grown woman by then, I could've gone to the police. Put a stop to him. Isobel didn't even know. She'd been playing up and she thought that was why they were sending her back. Drinking. Staying out late. She thought the Wylies just got tired of her. But the Wylies would have kept her. They *wanted* to keep her."

There was nothing you could say to make that better. The silence passed its own judgement.

"Where is she now?" Eileen's desperate glance bounced between Nicol and McCormack. "I mean, maybe I can help her? Make up for it in some way."

"She's dead, Miss Elliot."

"Oh God."

"Six years ago. Murdered."

Her voice was worn down almost to nothing. "Murdered?"

"She was killed by Walter Maitland. Maitland and another man decided to fake the death of a woman called Helen Thaney. They used Isobel Wylie. They killed Isobel Wylie and made her look like the other woman."

The words seemed to shrivel Eileen Elliot. She hugged herself, canting forward and keening almost silently.

"They killed her," McCormack said. "You didn't."

She shook her head. "I took her back. She was gone and I took her back. It was me."

She wasn't looking for sympathy. She was stating the facts, admitting to herself what she'd known all along.

"You were doing what they told you to do," McCormack told her. "You were a victim here too."

She was looking at the floor, rocking gently back and forth. "They took photos," she said. "They took photos of the girls. Some of the girls, they still had family. They still hoped their family would come back for them. They knew if they told anyone what was happening, they knew the photos would be sent to their families."

They heard a toilet flushing somewhere, footsteps in the hallway. Eileen Elliot's daughter. Her half-sister.

"You want a way to redeem this, Eileen. You want a way to make this better. There isn't one. But what you can do, what you're going to do, is this. Every name. Every man who preyed on those lassies, you tell us his name. And the names of the girls. And we'll put away as many of these men as we can."

She was breathless as if she'd just surfaced for air. She rubbed her hands up her face and her nails caught on the headscarf. She tugged it off. With her hair down and her mascara in streaks she looked like a girl again herself. She busied herself unknotting the headscarf then she stopped, looked up at Nicol, then at McCormack.

"I know what it was," she said softly. "I know what they were looking for."

"What who was looking for?"

"When they trashed his study. I know what it was." She paused. "You see, I found it."

McCormack felt the hairs on his arms stand up, as though a breeze had rippled through them. He remembered the man in the green suit, coming down the front steps of Elliot's house.

"It was a list," Eileen Elliot went on. "Guests who'd come to Auldpark. Names and dates. The Friends. The men who made charitable contributions to the Home and, well. You know how it worked."

She had found her handbag by the side of the sofa and was rooting in its depths. Her chin twisted with the effort of clamping her jaw and he saw the reddening of her eyes. She took some pages from her handbag and McCormack closed his hand over them.

"Thank you," he said.

They rose to go. At the door, McCormack turned. "While I remember," he said.

Elliot raised her blurry face to them. "What is it?"

"Did Chisholm ever contact you? About your father, I mean."

She wiped her eyes with the heel of her hand. "I think he did," she said.

McCormack waited.

"I received a letter. A couple of days before my father's body was dumped. I didn't keep it. I'm sorry."

"Do you remember what it said?"

"Word for word." She smiled weakly at them. "It said, *The pains your father suffered in his final days are nothing to those he will suffer in eternity*. I thought it referred to something else. To Auldpark. That's why I burned it. It wasn't signed. I'm sorry."

"That's all right," McCormack said. "It was Chisholm all right."

WEDNESDAY, 16 JULY 1975

58

M cCormack went back to work on the Wednesday. Skelton's report had cleared him; he was a polis again. *For what it's worth*, he thought. When he got to Temple he found that the other units—Armstrong's and Patterson's teams—had crowded into the Byre for a celebration. Cans of Export and Tennent's Lager. A bottle of whisky and paper cups. They toasted him and cheered him, forced drinks on him. He was no longer yesterday's man, the man who caught the Quaker in the distant past. He was the man who cracked the Elliot case, took out Gordon Chisholm. It had got messy at the end, but Walter Maitland was off the board, too. It was a result, of sorts.

Around lunchtime he hirpled down the corridor to the Gents. Haddow was busy at one of the urinals. McCormack left a urinal between them. Cordon sanitaire. Haddow zipped up and went to wash his hands. When McCormack arrived at the sinks, Haddow was smirking in the mirror.

"Well played, McCormack. Good for you. You got your man."

McCormack soaped his hands. "I didn't get my man, sir. I wanted Walter Maitland to see out his days in Peterhead."

"Right. That's why you sent your tout to kill him."

The paper towels made a rasping sound as McCormack tugged them from the dispenser.

"Christopher Kidd was gathering intelligence, so far as any of us knew."

Haddow laughed. "Really? Gathering intelligence? Don't insult mine, McCormack. You knew how Kidd felt about Maitland. What he'd done to Kidd's sister. You sent him anyway."

"I knew that Kidd had agreed to cooperate. Help us put Maitland away."

"Put him away is right. Judge, jury and executioner. That's not how we do things in this unit, McCormack. I won't stand for cowboys. Gunning folk down. It's not Carson fucking City out there."

McCormack balled the paper towels, dropped them in the basket. "And what would you know about that, sir, exactly? Out there?"

"You think 'cause your name's in the papers you're a fucking hero? Nothing's changed, McCormack."

"Nothing ever does, sir. Not if your head's as thick as reinforced concrete."

He let the door clang shut on whatever Haddow was saying or about to say. Through in the Byre the party was winding down, the other teams drifting back to their desks. McCormack untied his necktie and tugged it free. He rooted in his desk drawer for the black tie.

Half an hour later he was in the Eastern Necropolis, off the Gallowgate, standing beside Isobel Wylie's grave. He'd paid for the new headstone, just the name and dates, nothing fancy, but it was good to see the chiselled letters in the oxblood sandstone. The old headstone, the wrong one, that bore the name of a living woman, had been taken away. Maybe they could keep it in storage until Helen Thaney died again.

Nicol had come with him. Eileen Elliot was there, too, with Sarah, looking more like sisters than mother and daughter. Bob Wylie had been contacted but had chosen not to come. He didn't deserve to be there, he told Nicol; not after what he'd done.

The priest from St. Michael's was about to begin his blessing when a car door slammed. It was Rona Shaw, Yvonne Gray's old workmate from Healing Hands. She took her place at the graveside, next to Nicol.

"I knew Yvonne would want to be here," she whispered. "But since she can't, I figured, you know . . ."

Nicol reached out and squeezed her hand. "Thank you," she said.

The priest didn't waste much time. It wasn't a funeral service (the body had been buried here six years back), just a short consecration of the stone. When it was over the priest shook hands with the mourners—McCormack slipped him an envelope for the church funds—and started on the short walk back to St. Michael's.

The others left too. Nicol came up beside McCormack as he stood looking down at the headstone. She touched his arm. "I'll be in the car, sir," she said. "No hurry."

He nodded. When he was alone he bent his head. He tried to pray, but nothing came. Only the image of Isobel Wylie as he'd seen her last, dead on the floor of a Bridgeton tenement, the flash from the snapper's Leica bleaching her features. They had failed her, all of the men in her life, from her father and the staff at Auldpark to Gavin Elliot and Bob Wylie. McCormack himself. Only her brother, only Christopher, had tried to save her. But he'd been a boy, powerless against the men who did what they wanted with his sister.

He heard a van door slam and turned to see a man crossing from the car park with an outsize wreath. McCormack stepped aside to let him lay it against the gravestone. White roses and hydrangeas. He gave a little bow and McCormack nodded and the man walked back to his van with his hands clasped in front of him. McCormack was turning to go when he noticed the card sticking up from the wreath. He bent to inspect it and saw his own name on the envelope.

It was a plain white rectangle, slightly larger than a business card. It was signed "C.K." and the message was three words: "I stood up."

Young Lochinvar, thought McCormack.

He tucked the card into his breast pocket and picked his way through the graves towards the car.

UNSENT LETTERS #4

Flat 4c, 70 Craigpark
Glasgow
9 August 1969

Dear Chris,

Just a quick note this time. Walter's picking me up in twenty minutes. I could spend that twenty minutes in front of the bathroom mirror, but I've worn a hole in the lino there already, so I thought I'd put the time to better use!

How's things with you? Are you off to the dancing later on? Grab a granny night at the Barrowland! Maybe I'll see you there! Truth is, I've no idea where we're going. It's a big surprise. State secret. Must be somewhere fancy, though, as he wants me looking my best. And I'll let you into a secret of my own: I bloody am looking my best! (That's not saying much, says you!)

Honest to God, Chris, you'd hardly know me. I got my hair done this morning. Platinum blond. I look like Jayne bloody Mansfield. Well, my hair does! I'm wearing a new frock that Walter bought—grey crêpe-de-chine, since you ask—and Helen's Pierre Cardin coat. It's just the two of us tonight, not a foursome with Peter and Helen. I'm kind of glad about that. With the hair and the coat, I look like Helen's ghost. I think Walter must secretly fancy Helen and he's trying to turn me into her!

I shouldn't laugh. He's been good for me, Walter has. Not like I thought he'd be. When he's working the door at Whitehill Street he looks like a grizzly bear in a tux. But he's not like that at all. He's a sweetheart, really. A gentleman. He gave me this pendant—I think it was

516 · LIAM McILVANNEY

maybe his grannie's or something, it's a real antique—and you should have seen his smile when I put it on. Like I was his princess or something. I'm wearing it now. It's what I always say, Chris. You think you know a person, you think you've got their number, but you really don't.

Well, I was going to say that I had no other news but, listen, you'll be pleased to hear: I'm no longer a woman of ill-repute, aka a hoor! But that's just because I'm no longer anything. I'm nothing at all. They fired me! Can you believe it? I missed a couple of shifts. All right, I missed four shifts. I thought Walter would have a word but he says it's for the best. The job at Peter's restaurant's a certainty, and he'll sub me till the new job starts. It's like Dad's song again, "Bye Bye Blackbird". How does it go? "Pack up all my cares and woes". That's me, Chris. Packing up those woes.

I know haven't found you yet, Chris, but I will. You'll have an absolute stack of letters to read by the time I get a hold of you! And we'll make up for all the lost time. We'll put the past behind us, like I said. I know you think about what happened at Auldpark. I do too. I can't help it. But if you get all bogged down in hate and anger then that's no good. They're just stealing more of your life from you. That's the way I look at it. The best revenge is to live a happy life. Find someone you love. Maybe I've already found someone. Maybe you have, too. Anyway, there's Walter beeping. Wish me luck!

Bye bye, Blackbird.

Your sister,

Isobel

Acknowledgements

It remains a privilege to work with Jim Gill and Lucy Joyce at United Agents, and with Julia Wisdom and Sophie Churcher at HarperCollins. I am, once again, deeply indebted to the gimlet eye of the world's best copy editor, Anne O'Brien. David Goldie read a draft of this book and improved it with his acumen and insight. Nanette Pollock generously shared her knowledge of police procedures, as did Jim Fraser with his forensic expertise. Allan Macinnes and Calum MacLeod kept me right with matters Highland and Gaelic. Life at the University of Otago's Centre for Irish and Scottish Studies, where I ply my trade, is greatly enhanced by the congenial presence of Professor Sonja Tiernan and Charlotte Hall-Tiernan, and Visiting Professors Val McDermid and Jo Sharp. For help and advice of various kinds, I want to thank: Damian Barr, Bob Barrowman, Julia Bell, Ralph Bouhaidar, Claire and Gerard Campbell, Alastair Dinsmor, the Dunedin Detection Club, Edin Gay Book Group, Wendy English, Julie and Alan Hill, Barry Hurford, Liz Lammers, Abby Ludeman, Bob McDevitt, Hamish McNeilly, Denise Mina, the staff of the Mitchell Library, Ian Nicol, Alan Parks, Maureen Scott, John Stenhouse, the Stuart Residence Halls Council, and Dave Webb. I couldn't do what I do without the love and support of Valerie McIlvanney: all my love, as ever, to her, Andrew, Caleb, Isaac and Diarmid.